Worth The Drive

She leaned into him, her head as far forward as his. Her set-up identical to his, but instead of gripping an imaginary club, she gripped his arms. Her forehead swayed forward and was stopped by his. She felt feverish against him.

"Did you know?" she began again. "That when you're on the course, and you are over a shot, just like this." She stopped. Darío waited, not wanting to break the spell she was putting him under. "That your arms…your arms…are just about the sexiest thing I think I've ever seen."

He waited for her to say more. He wanted her to say more. When she didn't, he realized she must be waiting for him to say something. He couldn't. He absolutely could not think of any response to what she'd just said.

All thought of wanting Katie completely sober before taking her to bed flew out of his mind. She obviously wanted him. So she was a little drunk? She had been attracted to him on the course, well before she began drinking.

Just as he was about to break her hold on his arms by putting them around her, he heard a noise coming from her.

A snore. A soft, lady-like snore, but a snore nonetheless.

She had literally passed out on him.

OTHER TITLES BY
MARA JACOBS

The Worth Series
(Contemporary Romance)
Worth The Weight
Worth The Drive
Worth The Fall

Anna Dawson's Vegas Series
(Romantic Mystery)
Against The Odds
Against The Spread

Blackbird & Confessor Series
(Romantic Mystery)
Broken Wings

Countdown To A Kiss
(A New Year's Eve Anthology)

WORTH
THE DRIVE

The Worth Series, Book Two:
The Pretty One

MARA JACOBS

Published by Mara Jacobs
©Copyright 2012 Mara Jacobs
Cover design by Kim Killion

ISBN: 978-0-9852586-6-5

For more information on the author and her works, please
see www.marajacobs.com

For Kelly

Prologue

—⁓—

We were happily married for eight months.
Unfortunately, we were married for four and a half years.
~ Nick Faldo, professional golfer

"I'M NOT SURE I *ever* loved you."

Wow. She hadn't seen that one coming.

Still, Katie Lipton supposed, if you're stupid enough to ask the question, "Don't you love me anymore?" you ought to be prepared for the answer. Whatever it turned out to be. But she couldn't believe the words coming out of Ron's mouth.

She watched as he stood in the bedroom and continued to pack his suitcase. Like picking at a scab, she couldn't stop herself from pursuing his comment. "What do you mean you never loved me? What were the last seventeen years, then—a crush?"

"Don't, Katie. Don't do this to yourself. It's over." His look for her was patronizing, filled with false empathy. She wanted to put her fist through his Greek god face. Make his incredible good looks bloodied and bruised, to match her heart.

Her best friend Alison would have done it. Wound up and cold-cocked him right there, right now. Not caring if he bled all over their cream carpeting or their cream comforter in their cream-colored bedroom. Or she would hurt him with the words that wouldn't come to Katie. Alison's quick wit and razor-sharp mouth would bring Ron down to size. But Katie wasn't Alison.

Her other best friend, Lizzie, would probably have seen this coming months ago and had some kind of plan for when the moment arrived. Or she'd defuse the situation with her calming, soothing nature. But Katie wasn't Lizzie either.

While Alison's smarts and Lizzie's shining personality would have been so useful now, Katie's incredible beauty—what *she* was known for—did her no good in this situation. All she could do was sit on the bed, stunned, and watch as her boyfriend of four years, husband of thirteen, packed his tee-shirts and boxers into the his of their his-and-hers matching luggage.

"Ron, if this is about the baby…" Her voice trailed off. What? What could she say? Promise not to mention the baby again? Promise to abandon her dream of becoming a mother? Could she do that? If it meant keeping Ron, *would* she do that?

"See, Katie, you even say 'the' baby, not 'a' baby, as if one ever existed." His voice was harsh. "There is no baby, Katie. There never was a baby. There will never be a baby." He paused. "Not for us, anyway."

There was something in his voice as he made the last comment. Something cutting and mean. Katie had come to recognize that tone. It had been so foreign just a few years ago, when his voice had always conveyed his love for her. "What do you mean, 'not for us, anyway'?"

"It means no baby for *us*, Katie. Just like I said."

Don't do it. Don't ask. Don't jump at his baiting voice. But she couldn't help herself. "Is there a 'but' at the end of that?" she asked.

Obviously he'd been dying to get to this, knowing she would lead him there eventually.

"Yes, there is a but. There will be no baby for us, Katie, but," he dragged the word out, emphasizing every letter, "there will be a baby for me. In five months, to be exact."

She wanted to double over, the pain was so great. Her breath totally left her body. But some small shred of dignity made her sit still, not even flinching. In the back of her mind she wondered what hurt more, the knowledge that Ron had betrayed her or the thought that yet another woman would have a child and she would not.

Ron seemed disappointed that she hadn't crumbled, and that gave her a little bit of strength. Enough to say, "And just who is the mother of your child?"

He turned his back to her, going to a drawer in the dresser and taking out all of his socks. Socks she had bought for him. Socks she had washed. Socks she had picked up off this bedroom floor more times than she could remember.

"Amber Saari," he said.

Katie couldn't hide her shock this time as a small gasp escaped her. "Amber Saari? She's a child herself. She's one of your students."

"Was. Was one of my students. She's twenty," he said, hurt and indignant. Like how dare she believe he'd ever have anything to do with one of his students at the high school. Oh no, he'd wait until they were out for two years before sleeping with them. A man of honor, her Ron.

"If I recall correctly, she was something of a tramp when she was in the high school. Are you even sure the baby's yours?" She couldn't believe she was being so calm when every muscle in her body ached to throw something at him. She was just afraid that she'd throw herself at him. Whether to claw his eyes out or beg for mercy, she wasn't sure. That thought kept her perched on the bed.

He looked at her as if she were crazy. "Of course the baby's mine."

"Oh, I see. *You* were the only one who was unfaithful."

"Katie, let's not do this," he said. But it seemed that's exactly what he wanted to do. He wanted her to lose it, to become the shrieking fishwife he apparently had made her out to be. It would justify his walking out on her. It would then be he who left because of her obsession with having a baby, her instability, her shrewish behavior. When, in fact, he just didn't want to be with her anymore. He wanted to be with a twenty-year-old former student named Amber.

She wouldn't give him the satisfaction.

"You're right, Ron, let's not do this." She sat up straight on the bed as he zipped up the suitcase. She summoned every prideful gene she possessed and waited for him to leave. To leave her and their home.

To leave her alone for the first time in her life.

He stopped and looked at her, surprised by her tone and composure. His gaze raked across her face. "Jesus, you're beautiful, Katie." His voice was soft and tender, and for a moment it reminded her of the Ron she had fallen in love with. The Ron who had pursued her relentlessly their freshman year at Michigan State. The Ron who was the most handsome man at the enormous university, who had wooed her and caught her with that same soft, tender voice he was using now.

"So fucking beautiful," he whispered, and reached out to touch her face.

She winced, not sure if it was from the prospect of his touch or his language, which he knew she hated. Either way, her flinch broke whatever spell her splendor had just woven over him and he stepped back, dropping his hand.

"You keep the house. I'll keep the Hummer. The rest we can figure out later."

He set his sealed suitcase on the floor, stacked the smaller bag he'd packed earlier on top of it, and pulled up the handle, wheeling them both out of the room behind him.

Funny, the thoughts that go through your head, she mused. Here her husband had just walked out on her and all she was thinking was that it would have been so much more manly, so much more dramatic, if he'd picked both bags up by the handles and walked out instead of wheeling the bags behind him like a flight attendant traveling through an airport.

After she heard the front door close and the roar of that monstrosity leaving the driveway, Katie rolled over onto the bed, her knees to her chest, pulling one corner of the comforter over her. She finally let the pain of the knife he'd plunged into her heart wash over her.

Her husband had left her for some young tramp he'd knocked up.

Katie Maki Lipton. Known as the prettiest girl to ever come out of Hancock High. The most stunning woman in the Copper Country. They said she was a true original. A unique beauty.

And she was now nothing more than a bad cliché.

One

---~~~---

Give me golf clubs, fresh air, and a beautiful partner and
you can keep my golf clubs and the fresh air.

~ *Jack Benny*

"**YOU'RE RIGHT.** I am glad you talked me into this, but 6am?"
Katie said through a yawn. She secured her long hair into a ponytail and put a Michigan State baseball cap on, pulling her hair out
through the back opening of the hat.

"I know. Sorry. But this guy's tee time is 7:10 and I want to
make sure he sees that I'm there not only to watch him tee off, but
to hit some balls first, too," Lizzie said.

They had set their hotel alarm for five to make sure they had
time to shower, dress, and get to the course before six-thirty. Precious moments Katie would like to have back so she could have
slept on. Getting good sleep had become so hard lately.

"Besides, they flip-flop tee times on Thursdays and Fridays,
so he'll play in the afternoon tomorrow and you can sleep as late
as you want," Lizzie said, trying to placate Katie.

They parked their rental car ridiculously close to the country
club door—Lizzie had some kind of pilfered VIP parking pass—
and put on sunscreen. Back home, in the Copper Country of
Michigan, the May sun was neither hot nor abundant enough
to elicit a need for the protection. But here in Texas, the heat

was already hanging in the air, threatening to be stifling by mid-afternoon. Bring it on, Katie thought, as she covered every inch of her fair, Finnish skin with SPF forty-five. She dared the sun to sink into her soul, to thaw the chill in her bones that had taken up residence since Ron left and the long Upper Peninsula winter began.

Katie followed Lizzie behind the clubhouse. Lizzie seemed to know where she was going, although it was her first time here as well. Blooming flowers in glorious colors bordered the walkway to the driving range. Katie was astounded by the many different shades of green that adorned the golf course and its surrounding foliage.

"So this is what May looks like in the rest of the world," she murmured, aware that lowered voices seemed to be the norm based on the conversations of the scattered people they passed. There weren't many spectators at the course yet—it was too early—but those who were there spoke with hushed reverence. Katie and Lizzie walked to the driving range, where fifteen or twenty golfers were hitting balls.

"I know, isn't it beautiful?" Lizzie said. "Hard to believe that back home we had a snowstorm two weeks ago. It's like we don't even live in the same country or something."

Lizzie led Katie to the bleachers that overlooked the driving range. They settled onto seats in the first row and both started to look at the day's pairing sheet that they'd taken from the attendant at the gate.

"The UP might as well be a different country, Lizard," she said, with just a touch of disdain in her voice.

Lizzie caught the tone though, as Katie knew she would. Lizzie—and Alison too, for that matter—had been hyper-sensitive to her every intonation the last seven months, watching as Katie went through phases of disbelief, self-doubt, and rage.

The last two months had been the worst.

Being the features section editor at *The Copper Ingot*, it was among her myriad duties to do the final proofread of the living section of the daily paper. Of course, at a paper the size of *The Ingot*, the living section was only a page, but still, Katie proofed it diligently every evening before she left. That's when she'd seen it: the birth announcement of little Crystal Lipton, daughter of Ron Lipton and Amber Saari.

That had been two months ago, and she had been in a deep depression ever since. So much so that Lizzie and Alison brooked no arguments when they sent Katie to Texas—where Lizzie was meeting a new prospective client—for two days.

Lizzie looked at her. "I know everybody's a little sick of the weather at home this time of year, Kat, but you love the Yoop," Lizzie said in a soft, coaxing voice.

"No, you love the U.P., Lizard. I just put up with it." She had never said that before, had never really even thought it. She didn't know where it had come from, but realized it was the truth.

Not wanting to get into it with her friend right now, not willing to do anything to detract from the warm feeling the sun was bringing her, she perused the pairings sheet for something she could use to change the subject.

"What's the name of this guy you're pitching, again?"

"Chad Curtis," Lizzie said. At Katie's blank look, she continued, "You probably haven't heard of him. He just announced he's skipping his senior year in college to turn pro. This is his first tournament as a pro. He's here on a sponsor's exemption because he's from Irving. Hometown boy making his pro debut. Remember, we watched him on TV at the Masters? We were all excited that an amateur had done so well, placing in the top ten."

Katie vaguely remembered. She loved watching professional golf, and she and Ron had always hosted a brunch on the Sunday of the Masters. This year she had gone to Lizzie's home to watch, not wanting to be in her empty house.

Lizzie's husband of three months, Finn, spent most of the time asking questions, knowing nothing about golf. His kids, Stevie and Annie, had cheered Phil Mickelsen on to another green jacket, and Lizzie and Alison had hovered over Katie, aware of her precarious state.

"Chad's supposed to be pretty good, a real up-and-comer. I think he'd be just the player to branch Hampton PR into representing golfers," Lizzie said.

Katie nodded and looked through the sheet to find Chad Curtis's name. She knew he had an early tee time, and she found him near the top of the list. "Oh, he's paired with Darío Luna. I love him."

"You do?" Lizzie asked. "That surprises me."

"Why does that surprise you? He's been around forever, he's won three majors."

Lizzie shrugged. "I know, but you usually go for the really handsome guys, the pretty boys."

More like the pretty boys always went for her. And she'd always let them. Then Ron—the prettiest pretty boy she'd ever seen—went after her and the rest of them all just fell away, feeling they were unable to compete. She'd never looked beyond Ron. Had never wanted to.

Her gaze scanned down the line of early golfers warming up on the range. There were little placards with each player's name in front of them, presumably so the fans would know who was who. It also probably helped the bleary-eyed caddies find their employers on early mornings after late nights. The golfers looked refreshed and neatly pressed. The caddies looked rough and badly wrinkled.

Katie didn't need the placard to know Darío Luna. She'd been watching him play for years. He had played in his first Ryder Cup at twenty. Katie and Ron had watched it together, cuddled on the couch in the apartment she shared with Lizzie and Alison. They'd dated for two years by then, both also twenty, and juniors at State.

Darío won his first major, the British Open, at twenty-two. Katie and Ron had awakened at the hotel on their honeymoon and watched the early overseas telecast as they ate their room-service breakfast. While Darío lifted the Claret Jug in victory, Katie and Ron lifted their champagne glasses and toasted their new life together.

This past April, as Katie wallowed in her haze of self-pity, and Ron was probably playing with his new daughter, Darío Luna missed his first cut at a Masters—a tournament he'd won twice—since he'd turned pro.

They were both having bad seasons.

She spotted him at the far end of the range. It would be a stretch to call him handsome; his bit of a schnozz saw to that. But there was something about him that drew her eye. He was smaller than most the other golfers. Katie suspected that he wasn't much taller than her own five foot nine. His body was compact but muscular, almost coiled, like he could strike at any moment. He had the dark skin of his native Spain as well as the requisite black hair and brown eyes.

He was wearing a coral Lacoste shirt and perfectly tailored trousers. Katie knew that several of the Spanish players on tour wore Lacoste and figured the gator must make his home not in the Everglades, but in Spain. She hadn't worn a golf shirt with a reptile on it since her preppy days back in high school.

Katie had always liked watching him play and rooted for him when he was in contention, so she was excited that she'd spend the day following his threesome.

She sat, mesmerized, and watched as he warmed up, going through what was obviously a well-established routine. Lizzie was chattering beside her, talking about this player or that and pointing things out to her, but Katie wasn't paying attention. She couldn't take her eyes off Darío.

He and his caddy worked together in an easy rhythm, the caddy ready to throw him a ball as soon as Darío turned to him. At his side to clean the club Darío was done with and hand him the next one. After so many balls, Darío taped his ring finger and his pinky on his right hand. Katie chuckled, and Lizzie asked her what was so funny, following Katie's gaze to Darío Luna.

"You'd love this guy, Lizard, he's just as anal as you are. He's counted his clubs twice, making sure he's not carrying over the limit. Oh, look, now he's having the caddy count them too," she said, laughing. Lizzie harrumphed and tried to respond with some kind of witty comeback, but didn't. Katie figured it was because Lizzie knew it for the truth. Her friend probably even admired Darío for his foresight and planning.

"You don't think he's handsome?" Katie asked.

"Well, certainly not a gorgeous pretty boy, like…" She didn't finish her sentence. She didn't have to. Katie knew she was about to utter Ron's name. "But handsome? Yeah, definitely, but in an unorthodox kind of way, you know? Plus, he's got that whole European thing going on."

Katie nodded. There was something about him that was riveting to watch.

Darío and his caddy moved from the range to the bunker and chipping area, still in view of the bleachers, but closer to the first hole.

Katie moved to the seat behind her so she could stretch out her long legs onto the bleacher she had previously occupied. With no one behind her, she leaned back, resting her elbows on the hard plastic that was already heating up from the sun. By the end of the day, no one would be able to sit on them with shorts on for fear of losing a layer of skin. A poor man's chemical peel.

Katie dropped her head back and looked at the blue sky. The morning haze was quickly burning off and the sun played a game of peek-a-boo with the only cloud in the sky. A soothing warmth spread over her, and for the first time in seven months, she felt human. No, she felt like a woman again, and it had been much longer than seven months since she'd felt like that.

She was dressed for maximum sun in a tank top and khaki shorts, revealing a tremendous amount of her long legs. She was pale from the Michigan winter. Hopefully she'd be able to change that somewhat in the next two days. Her feet were adorned in flip-flops that would soon be slipped off for the feel of warm grass beneath her feet when they walked the course. She looked like a beach bum, and after months of wearing a minimum of three layers, it felt great.

Lizzie had dressed more conservatively, being here in a professional capacity. She wore longer black linen walking shorts and a crisp, white sleeveless blouse with cute anklets and black and white loafers. Her dark hair, cut in a short shag, was already starting to curl at the ends from the humidity. For once Katie was thankful to have her baby-fine Finnish hair. At least it would stay put all day in its ponytail.

As the sun came out from behind the lone cloud once more, Katie closed her eyes against the glare and breathed in deeply. The smell of freshly cut grass mixed with the scent of her suntan lotion. It smelled like summer. The thought cheered her immensely. "Thanks, Lizard," she said quietly, not even sure if her friend heard her. "Thanks for bringing me here."

She felt Lizzie's hand on her ankle, giving it a light squeeze, and then it was gone. Lizzie didn't say anything, and Katie didn't say any more. She didn't need to; they both understood how much Katie needed to get out of the Copper Country right now. How, if only for two short days, they could inhabit a world that held sunshine and laughter. Where great golf was played by the game's best. A world where rules counted and a person played with honor. Where cheating was considered the demise of humanity and was never tolerated.

A world where Ron did not reside.

Lizzie got up to go introduce herself to Chad Curtis as he left the range to head for the pitching area. Katie watched as her friend shook the young man's hand. The kid was probably no more than twenty. The thought that Chad Curtis was more age-appropriate for Amber Saari than Ron fluttered through Katie's head.

No. No. No. This is not about Ron. This was about a change of scenery, a change of attitude. She could enjoy her two days here and head back to Michigan on Saturday with a new outlook.

But what would really be different when she got back? Ron

would still be there with his new baby and his live-in girlfriend. It would be months before their divorce was final, but Katie had no doubt that Ron and Amber would be married the minute the ink was dry. As Hancock High School's hockey coach and math teacher, it was not wise to be shacking up with a former student, raising their illegitimate child together. Small towns would only tolerate so much, and this pressed its boundaries.

If this had happened to Lizzie, Ron would have been run out of town, tarred, and feathered. But whereas Lizzie was beloved in their hometown, Katie was revered, admired from afar. She had seen the sympathetic looks in the grocery store, but she had always been considered unapproachable, and so the possible good thoughts from her neighbors were just that—thoughts.

Those who really knew her—Lizzie, Alison, the crew at *The Ingot*—knew that beyond her looks was a human being capable of stumbling and falling just like the rest of them. With the scrapes and bruises to prove it.

Determined to put her inevitable return to the Copper Country out of her mind, Katie made her way over to the starting tee, realizing that Lizzie had been chatting with Chad for quite a while. It was now time for his threesome to tee off. Joining Chad and Darío was an Australian golfer, Barclay Something-or-other. She figured he was either up and coming or down and out, because she had followed the Tour for nearly fifteen years and had never heard of him.

As soon as she saw him, she had her answer. He was probably in his mid-to-late forties because otherwise he'd be playing on the Champions Tour, but years of the harsh sun on his face made him appear older. "Craggy" was the word Katie came up with when she looked at him. He was undoubtedly one of those players on tour who'd played for years on the fringe of the eligibility list, never becoming famous, hanging on until he turned fifty and could play the Champions Tour, yet still making five times what Katie made annually.

They made an interesting threesome. The fresh-faced Chad,

the seasoned veteran, Darío, and the world-weary Barclay. Katie found herself looking more forward to watching a simple round of golf than she had anything in a long, long time.

Lizzie joined her, and they made their way to the ropes. With such an early tee time and no superstars, the threesome had a relatively small gallery. At the first hole, it was comprised mostly of people who had staked out spots along the ropes at the tee and who would spend the entire day there, watching every group go through. Katie suspected the crowd would lessen as they followed this group farther out from the clubhouse.

There was a contingency of people who were clearly from Irving, here to cheer on one of their own. But they kept together, all wearing matching tee-shirts with Chad's face on it. Katie felt a pang of pity for the kid. He had probably died of embarrassment when he'd seen them.

The starter gave them their tee-off order, and the players went through their individual rituals. Darío took off his hat, emblazoned with a club manufacturer's logo, and approached the other two players.

"Gentlemen, play well." He shook their hands, looking them squarely in the eye as he did so, and giving them both a solemn nod.

His sincere gesture, accompanied by just a trace of Spanish accent, made Katie's belly do a little flip-flop, and she regretted that they hadn't had time for breakfast.

She and Lizzie stood on the left side of the tee box so the players faced them as they teed off. Chad hit a booming drive down the middle of the fairway. Barclay hit a drive that was on the same path as Chad's but some fifty yards shorter.

Darío stepped to his teed ball and Katie's eyes were drawn to his forearms as they took formation around the grip of his club. Corded muscles and tendons rippled as the sunlight glinted across the smattering of dark hair on his arms.

Katie had never been one for men's arms. Growing up in a hockey town, and marrying a hockey player turned hockey coach, she had always been a thigh and tush woman, those parts of the male anatomy being so sculpted on men who skated regularly.

She was ready to amend that opinion as she stared at Darío's hands and arms as he held on to his club. His dark skin—part Spanish heritage, part golfer's tan—was shown to perfection in the coral shirt.

With a quiet grace and fluidity, he effortlessly swung the club back and forward, making loud contact with the ball. As the entire gallery turned to watch the ball careen through the air, Katie's head stayed in place, watching Darío's backswing. Watching Darío watch his ball. Watching Darío cringe and yell out, "Fore, right," and motioning wildly to the spectators walking down the right side of the fairway. Watching as Darío dropped his head, shook it and said something under his breath that Katie couldn't hear, but certainly understood.

He handed his club to his caddy, and the entire group strolled down the fairway as the gallery began to move. Those who were following the group moved along the ropes, those who were staying, stretched and looked at pairing sheets to see who would be coming next.

"Hey Katie, come on," Lizzie said.

Katie looked up from where Darío had been. She turned to find Lizzie already thirty yards down the fairway. Shaking herself from thoughts of those strong arms wrapped around something other than a golf club, she followed her friend.

Two

Pressure is playing for $10 when you don't have
a dime in your pocket.

~ Lee Trevino, professional golfer

MIERDRA! ANOTHER *opening drive in the rough!* Just like last week. And the week before. And the three before that.

No, he couldn't think like that. Take it one shot at a time. One hole at a time. One round at a time. Last week was history. Today was a new tournament. A new course. A new chance.

And the same wicked slice off the tee.

Darío followed his caddy, Binky, to his ball, stepping under the ropes as Binky held them up. He hated walking under the ropes. It meant his drive had once again not only not found the fairway, but had probably found the neighboring hole's fairway.

"It's okay, Guv, you can handle a shot like this with no problem. That's your bread and butter. Here," Binky said, handing Darío the required four iron.

Darío's reputation as the game's most creative shot maker was a dubious honor, at best. Yes, he was capable of getting out of trouble better than any other golfer, but only because he was in trouble so much of the time to begin with.

"Bah!" He hated being out of the ropes on his first shot. It could be a very long day.

He made a spectacular recovery and managed to par the first hole. His next was better, a birdie, and he was on the tee at the third hole before he realized that the two women he'd seen at the first tee were following his threesome. They were far enough out from the clubhouse now to make no mistake.

"A nice distraction, hey Guv?" Binky, who always seemed to be reading his mind, commented.

Darío had always been a gallery watcher. He knew that many players never looked beyond the ropes that lined each hole, feeling it took away focus. Other players were just the opposite, chatting with members of the gallery through their entire round, feeling it made them relax. Darío fell somewhere in between the two philosophies.

He watched the gallery constantly when it wasn't his shot. Watched the people that followed his group through all eighteen holes. Looked at the spectators who staked their claim at one hole—usually at the tee or the green—and settled in their lawn chairs content not to leave the entire day.

He never allowed himself to think too deeply about who he was looking for in those galleries. He knew, deep down, that he'd never find him.

"Do you think they're following our group?" Binky asked.

Darío shrugged, pretending he didn't care, but that wasn't quite the truth. "Could be. It is unusual to see two women together out on the course, though, isn't it?" When Darío had first started on tour, women in the gallery at all were rare. Over the past eighteen years, women were much more prevalent, but they were usually with a man. Two women, without a man in their group, was indeed rare. Except for the case of groupies, which was more common than in years before, thanks to the higher profile of professional golf. And particularly after the whole Tiger incident.

"Suppose they're groupies?" Binky asked as they stepped to the next tee.

Darío's eyes followed the women as they walked along the ropes, waiting for the threesome to tee off. "I doubt it. They are not dressed like 20th Holes," Darío said.

The nineteenth hole was well known in all golfing circles as the bar one visited after a round. The 20th Holes were what the Tour players called the women who pursued professional golfers. Whether they had a one-night stand or a one-carat diamond on their minds, the name applied.

"Besides not being dressed like 20th Holes, they're already on the fourth hole with us. Groupies don't usually walk that far away from the clubhouse," Darío added to his assessment.

"Yeah, that's true. It's hard to walk a course wearing fuck-me pumps."

One of the women had on comfortable yet stylish loafers, while the other had on flip-flops, which she was now taking off and carrying. They were both good looking, but the one with the flip-flops was extraordinary, though she did much to conceal it, wearing a hat pulled low over her face, her white blond hair peeking out from behind in a ponytail.

He loved a ponytail on a grown woman. There was something so sexy about the way it swayed back and forth as the woman walked, in time with the movement of her behind.

It was all Darío could do to concentrate on his next shot as he watched the blonde walk along the ropes of the fairway ahead of him. Her long legs kept a tantalizing rhythm with her ponytail. Her legs, though gloriously long and shapely, were very pale.

"Maybe they're hometown girls out to see Chaddy boy?" Binky said as they walked down the fairway. Darío thought that Binky's eyes were following the women as much as his were. He and Binky had been together for many years.

Darío shook his head. "Both women have very fair skin. Either they're not from Texas, or they're very conscious of not getting any sun on themselves. But then why wear shorts and sleeveless tops today? No, they're definitely not hometown girls."

"Texas is full of blondes," Binky said. "But most of them have big hair to match their long legs."

It was true, Texas was full of leggy blondes, but this woman looked more Nordic than Texan. The European Tour currently didn't have any stops in Sweden, but if it did, the gallery would be full of women who looked like this one.

Well, perhaps in coloring, but even Sweden may be hard pressed to find a woman that beautiful.

When they made the turn at nine, Darío curiously watched to see if the women would continue on with his group. They were back at the clubhouse and many more golfers were now on the course. Phil was due to tee off soon, if he recalled correctly, so he'd probably lose the women to Phil's threesome.

He was amused at how he thought of the women as his to lose. And pleased when the women kept following.

"Huh. Yep, they're definitely with us," Binky said, needing no prodding from Darío.

His mind wandered as to why two women who were not from the area would not only be at the tournament, but be following his threesome. One of his playing partners, Chad Curtis, was from right here in Irving. The other, Barclay Ives, was from Australia. If the women were Australian, they'd have more sun on them than these two did.

Yes, he was definitely overthinking this.

His focus was so intent on the women and why they were following his group, he was startled to hear Binky say, "Hell of a round going today, Guv. Keep it up."

His mind came back to the game and he realized he was three shots under par through eleven holes. He didn't even remember making the shots. He pulled his scorecard out of his pocket, happy to see that the shots he recorded for Barclay and Chad matched what the sign bearer had.

Darío was stunned that he'd gone through the last eight holes on autopilot while he and Binky had contemplated the blonde. That was unlike him. He watched the gallery while he played, but never at the expense of total concentration to his game. Besides, when he scanned galleries, it was never a woman he was looking for.

He acknowledged Binky's compliment, then tried to put the blonde from his mind and focus on his livelihood for the rest of the round. He still had seven holes to play—lots of chances to make some birdies.

His body was fluid and the game seemed effortless. The pure physicality of his swing sang to him. His arms and shoulders became one with the club.

"A couple of fine Sheilas we've got with us today, hey mate?" Barclay said two hours later as they stood next to each other and watched the Curtis kid putt out on the eighteenth hole.

Darío knew exactly to which women Barclay was referring, but something in the man's lecherous tone made him shrug ignorance.

"Right behind you, mate. They're standing together by the ropes."

Darío snuck a look behind him, but he knew exactly where the women were. Though he had turned his mind back to the round, he had never lost track of the Swede, and was delighted that she was still with the group to the final hole.

"*Sí*, ees *muy* preeetty." He drawled the words, laying his Spanish accent on a little thick. His first few years that he'd played in the States, he'd been able to feign a language barrier when paired with a blowhard like Barclay. It was an easy way to have a nice, quiet, peaceful round.

As he started winning, and became more well known, the fact that he spoke impeccable English became common knowledge and he could no longer play that game. English was the language spoken on the European Tour as well, and Darío had been proficient since learning it as a child. He had been somewhat disturbed recently to realize that he now dreamt in English. It was nearly as innate to him as Spanish but, every now and then, he thickened his accent and pretended not to understand certain words to halt an unwelcome conversation.

It didn't work in this instance, as Barclay kept on. "Did you see the tits on the blonde? Well, both of them, actually, but the blonde. My God, do you think they're real? And those legs? Can you imagine those thrown over your shoulders?"

Darío was no prude, but his belief was that crude language, such as Barclay's, was best used between the sheets, not between the ropes. He had never partaken in locker-room talk, even as a youth.

The picture Barclay painted was indeed evocative. Just as long as he was in the starring role and not Barclay.

Barclay seemed not to notice Darío's bristle—or ignored it—and kept on. "My God, but I'd like to get my hands on her. Think I'll give it a whirl when we're done here. Lord knows I need something soft to lay my head on to take the sting out of this awful round. Those lovely tits seem just the thing." Barclay was four over to Darío's now four under.

Darío couldn't describe the flash of emotion that went through him when he thought of Barclay's clammy hands on *his* blonde. He chastised himself for the thoughts, but could not escape them. She wouldn't fall for some lame line that Barclay was likely to offer up, would she? He smiled to himself, thinking of how he'd assigned a deep intelligence and good taste to a woman he'd never met. Still, he knew his Swede—as he'd come to think of her—would not be fool enough to buy whatever Barclay Ives was selling.

Chad Curtis putted out, ending the round. The gallery had grown as the hour grew later, with more locals wishing well to their hometown boy. The cheers from the crowd were loud and boisterous for one of their own. They were also kind to Darío, appreciative of the stellar round he'd shot.

Chad had shot even par, playing very well for his first round as a professional in front of a nerve-inducing hometown crowd. Darío had ended up at four under, the best round he'd shot in nearly a year. Barclay finished at four over. Unless he had the round of his life tomorrow, Barclay would probably miss the cut, making an early exit from the tournament. Never one to be cruel, Darío was nonetheless cheered by that thought.

The three golfers made their way to the scorer's tent, which was actually a trailer, and checked, then signed their official scorecards. When they came out, they went to the ropes that led from the trailer to the clubhouse doors, giving the golfers a straight shot through the crowd. The ropes were always lined with autograph and memorabilia seekers. Darío typically gave a half dozen balls away to children after each round, making sure he gave one to any child who had followed his group during his round.

Half of the crowd went after Chad, which was only natural, him being a local. The other half went after Darío as crowds still did, even though Darío had not played well the last two years. Due to winning three majors, albeit several years ago, his name still carried a certain cache among golf fans.

Darío started to sign his name on hats and programs as he slowly made his way along the ropes, keeping an eye on Barclay, who was searching the crowd for the Swede. He knew the second Barclay spotted her, following Barclay's beady eyes to the Swede.

She stood away from the crowd, her eyes not following Barclay, but following Darío. He had thought he'd felt her eyes on him during his round, but it was hard to tell with her wearing that hat. She'd taken the hat off and it slapped lightly against her thigh. Her face was even more arresting than Darío had imagined. Stunning cheekbones, a cool beauty reminiscent of a woman his mother adored, Grace Kelly.

And she was looking straight at him.

The piercing blue of her eyes made the pen in his hand slide off the paper he was signing. She seemed to sense his reaction, because her head tilted back, as if their connection had been physical.

He finished the autograph and handed it back to the man, who looked puzzled when he saw the squiggly lines go off the edge of his program. Darío made toward the Swede. She was several steps beyond the crowd and to get to her Darío would either have to leave the safety of the ropes and brave the crush of the crowd, or somehow wave her over, through the avid autograph seekers, to the ropes.

While he was trying to figure out the best plan of action, the Swede's attention was drawn away by Barclay, who had already left the ropes and was at her side, touching her arm. Darío saw her stiffen at the touch, and was pleased to see her drop a cool façade on her beautiful face as Barclay made his play. He saw her head shaking no, at first slightly, then a bit more emphatically. She finally pointed to the woman she'd been walking with.

The woman was along the ropes not far from where Darío stood, talking intently with Chad Curtis. They seemed to be making plans to meet later. Chad was giving her directions to a restaurant and they both agreed on a time for later that evening. Darío couldn't help overhearing the directions to the meeting place as disappointment washed over him at the realization that the women had been following his threesome because of Chad Curtis.

He looked back toward the Swede, who was finally getting Barclay to take the hint. As Barclay made his way back to the ropes, the Swede looked back at Darío, seemingly not surprised to find Darío still looking at her. She rolled her eyes at Darío, as if to let him in on her amusement of Barclay. Darío grinned, sharing the Swede's humor, and watched as she rejoined her friend.

As the two women turned to leave the course, Darío quickly tried to commit the directions Chad Curtis had given the Swede's friend to memory.

It was time to try a new place for dinner.

Three

~~~

This is a game of misses.
The guy who misses the best is going to win.
~ *Ben Hogan, professional golfer*

YOU COULDN'T REALLY even call the Armadillo a restaurant. It was no more than a dive bar that happened to serve food. The chairs stuck to the floor, as did your shoes. The bartender had a front tooth missing. Her husband, also behind the bar, didn't look much better. George Strait blared out of the jukebox.

Katie loved it.

Plus, they made the most incredible margaritas.

Her first one went down fast. Too fast, but after a full day in the hot Texas sun walking a golf course that was over five miles long, the cool drink slid down her parched throat with ease. The salt on the rim of the glass stung her sunburned lips. She'd slathered enough sunscreen on her skin to escape the pink sting of sunburn, but she'd forgotten about her lips. The ice in the glass soothed the sting of the salt and the drink numbed her in all kinds of ways. She kept her mouth near or in the glass as she listened to Lizzie and Chad talk business.

She had tried to beg off, told Lizzie she'd order room service at the hotel, but to no avail. Lizzie was insistent that Katie join her and Chad.

Chad had flattered Katie by making an attempt to hit on her. Over the years, she'd gotten the graceful brush-off down pat, and Chad didn't seem to mind her subtle rejection. He only shrugged and mentioned that a bunch of his hometown buddies who still lived in the area would probably be stopping by later to help him celebrate his first official start as a PGA Tour player.

The thought of a bunch of twenty-one-year-old Texas yahoos in celebratory mode made Katie's second margarita slide down as smoothly as the Hank Williams song that now played on the jukebox.

"I love this place," she yelled. She was trying to be heard over Hank, but by the way Lizzie and Chad's heads bolted up, she figured she'd overshot her mark.

Lizzie eyed Katie's near-empty glass. "Careful, KitKat, those aren't made of water, you know."

Katie ignored her friend and instead leaned her head against the back of the chair, feeling her hair stick to something that she didn't want to think about. She let the warm buzz of the drink glide through her body, matching the heat the sun had left on her skin.

The music moved from Hank to Patsy, and Katie hummed along to Crazy. She could hear Lizzie and Chad discussing business, but only made out snatches of Lizzie's pitch.

Blah blah blah, national exposure. Blah blah blah world arena. Blah blah blah part of our family of athletes. Blah blah blah first golfer to be represented by…

She had no doubt Lizzie would land Chad Curtis as an account at Hampton PR. Or Hampton and Associates, as it had been known for several months since Lizzie had taken on partners to free herself up to move back to the Copper Country.

To marry Finn. To become stepmother to his children. To probably become mother to his child someday. To be happy.

Happy. The condition seemed foreign to Katie as she tried to remember the last time she'd been truly happy.

Was she happy seven months ago, when she didn't know

about Ron and Amber? When she'd thought her marriage safe? Safe. That was the word that she came up with when thinking about her marriage pre-bombshell. Safe, not happy.

So, if not happy seven months ago, when? Her mind began twirling a calendar back in her head, almost like the shuffling of a Rolodex containing years, images, incidents. Some elusive memory seemed almost within reach when she was pulled out of her reverie by a deep, definitely male voice coming from behind her chair.

"Hello, Chad. Apparently we didn't spend enough time together already today, for here we are again."

There was humor in the voice. The lilting Spanish accent and deep voice sent the same current through Katie as it had earlier when he'd wished his fellow players well on the first tee.

Katie's head sprung forward, some of her hair staying behind, indeed stuck to the chair as she'd feared. Her hands scrambled to free herself, but the movement was awkward, and before she was able to complete the task, the same voice said, "Allow me." Her hair was disentangled from whatever had made the back of the chair sticky to begin with. Katie didn't even want to begin to imagine what that substance could possibly be.

Chad rose from his seat, his hand stretched out over Katie's head. "*Hola,* Darío, I didn't know you'd be here tonight. Not too many people know about this place."

A strong brown forearm reached past Katie's head to shake Chad's hand. "You forget, I have been on Tour many years. There aren't many good restaurants that I have not been told about."

At the phrase "good restaurant" being used to describe the Armadillo, Katie and Lizzie exchanged smiles across the table from each other.

"Darío, Binky, I'd like you to meet Lizzie Hampton-Robbins and Katie Lipton," Chad said, indicating the two women. "Lizzie, Katie, this is…"

"Maki," Katie interrupted Chad.

"Excuse me?" Chad asked, looking at Katie, not quite sure

what she meant.

"Maki," she said again. At Chad's questioning look she added, "Katie Maki, not Lipton. Maki."

Chad was apologetic. "I'm sorry, I must have misheard Lizzie this morning."

"No, you heard her right, it's not your mistake. And it's not Lipton, it's Maki. Katie Maki," she said. She held out her hand as she swiveled in her seat, and came face to face with Darío Luna.

Well, not quite face to face, more like hand to crotch.

Her hand, held out to shake, came into direct contact with two-time Masters winner Darío Luna's penis.

His "oomph" and her simultaneous "oohh" stunned the rest of the table until the man standing next to Darío said, "If that's your idea of a greeting, luv, let me introduce myself."

It lightened the moment, and all laughed except for Katie and Darío who couldn't stop staring at each other.

"I'm so sorry…"

"I saw you on the course…"

They both spoke at the same time. Both put their heads down, flustered, then both tried again.

"I enjoyed watching…"

"No apology necessary…"

This time they both laughed. Darío held up his hand for Katie to go ahead. "I am so sorry," she said, indicating her hand and his crotch, which only furthered her embarrassment, and she groaned. "Please, you speak."

He laughed. "I was going to say, no need to apologize, but now you have done it twice. Also, I was going to say I saw you on the course today. Did you enjoy the round?"

Katie nodded her head, pleased, but not surprised that Darío remembered her. He had, after all, made eye contact with her afterward. She had been about to go over and introduce herself to him and congratulate him on a fine round when that awful Barclay Ives started hitting on her. "Yes. I enjoyed it very much. You had a great day."

He waved his hand, as if to brush away her compliment. She felt the breeze it created across her cheek. It felt cool against her flushed skin.

"Your approach shot on thirteen was brilliant," she said.

Chad, Lizzie and the caddy turned their heads to Katie in surprise.

"Thank you, but I must confess that the outcome was mostly luck on that shot. Luck and a good bounce."

"You're much too modest," Katie said.

The man next to Darío snorted. "Modest? Guv here, modest? Not bloody likely. By the way, I'm Binky, and you, as you said, are Katie. Not Lipton, but Maki, right?"

He was much taller than Darío, but that was not hard to accomplish. He was lanky, downright skinny, with none of Darío's brooding strength. He was probably a good ten years older than Darío, though his weathered face made him look even older. He wore Dockers and an oxford shirt. Much more dressed up than he had been earlier on the course, when he'd worn shorts and a golf shirt under the requisite apron that all caddies wore.

He was obviously British and Katie suspected he was playing up his thick accent. She already liked him immensely.

"Right, Binky, Katie Maki," she chuckled. "Will you gentlemen join us?" she asked, then remembered that it wasn't her party to invite people to and looked to Lizzie and Chad for reassurance.

Chad jumped to Katie's aid. "Yes. Please, join us."

Binky started to grab for a fifth chair from a neighboring table, but Darío cut him off. "No, thank you, but please enjoy your dinner." He moved beyond them, to a table farther down the length of the bar. A surprised Binky gave Katie a shrug and followed his boss.

Katie looked back at Chad and saw him give a sigh of what looked like relief. "I'm sorry, Chad, should I not have done that?"

He shook his head. "No, that's okay. It never occurred to me to invite them to join us. I'm glad you did. I'm just glad they said no, that's all."

"Oh. Don't you like Darío?" Lizzie asked Chad.

Katie realized she was holding her breath. She didn't know why, but it was very important to her that Chad not say anything bad about Darío.

"Oh no, it's not that at all. It's just, I was so nervous to begin with about playing today, and then to find out yesterday that I'd be paired with Darío Luna. I mean, my God, I was eight years old when I watched him win his first Masters, and now I'm playing with him?"

Katie and Lizzie exchanged "we're so old" glances with each other as they realized how old *they* had been when they watched Darío Luna win his first Masters. It was a lot older than eight.

"But he was so cool. Even asked me questions about growing up in Texas, if I played this course a lot, stuff like that," Chad said. "He was totally awesome, but I don't know if I could handle having to make dinner conversation with him. I think I'd be too nervous."

Chad's cool and totally awesome vocabulary made Katie feel even older than realizing she was Darío Luna's age, not anywhere near Chad Curtis's. She tried to alleviate that sting with some more margarita, only to find her glass had somehow mysteriously emptied.

She waved her empty glass toward Blanche, now on a first-name basis with the bartender. Blanche nodded and gave a, "Comin' up, sweetie," accompanied by a toothless grin.

Katie returned the smile. She loved this place. Women who looked like Blanche seldom called women who looked like Katie sweetie. Usually it was something like "stuck-up bitch" murmured low enough to hear, but not loud enough to be able to comment on.

But Blanche didn't think she was a stuck-up bitch. No, Blanche called her sweetie. She even patted Katie's head as she brought her the margarita. "Pace yourself, sweetie," she said. "I can tell you ain't from Texas, and these here is Texas margaritas. They pack a wallop."

Katie was touched at Blanche's concern. In fact, the warm glow of the liquor made her realize that no one in her entire life had ever cared for her as much as Blanche the Bartender did. Blanche loved her. Just look at the lovely drink she'd brought all the way over to the table for Katie. If that wasn't love, what was?

Katie got out of her chair, not an easy task, swayed just a little, quickly tried to cover it, and launched herself into a startled Blanche's arms for a huge hug.

"Oh Blanche, thank you. Thank you for taking care of me. Thank you for understanding me. You know, I think you're the most wonderful person. I want you to know that." She pulled away, but still clung to Blanche's arms. Blanche held Katie's gaze as if Katie were imparting deep words of wisdom. Katie felt she was. "Blanche, I think I should move to Texas. Is everyone in Texas like you Blanche? So lovely? So understanding?" She looked at Lizzie and Chad, whose eyes had grown big with amusement. "Lizard, I'm moving to Texas."

Lizzie only nodded, but Katie was already turned back to Blanche. "I will notify you the minute I relocate to Texas, Blanche. You will be my first call."

Blanche smiled, disentangling herself from Katie, got her seated once again and then turned to Lizzie and Chad and asked, "Did y'all want another one?"

—⚉—

At the other end of what could loosely be called a restaurant, Darío watched Katie hug the bartender and wondered if perhaps he had been mistaken and she was from around here after all. Then he saw her sway as she sat back down, her friend's hand instinctively reaching out to offer support, which was not heeded, and he realized the scene was one of a grateful drinker to an amused bartender.

He smiled. Katie Maki. Not Lipton. Maki.

So, she had either recently gotten married or divorced. Judging from the vehemence in her voice, and the bare ring finger, he guessed divorced. And the bitterness that he'd detected also led him to believe that perhaps the divorce had not been a friendly one.

Darío wondered what kind of fool would let a woman who looked like that walk out of his life? Her hand at his crotch now made more sense after seeing her sway as she stood to hug the bartender. Maybe she was a drinker? Was that the cause of her divorce?

He didn't think so. There was something almost…virgin… about her drunken movements, like it was a state she was not familiar with.

"Aaah, so that's why you dragged me out to this blasted shack, a bird?" Binky interrupted Darío's gaze and thoughts. "And the pretty bird who followed you all day, no less." There was a teasing gist to his voice.

Darío didn't pretend to misunderstand. "She was not following me. She was following Chad Curtis."

Binky smirked. "Yeah, maybe, but do you think she could tell us what approach shot Chaddy boy shot at thirteen?" He looked around the room and shuddered. "I've been in my fair share of dives in my time, but I can't say I've been in any worse than this one here. And you made me wear my church clothes to this place?"

Darío shrugged and ordered a beer from the man who came from the bar to their table. "I didn't know what it was like."

Binky slapped a hand down on the table. "Right. I knew you were telling tales when you said you'd been here before to Chaddy boy. This place is up my alley, all right, but not yours."

"I didn't say I'd been here before. I said I had been on the Tour a long time and had heard of most local establishments. All true."

"But you'd never heard of this one, have ya?"

"No," Darío admitted.

Binky laughed heartily. "By God, that may be as close to fibbin' that I'll ever see from ya, Guv. And for a bird?" He chuckled some more. "So then why not sit with them when they offered?"

Darío shrugged. "It seemed to me that Chad and Lizzie were conducting business. I didn't want to interfere." That and Katie's hand at his pants had made him so flustered that he felt it better to retreat and regain his composure. Hopefully before the night was over he would get to talk with her again. Plus, he enjoyed just watching her.

Their drinks were delivered and they ordered their dinners. Something that was fried and served in a red plastic basket. The beer tasted cool and refreshing, and Darío momentarily regretted that he only allowed himself one beer per night during a tournament. It was another one of his strict codes.

Darío was also in what Binky would call his church clothes, though Darío had not attended mass for several weeks now. He had assumed that by the business-like demeanor Chad and the Swede's friend had been using at the ropes after the round, that this was indeed to be a business dinner and would thus be held at a fine dining establishment. It was a good thing Darío didn't normally travel with a sports coat, or he would have been even more overdressed than he was in his tailored slacks and white dress shirt.

The women must not have been expecting the Armadillo to be quite so…colorful, either. The woman introduced to Darío as Lizzie wore a nice blouse and slacks, looking like she'd dressed for the business occasion Darío had assumed this dinner was. Katie was a little more casual, but still much more elaborate than Darío was sure the Armadillo was used to. She wore a pale blue sundress, which highlighted her exceptional body. Form-fitting without being obvious. Darío liked that. He had never been attracted to women who flaunted themselves. And lord knew she had plenty to flaunt if she so chose.

Her hair was loose from the ponytail she'd worn at the course and cascaded down her back, almost to her waist. Poker-straight and so blond it was nearly white. It almost seemed incandescent in the poor lighting of the Armadillo. It looked like a halo surrounding the Swede.

Katie Maki. Not Lipton. Maki.

Darío made himself as comfortable as possible in the hard chairs and sat back to let the evening unfold.

The wait was not long. Only an hour later, Katie and Lizzie's table had turned rowdy and lewd, with Chad's hometown buddies toasting their friend's debut on the Tour. Darío and Binky watched as Lizzie tried to leave, but Katie dragged her feet. Seeming to compromise, it looked like they decided to stay, but to move to another table. As they got up and looked around, Binky motioned for the women to join them.

"I think you're safe over here, ladies," Binky said.

Darío couldn't vouch for their safety, but kept his mouth shut when the women joined them. He often let others do the talking, and it would have been hard to get a word in anyway with Binky and Katie quickly becoming as acquainted as old friends.

When Katie waved for another drink, Lizzie stopped her with a head shake to the bartender and a quiet, "No, Kat, you'll be dying tomorrow. How about some water?"

"No, Kat. No, Kat. Did you hear that, Binky? I've just been shot down by someone I'm a whole four months older than. Do you think that's right?"

Before Binky could come back with what Darío presumed would be an unsuitable answer to one of the women, he defused the situation by asking, "Kat? That nickname came from Katie, I assume?"

Katie nodded, then broke into song, "Cat. Hat. In French, chat, chapeau." She smiled at Lizzie. A smile Darío knew bridged years of friendship. Lizzie caught her cue and joined in. "In Spanish, el gato in a sombrero." The two women giggled when they completed their song.

"From The Cat in the Hat," Lizzie explained to Darío and Binky. "It's been one of our favorites for years."

"I particularly like the Spanish interpretation," Darío said. "In my country, you would be known as *Gato*. Well, actually, *Gata* in your case."

Both women smiled at him, but he only saw Katie. He

watched the flush of her cheeks when he rolled the name out.

"*Gata*. Yes, I like that. You may address me as *Gata*." She declared this to the whole table, with a ceremonial wave of her hand that nearly toppled Darío's water glass.

"I must confess, I came to think of you as 'the Swede' today on the course, before I knew your name," he said, chagrinned.

She waved his comment aside, this time almost taking Lizzie's glass with her.

"That's okay. Lizzie's husband called me the Viking before he met me," she said. Her brow furrowed as she continued, "Actually, he still calls me the Viking, now that I think about it." She chuckled at this, and the furrow charmingly turned into laughter crinkles.

"Then I am forgiven for thinking of you as the Swede, eh?"

She smiled. "Where I'm from, we use 'eh' at the end of sentences too," Katie said. "But it doesn't sound as lyrical as when you do it."

"And where exactly is it that you come from?" he asked. He was replaying her voice in his head, seeing if he'd missed some sort of accent. He didn't think so. Years on both the European and American tours had exposed him to nearly every language spoken and he had become adept at recognizing each, and actually learning quite a few.

"From Michigan," she said.

Darío turned his right hand to her, palm facing them both. "Show me where," he said. He had seen a couple of the caddies that were from Michigan do this once, the upturned hand simulating Michigan's mitten shape.

She laughed again, a lovely, tinkling sound. "See, that's the thing. I'm from the *Upper* Peninsula." She took her left hand, palm facing them, and placed it above his, almost touching the bottom edge of her pinky to the tip of his middle finger. "There's a whole 'nother part to Michigan that nobody realizes."

He nodded. "That's right, now I remember, Michigan is in two parts. Where exactly is your home?"

She used her right hand to point to the base of her thumb. "I'm from Hancock, which is part of the Copper Country, right here."

The use of their combined hands to create the Great Lakes State had their heads in close proximity. Darío could smell her perfume, though it was soft, barely there. Some kind of tangy, fruity scent. Like oranges, or maybe some kind of berry. He was tempted to ask her the location of every single city in Michigan just so they could stay this way longer.

She looked at him and all thoughts of geography flew from Darío's mind. *Dios mio*, she had the most incredible…everything. He could list her exceptional attributes, but it would take too long. She was simply as exquisite up close as she had been from behind the ropes earlier that day.

Their heads were so close he could smell her sweet breath. It was lime and salt and something else he couldn't name. Her lips, puffy from sunburn, were so near his own, it would only take a small movement to capture them. His head moved another fraction.

"Oh no," Lizzie said from across the table.

Darío and Katie's heads popped apart, as if they were children caught with their fingers in the cookie jar. Lizzie was looking beyond them.

"Chad looks like he's trying to get out of here gracefully. I don't think he should drive, he's had quite a few beers since his buddies showed up," she said, her eyes never leaving Chad Curtis, halfway across the room.

"Lizzie, he's not even your client," Katie said.

"Yet. And if he's going to be my client, I can't let him walk out of here and drive after drinking." She grabbed her purse, opened her wallet, got her keys and made her goodbyes all at once.

Darío waved her hand away as she went to pay for the drinks she and Katie had consumed since joining the men. The drinks Katie had consumed. Lizzie had drunk only water all evening as far as Darío could tell. "Please, Lizzie, allow me," he said.

"Thanks, Darío. It was great to meet you. And you too, Binky. Come on, Kat," Lizzie said, rising from the table. "We'll take my car, leave his and then I'll pick him up in the morning and bring him back here. Yes. That will work." She said the last to herself more than her companions. She was still watching Chad who was fumbling with his keys. She didn't seem to notice that Katie made no move to leave. She had gone several steps toward Chad when she finally realized Katie was still sitting.

As their eyes met, Katie folded her arms across her chest and gave her friend a firm shake of her head. "Uh-uh. I don't want to leave yet, Lizard," Katie said.

"Kat, really, I can't let Chad drive. Please, we've got to go. This could ruin my plan."

Before Darío could, Binky jumped in, "We'll get Katie back to your hotel, Lizzie. Not to worry."

Lizzie looked from Katie, to Binky, then finally to Darío, who nodded. "We'd be happy to bring Katie back with us. We won't be too much longer." He saw Lizzie's eyes glance toward Darío's glass of water, which he'd switched to long ago after having his one beer. He liked that she was looking out for her friend as well as her prospective client.

Lizzie looked at her friend. "Are you sure you want to stay, Kat?" There was concern in her voice. Darío could see she was visibly torn between getting to Chad in time and making sure her friend would be all right.

"Please, Lizzie, Binky and I would be happy to bring Katie back to the hotel," Darío assured her.

"Okay. Thank you both. See you later, Kat. Stick to water from here on out, eh?"

Katie laughed. "Yes, mother."

He watched as Lizzie caught up with Chad at the entrance and gracefully removed the keys from his hands as she led him out the door. Darío turned back to the table to see Binky and Katie both staring at him. Binky had a mischievous grin on his face.

Katie was licking her sunburned lips. Her beautiful, full, tempting lips.

"Okay. Now that our resident stick-in-the-mud is gone, let's get this party started," Katie said and waved her empty margarita glass at the bartender, pushing her water glass aside.

Binky laughed and waved his glass as well, while Darío could only wonder what he'd just gotten himself into.

Four

—〰—

*Eighteen holes of match or medal play will teach you more
about your foe than will eighteen years
of dealing with him across a desk.*
~ Grantland Rice, former sportswriter

KATIE WASN'T SURE if she'd said goodbye to Blanche. And she
knew she'd wanted to. But here she was in the front seat of Darío's
courtesy car, provided for the players at each tournament, and she
wasn't exactly certain how she'd gotten there.

The car was stopped in front of room number 18 at a Motel
6.

Oh God, she hadn't just made a monumental mistake, had
she?

Headlines of pro athletes being accused of sexual transgres-
sions flashed through her head. Headlines she'd proofread herself.

"What…what are we doing here?" she asked. This was not
the Imperial, where she and Lizzie, as well as the golfers, were
staying.

Just as she was trying to remember all the things she knew
Alison and Lizzie had learned as single women about being alone
in this kind of situation, she saw movement in front of her. Binky
was motioning goodbye and disappearing into the motel room.
Darío gave his caddy a wave as Katie felt a wave of relief.

As he backed out of the lot, she saw that Darío realized she had awakened from her...uh cat nap...she decided to call it. He smiled at her. It was a soft smile, full of concern, and made her feel as warm as the sun had earlier in the day. It rushed through her body like the tequila. "Are you going to be okay?" he asked her.

Good question. She certainly didn't feel okay. Her mind was still a little fuzzy, but slowly coming back into focus.

This was so unlike her. She hardly ever drank, and when she did, it was always just one with the girls. But Lizzie had said that these two days were about getting away from everything, and she was determined to do that. She just hadn't thought she'd do it with alcohol. Oh well...spilt milk. Or spilt tequila in this case.

He asked if she was going to be okay. She didn't have the answer, but she nodded at Darío anyway. "Sorry I fell asleep."

He shrugged, seemingly not put off by either her inebriated state or her falling asleep. Maybe it was something he was used to. Binky certainly seemed no stranger to the bottle.

"Why is Binky staying here? How come he's not at the Imperial?" she asked.

Darío kept his eye on the road as he answered, "The caddies don't stay where the players stay. It's too expensive for them. They usually stay at a cheaper place."

Katie nodded. That made sense. They slowed, then stopped at a red light, and Darío turned to her. He studied her face with that same look of concern. She knew the moment the look changed from concern to desire. She thought it would startle her, even shock her, but it didn't. It made her tingle.

Of course, that could just be the residual effects of the margaritas, but she didn't think so. It had been a long time since she'd seen a man show that kind of want in his eyes.

Sure, she intercepted lecherous looks all the time. And nice gazes, ones of appreciation, that she returned with a soft, asexual smile. But to be this close to a man who was looking at her like he'd like to have her for dinner? It had been an awfully long time. And it felt...nice. More than nice, she realized as Darío moved a hand to her face.

He was going to kiss her! The thought literally made her toes curl and the straps of her sandals dug into the tops of her feet. God, she wished she had a mint.

His hand drew nearer. She could see it clearly from the streetlight. A strong, calloused hand, the indentation of the tape he'd worn earlier still evident. This one much lighter than the one still resting on the steering wheel due to wearing a golf glove so much of the time. She followed the hand down to his wrist and to his forearm. His shirtsleeve rolled nearly to the elbow gave her a clear view of that lovely arm. Which she couldn't take her eyes off of all day. The one he would surely anchor behind her neck and pull him to her for a scorching kiss.

But no, the hand went to her mouth, and she found she liked the thought of that even better. A little nibbling on his finger as he outlined her mouth? She and Ron had been past the point of seduction years ago.

Just a little bit more and he'd be touching her. Yes, that's it. He brought his thumb to the corner of her mouth. But instead of the gentle caress she'd been expecting, it was a rough draw across her mouth and cheek. She then watched as he took his hand away and wiped his thumb on his pants.

Oh, God! She had drooled while she'd slept and it was so obvious, he'd felt the need to wipe it off himself. The warm feeling running through her turned to a chill. His look wasn't desire, she decided, but disgust. If she'd had any idea where in the world they were, she might have just jumped out of the car right then and there and walked back to the hotel.

She was saved from having to say anything—and making a dash for it—by the car behind them honking. Katie didn't know how long the light had been green, but the cars behind them were not happy. The entrance for the expressway was just beyond and Darío turned his attention to the road.

They rode in silence for a while, until Darío finally spoke. "Tell me, why is it that you are Maki, not Lipton?"

"I drool in my sleep and my husband couldn't take it anymore."

Darío threw his head back and laughed, and Katie noticed the white skin peeking through at the juncture of neck and throat. "Somehow, I think that waking up next to you would not be dampened by something as inconsequential as a little drool."

She loved how he spoke. The slight accent was lovely, but his word usage…not too many people threw around the words dampened and inconsequential in the same sentence. And this was his second language.

Oh heck, why not tell him the truth. She'd never see this man again after tomorrow.

"My husband left me," she said quietly.

Darío didn't say anything, only nodded for her to go on.

Which she did, and then some.

It was a purge. And this time it was not quietly spoken.

"Not only did he leave me, but he left me for a twenty-year-old that he'd gotten pregnant."

Darío nodded.

"He couldn't handle us not being able to have a child. Or, I guess I should say, *me* not being able to have a child. Because it's darn sure obvious now that *he* can."

Darío nodded but kept his eyes on the road.

"We'd been together since we were freshmen in college. Married for thirteen years, and he comes home and tells me he's leaving me for some young thing. God, it's so cliché, so laughable."

Darío only nodded again soberly. Apparently he didn't think it was laughable.

"I should have known, though. It shouldn't have taken me so much by surprise."

Darío finally spoke. "Why should you have known?"

"Oh, little things. Like he had to 'go to the office' a lot last summer." At Darío's questioning frown she clarified, "He's a high school teacher and hockey coach. There's no school in the summer, and hockey's played in the winter." Darío nodded his understanding, and motioned with his hand for her to continue.

"Last summer he used the money we'd set aside for invitro fertilization for a Hummer."

"What is a Hummer?"

"They're these huge cars that kind of look like a tank, and no one with any sense would spend over $50,000 on one. Thank God they've stopped making them. Just not in time for me."

"Oh yes, a Hummer. Several players on the Tour own such vehicles."

Feeling she had just insulted his friends, she said, "Oh, I'm sorry."

He waved his hand. "It's fine. I too believe that these vehicles are a bit…" Just as the word popped into her head, he finished, "…Ostentatious."

"Anyway, I should have known then. But I thought it was just the stress of trying to conceive. They warn you about that when you first start seeing the doctors. They tell you that infertility can put a strain on a marriage."

"The man is a…what's the word you say here? Douche," Darío said.

Katie smiled. "No. That's just it, he isn't really. He's a good person, and was a good husband…"

"Until he impregnated another woman. A girl, really."

"Yes," her voice became quiet once more.

"The man is a fool," Darío whispered.

"No, he's not a fool. He's just a man. And when the going got tough…"

"Maybe he's not a fool. But the man has no character."

Katie was about to contradict Darío, to tell him that for most of their marriage, Ron had been a good husband. A great husband, even. That the pressure of trying to have a baby was too much for them. He broke in his way—by having an affair.

But she broke in her way as well. She became distant, she saw that now. She hadn't seen the signs of Ron's straying because she was immersed in her own self-pity. Knowing that their inability to have a child was her fault had made her withdraw from Ron. She'd felt she'd failed him. Failed herself. The only time they'd had sex was when it was conducive to conception. And even in those times it was cold and clinical, all intimacy gone.

He had reached out to her several times and she had always turned away.

Ron wasn't a douche. He was a man who made a mistake. But hey, if Darío wanted to think he was a fool with no character, well, she'd just let him.

—⚬—

Darío didn't even know this man Ron and yet he wanted to throttle him. As he pulled the car into the valet area at the Imperial he took another glance at Katie. Her outburst over, she was now deep in thought. That was not good. Her beautiful face no longer held the smile it had all evening. Her delicate brow was scrunched into a frown. He longed to bring her smile back, but was ignorant as to how.

As the valet took his keys, Darío hurried to the other side of the car to help Katie. He would have anyway—his Mamá had drummed that into his head well enough—but he thought Katie may actually need help getting out of the car and walking into the hotel.

She did need his help. She tried to wave him away and made it as far as the lobby door, but the huge revolving door was too much for her and she turned to him with a helpless look in her eyes.

He didn't say a word, just put one arm around her shoulder and tucked his other hand through her arm, pinning her to him, and proceeded through the doors and across the ornate lobby.

Two Tour players were just leaving the hotel bar and met Darío and Katie at the elevator banks.

They said their hellos, the players obviously waiting for an introduction to Katie, who only nodded and smiled at the two men. Darío knew Katie would never see these two men again. She would probably never see *him* again. And yet he felt a duty not to tell the players her name when they could obviously see she was severely inebriated, and had probably already labeled her for accompanying him to his hotel room.

He could have explained, but chose not to. Let the men think what they wanted. Many of the Tour players partook of the women at each tour stop, and the majority of them were married. Though the married ones were much more discreet after Tiger's scandal.

The elevator arrived and the other two players waited for Katie to board. Darío gently held her in place. "You two go ahead, we will wait for the next one."

The players gave him knowing grins, and stepped into the elevator. Darío pushed the up button again as soon as the one carrying his fellow players was on its way. When the next elevator arrived Darío nudged Katie inside.

Once inside he loosened his hold on her. She seemed to take it as some kind of cue and separated herself from him altogether. That had not been his intention. He liked holding her. Liked how her body fit with his. She was taller than the women he was usually attracted to, almost taller than himself, but that didn't bother him.

Her hips met his; her waist was at a perfect level for his arm to slide around. Her breasts met his chest. In theory. He had yet to feel that particularly tempting sensation.

She moved to a corner of the elevator and steadied each hand on the railing. Her knees bent slightly. She seemed to be bracing herself for the ride. She looked adorable, almost childlike.

"What room are you in, Katie?" he asked, his finger hovering over the button panel.

This seemed a very serious question to Katie and her eyes stared hard at the carpet in concentration. It came to her in a flash and she raised her head, smiling as though she had just solved a difficult equation. "Thirty-five fifteen."

Darío pushed the button for the thirty-fifth floor and then went to the other corner of the small cubicle, also resting his hands on the railing. He noticed that Katie's knuckles were nearly white with the effort to hold herself steady. Their hands almost met on the back wall railing. He tried to nonchalantly ease his fingers to hers, his body still lamenting the loss of contact. She seemed to notice the movement and her gaze moved to his hand. He held his hand in place.

She stared at his hand for a moment, then her eyes moved up his arms.

"Make like you're taking a swing," she whispered.

"Excuse me?"

"Pretend you're setting up at the ball." There was a small note of command in her voice. Darío liked that. "Please," she added, and he liked that even more.

She took her hands away from the railing and held them together in front of her, pretending to hold a nonexistent golf club, showing Darío what she wanted him to do. Then, as if she might lose her balance, she quickly grabbed for the railing again and only when she had her composure back did she nod for Darío to proceed.

This was not a completely unusual request for Darío. He was asked lots of times for tips on a swing, or to watch someone set up, or to look at their grip, or if he would show them his. But he was always asked by men, and very seldom in elevators. Still, if Katie wanted to see his set-up, fine.

He pushed away from the railing and stepped into the middle of the elevator where he then addressed an imaginary ball, as if it were the opening drive of the Masters. He looked up at Katie, waiting for her instructions, but did not meet her eyes. He could not make eye contact with her because she was staring at his forearms. He looked down at himself to see if he was doing something out of the ordinary. No, it was a usual set-up. He glanced at her again. Her eyes were still on his arms. She wasn't looking at his grip, either. No, it was definitely his arms.

He looked at them again, trying to figure out Katie's fascination. He could come up with nothing. He ventured another look at Katie, and this time...*Dios Mio*, this time she licked her lips as she watched his arms.

She was aroused? By his arms? It didn't seem possible, but she finally raised her gaze from his arms to his eyes and there was no mistaking the look in her sky-blue eyes. Unbelievable. His arms made her hot.

It had been a rollercoaster ride the entire evening trying to tell if Katie felt the same attraction he did, or whether she was just happy to meet a professional golfer and make new friends. He'd have sworn she felt the same heat he had when their eyes would meet at the Armadillo. Even as far back as earlier on the course. And when they had huddled together to create the state of Michigan with their hands, he was sure she had breathed him in as deeply as he had her.

He had thought he might get lucky.

But the ride back to the hotel had shot that idea down. First, she had fallen asleep, making Darío realize that she was drunker than he thought. Then she began ranting about her ex-husband, and he wondered if the sexual attraction was all in his head. Either that, or the bitterness she felt for her husband far outweighed her attraction to Darío.

He didn't want a revenge fuck. He wanted Katie in his bed, all right. But he wanted her sober, willing, involved.

But now, she was making eyes at him in the elevator. He stayed where he was, his body still locked in golf mode.

She slowly pushed her incredible body away from the wall, took her hands from the railing and made the two steps to where Darío stood. He started to break his formation, but her hands on his arms stopped him.

"Did you know," she began. She seemed to lose her train of thought as he stared into her eyes. She became flustered, and lowered her gaze back to his arms. She stood right in front of him, her head bowed, almost praying over his grip. That seemed fitting, he thought, because he often found himself praying over a shot as well.

She leaned into him, her head as far forward as his. Her set-up identical to his, but instead of gripping an imaginary club, she gripped his arms. Her forehead swayed forward and was stopped by his. She felt feverish against him.

"Did you know?" she began again. "That when you're on the course, and you are over a shot, just like this." She stopped. Darío waited, not wanting to break the spell she was putting him under. "That your arms...your arms...are just about the sexiest thing I think I've ever seen."

He waited for her to say more. He wanted her to say more. When she didn't, he realized she must be waiting for him to say something. He couldn't. He absolutely could not think of any response to what she'd just said.

All thought of wanting Katie completely sober before taking her to bed flew out of his mind. She obviously wanted him. So she was a little drunk? She had been attracted to him on the course, well before she began drinking.

Just as he was about to break her hold on his arms by putting them around her, he heard a noise coming from her.

A snore. A soft, lady-like snore, but a snore nonetheless.

She had literally passed out on him.

Five

—⚬—

I'm playing the best golf I've ever played right now,
except for when I was playing better.
~ Fred Couples, professional golfer

SHE WAS BLIND. All she could see was white. Just a glaring flash of white.

"Katie? Hey, Kat? You really need to get up."

Lizzie had opened the drapes. That was the blinding flash. "Lizard, close the drapes," she whispered.

"It's nearly eleven. I let you sleep as late as I could. I've already taken Chad to pick up his car. You need to get up and get going. We should be leaving for the course in an hour." Lizzie's voice sounded like a cannon in Katie's muddled head.

"An hour? It only takes me a half hour to get ready." She pulled the pillow over her head in an attempt to block out the sunlight. And Lizzie's voice. And the monumental hangover she was suffering from.

"I have a feeling it's going to be slow going for you today, KitKat," Lizzie said, a touch of sympathy in her voice. "Come on now. Step one, take the pillow from your head. Step two, open your eyes."

Not budging, Katie asked, "What's step three?"

Lizzie chuckled. "A shower. But I didn't think you could

handle hearing beyond one and two just yet."

"Very intuitive," Katie said, as she slowly removed the pillow from her head. Tentatively she raised her eyelids. They seemed so heavy, as if something were weighing them down. Sleep crust mixed with dried on mascara.

Taking the bull by the horns, she rubbed her eyes open, threw the blankets from the bed and started to get up.

Big mistake.

"Oh God, Lizard, I think I'm dying," she moaned. Even that caused her head to ache. She sat on the edge of the bed holding her head in her hands.

Lizzie sat next to her on the bed and began gently rubbing her neck. "You're not dying, Kat, but you're probably going to wish you had. Here, hold this to your forehead and eyes." She handed a cool, damp washcloth to Katie, which she immediately administered to her aching head.

"Thanks, that helps." Lizzie began massaging the back of Katie's neck and shoulders. "Oooh, that helps too." She was quiet a moment, letting her friend's soft touch work its magic. "And thanks for no 'I told you to stop drinking', too." Her voice mimicked a nagging shrew and Lizzie softly swatted Katie.

"First, I wouldn't say 'I told you so', and second, if I did, I would certainly never use that tone of voice. I've only been a stepmother three months, I haven't perfected that tone yet." She paused. "But both Stevie and Annie have certainly got me working on it. It'll be no time at all before I'm a pro at being a nag. Then, watch out."

After a few moments, Lizzie pried the washcloth from Katie and walked to the bathroom, presumably to run fresh cold water on it. Katie hoped so, because she thought that the cloth may be the only thing saving her from running into the bathroom and doing a little praying to the porcelain god.

She hadn't thought of that phrase in years. Probably since college and the last time she, or any of her friends had drunk so much that being bowed before the toilet on a Sunday morning was the only form of worship that happened that day.

Her thoughts quickly returned from the past, before they could turn to Ron. Instead, she tried to remember last night, and the events that put her in this sorry state.

Images blew past her. The Armadillo. Her new best friend, Blanche. Chad being in his glory amongst his hometown buds. Lizzie looking out for her potential new client, just as she looked out for all those in her close circle. Binky tempting her to another margarita. Binky?

Darío.

"Uh, Lizard? How did I get to the hotel room last night?" Lizzie was back at her side, handing her the fresh cloth. She sat down in a chair across from the bed, facing Katie.

She put her feet up on the bed, next to Katie's behind, nudging her. "I don't know, KitKat. How *did* you get back to the hotel room last night?" There was a wicked smile on Lizzie's face.

Katie looked around the room, taking in everything. "I don't remember, but I know you undressed me and put me to bed."

Lizzie looked surprised. "How do you know that?"

Katie shrugged her shoulders. Even that hurt. "Because my clothes, which undoubtedly reek from that bar, are neatly folded on the dresser. Only you would do that, Lizard."

"Busted. So, you figured that out. What do you actually remember?"

Katie sunk her head back down into her hands and the cool dampness of the washcloth. "Um, I remember you leaving to bring Chad back here. Did that go okay?" She realized for the first time that there were other people on her little adventure last night other than herself. And Darío. She felt guilty about not asking Lizzie about Chad sooner.

Lizzie waved her hand, dismissing Katie's guilt. "Fine. It was a little tense in the parking lot when he realized I had no intention of letting him drive. But I won out."

Like you always do, Katie thought to herself.

"When I took him to get his car he invited me to his parents' home for dinner this evening. I think he wants to close the deal."

Katie raised her head and smiled at her friend. "That's great. Congratulations. Though I'm not surprised. Lizzie Hampton always gets her man. Oops, I mean Robbins."

Lizzie smiled back at Katie. "Hardly. About always getting my man, that is."

"You did in the end, though, Lizard, that's what counts."

She was speaking about Chad, but by the dreamy look on Lizzie's face, Katie guessed her friend had her husband in mind when she nodded and said, "Yes. In the end, I got him."

"Wait. You got ready and left and came back and I didn't hear it?" The thought of not hearing the commotion made Katie realize just how dead to the world she'd been. That thought led back to how she'd come to be in that position.

"I remember staying on with Binky and Darío. Binky and I played a few drinking games…"

"What kind of games did you play with Darío?" Lizzie asked, once again nudging Katie's hip with her foot.

She was about to say "none", but she stopped herself. She searched her memory. Images of Darío's hand reaching to her mouth flashed through her mind. She decided to ignore her friend's last comment. "We left. We took Binky to his hotel and dropped him off." The memories were becoming sharper now, more in focus. She didn't feel the need to tell Lizzie about falling asleep, nor about her near hysterics as she told Darío about her marriage breaking up. She would just keep that bit of embarrassing information to herself.

"We came here. Took the elevator." She stopped. She didn't remember anything after that, but another flash, this one of Darío's strong arms reaching for her, went through her mind. He had brought her straight here, hadn't he? There had been no pit stop to his room, had there? Though the idea of sleeping with Darío Luna was not at all displeasing to her, she'd like to be able to remember it.

"And then I took over," Lizzie said. She sounded disappointed that there wasn't more to the story. "And here you are with a hangover. God, it's been so long since I've had a hangover. Are they as bad as I remember?"

"Worse. What do you mean then you took over?"

"From Darío." Katie gave Lizzie a questioning look. "When he brought you here. God, you were a sight, KitKat, thrown over his shoulder like a sack of potatoes, completely passed out. He was good enough to put you on the bed before he left. If you'd passed out on me in an elevator, I'd had probably left you there."

The fuzzy feeling rushed from Katie's head, replaced with pure mortification. "Oh no. I passed out in the elevator? He had to carry me here?" As Lizzie nodded, Katie closed her eyes and moaned.

Lizzie's snicker was interrupted by a knock at the door. Good thing, or Katie probably would have kicked her.

"That's probably housekeeping. I put the Do Not Disturb sign on, but it's getting so late they probably think we're dead in here," Lizzie said as she got up to cross the room.

"Who's to say we aren't?"

The nightmare continued for Katie as she looked up and saw Darío standing at the door holding a glass filled with green goop.

Lizzie waved him in while Katie said a silent prayer of thanks that Lizzie had dressed her in a huge tee-shirt last night. At least she was covered in all the important places. Except for her pride. That was naked and shivering.

Darío didn't seem to notice. He said a quick hello to Lizzie and moved past her to stand in front of Katie.

"Ah, the Kat is more of a kitten this morning, eh? No roar left?" He smiled at Katie, his voice teasing.

She forced a weak smile. "No more roar. If fact, I feel like I may cough up a hairball at any minute."

He laughed, a deep, throaty chuckle that should have made Katie's head ache more, but somehow it didn't. She didn't make any move to leave the bed, wasn't sure she could stand up even if she wanted to—which she didn't. She waved him to sit in the seat that Lizzie had just vacated, which he did. She eyed the glass he held in his hands. "Why do I think you come bearing gifts?" she asked, gesturing to the glass.

"Ah, yes. I am correct in assuming that you two ladies will be following my—Chad and my—pairing this afternoon?"

Katie was about to say no, that she couldn't possibly walk the course in the blazing afternoon sun, but Lizzie piped in. "Of course."

Darío nodded. "Then I thought that perhaps Katie may need some…uh, fortification before the round begins." He held the glass out to her with both hands.

Something about the way he held the glass. With both hands, arms extended, almost like he was holding a golf club. Something about that seemed so familiar to Katie. She looked from the glass to his hands, his arms and then to his face. He had a sly smile that Katie figured was some sort of private joke that she was supposed to know the punch line to. She didn't, so she ignored his look. "What's in that…fortification?" she asked, pointing to the glass of goop.

"I think it best if you don't know," he said. "I called Binky this morning to ask him what he uses. He gave me the recipe. The staff in the kitchen was kind enough to prepare this for me. For you."

If the man was thoughtful enough to call Binky then get the hotel kitchen to whip this junk up for her, then she'd have to toughen up and drink it. Taking a deep breath, she took the glass from his hands and drank the concoction in one, long drink. She waited a moment to see if she'd need to make a mad dash to the bathroom after all, but was pleasantly surprised to find that it stayed down.

"Thank you. That was very considerate of you," she said, meeting his soft brown eyes.

"It is nothing," he said as he rose to leave. "I will see you both later this afternoon." With a quick nod to Lizzie he was out the door.

Lizzie came back and sat across from Katie. She said nothing, only raised an eyebrow to Katie.

"What?" Katie said.

"What? What? That's my question. Exactly what happened last night?" Lizzie asked, a mischievous smile on her face.

"I told you everything that happened."

"Well maybe you left something out, 'cause he's definitely smitten, Kat."

Katie snorted. "He's not smitten. He's a good Samaritan, that's all."

"If you say so. Hey, I say go for it. It'd be just what you need to get a little attention from someone like Darío Luna."

Katie sighed. "Lizard, there is no way the guy is interested. First of all I shake his crotch instead of his hand when we're introduced. Then I get drunk. I fall asleep in his car and drool all over myself. Then I pass out on him in an elevator seconds after I tell him his arms are the…" That last missing piece of the previous night came flooding back to Katie. "Oh, God," she moaned, curling back on the bed and putting the pillow over her head.

"What?" Lizzie asked, sensing good scoop.

"I told him. Oh God! I told him when he sets up over a shot, his forearms are the sexiest thing I've ever seen."

Lizzie sat down with a plop. "And do you?"

"Do I what?" Katie said, the pillow muffling her reply.

"Think his arms are the sexiest thing you've ever seen?"

Almost a full minute went by until Katie slowly pulled the pillow from her head. "Yes. Yes, I believe I do."

—⁂—

He could do no wrong.

The hole looked four feet wide and his putts went in effortlessly. He sank the long ones. He sank the short ones. He sank everything.

But that wasn't even the amazing part. His drives were straight and right in the middle of the fairway.

And of course it would have to happen to him when he finally had a reason to want to walk near the ropes.

Katie. *Gata.*

She and Lizzie had been with his group from the start, and although Darío knew that Lizzie was there to follow Chad, he let himself believe that Katie was there to follow him.

Not that it mattered, of course, but he did feel a small burst of pride knowing he was shooting close to a course record today while she watched.

And she knew it too. She knew a truly good shot from just an okay shot. Much of the gallery would break into ecstatic clapping when he sank a long putt. But Katie would applaud a chip that didn't even get to the hole but had been a bear of a shot because of the lie. She knew the difference, and that pleased Darío.

She was again dressed for maximum sun and Darío kept an eye on her glorious shoulders, worried that the sweltering afternoon sun might get through any protection she wore.

On the thirteenth hole, a par three where players were forced to wait several minutes on the tee box for the green to clear of the group ahead of them, Darío watched as Katie licked her lips and grimaced. He had seen her do that several times, and remembered how tender and swollen her lips had looked last night.

He had thought they looked like they'd been kissed and kissed well. Now he realized they were sunburned.

He motioned for Katie to come to him, politely asking the fans who had glued themselves to the ropes for the entire day to let her through. They weren't very happy about relinquishing their sought-after positions, but the request was so out of place that they moved to the side and let Katie through.

She looked at him bewilderingly and with just a small touch of panic once she got to him. "What? What is it? Is something wrong? Are you sick? Is Binky?"

Darío chuckled. "No, nothing is wrong." He then pulled a Chapstick from his pocket and held it up for Katie to see. "You need to put some of this on your lips, *Gata.*"

She stared at him. He knew she didn't understand it. It was

very unorthodox for a player to talk with the gallery during a round. Look at, sure. Possibly even make eye contact with. But rarely did a player lose his focus and talk to anyone but his caddy. Even polite chit-chat with the other players was usually confined to the first three or four holes until the players found their groove.

He gestured for her to take the lip balm, but she stared at him, dumbfounded. Then she looked around the gallery and saw everyone staring at her and the most adorable flush rose up her neck and cheeks.

Darío figured they could stand like that for hours. Taking matters into his own hands, he uncapped the tube, gently held Katie's chin between his thumb and forefinger and applied the balm to her mouth.

Her lips, slightly swollen from the previous day, absorbed the balm at contact, and he made several swipes to build up a good coat. He took his time, enjoying the soft give of her mouth as the balm made contact. Enjoying, also, the feel of her soft skin where he held her chin. Finally satisfied, he looked from her tempting mouth into her crystal blue eyes.

Big mistake.

She felt the connection as well, and it shone in her eyes. Darío took a step back, so thrown off guard. He nearly tripped over his golf bag and was caught by a chuckling Binky. Darío's eyes never left Katie's.

He finally thought of something to say to break the connection, though he wasn't sure he wanted to. "And are you feeling better this afternoon?" he asked.

She nodded. "Yes. Thank you. Your remedy completely did the trick. Thank you for all the effort."

"It was no effort at all." He knew he should turn back to the course. Others from the gallery seemed to be getting bolder, moving closer, yearning to hear the conversation he was having with this beautiful woman. He couldn't seem to make himself move. "Are you enjoying the round?"

Her head nodded enthusiastically. "Very much. Is golf like

baseball where you can't mention to a pitcher with a no-hitter going how well he is doing?"

He was confused. "I am not familiar with that." He quickly glanced at the green and saw that in the group ahead of him, one of the players was having trouble with the treacherous bunkers. Good, he thought, more time.

"In baseball, if a pitcher has a no-hitter going, nobody talks to him in the dugout, or says anything to him, and they certainly don't mention that he's doing so well."

"Ahh, I see, a superstition?"

"Right. No one wants to jinx him. Is it the same in golf?"

He thought on that for a second. From the corner of his eye, he noticed Chad and Barclay standing to the side of him, watching. Barclay made a move to join him and Katie, but Binky cut him off with some inane question about Barclay's balls. Darío assumed Binky was referring to Barclay's golf balls, but with Binky one could never be sure.

"In golf, you really only talk to your caddy during the round. Some to the other players and caddies. Never to the gallery…" He stopped as Katie raised her eyebrows at him. "Very seldom to the gallery," he amended. "But your caddy does not see it as a jinx to mention how well you are doing."

"Oh, okay," she said. Then her beautiful face lit up into a huge smile and Darío heard audible gasps of delight from the men in the gallery who were positioned well enough to see her. "In that case, you're having a spectacular round. Keep it up!"

He did.

An unfortunate bounce on sixteen kept him from tying the course record, but he ended the round on Friday in the lead of the tournament. A position he hadn't been in for years. He motioned for Katie and Lizzie to meet him at the ropes at the finishing hole.

"We must celebrate, eh? Let me take you and Lizzie to dinner tonight. You two seem to be good-luck charms for me." He added Lizzie to his declaration, but his eyes were solely on Katie.

Lizzie smiled. "Thank you, but I can't. I'm having dinner

with Chad and his parents this evening. But it would be great if you would take Katie; that way I wouldn't feel so guilty about dumping her."

"You're not dumping me, Lizard. I'll be just fine alone," Katie said.

"But there's no need for you to dine alone," Darío added.

He saw her chew on her lip, knew that she must be tasting the cherry flavor of his lip balm, had tasted it on himself throughout the day. It had given him a perverse pleasure to know she was tasting the same thing as he.

Dios Mio, get a hold of yourself! It's only lip balm.

She still hadn't decided. "I promise not to let you drink any margaritas," he cajoled.

Katie laughed. "That won't be a problem. Believe me, if I never see another margarita again, I'll be happy."

"Famous last words, luv," Binky said. He had not been part of the conversation, but had walked by at that precise moment, dropped his one-liner, and kept on going toward the clubhouse with Darío's bag.

Katie smiled at his caddy's comment. "Will Binky be joining us?" she asked.

Good, she had accepted. Bad, she wanted Binky to come along as well.

Darío had no illusions about dinner. He had expected to take both women. That he was only taking Katie in no way led him to believe that anything more than dinner would be happening. After the way she ranted in the car last night about her ex-husband, Darío knew that Katie was a long way from wanting to be intimate with a man. Any man, let alone one she had just met the previous day. No, it would just be dinner. A chance for him to get to know her better. But it would be just the two of them.

"No. Binky spends Friday evenings playing poker with some of the other caddies. It is a contest, of sorts, to see which caddies are there on Friday nights and which are trunk slammers."

"Trunk slammers?" Lizzie asked.

"If a player doesn't make the cut on Friday, he puts his clubs in the trunk of the car to go home. In theory, slamming the trunk door shut on a bad week. The caddies who are still around on Friday night are there because their players made the cut, thus their paycheck will be more than the usual salary that week.

"A caddy is paid a weekly salary by a player, but if he makes the cut, then the caddy gets a percentage of the player's winnings as well. The percentage goes up based on how high the player finishes."

Katie and Lizzie nodded their understanding. Binky would be in a good position at this week's poker game.

"So, *Gata*, shall I come to get you at your room at, say, eight o'clock?" he asked.

Katie took a peek at Lizzie who seemed to be silently nudging her friend with her eyes. "Eight will be fine," she said. "But I can meet you in the lobby."

Darío nodded, then turned to the autograph seekers who had been waiting, some patiently, some not so patiently, for him to sign their various memorabilia. He began with the children, as he always did, then worked his way to the adults. He watched over the heads of the fans as Katie and Lizzie walked away from the group, toward the parking lot.

Six

—∿—

I owe a lot to my parents, especially my mother and father.
~ *Greg Norman, professional golfer*

"BOY, THIS IS KIND of like getting ready for dates at State all over again, eh?" Lizzie said as she nudged Katie's hip with her own to allow herself more room at the bathroom mirror.

Lizzie wore light cream slacks and a pale blue sweater set while Katie, wanting to show off the sun she'd gotten over the last two days, wore a sundress and sandals.

Katie laughed. "Except there isn't beer on the counter in front of us, and these aren't anything near dates. But yeah, it does kind of remind me of back then."

"Do you want a beer? Take one out of the mini-bar, or I could order something from room service for you," Lizzie, always one to please, offered.

"Ugh. No. Just the thought of alcohol gives me the heaves, but you go ahead, Lizard."

Lizzie ducked her head, looking away from Katie. "Um, no, none for me."

"Oh right, never drink in front of a client?" she asked re-membering Lizzie drinking only water the night before as well.

"God, no. You don't know how many clients I had to drink under the table to prove my worth. Thank God I'm a Yooper girl."

Lizzie put the lid down on the toilet and sat down so she could face Katie as she put the finishing touches on her makeup. "Kat, I need to tell you something." She waited until Katie sensed the seriousness in her voice, and put down her mascara tube to turn to Lizzie.

"I'm pregnant." Lizzie said, watching Katie's face for emotion.

Katie covered the flash of envy and hurt quickly. "Oh, Lizard, that's wonderful. You are happy about it, right? I didn't even know you guys were trying. How far along are you?" The questions tumbled out, and to get a hold of herself, she turned away from her best friend and once again began applying makeup. Her hand shook as she brought the mascara wand to her face and she steadied her other hand on the sink.

"I'm ecstatic about it. We started trying the minute we set a wedding date, knowing it was going to be a very short engagement, and I'm no spring chicken. I'm just over three months, so we think it's safe to start telling people." Lizzie got up from the seat and stepped behind Katie, wrapping her arms around Katie's waist, making her meet her eyes in the mirror. "Finn knows, of course, and the kids, but we haven't told anyone else. I wanted to tell you first, KitKat, and yet, I didn't want to have to tell you at all. Does that make sense?"

Katie put the makeup down and leaned back into her friend's embrace, allowing the hurt to now show on her face. She tried her best to answer Lizzie, trying to keep the tremble she felt out of her voice. "I understand, Lizard. And you do know that I really am happy for you, don't you? And Finn too, of course." Lizzie nodded and touched her head to Katie's. Their hair melded into a strange zebra pattern, Katie's so white and Lizzie's so black. "It's just…" Katie sighed.

"I know, KitKat, I know," Lizzie whispered.

They stood that way for a minute before Lizzie said, "I have to get going. Are you going to be okay?"

Katie stepped out of the warm embrace and pushed her friend to the bathroom door. "Of course I'll be okay. You go out there and sign that client, Little Mama."

Lizzie gave Katie one last, questioning glance. Katie gave a bright, reassuring smile and waved her friend off. She heard the hotel room door click shut.

The hurt came in waves, suffocating her. Lizzie would be a great mother, but she'd never cared about kids before getting together with Finn. Katie, on the other hand, had wanted children for forever it seemed. She slowly turned to the mirror, preparing to do her makeup all over again, as she watched the tears begin to roll down her face.

—⁂—

The restaurant Darío took her to was a far cry from the Armadillo. It was just as small, and off the beaten track of downtown Irving, but it was full of warmth and charm. And Spanish cooking, as Katie found out when she barely recognized a word on the menu.

"You don't care for Spanish food? We could go someplace else?" Darío asked.

"No, I love Mexican, I'm just not familiar with too much on the menu," Katie said.

Darío smiled, "That is because it is Spanish, not Mexican."

Katie thought of okra and grits, neither of which she'd ever tasted, and the pasties she was so used to in the U.P. "Point taken," she said. "Why don't you order for me? I like spicy, but not too spicy. I love beef, but not pork. And I prefer rice to beans." Darío nodded, perused the menu for a moment and gave their order to the waitress when she arrived.

They talked of the day's play. Besides Darío's great round, Chad made the cut in his first tournament as a pro—no small feat. Neither one of them expressed any regret in seeing Barclay head home, missing the cut by four shots.

Over a wonderful dinner that Katie readily admitted was one of the best she'd ever had, the conversation flowed comfortably.

"You don't play poker with Binky on Friday nights?" she asked.

He shook his head, wiping his mouth with his napkin. "No. It is a game for caddies only."

"I'll bet that's quite a picture. A room full of Binkys knowing they've got an extra paycheck to burn. I see a dark room with cigar smoke, empty beer bottles, and lots of foul language. Quite a boy's club, eh?"

Darío smiled. "Not entirely. There are a few women caddies on tour. More on the smaller training tour. In those cases, it is usually the players' wives, as they cannot yet afford to pay a regular caddy."

"Surely that's not the case at this level?" Katie asked.

"No. The caddies at this level have been doing this a while. And they get paid very well, though they do have to cover their own travel expenses. The women caddies are not the players' wives on the Tour."

"I saw one on the practice range yesterday. She had a long ponytail, sort of petite, incredible legs, about my age," Katie said.

Darío nodded. "*Sí*, that was Franny. She's been on the Tour with Rick for over ten years."

Katie noticed he didn't mention anything about her description of Franny. Did he like petite women? With great legs? She knew her legs could stand the comparison, but did she seem like an Amazon to him? He was her height. Maybe he was one of those men who liked to tower over their women.

Maybe she should get her mind back to the subject! "Rick? Rick Donaldson? She's *his* caddy?"

"Yes. For at least ten years now, probably more. You've heard of Rick?"

"Yes of course I've heard of Rick Donaldson. I know of his— what?—four majors?" Darío nodded. "He's known as Prick Donaldson on Tour, isn't he?" Her embarrassment at using the word in front of Darío about a man she'd never met was obvious as she felt the blush creep up her cheeks.

Funny, she'd always been known as something of an ice princess, and she'd probably blushed more in front of Darío in two days than she had in the past ten years combined.

He seemed amused at her discomfort. "Yes, that's his nickname," he said.

"Do you know him very well? Is he…is he…" She couldn't ask it.

"Is he really a prick?" he chuckled. Katie nodded. "It depends on who you ask. I've been on several Ryder Cup teams with Rick. He is just a few years older than I am. He was very generous and helpful to me during my first Ryder Cup experience. For that, I will always be grateful." He hesitated, then smiled. "But yes, he can be a prick."

"And this Franny, she's his caddy?"

"Yes, for many years now they have been a team. She may possibly be the only person who would put up with Rick so long."

"And are they a couple also?"

Darío shook his head. "No. Rick is currently going through his second divorce."

"So, there are two women out there who agree with the nickname," Katie said.

"At least," Darío said. "He tried to steal Binky from me years ago. That's when Binky introduced him to Franny. She was new on the Tour and Rick had gone through several caddies. No one would stay with him. I think Binky has always had a soft spot for Franny, so he saw that she got on with a relatively stable player."

"Two marriages is relatively stable?"

He grinned and Katie felt a flutter in her belly. "A relatively stable player on the Tour. The other," he waved his hand, "I cannot speak to."

Katie smiled. "Well, I can hardly talk about stable when it comes to marriage." She refused to fall into some kind of maudlin funk. Not when she was enjoying Darío's company so much. "So, Binky and Franny play poker together on Fridays, eh?"

"*Sí*. Most caddies socialize together and most players socialize together. There are exceptions, of course."

"Oh, so last night was a fluke? You and Binky going out together?"

"No. We have dinner together every Wednesday and Thursday night. Wednesday is after the last practice round, before the tournament begins and we discuss course strategy. Thursday is after we have played the first round, and we talk about any adjustments we need to make to that strategy. Usually we eat at the hotel, but last night..." His voice trailed off.

"Last night?" Katie prodded.

A sheepish smile crossed his face, making his mouth seem lopsided, emphasizing his large nose. Katie found it endearing.

"Last night," he sighed, "I'd overheard Chad telling Lizzie about the Armadillo at the golf course. I decided to give it a try."

Katie wondered at that. She didn't assume she was the reason why Darío wanted to give the Armadillo a try. But still...the place wasn't necessarily one that people put on the top of their must-eat-at lists.

"So, you only eat with Binky on two nights of the week. What players are you closest to? Who would you normally be eating with on a Friday evening if you hadn't taken pity on me?"

He shook his head, a warm compassion filling his chocolate eyes. "I have no pity for you, Katie." Before she could respond to that, he added, "Normally I eat alone the other nights. Occasionally one of the other Spanish players, or some other player I happen to know well, is at an event and we'll get together, but most times alone."

The concept of eating out alone was foreign to Katie. She had never in her life eaten at a restaurant alone. The thought terrified her. And yet, she knew that it was a very real possibility for her future.

Nah, not while Alison was still single. She'd always have someone to go to the Commodore with for some pizza and a drink.

"You must get very lonely," she whispered, thinking more of her future than addressing Darío.

He thought on that, took a sip of his water that he'd switched to after one beer. "I am alone ninety percent of the time. Of that time, I am lonely perhaps ten percent of that."

She wrinkled her brow, puzzled.

"There is a difference between being alone and being lonely, *Gata*," he said quietly, now sensing she was talking about herself as well as him.

"Is there?" she asked, not convinced.

"Yes. You'll get used to being alone, and then you will see the difference. Right now, to you, they are the same."

She stared at her empty plate, took a sip of her water. "Maybe. I hope so. I've never lived alone before. I'm somewhat ashamed to say I don't like it. Here I am, moments away from thirty-seven. I have a good job, great friends, a wonderful family who lives nearby," her voice dropped to a whisper, "and I'm so afraid to be in that house alone at night."

Darío's concern was evident. "Do you not live in a safe area?"

She laughed softly. "It's not anyone else I'm afraid of. It's… it's…it's just being with only me for all those hours that terrifies me."

She could tell that this concept was as foreign to Darío as his being alone so much of the time was to her.

He changed the subject, and she was grateful. "Tell me, what it is that you do for a living, Katie?"

"I'm an editor at the daily newspaper in town."

He smiled. "Ahh, a journalist, sometimes known as the enemy."

"In what way?" she asked.

He shrugged. "I have not had much problem with the press, but some players on the Tour—such as Rick Donaldson—feel they have been…misrepresented…in the press. They don't have overly friendly feelings toward journalists. And of course Tiger…"

She loved how the word "misrepresented" rolled off his

tongue, the accent not quite on the right syllable, his Rs rolled as flat as a pancake. His "is" and "it's" sounded more like "ees" and "eet". She could listen to this man read the phone book.

She waved her hand. "What I do is far removed from sports writing. Following a team or the Tour. Those guys are professionals." She was dismissive in her tone and he picked up on it.

"So what is it that you write exactly?" he prompted.

She raised her shoulders, as if her subject was unimportant. "Well, the *Ingot* is a small-town daily newspaper, so the local news is key. Town meetings, police and court reports, and of course the obituaries. Obituaries are big at the *Ingot*."

He chuckled. "You see. You cover matters of life and death, while these 'professionals', as you call them, only cover a silly game."

She smiled. "But it's not a silly game to you, is it?"

He returned her smile with one of his own, lopsided and adorable. "No. It's not a game to me. It is my livelihood, but even more importantly, it is…" He paused, searching. Katie wasn't sure if he was searching for the correct word in English, or trying to define his thoughts. She waited, silently. "It is who I am," he finally said.

Katie nodded, understanding. She wished she could define herself that simply. At one point, she'd hoped to define herself in three words…mother, wife, and journalist. Now, one was out of her reach, one had been ripped from her grasp, and the third wasn't what she'd thought it would be. How nice to say, "I am a golfer" and be done with it.

"Did you learn to play with your father, at his club, like most of the players on the Tour?" she asked. She knew that the majority of pro golfers grew up with silver spoons in their mouths, learning the game at their fathers' knees at country clubs. There were the exceptions, of course, but for the most part, golf at the professional level continued to be a game for the elite. You didn't see many players who battled their ways out of the inner city to join the PGA Tour.

But Darío didn't seem to have an attitude of entitlement about him. She didn't know much about his background, only that he was from northern Spain, had taken the golf world by storm at twenty, was currently thirty-six, and had never married. If her two best friends had not also been single at thirty-six— Lizzie marrying Finn only three months ago—she would have found Darío's being single suspect, wondered if maybe he was gay. But because of her friends, she knew that not everyone was destined to marry, or even to marry young, as she had.

And he sure wasn't giving off any gay vibes.

"No. Not from my father," Darío said. The curtness of his voice pulled Katie back from her silent reverie to watch him. He did not look at her as he spoke, but rather his gaze swept the room, not landing on anything or anyone in particular. "I learned golf from the greenskeeper at the club where my mother worked as a cook."

"Oh. Well your parents must be incredibly proud of all you've accomplished," she said, trying a different tack.

"*Sí*, my mother is very proud. We are very close," he said, still not looking at her.

"But not your father?" she asked. She knew he was dodging the subject, but her journalist's curiosity won out.

He finally looked at her, his warm eyes for a moment flashing cold. "I don't know who my father is, Katie. I don't know if he is proud of me." His shoulders slumped and the glare went out of his eyes, the gentleness returning. "I'm not sure if he even knows I exist."

She held his eyes for a moment, trying to convey the same empathy that he had given her earlier when talking about loneliness. Like him, she felt no pity, but she did feel the loss he must have felt as a child. A loss that obviously was still with him.

He gave a small smile, acknowledging her, then swept the matter aside. "So, tomorrow, Chad and I will no longer be paired together. Lizzie will be following his group. Will you be with her, or may I count you among my gallery? You have a good-luck charm reputation to uphold."

She was flattered that he asked, but sorry for the answer she had to give him. "We won't be going to the tournament tomorrow. We're leaving in the morning."

"You're leaving? But why?" Katie heard what she thought sounded like minor distress in her voice, and it perversely made her feel good.

"We have to get back. Lizzie planned this trip so that she could meet with Chad on days he would be sure to be here, in case he missed the cut. And…and we need to be back home on Sunday."

"What happens on Sunday?"

Katie looked away, took a deep breath and said, "Sunday is Mother's Day." She said the words like a poison she was trying to expell from her body. "It will be Lizzie's first Mother's Day since she got married, and became a stepmother. She didn't want to miss it."

She remembered Lizzie's earlier news and realized that the day had even more meaning for Lizzie and Finn than she had originally known. She tried to feel happy for her friend, and she was, but feelings like that were locked so deep down by now, she wasn't sure if she'd ever find them. Her own inability to conceive had left her bereft anytime a close friend or one of her brother's wives became pregnant. Now, with Ron becoming a father, the pain was even deeper.

Katie watched Darío watch her. She remembered that she had told him about her infertility in the car last night in the midst of her tirade. She searched his eyes for the pity she was sure to find, but didn't. She went on, "And it's also my birthday, and my parents and brothers and their families will want me there for dinner."

"Your birthday is on Mother's Day?" he asked.

He seemed to get the cruel joke played on Katie. "Every so many years it falls on Mother's Day. There's a celebration for me all right, but never the right one." She laughed at her joke, but it came out as more of a whimper. Darío did not smile at her attempt.

He reached across the table and laid his warm hand over hers. "To mark the day that you joined us in this world, *Gata*, that is most definitely cause for celebration."

She looked into his warm chocolate eyes. What would it be like to be held by this man? Could he take away the pain that hearing of Lizzie's pregnancy brought her? Could he make her body feel anything other than the numbing cold she'd felt since Ron had left? No, of course not. But maybe...maybe for just one night she could forget her traitorous, barren body, her friend's impending motherhood, and the family gathering on Sunday, which would surely be a birthday party for her and a Mother's Day party for her mother and sisters-in-law.

And maybe, one night in the arms of Darío Luna would help her forget the existence of little Crystal Lipton.

That was when Katie decided to seduce Darío.

Seven

—ᘑ—

It was one of those days you dream about.
Every hole seemed to be six inches wide.
~ Tom Purtzer, professional golfer

SHE WAS BREATHTAKING. She was exquisite. She was acting very very strangely.

The evening had been going along fine, she had enjoyed what he'd chosen for her for dinner, their conversation was comfortable and even. She had been very honest about her feelings about not being able to celebrate Mother's Day.

And then, something happened.

She seemed to come to some sort of decision. And then her manner changed dramatically. If he didn't know better, he would have sworn she was trying to seduce him. He knew that couldn't be it. For one thing, Katie didn't want to be with a man right now. Her venomous spewing the previous evening was proof of that. Also, what she was doing was a far cry from any seduction Darío had ever seen before. She didn't seem to know what she was doing. He thought for a moment that she was actually batting her eyes at him!

She attempted to put her hand over his that rested on the table and, in doing so, proceeded to knock over her water glass, dousing the table. She was not to be deterred, though, from whatever mission she was on, and Darío found himself admiring her tenacity. He was still confused, but admiring.

When she nearly set her hair on fire leaning across the candlelit table to whisper something to him that could easily have been said at a normal level, Darío was determined to put her out of her own misery. For her own safety, as well as for the fact that it was painful to watch her demonstration.

"*Gata*, what is it you are trying to say to me?" he asked.

She furrowed her brow. "Say to you? What do you mean? We were talking about your next tournament."

He maneuvered his hand around the battlefield of debris she'd made of the table and lightly touched her arm. "*Sí*, but what are you trying to *say* to me?"

She tried to put her head down, but he moved his hand from her arm to her chin and held it up. There was no way that he would not see her gorgeous eyes as she said whatever she was going to say.

Not being able to hide, she did the next best thing, and whispered her reply. Her voice was soft and light, and he was not able to hear her.

"I didn't hear you," he said, leaning closer.

The already quiet restaurant became even quieter, all diners feeling the need to stop talking and take bites of their food at that precise moment. It coincided with Katie raising her voice. "I said, 'I'm trying to seduce you'."

Not only did Darío hear her this time, but so did the entire restaurant.

He watched as her huge blue eyes became even larger. A look of panic and then mortification took up residence in the sky blue pools. Thinking quickly, Darío said loudly, "Did she really say that? No way. So what did *he* say?"

Katie immediately caught on to Darío's attempted rescue. She continued, "Well, she said…" and then leaned closer, as if to tell him the rest of the story. She only whispered, "Thank you."

"No, I believe the thank yous are all mine, Katie, if you

meant what you said," he teased, his eyes never leaving hers.

On the drive back to the hotel he kept glancing at her, waiting for her to change her mind, but she seemed determined. "Are you certain about this?" he asked at a red light when he could turn to face her.

"Yes," she said. Then she seemed to realize that more than just her consent was needed. "Unless...unless you don't want to."

He saw a tremor of doubt flash across her beautiful face. "Katie, you're a remarkable woman, any man would jump at the chance to spend the night with you."

"I didn't even ask if you were involved with someone. Oh God, maybe you're not even available," she groaned. She dropped her head back against the headrest, closing her eyes.

"It's fine. I'm not seeing anyone. If I weren't available, we wouldn't even be having this conversation. I wouldn't have invited you to dinner, innocent as I thought it would be. I don't mess around, Katie." He moved to brush his hand across her cheek, to give her some sign of his interest, but the car behind them honked and Darío realized the light had turned green.

Back in his own thoughts, he could not wrap his mind around the idea that Katie indeed needed a sign of his attraction to her. Had she never looked in the mirror? Didn't she know how stunning a woman she was? Had this Ron person done damage so deep that she needed affirmation that she was desirable?

Was this what her seduction was all about? Her ex-husband?

Yes, probably. He didn't care. She needed to feel desired, and he most definitely could do that for her. He had slept with women out of boredom, loneliness, and other reasons much less definable than this.

He snuck a peek at her, watching her elegant neck arch as she rested her head, her heavy lashes at rest against her smooth cheeks. He found himself growing hard, and knew that this seduction may have been her idea, but he was a very willing participant.

In the elevator, he hesitated to push the button, giving her one more chance to change her mind. Instead, she sidled in front of him, facing the panel herself and said, "What floor is your room on?"

"Fourteen," he answered, and watched as she pushed that button and no other.

So, it was going to happen. He watched her go to the opposite corner of the elevator, like two boxers returning to neutral corners. She gripped the metal rails like she had the night before, but this time it was not to find balance. Tonight, Katie was sober, but her grip on the railing still made her knuckles turn white.

Darío tried to think of something that might ease her nervousness. He wasn't sure it was the right move, but he stepped to the center of the elevator and took up a golf stance, addressing an invisible ball, just as Katie had asked him to do the previous night. He heard her make a small gasp of recognition. He lifted his head—a definite no-no if he were really going to hit a ball—and met her eyes.

She looked horrified to be reminded of her forwardness. That wasn't his intention; he was trying to lighten the mood. He gave the imaginary club an exaggerated waggle and gave Katie an exaggerated wink. Finally, the desired effect spread across her face as she burst out laughing.

She buried her face in her hands. "Oh God, I can't believe I did that."

He stepped out of his stance and to her side of the elevator, pinning her to the wall. "I have to tell you, I've had many instructors over my career, some world famous, some locals at driving ranges who could not resist giving me advice. But I have never, ever enjoyed setting up for someone to look at my form like I did last night." He hoped she could hear the tease in his voice.

She looked up from her hands with a bright smile on her face. "We never did get around to your form, did we?" she teased in return.

"I was hoping that would happen very soon," he said, just as the elevator came to rest on his floor.

They didn't speak as he led her to his room, his hand on the small of her back. He allowed her to go first through the door. He reached for the light switch on the wall the same time Katie did and her arm knocked him in the gut, causing a soft "oomph". He thought of their introduction last night at the Armadillo and how her hand collided with his crotch. What was it with this woman and her dangerous limbs?

"Oh, I'm so sorry. What is it with me and my clumsiness around you? I'm never like this, really. Ask any of my friends, 'klutz' is never a word that they'd use to describe me," she said, moving into the living area of the large room.

Saddened by her moving away from him, but determined to go at her pace, he followed. "And what words would they use to describe you?" Darío asked, rubbing his stomach as he turned the lights on to their softest dimmer setting and following Katie to the small couch, where he sat next to her.

He waited. She shrugged and looked away. "I'm not really sure. It depends on who you'd ask."

"What if I were to ask Lizzie? What word or words would she use to describe you?"

"That's easy. Friend. Loyal. Caring. Nurturing. She and Alison always say I mother them too much, but I guess it's my nature." She was quiet for a moment, wouldn't meet his eyes. "At least I get to mother someone."

It was almost a whisper, one Darío wasn't sure he was meant to hear, but he did, and the hurt in her voice tugged at him. "And other than Lizzie, the people in your town, what words would they use to describe you?"

She sighed heavily. "I suppose that's easy as well. 'The pretty one.' That's exactly what they call me, have since high school."

Darío was confused. "There is only one pretty person in this town, and thus you are the pretty one? What an odd town."

Katie laughed. "No, not the pretty one of the town, the pretty one of the three of us, Lizzie, myself, and our other friend, Alison. It's a stupid thing. The three of us were always together since kindergarten. Somewhere along the line someone dubbed us

'The Smart One', 'The Pretty One' and 'The Nice One'."

"Lizzie is…" Darío asked, not willing to put a label on a woman he had just met, not willing to guess the wrong one.

"'The Nice One', can't you tell?"

"Yes, of course, Lizzie seems very nice, but she's also very pretty. Not beautiful like yourself, but…"

"Yes, she is, and so is Alison—pretty, I mean. That's exactly what I'm saying. We hated it, still hate it, but some people still refer to us that way. It's humiliating, actually."

Darío stretched his arm across the back of the couch, touching Katie's hair. It looked like softly fallen snow, so white and pure. "In what way humiliating?" he asked, but he could already see how living within a label like that could have limitations.

He had lived with one all his life and everything he had done, everything he had achieved, could not erase it.

"It's a no-win situation. You're secretly pleased you are the one you are, and yet you think 'Hey, I'm smart too, you know.' It's kind of a crutch. Why did I have to work on being outgoing and personable when Lizzie already had that covered for us? Why should I knock myself out over books when Alison would always outshine everyone academically?

"And being 'The Pretty One'…" The disgust was evident in her voice. "What did I do to earn that? Nothing. Genes, that's it. Good genes, freak of nature, whatever, it's nothing I *did*."

He could see her point. His label was nothing he had done either, and yet he could not escape it anymore than Katie could escape being beautiful.

He tried to turn her thoughts. "Yes, but you see, *Gata*, if you were 'The Smart One' you probably would have thought twice about coming to my room." His words made her laugh as he'd hoped.

"And if I were 'The Nice One'?" she asked. She turned her body into his, leaned her head against his hand along the back of the couch.

"Then I would feel like a heel taking advantage of you at

such a vulnerable time in your life," he said, smiling. His hand circled the back of her head through the softness of her hair, cradling her.

She smiled. "But you don't feel bad taking of advantage of me because I'm good looking?" She nuzzled her head against his hand, seeming to enjoy the feel of contact as much as Darío was.

He moved even closer, so that his face was mere inches from hers. "Am I taking advantage, *Gata*? I don't think so. Because, you see, though you may be 'The Pretty One', you are also very strong." He saw the dubious look on her face. "It takes a strong woman to start over, to be alone, to tell a man she has known for a short time that she wishes to seduce him."

She dropped her head in embarrassment, shaking it. "No, not strong. Maybe crazy, but not strong."

He took his hand from the couch and lifted her face, gently caressing her cheek. "Crazy? Strong? Perhaps they are the same. They both suggest lack of fear." He brushed his lips over hers. She felt so warm, so soft. "Are you afraid to be here, *Gata*?" he whispered.

She returned the soft kiss, using the exact same pressure, the same movement, he had. "No. I want to be here. I want to do this." She raised her eyes, meeting his. "I want you."

He brought her mouth to his. They were nearly the same height, but he was slightly above her when they sat. Her height must be in those gloriously long legs.

She tasted of wonderful Spanish spices. No doubt it was from their dinner, but Darío allowed himself to think she tasted like home. Her lips parted with no prodding and he was encased in her warmth. His tongue met hers in a dance reminiscent of his country's famous tango.

A flash of Katie dressed in full flamenco regalia made him go hard. He got up from the couch and held out his hand to her. She took it, like she was accepting his invitation to dance, which in a way she was. The oldest dance there was.

Either he pulled a little too hard, or she was a bit too enthusiastic, because she barreled into him, causing him to stumble backward, pulling her with him. "Sorry," she whispered, when they had finally righted themselves.

He waved her apology away then took her in his arms. He kissed her again, walking backward to the bed. She fit so well in his arms, just as he thought she would. She wrapped her arms around his neck, her fingers slid around his nape, sending a chill through him.

She stepped on his feet twice and the image of her as a graceful Flamenco dancer swiftly left his mind.

"Oops, sor —," she started to say, but he cut her off with another kiss. Her breasts crushed against his chest, her hips aligned with his, their thighs tangled. His legs reached the edge of the bed. He stopped.

Katie kept going.

They tumbled onto the bed, Darío able to keep Katie on top of him, cushioning her fall. "Sorry," she said again. Darío wasn't sure, but he thought he heard amusement in her voice. His hands found the zipper of her dress at the same time his mouth found the soft nook of her neck where it met her shoulder. He felt her tremble. He sucked on her flesh and felt the shimmer go through her again. He licked her warm skin as he lowered the zipper.

He felt her tense when his hands moved to her bare back, but her hesitance was quickly gone. He spread his legs and she kneeled between them. He raised her dress, past her thighs, so toned, so lean. Over her full hips. Along her trim waist, and beyond her plentiful breasts. She raised her arms for him, and he tossed the dress to the chair across from the bed.

She was kneeling in only her bra and panties. White, plain cotton. He smiled. He wasn't sure what he'd been expecting, but such serviceable lingerie was not it.

She saw his grin, and as if reading his thoughts, said, "You were expecting what? Maybe leopard print? Cut outs?" She laughed. "I'm a Plain Jane girl underneath. Sorry to disappoint you."

He sat up, his face level with her breasts, and tugged his shirt out of his pants and over his head. He took her hand and placed it on top of his bulging erection. "Does it feel like I'm disappointed?"

She grinned and began to move her hand along him. *Dios Mio*, it felt wonderful. He removed his hand from hers and moved to undo her bra. "Plain Jane white cotton or leopard skin, the damned thing has to go!"

She threw her head back and laughed, highlighting her graceful neck. If he wasn't so close to paradise, he would have moved to kiss her neck again, but his nimble hands had made quick work of her bra clasp and he was now slowly unveiling her like a fine work of art. Her breasts were full and firm, had the shape and tone of a woman of twenty. He nestled his head between them.

He lifted her right breast in his hand, weighing, learning, committing to memory the shape and feel of her. He felt, rather than heard, a small breath escape her. He laid her down, resting on top of her. Limbs tangled, then righted themselves as they found comfort. He could wait no longer to taste her, and took her nipple into his mouth.

She moaned softly, which became louder as Darío began to suck. He caressed her other breast and then switched his mouth and hand.

Katie began to move against him and he knew it wouldn't be hours of foreplay before they were both ready. They were both ready now. He moved one hand down her stomach, felt it flinch then relax, and continued down to slip a finger inside her panties. Yes, they were both ready now, her wetness tipping him off, as well as her hands plastering his head to her breasts.

He needed to be inside her. To feel her. Be a part of her.

"What about protection?" he asked, taking his mouth from her bountiful breasts to speak.

Eight

—⚉—

Golf is like making love.
One day you think you are too old,
and the next day you want to do it again.
~ *Roberto De Vicenzo, professional golfer*

PROTECTION? What a joke.

Thoughts of numerous doctors' offices, pokings, proddings, and devastating periods swept through Katie's mind.

It was almost enough to kill the mood for her until Darío nibbled on her breast once more. That delicious sensation brought her right back to the moment at hand.

"It's not an issue," she murmured.

"What?" he asked, still intent on her breasts.

"Protection. It's not an issue," she said. More like gasped, really, as Darío moved to her other breast, his tongue circling her tender nipple. "I…I can't…get pregnant, remember?" Her voice quivered, but from passion, not from the pain that usually accompanied such announcements of her infertility.

He lifted his head, stared at her, and nodded, understanding. Looking sorry that he'd brought up the subject. "And the other?"

Other? What other? Then Katie remembered protection was used for more than unwanted pregnancies. It had been so long since unprotected sex was any kind of issue for her.

"I was tested after I found out Ron had cheated. I'm fine." She wouldn't go into the humiliation she'd felt at asking for STD and HIV tests after being married for so long. The nurses had heard, of course, that Ron had left her, had found someone who could bear him a child. They treated her with respect and just a touch of pity. It was another one of those times she hated living in a small town.

"I was tested for my yearly physical a few months ago, and have been with no one since," Darío said.

She believed him. Maybe that was naïve of her. But *he* believed *her*. Plus, she desperately wanted this man inside her. To pound into her. To pound out all thoughts. To pound away everything and everybody else. If only for now. If only for one night.

"Then we're good to go," she said, wriggling under him. She took a hand from his head and stroked down his back. "Or we will be when you get those pants off."

He chuckled and kneeled up to undo his belt and fly. She brushed his hands away, undid the zipper and eased his pants and briefs down to his knees just as he made a move to stand up. Her movement made him lose his balance and he fell on the floor, his pants wrapped around his knees.

"Oh God, Darío, I'm so sorry. Are you okay?" She peered over the edge of the bed to see him sprawled on the floor, legs held akimbo by his pants, his penis jutting and hard.

He waved away her offer of a helping hand and stood, taking his pants off at the same time. "You know, *Gata*, making love with you could be *muy* dangerous."

Katie was almost offended until she saw the twinkle of humor in his warm, brown eyes. She sat back on her haunches and deliberately eyed his erection. "Enter at your own risk, then," she purred.

His crooked smile ran through her, leaving her tingling almost as much as when he sucked on her nipple. "I believe I'll take that risk." He knelt on the bed, coming eye to eye with her. Without touching her body, he leaned forward to claim her mouth.

His kiss was hungry, urgent. He tasted of coffee and he smelled like sunshine and grass. It had been so long since Katie had been kissed by anyone other than Ron. Darío kissed so differently. He was raw, untamed. It was such a contrast to the poised, controlled man Katie had watched on the golf course for two days. This man did not kiss like a man who limited his beer intake. This man did not kiss like a man so disciplined he would shoot balls well into the twilight until he holed ten bunker shots in a row.

This man did not kiss like Ron.

That was the main thing. There would be nothing with Darío that would remind her of Ron. They were too different. Darío was dark, for one. His arms were much darker than the rest of him, of course, due to being on the course in golf shirts every day. A farmer's tan was what they called it in Michigan. But the rest of his skin was still a golden brown.

Ron was fair, blond, and blue-eyed just like herself. The golden couple, people had called them.

She'd thought they were.

Darío was smaller than Ron in height, his body more compact, his strength lean and compressed. No bulging biceps that Ron had worked so hard to keep up. She ran her hands up Darío's arms, as if to prove the difference to herself. She liked the way they felt. There was no denying his strength, it just wasn't so blatant.

His hands went to her waist, gently pushing her down to her back, then skimmed her panties off. He knelt between her legs, looking at her. She opened her eyes, knowing what look she'd see on his face. She'd seen it on Ron's face every time they made love, even in the end. Awe. Reverence.

She supposed she should like that, but it always unsettled her. She knew she had a great body by society's standards, and if she'd had to work for it, she'd take more pride in it. But, like her high cheekbones and startling blue eyes, she'd been born with these genes, and her body was no more her doing than the shape of her mouth.

But Darío's look was not one of awe or reverence. He did not look at her like she was a prize that he'd won, one he did not deserve. He looked at her with appreciation, sure, but more desire than devotion. More wanting than worshipping. And then he gave her that smile and she knew this would not be anywhere near what she'd experienced with Ron.

His hand went to her blond curls, fingers probing, separating, searching. He found her wet and swollen. A soft moan escaped her lips; her head fell back.

"No, Katie, look at me," he whispered. When she did, he flashed her another smile and began stroking her on her bud which was quickly becoming inflamed. "You feel so good. You are so wet, so ready for me. Do you want me inside of you?"

She could only nod her head, so swept up in the sensation. "Tell me, Katie."

She could barely gasp out the words, he had her so close to the edge now, his fingers circling her clitoris with expert care, quickening his rhythm. "I want…I want…oh God, that feels so good, don't stop doing that." She dropped her head back again, her neck unable to bear the weight.

"Look at me, Katie, watch while I make you come. Watch my fingers dance on you. Watch what they do to you. What you make happen, Katie." His smile was gone now, but there was no edge in his voice. He didn't seem to be playing power games, but more that he just wanted Katie to share this moment with him.

She raised her head, came up on her elbows and watched as Darío stroked her into oblivion. When the shudders overtook her, her elbows gave out and she flopped, gracelessly back onto the bed. She didn't care. She only cared that this feeling went on and on. He tried to oblige her, coaxing and teasing more out of her, finally letting her come down.

When her breathing felt as though it may—someday—return to normal, she looked up at him, expecting to find a self-satisfied smile. He only looked back at her with a heat and desire that took her breath away. "I want you inside me," she whispered.

He nodded and removed his hands from her, causing her to moan again. He ran his hands down her legs, leaving a trail of heat, and took hold of her ankles. He brought them up to his body, kissing the soles of both her feet, then placing them over his shoulders. He saw the look of shock in Katie's eyes. "Trust me, this will be good."

It wasn't as if she and Ron hadn't tried every position imaginable. *But over seventeen years.* This man had her doing creative things with him on their first night together.

Their only night together, she reminded herself, and allowed her legs to relax, his shoulders taking their weight.

He entered slowly, but without hesitation. "*Sí*, you are *muy* dangerous, *Gata.*"

It had been so long. To have a man inside of her, to feel his pulse deep within her. To be joined. To belong to someone, if only for a while.

He began to move, his eyes never leaving hers. He found different rhythms, tried different speeds, teased her with pulling out till she moaned for more. When she was near to another climax, he seemed to know, letting himself go at his natural pace, pounding into her as she'd wanted, grasping her hips as she watched her ankles bounce on his shoulders until they both came in deep, loud gasps.

It wasn't love. It wasn't undying passion. It was physical. It was raw. It was exactly what she needed.

There was no warmth, but there was definitely heat.

Heat that caused a thaw in Katie's soul. She thought of those cold commercials where the person freezes solid and then with the right remedy, the ice around them cracks and they go on with their daily lives. Her body felt like it was cracking, as if something cold was falling away and she could now go on with her daily life. She could live again.

Darío was her remedy.

—∽—

He played on, his groove just a little off from what it had

been the previous two days, but no one seemed to be making a charge up the leaderboard, so he'd probably be in the final pairing tomorrow.

"Not quite what it was the last two days, Guv, but no one seems to be making a game of it," Binky said, echoing Darío's thoughts.

"A bit different today without your good-luck charm here, right?" Binky teased.

He pulled his eyes from the gallery to nod at Binky as they walked to the green on eighteen. He'd watched the crowd today much more than he normally did. He knew Katie wouldn't be there, that at this moment she was on a plane headed back to Michigan? Perhaps she'd even landed by now. But a small part of him had held out hope that maybe she would change her plans, maybe she'd decide to stay for the weekend.

He'd seen a flash of blond hair the exact shade as Katie's when he'd been on the third hole, but had been disappointed. He had an image of Katie below him, her slender ankles hooked over his shoulders. If he was honest with himself, he'd been thinking about her in that position since Barclay had mentioned it on the course Thursday. He was immensely relieved that they were his shoulders and not Barclay's.

Bah! He should not let a woman take away his focus on the course like this. It was certainly not the first time he had ended up in bed with a woman he'd met on the course. It wasn't a regular occurrence, but when you were on the road over thirty weeks a year, sometimes it became a necessity. Still, Darío much preferred bedding a woman he knew and liked rather than one for the physical comfort.

But Katie was not like those women, of that he was sure. And that was why he was thinking about her rather than possibly winning a golf tournament for the first time in a very, very long time.

He needed to win this tournament. Winning was important to him. That's what got him on the cover of magazines and newspapers. The third-place finisher didn't have his name and picture on the front page. And that was important to Darío. There was someone out there he wanted to show that he was a winner.

Determined to shake Katie from his mind and get back to the task at hand, he asked, "How was the poker game last night, Binky?"

Binky shrugged as he cleaned off Darío's four iron he'd just used to knock the ball four feet from the pin. "Same as always. We all thought we had a chance, but Franny walked off with all our money."

Darío smiled. He didn't ask about the game every week, but it seemed that whenever he did the story was the same. Leave it to a woman to walk into a man's domain and leave him destitute.

Yes, today, without Katie on the course, even leading the tournament, he felt destitute. He'd felt it when he'd woken to find her gone from his bed, and he'd not been able to shake the feeling all day. Images again rose of Katie, of her long limbs slung over his shoulders, of her body shuddering beneath his. It was a night he would not soon forget.

It had been wonderful.

—⚉—

It had been awful.

Well, not exactly awful, but awkward, different. So unlike what she was used to.

Different from Ron is what you really mean.

Her body still tingled in places that Darío had paid close attention to. No, definitely not awful. But very, very different.

Katie looked out the window of the plane. They were over the heartland, but it looked like one big brown blob to her. She slid down the window shade and leaned her head back, thinking maybe she could catch up on some of the sleep she missed last night.

"What time did you come into the room? You look so tired, KitKat," Lizzie asked from the seat next to her.

Lizzie'd been sound asleep when Katie had crept into the

room at six-thirty in the morning. She'd been able to use the bathroom and slide into her bed without waking Lizzie. "I'm not sure, it wasn't very late. What time did you go to sleep?"

"I've been so tired lately, I fell asleep at ten-thirty, can you believe that? How lame, eh?"

"Not so lame. It must have been shortly after that when I got in. I was out the minute my head hit the pillow. All that fresh air and walking the course did me in."

"So, how was last night? Was I right, did Darío have something more in mind than just dinner?" Lizzie nudged her in the universal "hanky-panky" way, while raising her eyebrows.

Katie laughed. No, Darío had nothing more than dinner in mind. It was *she* who'd changed his mind. "Nope. All he was after was dinner. Sorry, no scoop here."

Lizzie leaned back, disappointed. "Man, we're so old, no good scoop after a two-day whirlwind of meeting pro golfers. We needed Alison here to liven things up."

Katie thought about how lively things had gotten last night, but kept her mouth shut, only nodding in agreement with Lizzie. She wasn't sure why she didn't tell Lizzie about sleeping with Darío. Lizzie wouldn't think any less of her. In fact, Lizzie and Alison both had been encouraging her for the last couple of months to get back into the dating scene.

She'd never had a one-night stand before. She supposed she should feel bad about it, but she didn't. Only one hit and run in her thirty-six years, that wasn't too bad. She didn't think they'd be making her wear a scarlet "A" just yet.

It wasn't like there was any kind of future with Darío. She'd left his room without waking him to make sure of not having to talk with him. She had been so uncharacteristically clumsy with him she was afraid what a tender goodbye could have turned into. The way she'd been going, blood could possibly have been drawn.

Funny how clumsy she was with Darío. She'd never been that way before, and certainly not when being intimate with Ron. Well, first times with people can be awkward, she told herself.

Even as she did, the memory of her first time with Ron came flooding back.

He'd gotten a room at a bed and breakfast in Saugatuck, a couple of hours from East Lansing. It was a rare Friday night without a hockey game for him. They'd been dating about three weeks and they both knew that going away for the night could only mean one thing.

The room was quaint, filled with antiques and a white eyelet duvet on the brass bed. They were both fueled by their growing feelings for each other and came together before the B&B keeper had closed the door behind her after showing them their room.

Candlelight glowed as they took their time undressing each other, paying homage to each other's bodies. "You're so beautiful, Katie, the most beautiful thing I've ever seen," he whispered to her.

She didn't want to say "you too", but the fact was Ron was the most beautiful thing *she'd* ever seen. Blond hair, a tad long in the back, short over the ears, like every hockey player she'd ever known wore their hair at the time. Blue eyes, so clear, so penetrating when they looked into hers. His nineteen-year-old physique held testament to a daily skating regimen that went above and beyond team practice. The man was a Greek god come to life.

Come to *her* life.

Their lovemaking was long and sweet and they held each other for hours afterward, whispering words of commitment. It was the first time she'd ever told a man she loved him. He said it was the first for him too. "This is only the beginning for us, Katie, we have our whole lives ahead of us," Ron told her. "Our whole lives to spend making love like this."

She'd believed him.

Nine

—⟋⟍—

Sometimes it seems like a man ain't the master of his own destiny…the ball takes a funny little bounce here or a putt takes a funny little turn.

~ Sam Snead, professional golfer

"I'M PREGNANT."

The three women were at the Commodore. Alison had her head buried in her purse, but she directed her answer to Lizzie seated across from her. "Yes, Lizard, of course you are, you can hardly hide that girth. Besides, why do you think Katie and I brought you along if not to be our designated driver?" She found her lipstick and brought her head up to face Katie and Lizzie on the opposite side of the booth.

She stopped short as she saw the dropped jaw of Lizzie's face. "Jeez, Lizard, I was just kidding, you're not *that* big. And we'd want you here whether you were the DD or not. It's just awfully nice for us, eh, Kit Kat?"

Lizzie was shaking her head at Alison "I…I…I didn't say it."

Alison looked confused. "Say what?"

"I didn't say 'I'm pregnant'," Lizzie said.

"Well, it's kind of obvious," Alison said, motioning to Lizzie's rounded belly peeking out from behind the table.

Lizzie continued shaking her head, then turned to stare at

Katie.

"I said it, Al. *I'm* pregnant," Katie clarified. She watched as Alison realized her mistake and then both Lizzie and Alison turned on her.

"Start talking," Alison said. She had quickly gotten her shock under control, but Lizzie, poor Lizzie, was staring at Katie with huge hazel eyes, her hands instinctively cradling her own belly.

The waitress appeared and Alison held her hand up to stop Katie from beginning her saga. "Hang on, Kat, I gotta have some alcohol to hear about this." She ordered one of the Commodore's famed Fishbowl drinks – a Long Island iced tea in a huge brandy snifter. Katie and Lizzie both ordered waters. "Jesus, I can see you two are going to be a barrel of laughs for the next few months," Alison said, indicating their tame orders.

"Okay, spill," Alison said and she sat back, her arms across her chest, as if she wasn't going to believe what Katie had to say.

Katie could hardly believe it herself. "I'm pregnant," she repeated.

"I got that much. A few details, please. When? Where? And most importantly, with whom?" Alison said.

Katie took a small sip of her water when it arrived. Alison took a large gulp of her drink, then sat back again, arms crossed once more. Lizzie stared at Alison's glass with envy, but sipped at her water as well. Katie knew how Lizzie felt. She could really use some Dutch courage to tell her friends about her miracle.

"I'm two months along. Really too soon to tell anyone, but…"

"We're not just anyone," Lizzie said, laying her hand on Katie's.

Katie smiled. "Exactly. And the doctor said there was no reason to think that I can't carry to full term without any problems. It was the getting pregnant part that was the problem, not necessarily the staying pregnant part."

"Which leads us to the getting pregnant part," Alison prodded.

Katie flushed remembering her night with Darío. She wasn't quite ready to tell that part first. She'd get to it. There was no way Alison—or Lizzie for that matter—was going to let her out of here without all the details. But first, she'd start with the stuff that she could put into words. "At first I thought I was sick. I mean really sick. Like cancer or something. I was tired, a little nauseous, had missed my period, and you know how regular I am."

The other women nodded. They had absolutely no secrets from each other since before puberty, and certainly none after.

"Typical signs of pregnancy," Lizzie said, having recently gone through them all herself.

"Yes. But of course, that thought never occurred to me, for obvious reasons. I thought maybe the infertility had brought on something else. Something…I don't know…I was thinking ovarian cancer." At the look of fear that crossed Lizzie's face, Katie quickly added, "I'm fine. Fine. Just…pregnant."

"Are we talking Immaculate Conception here, or is there a little something you've left out?" Alison asked.

Lizzie gasped. "Oh God, it isn't Ron is it? He didn't show up one night and you went at it for old time's sake, did he?"

"Jesus, Lizard, she wouldn't be that stupid," Alison chided their friend. Her eyes turned to Katie. "Would you?"

"No. Of course not." Katie said, though her voice lacked the conviction she knew Alison sought. Truth was, if she knew a pregnancy would result, she didn't know if she'd turn Ron away or not. She was immensely grateful that it had not been an option. "It's funny though, that was the first thought in my head when the doctor told me. I thought, 'I can't wait to tell Ron'. It took me a few seconds to remember he'd left me and that there was no way the baby could possibly be his. Isn't that pathetic?"

Lizzie and Alison gave sympathetic looks, but said nothing. Probably because they thought it was pathetic, too.

"How does this happen after years of infertility? Were the doctors all wrong?" Lizzie asked.

"Well, the doctors had always said they couldn't find anything physically wrong with either of us. Ron did have a low sperm count, but not so low that it would keep us from conceiving. That's why they hesitated to do IVF, why they tried artificial insemination first. But I kept saving money for invitro, figuring we'd have that as a last option."

"The money for that can be seen driving down the main street of Hancock every day at three-thirty in the afternoon, the second school's out," Alison said. At Katie's look of hurt over remembering the Hummer and how it symbolized the beginning of the end of their marriage, Alison backpedaled. "I'm sorry, Kat, but that whole Hummer thing still pisses me off," she said.

Katie gave a small smile. "That's okay, it still ticks me off too. First, that he did it. Second, that I didn't see the huge red flag it turned out to be." She shrugged. "Enough about Ron. I'm happy to say, that the doctors were right about one thing. Our problems in conceiving were probably due to his sperm and my eggs not being compatible, which was another thing they mentioned as a possibility."

Alison grunted, "If only it were just his sperm that was incompatible. What does that mean exactly?"

"That my body, my eggs, are not compatible with the make-up of Ron's sperm. That every time we'd try to conceive, my body would reject his." She looked at Alison, waiting for the crack that was bound to come.

Alison waved the lob Katie had tossed her aside. "Too easy."

Katie smiled. "Plus, they'd been telling me all along that the stress of trying to conceive was only hurting my chances. 'Relax,' they'd say, as if I could. Well, the pressure was off, and the doctor's sure that that was a huge factor in me getting pregnant."

Both women nodded their understanding. "So, if not Ron…?" Alison asked

Katie watched Lizzie and Alison trying to call up a mental calendar of two months ago. It didn't take Lizzie long, she always had her mental calendar up to date and could easily flip through it. She let out a gasp. "Darío!"

"Bingo," Katie said. "Although, it's not like there are any other candidates."

"Holy shit," Alison said. "You got knocked up by Darío Luna? You didn't say you slept together, you just said you met him and went for dinner." There was an accusing tone in her voice aimed at Katie for holding back such crucial information.

"And that's true," Katie said, ignoring Alison's profanity, as she always did. She'd given up trying to tame Alison's mouth back in high school. "But, after dinner we went back to his room…" She didn't quite know how to finish the sentence, so she just let it trail off.

"Obviously," Lizzie said. "How come you didn't tell me in the morning? It never occurred to me to ask specifically, but still, you could have said something."

Katie had struggled with this herself. "I'm not really sure. I felt kind of trampy, I guess. A one-night stand and all."

Alison shrugged, "Happens all the time. You were due."

"Well it was my first time," Katie said. "And my last." She patted her tummy, still flat as a board, which would soon be round like Lizzie's.

She couldn't wait to get huge. To swell up. To have to re-move her rings. To not have her clothes fit. All of it. She wanted outward signs of her impending motherhood. Something more than the nausea. Though it had been mild enough, and was now almost completely past. It was a good thing she missed her period, because she was experiencing so few other side effects, she might have gone on quite some time before she'd gone to the doctor.

"I can't regret it. Sleeping with Darío. Not for a second." She had to stop and wait, till her throat opened again and she could speak. Even then, her voice was hoarse with emotion. "You guys, I'm going to have a baby!"

An hour later, after many tears, another drink for Alison and the largest pizza the Commodore made, Lizzie started mak-ing plans. Lizzie always made plans.

"Let's see. I can get a number for Darío from Chad. That's

probably the easiest way to get it. Unless he gave you his number?" Lizzie said to Katie.

Katie shook her head. "No, he didn't give me a number. I didn't give him one either. Why would I want Darío's number?"

"To call him and tell him, of course. Unless you're planning on telling him in person? That's probably the better way to go. Let's see, the Tour's in Memphis this week, I think. No, wait, maybe it's South Carolina—"

Katie interrupted her. "But I'm not going to tell Darío."

That brought complete silence to the table. Both Alison and Lizzie stared at her.

"There's no need to tell him. I'm having the child. Obviously. And I'm raising it alone. There's no reason why he ever needs to know. It would just complicate everything. For him and me."

"Well, duh. Having a baby tends to complicates things, Kat," Alison said.

Lizzie was beside herself. "You have to tell him. He's the father. He has a right to know."

Katie patted her hand. "Lizzie, Darío doesn't want this baby. If he wanted kids he'd be married by now. It would just force him to take responsibility for something when there's no need."

"You can't possibly know if he wants children or not. That's not for you to decide. You have to tell him, Katie." Lizzie was almost in tears now, and she took her hand out from under Katie's, clutching it to her waist. "I'm sorry. I know I'm emotional right now. But, my God, Kat, you have to see that he has a right to know he's fathering a child."

Katie looked at Alison, "What do you think?"

Alison took a deep breath. "I'm with Lizzie." At Katie's look of disbelief, Alison continued. "But not for the same reasons. Although she has a valid point, I'm not as much into father's rights as Lizzie. I've seen too many deadbeat dads and how that messes a kid up. But Kat, these things always have a way of coming around to bite you in the ass. I'm afraid that's what would happen in this case."

"What do you mean?" Katie asked.

"It's like on soap operas, nothing ever stays a secret. Obviously, you're going to start showing, people will ask who the father is. Either you come up with some lie—which you know is bound to blow up at some point—or you tell the truth. Now, if you tell the truth, it will get back to Darío somehow, someday. Stuff like that always does."

"Come on. I live in little podunk Hancock, Michigan. He lives in Spain and is traveling all over Europe and the States most of the time. How would he ever find that out?"

"Six degrees of separation. It ain't just a fun game to play in the car. It is a small world, after all." Alison sat back in the booth, took a long drag from her straw, and saw Katie's look of disbelief. "Off the top of my head? Petey's always golfing in those pro-am thingies isn't he, Lizard? And you know what kind of mouth Petey has on him. He mentions to someone from the Tour that a good friend of his back in his hometown is having Darío's baby and it's all over."

Katie stewed about that, then disregarded the scenario as implausible. Alison pushed her point. "I don't know how he'd find out, but come on, you've watched enough television and read enough romance novels to know *they always find out!*"

"So I'll have to lie. I'll say I went to a sperm bank," Katie said.

"Oh please. You're the worst liar of the three of us, and I suck at it," Lizzie said.

"She's right, Kat, you stink at lying. The first time your mother puts the third degree to you…I hate to think about how quickly you'll crack."

The three were silent. Lizzie took the last piece of pizza while murmuring something about the injustice of finally getting to her goal weight after three years of dieting to then get pregnant.

Katie hoped she'd start showing early. She'd waited so long to get pregnant, that she wanted to enjoy every minute of it. She was glad she'd found out about it so early into the pregnancy.

She'd be able to cherish every change in her body, every nuance.

"Katie, why don't you want Darío to know? What is your worst 'what if' about telling him?" Lizzie asked, throwing down her napkin like a white flag of surrender as she finished her pizza.

Katie wasn't sure how to answer. Wasn't sure what the answer was. "I don't know. Nothing in particular. He just seems like a pretty decent guy, and I don't want to dump something on him that he doesn't want. That, and I have no intention of sharing this child with anyone." She placed her hand protectively on her stomach.

"You don't *share* a child with its father. The child shares its mother and its father."

Both Katie and Alison gave Lizzie puzzled looks. "What kind of bullshit touchy-feely crap is that?" said Alison.

Lizzie chuckled. "I don't know. And I'm certainly not the best one to be talking about this." She smoothed her t-shirt over her tummy. "Or maybe I'm exactly the right person." She paused, her hand starting a rhythmic circling on her belly. "You have to tell him, Katie," she softly said.

Katie looked at Lizzie's belly, burgeoning with life, then her own, which would soon be as large. She sighed heavily, her shoulders dropping in defeat. "Yeah, I know. I have to tell him."

—⚉—

The Memphis sun was even hotter than the Texas one had been. Sultry. That's the word Katie used to describe the Memphis heat. Warm, sticky, wet. Sultry. Not a word often used when describing the weather in the Copper Country.

She put on a heavy dose of sunscreen and pulled on her hat, feeling a small sense of deja vu as she walked to the first tee area. The internet had said Darío's tee time was 1:40, and she hadn't wanted to get to the course much before then. She'd flown in early this morning, rented a car, found a vacancy at a Motel Six by the airport, and left her things there, getting to the course right when Darío was teeing off.

She hung back, not wanting him to see her too soon. She

wanted to watch his round, but she didn't want to speak to him until he was done. Actually, she didn't want to speak to him at all. No, that wasn't true. She did want to speak to Darío, to see him again. On some level she even wanted to sleep with him again. She just didn't want to speak with him about the baby.

But, that's why she'd come.

Back in the hotel sat a pile of papers that a lawyer Lizzie had recommended had drawn up for Katie. Lizzie's husband, Finn, had used the same lawyer years ago to have Stevie and Annie's mother give up all rights to their kids.

Katie had the lawyer draft a similar set for her. In them, Darío would give up all claim to the baby and Katie would give up all financial claim on Darío as father of the child. If she could just get Darío's signature on those papers and then get out of Memphis, she'd never have to see Darío Luna again.

The thought did not necessarily make her happy. She liked Darío. Very much. Had enjoyed the time she'd spent with him. Would love to spend more time with him. But she couldn't. Not with her baby's future at stake. She couldn't afford to become too attached to Darío. He would undoubtedly be thrilled to see the back of her, wouldn't be able to sign those papers fast enough when he learned he was about to be the father of a child with a woman he barely knew. One who'd told him there was no chance of pregnancy.

That's what bothered Katie the most. The possibility that Darío might think she hadn't been honest with him. That she had somehow tricked him into having unprotected sex. She supposed women did it all the time to professional athletes and celebrities.

That's why she'd made sure the legal documents were airtight. There was no way Darío could think she was after his money or his famous name—she was signing away all rights to it. Forever.

The crowd was much thicker than it had been in Texas. It was an afternoon tee time, so more people were on the course for one thing. For another, Darío had been playing well since Texas. People knew he was a player on a roll, and they wanted to watch him.

By the fourth hole, she was sure she'd been made. She hadn't made eye contact or anything, and she thought she'd blended in well with the crowd. It was just a feeling that she was being watched. When she'd turn to Darío, though, he was always concentrating over a shot, or talking yardage with Binky.

By the fifth hole, Binky strolled up to the ropes where Katie had buried herself behind a crowd of people and said, "Hello, luv." When Katie didn't answer, and ducked her head further down, he said a bit louder, "Hello Katie Maki-not Lipton-Maki." Katie burst into laughter, causing her to get a stern look from the volunteer along the green even though none of the players had even reached the green yet.

"Come closer, luv, Darío asked me to give you something," Binky said.

Katie made her way through the people. So, Darío had seen her. What did he want Binky to give her? Money? No. His hotel key? She couldn't think of anything else it could possibly be. What else would he even have on him out here on the course?

She got up to the ropes while Binky dug into the pocket of the apron he was required to wear. She held her hand out and he passed the key on to her while squeezing her hand. "It's good to see you, luv. You're our good-luck charm, you know. We've been playing right well since Texas, but he's playing in that same zone today with you in the crowd."

She gave him a smile, still not opening her hand to look at the key. "It's good to see you too, Binky," she said. With a wolfish grin, he turned and made his way over to the green, where Darío and the two other players were marking their balls, reading their lines.

Binky turned a head over his shoulder. "Darío said to make sure you use that," he said, nodding to her still closed fist.

Katie turned her palm over and uncurled her fingers. She saw several people next to her in the crowd crane their necks to see what had made a caddie come over and talk to someone in the gallery. Katie could only imagine their shock when they saw a hotel room key and she tried to pull her fist into her stomach, slowly unwrapping her fingers so only she would see the key.

But it wasn't a key. Or one of those key card things.

Lying on Katie's palm was a tube of cherry Chapstick.

—∞—

Another drive right down the middle. Yes, he definitely played better when Katie was in the gallery. Darío had picked her out right away, though it was obvious she was trying to blend in with the crowd. Darío realized that he'd been watching every gallery since Texas. Waiting for her to turn up.

Hoping she would turn up.

She was wearing khaki shorts and a sleeveless blouse that was already damp down her back from the sweltering heat. Her skin had more color than in Texas and Darío figured the sun had eventually found its way to Michigan's Upper Peninsula.

He remembered the night they met, in the Armadillo, creating the state of Michigan with their two hands. Then he thought about the other things their hands had done to each other. He stumbled as he walked down the fairway. Binky chuckled, knowing what was wreaking havoc on Darío's mind.

Why had she come here, to Memphis? Perhaps she was accompanying her friend on another business trip? Could he dare hope that she'd come alone? To see him? He'd been playing some of the best golf of his career in the last two months. He'd come at the game with a renewed vigor, his drive returned. The drive that had made him succeed so young. The drive that had been lacking for the last few years.

It couldn't all be because of his one night with Katie Maki, could it?

Darío tried to focus on the round, but couldn't. When he saw Katie lick her lips at the third hole, his mouth went dry. He had to ask Binky for the yardage three times. Then he'd stuck the ball within four inches of the pin.

He'd sent Binky to Katie with the lip balm, not wanting her

lips to sunburn. He was hoping he'd get a chance to taste those lips once more. And this time, he wouldn't let her sneak out in the middle of the night. This time he'd get her to stay. For how long, he didn't know. He only knew Katie was once again in his gallery and all was well.

—⁓—

After his round—the lowest of the day, putting him atop the leaderboard—Katie waited by the ropes until Darío made his way to her through the autograph seekers.

He kissed her on both cheeks. "Katie, it's great to see you here. Is Lizzie here, too?"

Katie felt a bit of relief that he thought she was here with Lizzie and hadn't turned into some crazy fan stalking him. "No. I'm here alone," she said, watching his reaction.

He looked at her for a moment, then that crooked smile made its way onto his face and Katie couldn't help but smile back. "Let's have some dinner. I have to clean up, will you wait?"

Of course she'd wait. She'd been waiting for this for two weeks, ever since the girls had made her realize she had to tell Darío about the baby.

—⁓—

After a day in the Memphis sun, she'd cleaned herself up as much as possible in the clubhouse ladies room that Darío had gotten her into, driven her own rental car to the restaurant he'd told her about, had a lovely dinner, and now they sat over coffee—decaf for her—and she still hadn't gotten the courage up to tell him he was going to be a father.

She'd been enjoying herself too much. It felt wonderful to see him. His tan had deepened in the two and a half months since she'd seen him in Texas. The white on his forehead where his hat perched during rounds was a bit more pronounced. But those eyes. Those eyes were still the exact shade of milk chocolate that she remembered.

He paid the bill and made a move to leave. "Katie, would you like to follow me back to the hotel?" he asked.

She could see the question in his eyes. She so badly wanted to just say yes and worry about telling him tomorrow. She couldn't be that cowardly.

"No, let's go back to my motel. I'm sure it's not nearly as nice as yours. In fact, it's a dive, but it was the only thing I could get on such short notice. Anyway, I have something there I need you to see." She watched him digest this, saw his look of curiosity. *He probably figures I have some kind of crazy sex toys there. Ah, if only.* "I'm at the Motel Six just off the freeway, by the airport," she said.

A look of concern crossed his face. "My God, you should not stay in that area. We'll go get your things, and this 'something' you wish to show me and then I'll bring you back to my hotel," he said.

"There aren't any vacancies at your hotel. It's all booked up with Tour people," Katie explained.

"I'm not suggesting you get your own room, *Gata*," he said, his accent heavy at the end, lulling Katie.

It would be so easy to do that. Not tell Darío about the baby until tomorrow. Have one more night of heated sex with the man who had made her feel again. The man who had brought her out of her deep freeze. The man who was the father of the miracle growing inside her.

She was a coward to even entertain the thought, but entertain it she did. "Well, let's play it by ear. If you still want me to come and stay with you once we've talked, I'd like that very much," she said.

She had once again piqued his curiosity and he gave her a questioning look, but didn't say anything else.

He led her to the parking lot, putting her in her car and then heading to his. "I'll follow you Katie, but if we get separated, what room are you in?"

She told him and then started on her way. It was almost as if she could hear a drum roll in her head the entire drive to the motel.

Or Taps on a trumpet. Something ominuous and foreboding.

He pulled in right behind her and she waited at the door to her room for him. She led him inside and turned on the lights to the dingy room, embarrassed for him to see where she was staying. She'd tried to get in to a nicer place, but with a Tour event in town and apparently some sort of dental conference, this was the best she could do.

He closed the door behind him and turned Katie, taking her into his arms. He nuzzled her neck. "You feel so good, *Gata*. Smell so good." He breathed her in deeply and she found her arms curling around her neck, copying his actions and breathing in the scent of him.

He smelled of aftershave, soap, and man. She held on tight, not wanting to let go. To lose the feelings of warmth he brought out in her. Fearing she'd never feel this warm again once she dropped her bombshell.

Determined to get it over with, she took a deep breath and stepped away from Darío's embrace. His arms reached for her again, but she took another step back. He looked at her, tilting his head in question.

"Darío, I have to tell you something. Something that I'm very happy about and I hope you'll be happy for me."

His brow furrowed. "You have reconciled with your husband," he said, his voice flat.

Katie almost laughed. "God, no. No, that isn't it." She thought she saw him sigh in relief. "Darío," she continued, "I'm pregnant."

He looked puzzled at first and Katie waited. Soon, his eyes narrowed on her. "I thought you were not able to conceive?" he said.

She bit her lip, glad that she'd used the Chapstick he'd given her to protect the skin that she was biting off in her nervousness. "I thought so, too, but apparently not. I'm going to have a child. I'm going to be a mother."

His shoulders came back, as if bracing himself. His eyes narrowed even more, producing only brown slits. He waited for her to finish. She did.

"It's your baby, Darío."

Ten

—⚭—

Never give a golfer an ultimatum unless you're prepared to lose.
~ Abigail Van Buren, advice columnist

DARÍO COULDN'T BELIEVE IT. He was going to be a father? Him?

A moment of elation flooded through him before a black shadow encased all thoughts. What did he know of fatherhood? Then his thoughts turned from himself back to Katie.

She stood in front of him, biting on those succulent lips, her blue eyes huge with…what? Excitement? Trepidation? She didn't look pregnant, she looked sexy as hell. She wasn't showing at all, but if indeed this was his child, she wouldn't be showing yet anyway.

He knew nothing of pregnant women, but he seemed to remember that they began to show outwardly around the third or fourth month, sometimes even later.

He still hadn't said a word, trying to take in the news. She walked toward the small round table in the room and took a folder out of a large envelope, holding it loosely in front of her. The folder cover sagged and Darío could see several papers inside. Still not able to comprehend that he was to be a father, Darío's mind swam as he tried to make sense of the legal-looking papers she held.

"There's no need to worry. I've seen a lawyer, and taken care of everything."

"Taken care of everything?" Darío repeated. That could encompass a myriad of decisions concerning his child, none of which he was going to allow without his consent.

She wouldn't be considering aborting his child, would she? Darío was sickened by the idea, and quickly dismissed it. Katie had always wanted a child, she would not dream of getting rid of one now. And why would she need to see him and be waving some legal documents at him if that were the case. She'd simply do it and he'd never be the wiser.

The thought that a child of his could be aborted without his knowledge ran a chill through him. Katie saw him bristle and misunderstood.

"Really, these are airtight. There's no need to worry, once you sign them I'll never bother you again. It'll be like we," she rubbed her belly as she made the plural, "never existed."

"What do you mean?" he asked.

"We'll just go back to Hancock and you'll never hear from us again. I promise. And signing those papers will guarantee it."

What the hell was she trying to pull? Was this some sort of extortion? He looked at the papers she was holding out to him and then back to her face. He still thought she was the most exquisite woman he'd ever seen. Even the ugliness of this situation could not affect her serene, flawless beauty.

"Just what exactly do these papers say?" he asked. The golfers on Tour were warned all the time about women who preyed on professional athletes, trying to become pregnant so that they could sue the father for astronomical amounts of child support. It was particularly prevalent in the NBA where the players, because of their size, were such easy targets in bars and restaurants. Darío knew of at least one player on the Tour who was paying huge sums monthly to a woman he barely knew but for the one night they created a child.

And they'd seen what kind of women Tiger had slept with

when they all started coming out of the woodwork after the scandal broke.

Was this what Katie was doing? Was her talk about her infertility just a ruse to get him to have unprotected sex? If that indeed was her game, what were the chances that this child was even his?

"The papers basically say that you relinquish all rights, legal and otherwise, to this child and that I give up all rights to ask you for any type of monetary or emotional support."

Ah. Well, that put a different spin on it. Could what she was saying be true, that she didn't want anything from him? He corrected himself. She wanted one thing from him—his child.

If this *was* his child, that was one thing he would never give her.

"I cannot sign these papers," he said.

She looked down at the folder, trying to see what Darío found offensive. She must not realize how offended he was that she wanted him out of his child's life. And he wouldn't tell her, his pride would not allow it.

She put the folder back on the table. "Of course you'll want to have someone look them over. All the legal mumbo-jumbo was a bit confusing for me, too."

He waved her words away. "It is not that, although I will look them over and if I have any questions, I will call my attorney." He led her to the bed and gently pushed her shoulders so that she sat on the edge. He pulled a straight chair from the table and dragged it toward the bed. He sat down facing her.

The room was cool from the air conditioner and Katie's bare arms were covered in gooseflesh. He got up and turned down the air conditioner and sat once more in front of Katie. "Now, Katie, explain to me how this could happen."

A smile lit her face and Darío lost his train of thought, just staring at the transformation that talking about being pregnant brought out in her. Her cheeks bloomed with color as she explained her concerns about her symptoms—never considering being pregnant—her visit to the doctor's office, and telling her friends.

"And, you didn't know this when you met her, 'cause she wasn't showing yet, but Lizzie is pregnant too. She's five months along—no, wait—closer to six, so she'll deliver before I will, but our babies will be close in age. Isn't that great?"

Darío was ashamed of the mercenary motivations he'd assigned to Katie. This woman was born to be a mother. Everything in her demeanor changed as she talked about her pregnancy. How lucky she was to have very little nausea, the vitamins she was taking, and on and on. She became relaxed and animated right before Darío's eyes. He had thought it an old wive's tale about pregnant women giving off a glow, but now knew it to be true. Katie was radiant, and Darío was pleased that in a small way, he was responsible for making this woman so happy.

"Which brings us back to the papers. I know this is all a lot to take in," she finished.

"*Sí*," Darío said. "I am a bit shocked."

Katie rose from the bed and went again to the table and the folder. This time when she held it out to Darío, he took it. "Take your time, there's no hurry. Well, I guess there sort of is," she chuckled. "You have about six and a half months to sign them." She smiled, her white teeth sparkling.

"I'll look them over tonight. Can you meet me for breakfast tomorrow?" he asked. She nodded and they agreed on a time and place to meet the next morning. Being Saturday, the tournament's parings would be done by standings, and Darío was at the top, which guaranteed him a later tee time.

He'd checked the tee times before he'd left the clubhouse. He had until one-forty the next day to try to come to terms with Katie.

It could be a very long breakfast.

He turned to leave, then stopped and turned back to Katie. "Katie, I feel I must be honest with you. I'll look over these papers, but know this. If this is my child—and that will have to be proven to me by more than just your say-so—I will not be giving up any rights to it. And I will expect this child to bear my name. And if that means marriage, then so be it."

He turned again to leave, but not before he saw a look of shock and dismay cross Katie's radiant face.

—∞—

He brought Binky with him to breakfast. Moral support, Katie figured. That was okay, she liked Binky. She even thought she might get him on her side.

Her side? Had this really come down to sides? She was still in shock that Darío had mentioned marriage. Of course it was unthinkable; they barely knew each other. She had a small job in a small town. He traveled internationally and was a professional athlete. The only thing they had in common was this baby growing inside of her.

The pleasantries, such as they were, were over quickly. Breakfast ordered and eaten in near silence. Binky, the only one who spoke, kept up a running monologue of what Darío needed to look for in the round later today. Katie could see Darío was only pretending to listen.

He was wearing the same coral Lacoste shirt he had worn the first day she'd met him in Texas. Two months of hot sun made the white laugh lines around his eyes more pronounced. He held himself straight and tall, as he barely touched his food. He looked tired. Katie wondered if he'd gotten as little sleep as she had last night.

Their dishes cleared away, Darío sipped on his coffee and Katie struggled with finishing her huge glass of milk. "I'm assuming you've brought Binky up to speed with my situation?" she asked.

As Binky nodded, Darío added, "*Our* situation."

Katie nodded her understanding. "Right. Our situation." She took another gulp of milk, then leveled her shoulders, hoping for the best, but prepared for the worst. "And, after looking over the papers, are you ready to sign them?" She held her breath, waiting for his answer.

He placed his coffee cup down on the saucer. His rough hands smoothed the already smooth paper placemat. "I will not sign your papers. No child of mine will be raised without a father."

She felt she knew what he was thinking. He was a traditionalist, and he would feel that the child would need a strong father figure. Plus he came from a very male-oriented culture. She wanted to explain to him that his child would be surrounded by strong male influences.

"I understand that the role of a father is probably very important to you because you didn't know yours." She waited for Darío to break in. When he didn't, she continued on, not sure if she was helping or hurting her case. "But I have four brothers, all of them married and with kids of their own. This child will be surrounded by uncles and a grandfather, and have tons of cousins to play with." She waited. He said nothing. His steely look had left, but his jaw was still taut, filled with determination. Fine, so was Katie. "This child will be loved by a large family, Darío, there is no need for concern."

His eyes returned to the soft chocolate-brown she'd been so drawn to in Texas. They seemed to be full of hurt. He let out a loud sigh. Katie wasn't sure what nerve she'd hit, but she knew she'd trampled on one.

"Don't be concerned? Do you think I'm the type of man that by just knowing my child has uncles around him to teach him to play baseball I won't be concerned?"

Katie knew she'd made a huge mistake. She'd taken the position of letting Darío off the hook for any responsibility, assuring him that their child would be loved and guided by father figures. It would be enough for any man who was looking for a loophole, but Darío wasn't that kind of man. He played a game of honor, and tried to live his life as such. Shirking a duty was not the way he operated.

But Katie suspected that it was even more than that. Could it be that this was something Darío didn't want to shirk?

"I will say this once more only," his voice was soft, but firm.

"If this is indeed my child, we will be married. My baby will not be born a bastard." He got up before Katie could argue the paternity once again and left the table.

"A bastard. He called my baby a bastard," Katie said.

"Well, luv, it is his baby, too," Binky quietly added.

Katie was grateful Binky sounded so sure of that fact. Surer than Darío had. "Yes, but, the stigma of being born outside of wedlock is not what it used to be. With divorces and no marriages, more kids are being raised by one parent now than are by two. I mean, who even uses the word bastard anymore?" she said incredulously.

There was a small glimmer of compassion in the caddy's eyes. "He does. Because he is one," Binky said, turning to follow Darío as Katie stared after them.

—⚬w—

Darío drove to Katie's motel later that evening. He would have put up a fight about her staying in such a rough area, but knew he didn't really want her staying in his room with him. Well, he did want her in his bed, that much hadn't changed, damn it. How could he be so furious with her, and still want to sleep with her? *Bah!*

When he pulled the courtesy car in front of her room he saw her peek out the window and he could imagine her, standing at the door, not knowing if she should let him in or not.

He didn't blame her. He took great pride in his ability to control his emotions. He was a Basque, from the northern part of Spain, and they were especially known for passion ruling over reason. He never let himself fall into the stereotype of Latin hothead, governed by emotions. He could put a steely shield in place in seconds.

It had helped him win tournaments.

It had helped him survive childhood.

He had come very close to losing that control this morning in the restaurant. That was why he'd left. He'd been able to put his shield in place on the course this afternoon, though, and had shot a respectable three under par. Unfortunately, several players shot much lower and he had dropped down to tenth place going into the final round tomorrow.

He was surprised to see Katie in his gallery. She'd followed his entire round, though she stood well away from the greens when he was on them. He was mad with himself that he noticed and cared when he saw her reapply sunscreen to her lips and her skin several times throughout the day. He was happy to see she went through several bottles of water in the sweltering heat as well.

Regardless of who the father was, he would want any woman to have a healthy child. Even Katie.

Especially Katie.

He sat in the car debating what to say, when Katie opened the door. He got out of the car and made his way into her room. She shut the door behind him. She looked tired. It was the first flaw, slight as it was, that Darío had ever seen in her beautiful face. He cursed himself to know he was the one who'd put it there. Concern that maybe she hadn't gotten enough sleep, which he assumed was important for pregnant women, made him feel like an even bigger heel.

She started to speak but he held up a hand to stop her. He motioned for her to sit on the bed, noticing her open suitcase, obviously being packed. He sat on a chair, turning it to face her on the bed.

"Katie, please. First, I apologize for my behavior this morning. It's not my nature to become so emotional. I'm sorry for, as you say over here, 'losing it'."

Her eyes widened, and Darío could now definitely see the circles underneath.

"That was you losing it?" She chuckled, though Darío could see nothing funny in his apology. The chuckle turned into a full-blown laugh. "Oh Darío, if that's your idea of losing it, I'd love to see you at one of my family dinners. By that barometer, people are losing it all night long at one of the Maki gatherings." She stopped laughing, but a smile still played on her face. "I thought you Basques were fiery people."

"You know I am Basque?" he asked. He felt an unexplain-able pleasure to know she'd found out that much about him. Then a niggling thought crept in. What else had she learned, and why? And more importantly, when? Before she'd come to Texas? Had she done research on him, found out what it would take to seduce him?

Surprisingly little, as it turned out. Just telling him he had the sexiest forearms she'd ever seen was all it took.

"Yes, I know you're a Basque, though you surely don't seem like what I've read of them." She hesitated. "I take that back. They're known as a very proud people, and you are certainly that."

"Why have you learned so much about Basques? About me?" He couldn't help the small thread of suspicion that escaped and hoped Katie would not catch it.

She shrugged. "I don't know. I just thought it important to learn about traits that my baby may have."

Of course, the baby. Darío was a fool to think that her inter-est in his heritage had anything to do with him.

She waved a hand, as if to erase their current line of topic. "Anyway, no apology necessary for this morning. I honestly didn't know what to expect when I came here, but you've totally sur-prised me. It never occurred to me that you would feel so strongly about this baby."

She didn't know what a statement like that could do to him. She couldn't have, or she would never have thrown such a dagger at his heart. He was not the kind of man his father was. He would not turn away from his child. If this was his child—and Darío was not totally convinced of that—then he would never abandon it, would never allow his role to be played by uncles or a grandfather. The fact that Katie thought he could ripped him apart.

That she lumped him in with the son of a bitch who had fathered him made him furious.

Determined to stay in control this time, he rose from the chair. "I see you're planning on leaving tonight?" he asked. She nodded, and opened her mouth to speak, but Darío cut her off. "Have a safe trip back to Michigan, Katie. Please take care of yourself and the baby."

She must have sensed his slipping control, his barely masked rage. She unconsciously placed her hand across her abdomen as if to protect the baby from him. The thought made him even angrier.

"But if you think that you will keep me away from a child of mine, you are sadly mistaken. You'll be hearing from my lawyers."

He left the room, turning his back on her gasp.

—⁊⁊⁊—

"Mamá, what's a bastard?" four-year-old Darío asked his mother.

She dropped the pot she'd taken from the tiny stove in the cramped kitchen, paella spilling everywhere, but she didn't seem to notice. That in itself worried Darío. His mother was always so tidy in the kitchen, for her to not even seem to notice that their dinner was now all over her spotless floor…something was definitely wrong.

She stepped through the rice, gobs of it sticking to her shoes—another sign that this was serious stuff. Mamá loved shoes, and she only owned two pairs. She knelt down and pulled Darío to her, clutching his skinny arms in her warm hands. "Darío, where did you hear such a word?" she asked.

Darío could see the color start to rise in her cheeks, just like when he had done something wrong and was about to be scolded. He didn't know what he'd said, but he knew it wasn't good. Best to come clean, he figured. "The women in the kitchen said it today, while you went down to the office."

"Those bitches," she whispered, but Darío heard her. His eyes grew big. Mamá never said bad words. At least he thought that was a bad word. He didn't dare ask now.

"You shouldn't be listening like that," she said, but there was warmth in her voice.

"I didn't mean to. Sergio sent me to tell you that he was taking me out on the back nine with him."

His mother nodded. "Yes, of course. It was good you came to ask my permission."

Darío didn't bother to say he wasn't really asking for permission, more like telling her. There was no way he would miss going out on the course with Sergio, it was the best.

"What else did you hear the women say, *mi corazón*?" his mother asked.

Darío shrugged, his arms falling free from his mother's grip. "They said I was a bastard and you were a fool. But that I couldn't help being a bastard and you could help being a fool."

His mother crushed him to her. His arms were trapped between their bodies so he couldn't even hug her back. His face was buried in her hair, which she always let loose from the tight bun the minute they stepped into their tiny cottage. It smelled good, like flowers, and Darío buried his nose in it as he listened to his mother croon to him.

"No, no, you are not a bastard. You are a gift. The most precious gift. You are a miracle. My miracle."

She released him and held him away from her, her grip once again strong on his arms. "You are a miracle. Tell me, are miracles wasted on fools?" Before Darío could shake his head—that was the answer he thought she was looking for—she went on. "No, of course not."

Her face was bright red now. Darío had never seen her this upset and it scared him. He reached out to touch her face and realized tears were streaming down her cheeks.

"Don't cry Mamá, you're not a fool."

His mother wiped her eyes across her sleeve—something she always scolded Darío for when he did it with a runny nose. "No. I am no fool. And you are no bastard. You are my son, and you are my everything, *mi corazón*." Her heart.

Later that night, when he was supposed to be asleep, Darío crept out of the bed he shared with his mother and poked his head around the flimsy partition that pretended to separate the one-room apartment into two. His mother was at the kitchen table, her head in her hands, her beautiful black hair swung forward, ruining any chance Darío had of seeing her face.

But he didn't need to see her face to know she was crying.

It was the earliest memory Darío had. And the hardest one to forget.

Eleven

—⁂—

The trouble with me is I think too much.
I always said you have to be dumb to play good golf.
- JoAnne Carner, professional golfer

KATIE PUSHED THE GROCERY cart down the dairy aisle. She'd never been one for milk, but she was now drinking a couple of glasses a day. The stupid wheel on the cart did another three-sixty, sending her nearly into the butter. Nothing was going right today.

A typo in an obit had gotten through. Not good to have someone's last statement to the world have the wrong name. They'd already gotten seventeen calls on it before she'd left the office. No telling how many more they'd get tomorrow. Ah, the joys of a small-town paper.

It had been three weeks since she'd seen Darío. Three weeks and she still hadn't heard anything from him, and that made her nervous. That last evening in her motel room, he hadn't seemed like he was going to let the subject of giving up rights drop. The papers she'd taken to Memphis sat on her dining room table, untouched since she'd thrown them there after returning home.

Nearing the checkout, she remembered she needed toilet paper and returned to that aisle, nearly colliding carts with someone as she rounded the corner.

"Oh, I'm sorry, I…" The words died in her throat as she

recognized the driver of the other cart, and more importantly, its passenger. Strapped into a car seat that settled into the purse compartment of the cart was Crystal Lipton, being driven by her proud papa.

"Ron," Katie gasped. She was lucky she'd avoided him this long. She'd obviously seen him since he'd left her, to talk with their lawyers, to hash out financial arrangements, even in the Commodore one night having a beer with his friends. But she'd been fortunate not to have seen him or the baby since she was born. Now, her eyes were drawn to the pudgy arms waving, seemingly to her.

"Katie," Ron said. He looked uncomfortable to see her. Good, this was no picnic for her, either.

But he still looked good. Great. His blond hair was made even lighter from the summer sun. He wore a tee-shirt with the arms ripped out, showing off his muscular, tanned biceps. Denim cutoffs hugged his toned thighs; flip-flops adorned his long feet.

He looked casual, carefree, gorgeous. He also looked like the man who had broken her heart.

She tried to think of something to say. Something that wouldn't come out in a shriek of recriminations. She could think of nothing and her eyes once again turned to the baby. Her cheeks were huge and solid, her arms never rested and she was bound and determined to stuff her entire fist into her mouth. Miniature versions of her father's blue eyes twinkled and a cropping of blond fuzz peeked through a pink, elastic headband. "She's beautiful, Ron."

He looked at his daughter, then at Katie. For a moment, the past year fell away, and they looked at each other with the mutual affection they'd once shared. "Thanks. I think so too."

Maybe it would feel different if she weren't pregnant herself, but Katie felt a little of the animosity she'd felt for Ron slip away. If given the choice, would she have cheated on Ron to have a bundle like Crystal looking up at her? Would her desire to have a child have allowed her to be unfaithful if she'd known that Ron's sperm and her body weren't in sync?

It was a question she could not answer, did not want to even think about, afraid she might say yes. She'd wanted a child for so long, she wasn't sure that she wouldn't sacrifice her marriage vows to have one. Inadvertently, that was what Ron had done. She could—almost—forgive him. She could certainly understand him a little bit better.

"Well…" She disengaged her cart from his and started to roll past him.

He reached out and placed his hand on her arm, stopping her. "You have no idea how much I wish she was yours, Katie. Yours and mine."

"I…I have to go," she said, and went down the aisle. Her mind buzzed and her heart seemed to slow. Hadn't she secretly had the same thoughts? Certainly when she'd first found out about Crystal, but even about the baby she now carried? How she wished this baby were hers and Ron's, conceived in love, not out of a one-night stand. She felt she was betraying Darío to have such thoughts, but her history with Ron was much more complex and layered than anything she and Darío had shared.

Like a coward, she hid in the back of the store, behind a deli display, until there was no way Ron could possibly still be shopping. When she got home, she only had enough energy to put the perishable foods in the fridge, letting the dry goods sit on the counter. She didn't have any desire to make herself dinner, though she knew she had to eat. She sat down on the couch and tried to relax, willing the bad day away.

She'd gotten used to living alone, but she still didn't like it. Coming from a big family, she'd never been alone, though with four brothers she'd always had her own bedroom. She'd lived with Lizzie and Alison at State and then she and Ron had married after graduation.

Lizzie's husband, Finn, and his son, Stevie, came over on a Saturday now and then with a tool box in his Jeep and asked if she needed anything done. Lizzie and Alison and she still went out once a week for pizza at the Commodore, even with Lizzie now married and with kids. But Katie always came home to an empty house. Slept alone in bed. Made meals for one.

She thought back to seeing Ron at the store and wondered why she didn't tell him she was pregnant. It was still early in her pregnancy and something could go wrong, but she knew that wasn't why. She tried to come up with an answer when the doorbell rang.

That was odd. She couldn't remember the last time anyone rang the bell. Alison and Lizzie barged right in, as did her family.

Lifting herself from the couch, she made her way to the door, only to open it to Darío Luna. He looked tired, Katie thought, and his face didn't hold the teasing, crooked smile that he'd given her in the past.

"Katie, we must talk. And this time *I* brought the legal documents," he said.

―⁓―

Katie looked across the car to Darío sitting silently in the passenger seat as she drove. She hadn't even let him pass the front foyer of her home before grabbing her keys and hustling him out the door. She didn't want to have this conversation—whatever it turned out to be—in the home she had shared with Ron. Somehow, sitting amongst the accumulation of thirteen years of marriage while you discussed the pregnancy that was the result of a one-night stand with a near stranger seemed inappropriate.

Katie inwardly snorted. Nothing about this situation was appropriate. It would be appropriate that the child she was carrying were Ron's. It would be appropriate that the child she'd seen with Ron earlier were hers. And it would be appropriate if it were Katie, Ron, Crystal, and the baby on the way in the car driving to dinner.

She didn't take Darío to the Commodore. She'd know too many people there. Anywhere she went she was bound to run into somebody she knew. That was the price of living in a small town your whole life. Not to mention working at its only daily newspaper.

Katie didn't want to pay that price tonight. She wasn't quite ready to explain to the Copper Country why Darío Luna had come to town. She wasn't sure herself. To lessen her chances of bumping into any acquaintances, she drove Darío along the man-made Portage Canal, past Hancock to the town of Calumet. The drive was beautiful, the water sparkling like diamonds in the early evening light. A sight that usually soothed Katie, but not tonight.

Neither of them said much during the drive. Katie wasn't sure if that was because Darío seemed to be intent on the view, or if they had nothing to say to each other.

They were having a child together. Certainly they had something else in common that they could talk about. Something besides the baby.

But the twenty-minute ride remained silent as Katie racked her brain and came up empty.

They got lucky—the small pizza joint Katie picked was near deserted, and those few people eating were strangers to her. They chose a booth near the back, and they both studied their menus like they held the secrets of the universe. It was a no-frills pizza joint with only about six items on the menu, but Katie and Darío both perused the laminated sheets for several minutes, hesitant to put them down and start a conversation.

Soon the waiter, a teenager fighting the worst case of acne Katie could remember seeing, took their order and they were left to stare at each other. Katie's pregnancy resembled a pink elephant that pulled up a chair and joined their table.

Just as Katie prepared to start off with Darío's latest top-ten finish, and Darío opened his mouth to say something, a man and what appeared to be his daughter entered the restaurant and sat down at a table parallel to Darío and Katie's booth. Katie and Darío both seemed relieved to have something else to look at besides each other and their menus.

They both watched as the father and daughter sat down and immediately picked up their menus, hiding their faces behind them. Katie smiled as she thought the scene similar to her and

Darío. She sneaked a glance at Darío and saw him watching the little girl.

She was probably about ten, Katie guessed, with jet-black hair that probably made her stand out in her class of what would most likely be fair-headed Finns. Lizzie had stood out like that in their class years ago.

The little girl faced Katie, but Katie was only able to see the top of her head. Everything below her enormous green eyes was hidden by the menu. The little girl's forehead was furrowed. In concentration, Katie wondered? That much work over the menu? But that wasn't it, for soon, the little girl took a deep breath, braced the bony shoulders that stuck out of her pink tee-shirt and placed the menu down on the table. Her brow was still furrowed, but now Katie recognized the emotion. Determination.

"You know what you're having, Peaches?" the father asked from behind his menu.

Katie saw the little girl's grimace at her father's pet name. She had probably outgrown it years ago, Katie thought, but the father didn't realize it. Of course not, how could he possibly notice it when he doesn't look at the girl?

"Yes. I'll have the personal pizza, plain cheese." Her voice was small, quiet, and Katie felt herself leaning toward the table to hear her. Catching herself, she took a sip of her water, sat back and looked at Darío, only to find his gaze on the twosome as well.

She tried to think of something to say to him. "You had a great showing at the British last week. Another top ten, that's great. I'm sort of surprised you're back in the States so soon. I would have thought you'd play a few more tournaments in Europe while you were over there," Katie said.

Darío turned his attention back to Katie as she spoke. He nodded at her congratulations. "*Sí*, it was a good tournament for me." He paused, watching as the father finally put down his menu when the waiter came and took their order. "I usually do play in Europe from the British until the PGA, but, I decided to play over here instead," he said.

It being a Wednesday, and Darío being a thousand miles from Connecticut where the Tour was playing this week, Katie deduced he was taking a week off. And had decided to spend part of that time in the Copper Country. Great. Just what she needed on top of her crappy day.

Not that she didn't want to see Darío. She had to admit, her insides had done a tiny flip-flop when she'd opened the door and saw him standing there. After his initial pronouncement, her eyes had gone straight to his forearms, even more deeply tanned than they'd been in Memphis. He'd followed her gaze and smiled that crooked smile. She hadn't thought she could feel more vulnerable than she had earlier that day when she'd seen Ron in the aisle of Pat's IGA, but seeing Darío at her door, in her hometown, on her turf, smiling at her, made her curse the hormones that coursed through her body.

"Not playing Hartford?" she asked, though the answer was obvious. He wouldn't be here right now if he were teeing off in Hartford tomorrow morning.

"No, not playing this week." His attention was back on the father and daughter, and Katie followed his gaze. The father was asking questions of the little girl. Stuff about her everyday life that he'd have known if he were in the house. A quick look at the man's bare ring finger and Katie's suspicions of a divorced father out with his daughter for their weekly Wednesday night dinner were confirmed.

"So, Peaches, what'd you do today?" he asked his daughter.

"Um…played on the computer, watched a video," she trailed off.

"You didn't go swimming today? Not to the beach? It was a beautiful day," the father said.

Katie agreed with the man. It had been one of those idyllic days in the Copper Country. Mid-eighties with a nice breeze coming off Lake Superior, so no humidity. A day to be at the beach. Certainly not a day to go grocery shopping at Pat's.

"There are too many of us at daycare to go to the beach."

Peaches took a sip of her Mountain Dew. A pop that Peaches' mother probably wouldn't have let her drink so late in the evening, Katie thought, but how was the father to know that you didn't let a ten-year-old have so much caffeine and sugar at nine o'clock at night?

And just why was this father feeding his daughter so late, anyway? Katie had a momentary pang for the mother who would be getting back a hyped-up daughter well past her bedtime later on this evening. But then, Katie didn't know the circumstances that surrounded this broken family.

She wondered how many single-parent mistakes she'd make out of necessity or just to keep her sanity. She decided to cut this father a little slack.

"Oh. Daycare, that's right. Of course." The father seemed disturbed that he hadn't realized how his daughter spent her days during summer vacation. Katie's heart thawed even more toward the father. There was no bad guy here, just a bad situation.

Katie and Darío's food arrived, and they were again spared the need to speak to each other. Their silence was almost comfortable by now, certainly familiar, and the pizza was good. Moments later, Peaches' pizza and her father's burger arrived and their table fell into a hushed silence broken only by slurps of Peaches' straw.

Both tables ate with deliberation, as if they didn't want the meal to end. Katie knew it wasn't because of the food—excellent as it was. For her part, she stalled while eating dinner because she didn't want to hear why Darío was here, in the Copper Country. He said he'd come with papers of his own for her to sign. She couldn't really blame him. He'd had some time to think about the situation, cool down after the initial bomb she'd dropped on him in Memphis, realized that marriage was indeed out of the question, and had come up with an agreement of his own. Instinctively, she knew it would be more than fair, and that she would probably sign it. She knew Darío would want to do the honorable thing by his child, his announcement about marriage had proven that, but common sense would prevail. He'd obviously seen that, in their case, honorable did not necessarily mean marriage.

When their table had been cleared and the suspense was near killing Katie, she began, "Darío, I think I know why you're here, and…" She stopped when she realized he was not paying attention to her, but had once again turned his head to Peaches' table.

Katie, happy for the reprieve, looked to see Peaches alone at the table, the father's back disappearing down the hallway leading to the restrooms. But Peaches was talking. To herself.

She was nervously twisting her napkin beyond the point of recognition, the paper shredding about her place setting. Katie noticed several other napkins had also received the same fate and were littered across Peaches' side of the table. Katie leaned a little to her right to be able to hear what the girl was saying to herself.

"You see, Dad. I really need a new pair of sneakers. And um…" She stopped, seemed to rethink her opening, and tried again. "Dad, it's been almost a year since I got the shoes I'm wearing, and…" She stopped again. Peaches shook her little head, dismissing this latest try. Her hair lightly slapped her face as she shook and a clump of strands lodged in her open mouth, which she summarily began to chew on as she thought of her next approach.

Katie looked under the table and noticed the girl's shoes. They were indeed worn. They were also Nikes. Katie wondered why, if money was such a problem, would the girl would be wearing Nikes? She then remembered that the father was dressed very fashionably and expensively as well, and thought that maybe the rehearsing of a request for shoes wasn't about money at all, but about not being able to communicate with your father.

Katie felt a chill go through her and instinctively placed her hand on her abdomen. She looked across at Darío and saw a questioning look on his face. He knew something was wrong with Peaches' situation, he just hadn't come to the conclusion that Katie did.

"Daddy, my shoes…" Peaches trailed off again. Katie, being a journalist and having a way with words, wanted to jump in and help the kid out, but the father was headed back to the table.

"Ready to go, Peaches?" he asked as he started reaching for his wallet with one hand and the check with the other.

"Um, yeah, I guess," she said.

The father looked at his daughter's empty glass and empty plate, but didn't seem to notice the shredded napkins or the anxious look on his daughter's face. He saw his daughter was making no move to leave. "Did you want some dessert, honey?" he asked.

"No. I mean, no thank you."

Katie smiled at the girl's remembrance of good manners. The kid was tied up in knots, but caught herself on the thank yous.

"Um, Daddy..." she tried. She had her father's attention. He watched and waited patiently, trying to help her with the words, but he didn't know what they were.

"Yes, honey, what is it?"

"Um..."

Katie and Darío squirmed in their seats, feeling as uncomfortable for so obviously eavesdropping as they felt for the father and daughter next to them. As if both realizing they were staring, they looked at each other, but their ears were tuned to Peaches and her father.

"Did you get enough to eat?" The father's concern was genuine. He seemed to pick up on his daughter's unease. He wanted to help her, he just didn't know what she needed.

"Yeah. I mean, yes, thank you. Um...you see..." She had turned her voice to the sales pitch voice she'd been practicing while her father was away. "Um..." Her green eyes stared at her father. He looked back at her, waiting, a sympathetic look on his face.

Katie saw the moment the girl gave up. Her shoulders slumped. She reached for a clump of hair and began to chew it again. "The pizza was really good, Daddy, thanks. I'm ready to go now."

Katie watched as the father struggled with the decision to push his daughter into telling him what was wrong or to let it go.

He looked bewildered and Katie's heart, though none too pro-man on this day, went out to him. She saw nearly the same body movements of defeat come over the father that had just come over Peaches. All except the hair chewing.

"Okay, Peaches, let's get you home to your mother, then."

Katie watched them leave then turned to Darío, finally ready to hear what he had to say. Anything to take her mind off the heartbreaking scene she'd just witnessed.

"Do you think they can not afford new shoes?" Darío asked. "Do you know that family? Could we perhaps get the shoes for the little girl without their knowledge?"

Katie's throat clenched with emotion. She took a long swallow of her water and waited for it to pass. She wasn't sure if it would ever completely pass. She sensed that with impending motherhood she was destined to have her heart broken and then mended, daily.

"I don't think it was about the money for the shoes. She was wearing expensive shoes and clothes and so was he."

Darío nodded, he'd apparently noticed the same thing. "So…?" he asked. Katie knew he was looking for an easy answer as to what had just happened, but she didn't have one.

"I think…" She hesitated, choosing her words carefully. "I think she just doesn't know how to talk to her father. Not beyond 'yes please' and 'thank you'."

Darío continued nodding, his face drawn. His forehead, so tan until the top three inches where his hat rested while he golfed, was furrowed; much like Peaches' had been when she'd been mustering up her courage. "And the father?"

"I'm pretty sure it's a divorce situation. Apparently, he can't read his daughter any better than she can communicate with him." Katie breathed deeply, took another sip of water and placed her hands on the table, as if to steady them. "It's very sad."

Darío looked into her eyes, placed a large, dark hand on top of hers and said, "It is too sad, Katie. That must not happen to our child. That must not ever be our daughter."

As Katie moved to answer, Darío cut her off with a soft squeeze of her hand under his. "Please, *Gata*, don't let me ever be that father. Not knowing what his daughter needs. Only able to watch helplessly."

It wasn't fair. It should be Ron's child growing inside her. It should have been her child Ron pushed in the cart at the grocery store. And it should be easy for Peaches to ask her dad for gym shoes.

But life was not fair.

Or maybe it was. She was, after years of wishing and dreaming, going to become a mother. Maybe life was fair, just twisted.

Katie nodded, knowing she would do whatever it took to never put her child in the position of rehearsing a simple request of her father.

—⚒—

"I'm going on tour with Darío," Katie said.

She waited for Lizzie and Alison's reactions. When she got none, she hurried on. "In fact, he's meeting me here in a half hour, but I wanted to have a chance to tell you guys alone first. So you can tell me if I'm making the biggest mistake of my life or not."

They were at the Commodore, in their usual booth. She'd told them of Darío's unexpected arrival the day before, of Peaches' saga and how when they got back to Katie's house they'd talked for hours and come up with a plan. Then Darío had spent the night in the hotel across the street from the Commodore.

"Go on, tell us everything before we can tell you what we think," Lizzie said.

"First, let me say how amazing it was to talk this out with him. When I went to Memphis and he shot me down, I thought it'd be like Ron all over again. Well, no, not like Ron, he and I ignored our problems, Darío just dismissed them. At the time I thought it was the same thing, but he was just caught off-guard. Once he had time to digest the situation we were able to sit and talk this whole thing out. I tell you, it was pretty refreshing to hash out a problem with a man for hours.

"I'll travel with him until my sixth month. The doctor said travel until then would be fine, plus I'll be getting tons of good exercise walking the course during rounds. That gives us just over three months to get to know each other better. We agreed not to bring up legal papers or rights or visitation or anything like that for the entire time. When I get to six months, hopefully we can decide how to proceed, whether I'll live here and Darío will buy a home in Hancock so he can spend time with the baby."

"Or what?" Alison asked. "What's the alternative to you staying in Hancock? We just got Lizard back up here. Don't tell me we're going to lose you?"

"Well, he said he was still going to try to convince me to marry him, so that's an option."

Lizzie piped in, "You say 'that's an option' like marriage is just another choice for dinner. 'Well, honey, there's roast beef, chicken or, I suppose we could get married.'"

Katie placed a hand on Lizzie's arm, "Lizard, you're in a great marriage. I thought I was too once upon a time. Truth is, maybe marriage should be looked upon more like a business agreement than a love match."

"You can't mean that," Lizzie said.

Katie shrugged. "What's that saying? First time marry for love, second time marry for companionship."

"I thought it was second time marry for money," Alison said.

"I thought it was for friendship," Lizzie added.

Katie waved them both away. "Whatever. Anyway, I had my marriage for love, and it was lovely." She saw Alison opening her mouth and cut her off. "For most of it, anyway." Alison raised her eyebrows, but kept silent. "But we're getting ahead of ourselves. I can't marry a man who feels about me the way he does right now. Not to mention I barely know the man."

Alison took a sip of her drink. "Oh, I don't know, apparently you know him pretty well if that bun in your oven is any indication."

Katie only laughed as Lizzie chastised Alison with a look.

"That's what's so weird about it. Like last night. When he was leaving to go to the hotel…" She stopped at both Lizzie and Alison's questioning glances. "Yes, hotel. He'd already checked in before he came to see me. I liked that he didn't assume. So, anyway, he goes to leave and it was like a first date. Should we kiss? Handshake? Kiss on the cheek? I mean, we're having a baby together and we didn't know how to say goodnight."

"So what happened?" Lizzie asked.

Katie ducked her head, her face flushing with the memory. "He kissed me on both cheeks." It had sent heat through her at the time as well.

"How very European," Lizzie teased.

Alison, ever practical, asked, "What about your job?"

"I talked with Don a long time today. We talked about a leave of absence, but we came up with something else. So I can stay on staff and keep my benefits, I'll file a story or two each week while I'm gone. Sort of a slice-of-life thing from the Tour. We're not sure if it will be more travel-oriented or sports-oriented. We're going to talk about it more tomorrow, nail out the details before Darío and I head out on Monday. He was great about it, even with no notice."

Katie had hated doing that to Don, he'd been so good to her at the *Ingot*, but he'd been very understanding. They were more than boss and worker. They were friends, and Don knew what this pregnancy meant to Katie. She'd take her laptop on the road with her and be in constant touch with Don about different story ideas.

The thought of doing some writing other than obits and wedding announcements stirred Katie with an excitement about her job she hadn't felt in years.

"Okay, back to Darío," Lizzie said.

Katie waited. She knew her friends would support whatever decision she made, but she also knew that they'd certainly voice their opinions with no problem.

"Did he make any demands about a paternity test?"

"Not really demands. I explained we could do blood tests after the baby was born, but the only thing we could do while the baby was in-utero was an amnio and I wasn't prepared to do that. There's a risk it could hurt the baby and I'm not going to take that chance for something we can find out right after the baby's born. Something I know for certain, anyway."

"And he was okay with that?"

Katie nodded. "He agreed that we'd wait till after the baby was born before we'd even discuss paternity tests."

"You said he showed up with papers for you to sign, what was in them?" Alison asked.

Katie shook her head. "I don't know. I never ended up reading them. At the end of our talk, Darío took his papers and the set I'd taken to Memphis for him to sign and tore them up. Then he held out his hand and said, 'This should be our agreement alone. No lawyers, no judges.' I shook on it. That's all he needed. For now."

Alison and Lizzie both looked dumbfounded. "Are you kidding? A handshake? Wow. And you trust him?"

Katie sipped on her water and took a bite of pizza, all the while thinking. "I know it's crazy. But yeah, I trust him. I know he'll never go back on his word. That's why I allowed him to tear up the papers. That he *wanted* to tear up the papers says a lot, because, the thing is, *he* doesn't trust *me*, not yet, not completely. I think a part of him still thinks I trapped him."

Lizzie waved that away. "That's preposterous. Not in a million years would you have guessed you'd get pregnant that night."

"*We* know that…" Katie left the sentence unfinished.

Alison leaned forward, and Katie went on guard for the question she was about to ask. "So, if you think he doesn't trust you, why are you willing to have just a handshake deal?"

Katie met Alison head on, knowing she couldn't hide from her psychologist friend. "Because in the next three months, I'm going to make him trust me."

"That's important to you?"

"Yes."

"Why?"

Katie sat back in her seat, put her hands on the table, fingers clasped together. She looked at her two best friends in the world. Women she'd shared everything with since kindergarten. She gave them the only answer she had. "Because he's the father of my child."

Twelve

—∽—

I don't like watching golf on TV. I can't stand whispering.
                                    - David Brenner, comedian

DARÍO WALKED INTO the Commodore and immediately saw Katie and her friends. It was as if he sensed her more than saw her. He'd had the same feeling in Memphis when she'd walked in his gallery. He was drawn to her by some invisible force.

She threw her head back and laughed at something one of the women across from her said. Even across the entire restaurant her golden beauty was obvious.

The knot that had been in his stomach all day eased at the sight of her.

Actually, it has eased greatly last night when they'd made their decision.

Katie was going on tour with him. She was giving him a chance. Was giving them a chance to perhaps become a family. Something he had never been a part of. Not really. He wouldn't trade his mother for the world, but it had always just been the two of them. They were more of a team than a family.

He honestly didn't think this day would come. He'd certainly never gone looking for it. But he was about to have a family of his own. And he was going to try like hell to make sure his family stayed together, that he was a part of the decisions being made about his child and its future. He'd make sure his child never felt the awkwardness that Peaches had felt last night with her own father.

He'd spent most of the day thinking about her as he drove around the area where Katie lived. The Copper Country consisted of mainly Hancock, where Katie had grown up and still lived, Calumet, where they'd gone for dinner last night, and Houghton, which was home to the university.

In some ways, the area reminded him of the small town in Spain he'd grown up in and where he still resided when not traveling. Houghton was quaint, with just one main thoroughfare, and only one stoplight that Darío had seen.

Water was everywhere, from the man-made canal that divided Houghton and Hancock, to Lake Superior, just twelve miles from the Hancock city limits. Darío loved water, had grown up around it, and although he knew Lake Superior was a fresh-water lake, it could easily pass for an ocean. He found himself lonesome for the Bay of Biscay near his home. He'd stayed at the lake for hours this afternoon as he thought about Peaches and Katie and his unborn child.

Katie's unborn child. He could not be sure this child was his. Not yet.

And yet, all his thoughts were of that child's future, and what part he would play in it.

Katie's laughter from across the room pulled Darío from his thoughts, and he made his way to the booth. She had come directly from work, wearing a skirt with a floral print and a baby blue, short-sleeved blouse. It was plain, but it looked spectacular on her. The other two women were dressed more casually, in shorts and tee-shirts.

Darío wore a golf shirt and shorts. He wore shorts whenever he could during the summer. Players were not allowed to wear them on the course during events, even practice rounds. He missed the days of his youth when he played in shorts and a tee-shirt, soaking up the sun.

Katie saw him as he approached. Her face lit up as he walked toward her and he nearly stumbled. She slid over allowing him to sit next to her, across from her friends.

"Hey," she said softly, "you found us okay?"

He nodded. "You were right. Right across the street from the hotel."

"Darío, let me introduce you to Alison Jukuri. And of course you remember Lizzie."

Darío stood once again, moving to the other side of the booth. The women looked startled that he'd risen for the introductions. What kind of men were they used to up here?

Alison was closest to him; she stuck her hand out and gave him a sly smile. "Darío, it's a pleasure to meet you."

"Alison, the pleasure is all mine."

He then shook Lizzie's hand. "It is nice to see you again, Lizzie. Though I must say you have certainly changed since the last time I saw you." He sat once again next to Katie.

Lizzie rested a hand on her protruding belly and laughed. "Yeah, I guess so. But a good change."

From the corner of his eyes, he saw Katie also place her hand on her still-flat belly, not even realizing she'd done so. The movement pleased him, though he could not say why. Darío nodded. "*Sí*, a very good change. You are radiant, and have my congratulations."

Lizzie bowed her head, accepting his good wishes. He meant it, she glowed. Much like Katie did. And would even more so as she ripened with child. His child. Maybe.

"And congratulations to you too, Darío. We can't tell you how happy we are for Katie. And you too, of course."

Congratulations. He'd not heard the words before. Not about the baby. Binky had sensed he didn't want to talk about it, and had wisely stayed away from the subject for the past few weeks.

When he'd spent a few days at his home in Spain while in Europe for the British Open, he'd fully intended to tell his mother, but never found the right words. He needed to be able to answer more of her sure-to-come questions before he could tell her about Katie.

The lawyer he'd hired to draw up the papers he'd brought to the Copper Country had offered no congratulations, but, given the nature of the visit, it didn't seem like congratulations were in order.

Lizzie offering her congratulations was the first time someone other than Katie and his lawyer had spoken to him about his child, and he took a moment before speaking. In fact all he could do was nod back to Lizzie and murmur, "Thank you."

The women seemed to take his silence as reluctance, Alison and Lizzie's eyes darting carefully to Katie. Darío could see the protectiveness in their glances. He tried to put them at ease. Tried to alleviate some of their obvious fear for their friend. "Despite the…unusual circumstances, I'm very pleased."

That seemed to work. Lizzie sat back in her seat. Alison picked up her drink—which was in a huge glass—and took a long swallow.

Katie brought him up to speed, that she'd explained everything they'd agreed on last night to her friends before he'd arrived. They ordered dinner and another round of drinks, though Alison was the only one really drinking, Darío choosing to have a soft drink.

Alison groaned when he gave his beverage order to the waitress. "You're not going to be one of those expectant fathers who gives up drinking because his wife has to are you?" She shot a look to Katie. "Not that she's your wife, but you know what I mean."

Darío shook his head. "I had not thought to do such a thing." He turned to Katie, she was glowering at Alison. He placed a hand on her arm. Her skin was so soft, warm from the summer heat. "Is that something you'd like me to do?" he asked her.

She looked away from Alison and to him and his breath caught as she gave him one of her huge smiles. "No. Of course not. That doesn't bother me at all."

He nodded, but made a mental note to go ahead and cut out that one beer a night on Fridays and Saturdays.

"Okay. You gave us the broad idea, but just when are you leaving to go on tour?" Lizzie asked.

Darío waited for Katie to answer, still thrilled that she'd agreed to travel with him. "We're leaving Monday for Denver," she said.

"So you'll be here through the weekend. Both of you?" Lizzie asked.

"Yes. I'm taking Darío to meet my parents tomorrow," Katie said.

Alison chuckled. "Ooh, meeting the parents. Are ya nervous, Darío?"

Darío realized that maybe he should be. Before he could verbalize that thought, Katie came to his rescue. "What's there to be nervous about? They'll be thrilled for me. They know how long I've wanted a baby."

"Yes, but that was when you were married," Alison offered.

The table was silent.

"Friday night pasty party at the Makis'. And all those overprotective brothers. She did tell you about her brothers, didn't she Darío?"

"Al, stop. You're scaring him."

He hadn't really thought beyond the arrangements he and Katie made last night after watching that poor girl at dinner with her father. Of course Katie's family would have questions for him. But they'd be satisfied that he'd asked Katie to marry him, wouldn't they?

And just what was a pasty?

"You can't tell them that you asked me to marry you," Katie said.

"Why not?" both he and Lizzie asked at the same time.

"I just don't want them pressuring me to marry you just because they think I should for the baby."

The "too" at the end of her sentence was left off, but Darío heard it clearly.

She was right. They'd agreed not to bring up marriage, or any other permanent arrangements, for three months. It might as well count for her parents as well.

"Well, KitKat, *they'll* obviously bring it up. I wouldn't put it past your dad to bring out his shotgun," Alison teased. At least, Darío thought she was teasing.

"I'll just tell them nothing has been decided for certain. And then I'll try to distract them with talk about the baby and how happy I am."

Darío looked at her. He hadn't known her long, didn't know her moods or her nuances. But he guessed that right now was maybe the happiest she'd looked in years. Maybe ever. Her radiance was obvious. Surely her family would see it too.

Her friends seemed to agree with his unspoken thought. Lizzie reached across the table and laid her hand over Katie's. "I know. It's wonderful, isn't it?"

"Oh jeez, here they go again. I'm going to need another drink," Alison said. Darío could see the warmth behind the sarcasm as Alison looked at her two best friends, both pregnant, both wearing huge grins.

"Hey. If Darío's going to be in town this weekend, he could play in Annie Aid," Alison said. Both Katie and Lizzie looked at her then at each other. Lizzie raised a questioning brow at Katie and Darío felt Katie shrug back at her friend. "Ask him," she said to Lizzie.

"Darío, my company puts on a fundraiser for a needy child each year. Well, actually this is only the second year. But last year was a huge success and we've got even more professional athletes coming this year. There's a golf outing on Saturday. Followed by a dinner dance. Would you play in the outing for us? You'd be the only pro golfer. We've never thought to ask any because there's a tournament going on the same weekend."

Ah, golf. That would put him back on familiar ground. On the course he was sure of himself. He needed that right now after the past twenty-four hours with Katie. She, and the situation, had made him more unsure of himself since he'd first taken up the game of golf. That he had mastered in three years. Would it take as long to get a firm handle on Katie? On fatherhood?

"I'd be happy to play. I have to make sure I can, though. I'll call the PGA Tour offices tomorrow and make sure I have clearance."

"Oh, that's right, I forgot about that rule," Lizzie said. "Listen, if you think it'll be a hassle, forget about it. We wouldn't have time to properly promote the heck out of you anyway."

"What rule?" Katie asked. Her shoulder brushed Darío's and he reached across her for a napkin that he had no use for to prolong the contact. When he brought his arm back, he kept it attached to hers.

Lizzie waited for Darío to answer Katie, but he was too preoccupied with finding a way to press his thigh against hers. "The Tour has a rule that you must get clearance if you are going to play in any other tournament other than the Tour tournament."

"Even some rinky-dink charity thing in the U.P.?" Alison asked.

"Hey!" Lizzie chided. "Watch what you call my pride and joy."

Alison nudged Lizzie. "You know I'm just kidding, Lizard. You've done a great job with Annie Aid, this year and last year."

"Yes, even a smaller tournament"—he emphasized the word "smaller" for Lizzie, saw her nod her approval, then went on—"must have clearance from the Tour. I'll need some details to give them, Lizzie."

Lizzie nodded. "Sure. In fact, why don't I go ahead and fax the information sheet to the Tour headquarters tonight when I get home, that way when you call tomorrow, they'll at least have some idea of what you're talking about. I've got their fax number because of Chad."

"And exactly what am I talking about?" Darío asked. Though it really didn't matter. If Katie thought it was a worthwhile event, he would play. He wasn't going to do anything to break their tentative truce. At least he'd be on a golf course.

Katie explained what he'd just signed on for. "Lizzie's stepdaughter, Annie, needed a very expensive operation around this time last year. This was before Lizzie had married her husband, Finn. Lizzie's PR company put on a fundraiser up here, got in some of her clients for a celebrity golf outing, even got the Stanley Cup up here. It was a huge success. Annie got her operation, and is walking."

Her voice turned ragged at the end. Darío watched as she dabbed at her eyes, then turned to look at her friend, Lizzie, who also had tears streaming down her cheeks.

"I'm sorry, I thought if I explained it to him, it wouldn't be so emotional for you," Katie said, holding her hand out to Lizzie. "I didn't mean to make you cry." Darío didn't point out that Katie was crying as well.

Lizzie sniffled. "It's okay. Pretty much everything makes me cry these days. Hormones, you know." Katie nodded her head knowingly. Darío watched as Alison rolled her eyes at her friends, but then shot him a playful wink. He shrugged his shoulders at her in a silent bonding of the only two not being led around by hormones.

He was being led around by Katie. And a very different kind of hormone.

"Anyway," Katie continued, "it was such a success that Hampton PR is doing it again. But for a different child in need this year. Lizzie and Finn had Annie choose the child herself."

"With a little help," Lizzie said. "The Hannah Robbins Foundation found the candidates, all kids from the U.P., and we left the final decision to Annie. But she had to give us reasons as to why she picked that child. Otherwise, the kid who got help would probably be the one who most resembled Justin Bieber."

"Justin who?" came from both Alison and Darío.

"Ah, you obviously live in households without kids," Katie said. "He's all the rage with the pre-teen set. My nieces adore him.

This week, anyway."

"Yeah, remember how fickle we were at that age? One week it was Kirk Cameron. The next week River Phoenix," Lizzie said, her face serene as she remembered.

Alison smiled. "Except for Katie. It was Patrick Swayze from beginning to end for her, she never wavered."

Katie lifted her chin, ready to defend herself. "Hey, nobody puts Baby in a corner. Rest in peace, Patrick."

Darío studied Alison while Alison studied Katie. "No, that's not it. It's you, KitKat, once you make a choice, that's it, no going back."

Katie brushed Alison's words aside with her hands, but Alison kept nodding and Lizzie looked at Katie with a questioning brow.

The words permeated Darío's mind. He found himself irrationally hoping that Alison's statement was true, and that it also included Darío.

—◊◊◊—

Katie had only told her parents she was bringing someone for dinner—she'd given no details on who or why. Darío had been deeply amused to see the look on her family's faces when they discovered that their dinner companion was Darío Luna. But that look had been nothing when compared with the dropped jaws when Katie explained to her family that she was going on tour with Darío for a few months.

They were an intimidating bunch. Leo, Katie's father, and her four older brothers, all with Katie's white blond hair and towering good looks.

But Darío had gone against Phil Mickelson in match play and won. A large Finnish family shouldn't be intimidating to him. Right?

Most of the wives were also towheads, and every last one of the many nieces and nephews also sported the stick-straight white locks. Darío took a perverse delight in the thought that his child, surely with some of his dark coloring and hair, would break family tradition.

The house was a large, older Victorian on the east side of the small town, in an older neighborhood that rose above the man-made canal and the lift bridge that connected Houghton and Hancock. Large as the house was, Darío couldn't imagine growing up with four brothers, as large and active as Katie's brothers seemed to be, in one house.

The living room was full of reminders of the Maki children. The bookshelves held more art class projects than books. A ceramic animal that Darío guessed was supposed to be a duck was prominently on display on the coffee table. Darío picked it up, feeling its weight. As he put it back, he noticed the name Chris M. etched on the bottom. He looked over at Katie's eldest brother, Chris, who at the moment was chastising his thirteen-year-old son, Jordan.

Katie tried to head off the barrage of questions with a story that sounded rehearsed to Darío. It was technically true, but left out a great many details.

She told them they'd met in Texas when she'd gone with Lizzie to meet a prospective client.

True.

She told them they'd hit it off right away.

He remembered Katie's comment about his forearms, then how she passed out on him in the elevator the night they met. Memories of the next night, of looking down at Katie as he thrust deep inside of her flashed through his mind. Of her reaching her peak.

True. They'd hit if off right away.

She told them that she and Darío had kept in touch after Texas.

He thought about seeing her in the gallery at Memphis, the flood of gratitude he'd felt at getting another chance to see her, be with her. Then he thought of the rage he'd felt the next day at her hotel when she'd assumed he'd want no part of his child. He'd left swearing his lawyer would be contacting her.

So, true, they had kept in touch.

She told them that Darío had shown up out of the blue two days ago and after a very long discussion they'd decided they wanted to see where—"this thing" is what she called it—could lead, and the only way to do that would be for Katie to travel with Darío. She'd made arrangements with her boss at the paper to do some work from the road, and she was having Alison look in on her house and collect her mail.

Other than having his child vaguely referred to as "this thing", Darío figured that was all true.

What she didn't mention was the baby. No word of pregnancy at all. Darío waited, watched. Katie shot him a look that showed him she'd changed her mind. He followed her lead.

Katie dragged him into the kitchen with all the women to make pasties. She used the excuse that Darío had never even heard of pasties before, let alone seen them made.

A pasty, Darío found out, was a meat pie of sorts. He watched as Katie's mom and sisters-in-law rolled out the dough of the crusts, filled each with a meat, carrot, onion, and rutabaga mixture, then sealed it up into a crescent moon shape. Darío had tried cuisines the world over. The closest thing he'd seen to a pasty was an Italian calzone, but with a much different filling.

"It's Cornish originally. Cornish men came over to work the copper mines here, and their wives would make these for them to take down in the mines with them. They're hearty, but because of the crust, easy to carry and eat in such cramped quarters. The miners would heat them up on their shovels, by holding them over the candles on their helmets," Mrs. Maki—Ellen, she'd told Darío to call her—explained.

Darío only nodded and watched the women work. They'd obviously been doing this together for many years, each woman knew exactly her part, or ingredient as the case may be, to play.

Katie was the last person on the make-shift assembly line that'd been set up at the Maki's long, well-used pine kitchen table. He watched her elegant fingers seal the pasty, two fingers pressing down the opening, creating a wave effect of the crust. Her hands were lightly tanned, her nails trimmed and unpolished. He looked down at his own hands, roughened by years of handling clubs, his left hand much lighter than his right from years of wearing a golf glove.

As he watched the women work, biting their tongues, Darío saw the genius of Katie's plan. By having Darío in here with her, her mother and sisters-in-law couldn't ask her questions about him. And, maybe more importantly, he wasn't left alone in a living room full of Maki men just waiting to ask him his intentions toward their daughter and sister.

As if sensing his thoughts, Katie looked up from her work, and blew some hair out of her face as she caught Darío's eyes. She gave him a small smile, and mouthed the words "You okay?" to him. He returned her smile, nodded and mouthed "You?" She shrugged her shoulders, smiled again and returned to her chore.

Darío never did get the final tally on the number of nieces and nephews Katie had. He knew she had four brothers, all married, all with children. But amid the chaos, he lost track of what child belonged to what brother and which children couldn't be there because of swimming lessons or babysitting or something called T-ball. They seemed to range in age from three or four to around fourteen or fifteen. And someone had mentioned that one of the nephews had his mother's car to take some of the others to swimming lessons. So there was at least one old enough to drive.

Katie had not exaggerated when she told Darío in Memphis that their child would be surrounded by a large, loving family with lots of male influences. Her family seemed great. But her father, brothers and nephews were not the primary male influence that he wanted for his child.

He would be his child's male role model. Even if he had to move to this small town to do it.

He realized with that thought that although a time would come when proof would be needed, he was going to operate for the next few months under the conviction that the child Katie carried was indeed his. The decision gave him a lightness, a freedom, and he chose not to question the feeling.

Some of the children went out to play on the lawn after dinner while the adults cleaned up and then had coffee and some kind of Finnish cake in the living room. The two smallest children went instead to their aunt Katie, who seemed to know what was coming as she had set herself up in the largest chair in the room. The two kids—one was Molly, Darío thought he remembered, and the other Kyle—climbed up on Katie's lap, snuggled in on each side of her and demanded, "Tell us a story, Auntie Katie."

Darío watched, mesmerized, from across the room as Auntie Katie told her niece and nephew a story complete with ogres and dragons and—Darío figured an apt twist for today's times—a prince in distress and a maiden who saved him.

"She's something, isn't she?" Katie's brother Chris whispered. Darío only nodded, still trying to hear Katie's sweet, lyrical voice, even though it had grown softer as the adults started their own conversations and Molly and Kyle's eyes grew heavier.

"You know, normally we'd all be ganging up on you, giving you shit about taking care of our sister, but I got to tell you, this is the best I've seen Katie looking since that piece of shit Ron ran out on her."

Darío didn't let Chris know that the reason Katie glowed was from an entirely different reason than her going away with Darío.

"I mean, he really did a number on her. I wasn't even sure the old Katie was still in there. But hey, if shacking up with you for a few months can bring her out of it, then you've got my blessing." He held out his hand for Darío to shake, which Darío did, thinking how odd to be getting this brother's blessing to take his sister away for what they thought would be a three month fling.

Darío wondered if he'd be getting the same treatment if they knew that he'd gotten their beloved baby sister pregnant? Perhaps he would.

He kept his eye on Katie. She made a lovely picture, golden

and shimmering with two bundles of lightness on her knees. One of the children—Molly, he thought—sneezed and Katie took a tissue from her shorts pocket, held it to her, waited for her to blow and then put the tissue back in her pocket, all without breaking her telling of the story. The woman, though looking like an untouchable goddess, was a born mother.

The purity of the moment made Darío's throat catch. It was a beautiful picture, Katie with children on her lap. Could he be a part of that picture? Did he want to be? He knew the answer before he'd even finished the thought.

An image of Katie sitting, cradling his child, while Darío handed her a tissue after the child sneezed flashed through Darío's mind.

Yes. He wanted to be in the picture.

Thirteen

—⚍—

I played as much golf as I could in North Dakota,
but summer up there is pretty short.
It usually falls on a Tuesday.
~ *Mike Morley, pro golfer from North Dakota*

KATIE PICKED DARÍO UP bright and early Saturday morning to get breakfast before heading to the golf course for the Annie Aid golf outing. When he opened the door to her, Darío looked frazzled, something that Katie had not seen on Darío before.

"What's wrong?" she asked, stepping into the room as he held the door for her.

"It seems I have to check out this morning. All their rooms are completely booked for tonight because of the fundraiser."

"Oh. Of course, every hotel in town is booked solid. Not only do we have all the athletes coming in, but people come from all over the U.P. and Wisconsin to golf in this thing and then go to the dinner dance."

"It would seem so." Darío indicated the phone and phonebook on the bed. The phonebook was thin and the yellow pages section only about 20 pages. It was flipped open to the motel section.

"They should have told you that when you checked in," Katie said.

Darío looked sheepish. "They did, actually. But I honestly did not know when I checked in if I would still be here on Saturday. They also told me there were no places in town that had an opening for Saturday night, so I took my chances here."

Of course she knew the solution. It was silly, really, that he'd even stayed in the hotel this long after they'd decided Wednesday night that she'd go on tour with him. She just hadn't liked the idea of Darío staying in the house that she'd shared with Ron.

Time to grow up, Katie. She was going to be traveling with this man. Staying in the same hotel rooms with him. The whole idea was to get know him better. Starting now. "Well, you'll simply stay with me tonight and tomorrow before we leave on Monday," Katie said.

He watched her. Katie could feel the depth of his stare. She lifted her chin, daring him to argue with her, but he seemed resigned to the idea. "*Sí*, that is probably the only solution. I have been trying to see if there were any cancellations anywhere, but no luck."

"Of course not. It's Annie Aid. Lizzie wouldn't stand for any cancellations." Darío laughed at her joke. He must have noticed Lizzie's propensity for making a plan and sticking to it. "Let's throw your luggage in your trunk, and your golf bag in my car. We can leave your rental here and pick it up after the golf outing."

He nodded his head and stuck out his hand. "Your keys?"

"It's unlocked. The keys are in the ignition." Darío only chuckled at this and made for his golf bag. Katie went for the suitcase.

"What do you think you're doing?" Darío nearly screamed. "That's very heavy, you can't carry that." He rushed toward her, which was difficult in the small room.

"Okay, you take suitcase, I'll take the golf bag," Katie said.

Darío shook his head in disbelief. "You can't take that either. You shouldn't lift anything so heavy."

Katie sighed and sat on the bed, holding her hands up in surrender. "Okay, fine, you haul them both. I'll just sit here and be pregnant."

Darío smiled, the warmth returning to his face. "Thank you. If you want to help, I hadn't gotten to my carry-on bag, yet. My shaving kit from the bathroom, those papers over there," he pointed to a sheaf of papers on the credenza, "and anything else you see laying around."

Darío picked up the suitcase and went out the door. Katie went to the bathroom. His shaving kit was mostly packed. Only a canister of deodorant, his toothbrush, toothpaste, and aftershave were left on the counter. Katie was shocked by the overwhelming sense of intimacy she felt as she packed his toothbrush in the travel case she found in the kit. Her fingers gently stroked the bottle as she brought the aftershave to her nose, breathing deep. Darío always smelled so good, and now she knew why. The label was in Spanish and looked expensive. Not something she'd be able to pick up for him at Walmart.

She stepped out of the bathroom, put the now-complete shaving kit into the carry on bag and collected the papers off the credenza, adding them. She looked around for anything that wasn't hotel issue. There was a stack of magazines on the bedside table. Not sure if he'd read them or not, she scooped them up to take.

Covered by the magazines, at the bottom of the pile were two books.

Always interested in what other people were reading, Katie sat on the bed to look them over. She heard Darío behind her come in for his golf bag, then leave again. The first book was a thriller currently on the bestseller list. It had a price sticker on it from an airport bookstore. She guessed that's where Darío bought most of his books, not getting a chance to actually go to bookstores and browse for hours as she loved to do.

She tossed the book into the carry on bag, on top of the magazines. Her breath caught as she looked at the second book.

What to Expect When You're Expecting.

She knew the book well. She'd read it once all the way

through, years ago. And had read the first few chapters again and again every time she and Ron would await either the news of pregnancy, or the inevitable onset of her period.

It seemed Darío had read the beginning several times himself. The pages in the front of the book were somewhat ragged and dog-eared, and Katie saw that some pages were actually turned down to mark certain spots.

She flipped to the first marked page. *Nutrition in the First Trimester.* Surely Darío would find no fault with her there. She'd been religious about her diet from the moment she'd found out she was pregnant. In all honesty, she ate pretty healthily before that as well. The hangover in Texas had mentally stayed with her long enough that she hadn't even had a beer at the Commodore during Friday night pizza with the girls before she'd found out she was pregnant. She was even drinking milk for goodness sake, and she hated milk.

She flipped a few pages until the next bent-down page stopped her. *Mood Swings.* Ah, she'd had those all right. But they'd been from deliriously happy to euphoria. Having struggled with infertility so long, there were none of the doubts that could wiggle their way into a snit. No thoughts about the changes to her body. No second-guessing about the kind of mother she'd make.

The only swing her psyche had taken was in respect to Darío. But then, Katie had the sneaking suspicion that Darío could wreak havoc with her mood regardless of pregnancy. His physical presence anywhere in her vicinity did funny things to her body. Things not pregnancy-induced.

She thumbed through the well-read pages and stopped at the next marked page. *Sex in Early Pregnancy.* She chuckled to herself. It was nice to know that Darío still thought of her in that way. After another chaste good night kiss at her door last night after the visit to her parents', she was beginning to wonder.

She didn't need to read the pages. She knew what they said. In some cases, women would become sexually hungry during the first trimester. In other cases, some women would display a decrease in their libido during the first trimester, then a sexual awakening of sorts would take place and desire would return.

Katie didn't know if she fell into the later category or if the timing of Darío's appearance played a part, she only knew the last two days she'd felt a "sexual hunger" like she hadn't experienced in years.

She heard Darío coming down the hallway and threw the book into the carry-on bag, zipped it up and headed to the door to meet him. To take him away from the hotel and to her home.

—⁂—

"What a difference a year makes, eh?" Alison said.

The three women were seated at a long banquet table, one of at least fifty at the Annie Aid dinner dance in the Hancock Rec Center, a hockey arena used for weddings and banquets in the summer when the ice was taken out. The table was strewn with the remnants of a delicious dinner catered by an old high school friend.

Darío was across the hall, sitting at a table amongst several professional hockey and football players graciously signing autographs for anyone who wished. Occasionally he'd glance up, and give her a questioning "you okay?" look, to which she'd smile and nod.

Annie Aid was a rousing success, as Katie knew it would be. The sun had shone bright and strong on the Copper Country for the well-attended golf outing earlier in the day. The dinner dance was going great. The only event left was the celebrity memorabilia auction. Lizzie had scheduled that for last, figuring with a good dinner and a few drinks, people would feel like opening their checkbooks a little wider.

Katie figured if that's what Lizzie planned, then it was surely a good strategy. Anything Lizzie planned seemed to come off with a hitch. But now, with Alison's remark, she remembered the same night a year ago, and was reminded of one of Lizzie's plans that had blown up in her face.

Remembering her own entrance to the dinner dance a year

ago—in the brand new Hummer that Ron had just purchased—Katie shivered.

"Worst night of my life, easily," Lizzie said. Katie thought maybe Lizzie shivered as well.

"Not one of my best, either," Katie said. The other women looked at her. They all knew why Lizzie had hated that night—it was the night she and Finn had broken up, albeit temporarily. Their questioning glances wondered why Katie felt so strongly.

Explaining, Katie said, "Ron had just come home with the monstrosity that day. It was the beginning of the end, even though I didn't know it at the time." But that wasn't the entire truth. Looking back, she could remember the way her stomach contracted as he smooth-talked his way out of spending their in-vitro fund on a yellow school bus. Though she hadn't put it into a conscious thought, she'd known that day there'd be no baby.

She rubbed her tummy, looked across the civic center, and saw Darío once again watching her, a small smile on his face. She patted her non-existent belly and raised her glass of milk to him in a toast. He laughed. She couldn't hear the sound way over here, but she knew it by heart.

The girls had their concerns about her going off with Darío, and her parents had voiced theirs. But Katie didn't want to think too much about her decision to travel with Darío, didn't want to make plans for anything beyond the next Tour stop.

Lizzie was the one who was the plan maker, and this smoothly run night was a testament to that fact. Life just seemed to happen to Katie. Sure, she had plans, but things seemed to always turn in a different direction for her.

She'd met Ron her freshman year at State and it had seemed so right, so natural to marry after graduation, even though Lizzie and Alison were starting exciting new careers.

Moving back to Hancock just sort of happened to them as well. They'd thought they'd spend the first five or six years of their marriage with Ron playing in the NHL and Katie traveling to games. Ron had wanted her with him and Katie, her experiences limited to the Copper Country and East Lansing, wanted to see the country.

A dirty crosscheck by a University of Michigan player left Ron's NHL dreams in the dust. Katie lamented the lost opportunity to travel, but when Ron said he thought they should move to Katie's hometown, she'd agreed. After all, Ron had been so devastated at his career-ending injury that Katie felt ashamed to express her disappointment at not being able to travel a little before settling down.

They'd settled in easily, Katie getting on at the *Ingot*—which was ecstatic to actually have someone with a journalism degree in their midst. Ron became a math teacher at Katie's alma mater, Hancock High School. Three years later when the hockey coach retired, Ron took that on as well.

Their lives were smooth, envied, blessed.

Until they'd decided it was time to start a family.

Katie'd wanted to start after three years of marriage, Ron after five, so they'd compromised and began trying right after their fourth anniversary.

She'd never imagined there'd be any problems. Her mother had borne five children with no problems. Her brothers had already begun their families. Having her nieces and nephews around her made her yearn for a child of her own.

She hadn't been concerned until a year had gone by. They hadn't done any temperature taking or any hormone charting, but they'd made love nearly every night, and not just for the sole purpose of conception. There were certainly no problems in the bedroom which could be attributed to her infertility.

Katie remembered the following years, the tests that never concluded anything, the stress, the shame she felt that her outwardly perfect body was failing her.

She took a sip of milk and pulled herself back. It didn't matter now. She was pregnant. She would have a child. She'd never really given up her dream, even in those times when she'd turned away from Ron, ashamed at her own feelings of inadequacy.

She'd just never thought her dream would contain Darío Luna.

And that it wouldn't contain Ron.

As if conjured up from her reminiscing, Ron stepped into her line of vision, his large, hulking frame completely blocking out Darío. He walked toward her table, his eyes set on Katie. She looked at him with a dispassionate eye for the first time since she was eighteen years old. She didn't feel the sharp intake of breath that she'd always felt when looking at Ron. Her heart didn't leap at the sight of his sheer masculinity. Her knees were strong, solid, not weak.

Even three days ago, when she'd seen him at the grocery store with his baby daughter, Katie had felt that strange rush of excitement that just seeing Ron had always brought her.

A lot had happened in those three days.

He sat down at the table, next to Lizzie, across from her and Alison. Katie had to put a hand on Alison's arm that was slowly stretching toward her drink. Katie didn't know if Al was going for a guzzle or for ammunition, but she didn't want any drinks thrown at Ron. Well, not tonight, anyway.

"I know, I know, I'll play nice. Besides, it'd be a waste of perfectly good vodka," Alison said, reading Katie's thoughts, and the squeeze to Alison's arm.

"Ladies," Ron said in greeting. "Great success Lizzie, you should be very proud."

Lizzie, always the peacemaker, replied, "Thanks, Ron, it's been a great day. Did you have a good time golfing?"

He snorted. "Good time? It was amazing. I got paired with Steve Yzerman! Can you imagine playing golf with Steve Yzerman?" The women all shook their heads. "I mean, the only way this could have been any better was if I'd been paired with Darío Luna."

Alison choked on her drink. Lizzie looked away, as if checking out the enormous party she was giving, but in reality she was trying to hide a smile.

Katie swallowed loudly, uncomfortably. "But you've always loved Steve Yzerman. That would have been your dream pairing. You're not *that* big of a fan of Darío's." She hoped the proprietary way in which she said Darío's name was evident only to herself.

"Well, yeah. To meet, to spend some time with, then definitely Steve Yzerman. He's been my hero forever. But to play a round of golf with? Can you imagine playing a round of golf with a guy who's won three majors?"

"I can imagine playing all sorts of games with Darío. Can't you, Kat?" Alison joked. Katie lightly kicked Alison's shin under the table.

Ron rolled his eyes at Alison's double entendre. He'd never really liked Alison. He loved Lizzie, but then, everyone loved Lizzie. And Lizzie hadn't been around for most of the years she and Ron had lived in the Copper Country. Lizzie hadn't been there to distract Katie from Ron. Alison had. Alison had been the one Katie turned to when struggling with infertility, not Ron. Ron still resented Alison for taking the place in Katie's life that he couldn't fill. Katie supposed it was easier for Ron to blame Alison than to blame Katie herself. Or himself.

Lizzie seemed to take great interest in what Ron had just said. "Ron, do you think a lot of people feel that way? Would they have all liked to play with a professional golfer rather than a hockey or football player?" Lizzie asked. Lizzie was formulating some kind of plan, but then, when wasn't she?

"Anybody serious about golf would," Ron answered. "I'd pay good money to play a round of golf with him." He spoke to Lizzie beside him, but he didn't take his eyes from Katie. Katie now realized that he hadn't since he sat down with them. She wondered if she looked different outwardly. If someone who knew her as well as Ron did could tell she was pregnant just by looking at her. Did she glow as much on the outside as she did on the inside?

"Do you think Darío would play a round of golf with someone tomorrow and we could put it into the auction tonight?" Lizzie asked Katie and Alison.

"Lizard, that's a great idea," Alison said, then looked at Katie for her reaction.

Katie nodded. "A great idea," she added. "Do you want me to ask him?" She hoped Lizzie would say yes so she could leave the table.

But Lizzie was already rising. "No, I'll do it," she said, and was halfway across the room before Katie could move.

Ron gave her a puzzling look. "Did you meet Darío while helping Lizzie out?" he asked.

She gave a noncommittal shrug and took a drink of her milk, left over from her dinner. She swallowed the liquid, praying the stuff would go down her rapidly closing throat.

Ron knew something was up. He looked at her with suspicious eyes. There was almost a sweet kind of symmetry to that. That Ron would be suspicious of her! Katie desperately wanted to blurt out that she and Darío were a couple. Wanted to see Ron's reaction to that. She also wanted to shout out her pregnancy to the man who thought such a thing literally inconceivable.

She held herself back. She wasn't going to tell him about the baby, much as she wanted to. She'd made a spur-of-the-moment decision at her parents' place on Friday not to tell even her family until she got back from her three months with Darío. Only Lizzie and Alison, and Don at work, would know, and they had promised complete secrecy. Katie wasn't even sure Lizzie had told Finn, but even if she had, he wouldn't say a word if Lizzie asked it of him. She was at the end of her first trimester, it should be fine to tell people, but it wasn't the fear of miscarriage that kept Katie from wanting her family and, by extension—with her well-meaning but gossipy sisters-in-law—the rest of the Copper Country to know she was pregnant.

In fact, Katie had no real fear of a miscarriage at all. She had nothing to base her security on other than a deep-seated sense of calm. She knew, just absolutely *knew* with complete clarity, that her baby would be fine.

She didn't tell her family because she wanted to keep it to

herself for just a while longer. She wanted to share this only with the two women she loved more than sisters.

And Darío.

But not Ron. Even if seeing his beautiful face register his shock would have brought her a sadistic pleasure.

She took another sip of milk, wincing at the taste, and prayed Ron would leave the table soon so that her resolve to not taunt him with her news would hold. And that Alison's resolve not to throw her drink in his face would hang in there, too.

"You hate milk," Ron said suspiciously.

"I've acquired a taste for it," Katie said, her eyes lowered. She never could lie worth a darn, and never to Ron.

"Acquired a taste for it?" Ron said, disbelieving.

"Yes, acquired a taste for it," Katie echoed, her chin raised in defiance.

"So Ron, how are those divorce papers coming along?" Alison asked. Katie gasped at the abrupt change of subject, and the new topic, then realized that Alison had done it on purpose. She was trying to take Ron off the track that Katie's sudden taste for milk might take him. Katie sent a telepathic "thank you" to Alison and swore that she heard a "you're welcome" in return.

"Actually, that's what I came to talk to you about," he said to Katie, totally ignoring Alison, as if it were Katie who had asked the question. He turned to Alison, as if seeing her for the first time—though Alison wasn't someone you could ignore—and said, "Do you mind, Al? Could you give us a minute?"

"Yes, I think I do mind," Alison said.

Katie was grateful. She didn't want to be alone with Ron. She didn't completely trust herself not to lose her resolve and tell him she was pregnant and that she was going away with Darío. Especially if they were going to be talking divorce. "Alison can stay, she knows all the gory details anyway."

Ron snorted. "Of course she does. And so does Lizzie. So does the whole damn town. I'm surprised your brothers haven't come to string me up."

"They wanted to, believe me," Katie said.

Ron smiled. A small, sad smile. "Well, I guess I can't really blame them," he said. "Thanks for keeping them away from me." Katie nodded in response.

"So, back to the divorce," Alison said.

Ron shot her a dirty look, then looked back to Katie. "The papers should be ready to sign in three to four weeks. I'll bring them by the house when they're ready."

Katie assumed, but didn't ask, that Ron's wedding to Amber Saari would take place soon after that. Just another good reason to be out on the road with Darío. Katie shook her head. "No, that won't work."

Ron sighed, "Okay, I'll bring them to the *Ingot*."

"No, that won't work either. Bring them to Alison. She'll forward them on to me." She looked at Alison for consent and got her nod of approval.

"Where will you be?" he asked, suspicion returning to his voice. "I'll send them to you myself, just tell me where you'll be."

Katie fidgeted on the hard, metal folding chair. She wasn't going to tell him about the baby, but should she tell him about Darío? Her family knew. The people at the Ingot knew. It was just a matter of time before the rest of the town knew too. But not yet. Not Ron. It wasn't something she could talk to Ron about.

"Well, that's just it. I'll be moving around a lot, so if you don't know the exact date you'll be sending them, it'd be better to give them to Alison, and she can contact me and I can give her the address of the hotel where I'll be."

Ron looked from Katie to Alison, trying to figure out what tactic to take, and which woman was more likely to spill. Knowing Katie could never lie to him, he said to her, "What hotels? What's going on, Katie?"

"I'm going to be traveling for a few months, doing some correspondence work. I have the itinerary, but if you're not sure exactly when the papers will be ready, I can't tell you where to send them."

Ron shook his head, as if to clear it. "Traveling? Correspondence work? You mean like a writing assignment for the *Ingot*?"

Katie saw her hands shredding her paper napkin into bits. Reminded of Peaches, she put the napkin down, straightened her back and said, "Exactly." Well, not exactly, but close enough.

"Since when does the *Ingot* have the budget for a traveling correspondent?"

Katie shrugged again. "It's not coming out of the *Ingot*'s budget. It's something I'm doing for myself."

Before Ron could answer, Alison piped in, "Don't worry, Ron, it won't affect the settlement."

Ron looked at Alison with contempt, then to Katie. When he turned to her, the disdain left his eyes and the blue pools of warmth that she'd once gazed into by the hour returned. "Traveling, eh? That's great, Katie. You always wanted to travel."

It'd been so long since she'd given up that dream that she was surprised Ron even remembered it. "It should be fun," she said, her uncertainty clear in her voice.

"It's something you want to do, isn't it? I mean, you're not just leaving town to…to…" He didn't finish his sentence.

"Get away from you? She should be," Alison barked.

Ron let out a heavy sigh, looking at Katie, trying to ignore Alison.

Katie shook her head. "No, I'm not leaving town for any other reason. I have this opportunity, it's something I want to do." That was all true, at least.

"Well, then, I'm happy for you. Finally getting to do something you always wanted." She waited to hear the mocking in his voice, but it wasn't there. What she'd always wanted most—what *they* had always wanted most—was a child together. She looked at him and saw the hurt in his eyes, the pain that she felt too. He was sincere, she realized. He knew that traveling was a poor second place prize. He reached his hand across the table, as if to capture hers. "Katie," he whispered.

Alison made a grab for a napkin dispenser, knocking Ron's

hand back to his side of the table. Ron shook his head, rose, and nodded a goodbye.

—∽—

That must be Ron. The bastard. The enormously tall, well-built, handsome bastard. Darío chuckled to himself. It wasn't like him to be insecure, and he wasn't really. He knew he could offer Katie things that Ron never could. He was rich, for one thing. And famous—or at least to those who followed professional golf. But Darío sensed that those things weren't important to Katie.

No, the only thing of importance that Darío could do for Katie that Ron could not was give her a child.

And be faithful.

Darío knew he would never look at another woman once Katie was his. And he had every intention of making her his as soon as they got out of her hometown. He'd thought that maybe they'd be together tonight now that he was staying at her house, but it would probably be better to wait until they were on neutral ground. Besides, would she be ready to make love to Darío in the house she shared with Ron? Did he want those ghosts to contend with?

He watched as Ron left the table Katie and Alison sat at. He watched Katie's eyes follow Ron as he disappeared into the crowd on the other side of the room. Alison placed an arm around Katie, comforting her. Had the bastard said something to upset Katie?

After a moment, Katie and Alison both rose from the table, Alison heading toward the lobby. Katie scanned the room and Darío was pleased when her gaze rested on him. She smiled and walked toward him. He rose and met her halfway.

"Is your hand ready to fall off yet?" she asked.

In fact, his hand was cramping up a bit from signing so many autographs, but it came with the territory, so he wasn't about to complain. "It's not so bad. Did Lizzie tell you I'll be playing golf tomorrow? Is that okay with you?" He wanted to ask about Ron, but kept his mouth shut. If it wasn't something Katie wanted to talk about, he'd let it drop.

Katie stared at Darío for a moment, then laughed. "I'm sorry, but I was momentarily stunned at the idea of a man actually asking my permission to spend his Sunday playing golf." Darío started to make a comment to the types of men who'd been in her life before, but she hurried on. "That's fine. I can finish up my packing and take care of odds and ends. Thank you for doing it, Lizzie thinks it will go for a good price in the auction."

Darío shrugged. "We will see. Your Copper Country appears to be more of a hockey town than golf."

Katie smiled. "That's true, but a big part of that is because the golf season is so short up here. There's snow on the course as late as mid-May most years, and it gets too cold to play by mid-September."

They were interrupted by Lizzie's arrival onstage, welcoming everyone to the second annual Annie Aid. Katie led Darío to seats in a deserted corner to watch the festivities. He liked being private with her, but assumed it was out of a need to get away from people asking questions as opposed to wanting to be alone with him.

Things were happening on the stage, applause sounded every few minutes, but all Darío noticed was Katie sitting close to him. He slung his arm across the back of her chair and her hair lightly brushed his skin. It felt cool, soft, and he leaned his head closer to her to take in the scent of her shampoo. A fruity aroma assailed him. He hoped she brought whatever shampoo she used with her when they traveled. He took another deep breath then leaned back and watched Lizzie raise funds for her worthy cause.

—❧—

Katie's house reminded him of Katie herself—beautiful, classy, and yet comfortable.

He picked up his suitcase bag from the kitchen floor where they'd piled his things. He looked at Katie with questioning eyes. She only stared at his bag as if just now realizing that he was staying in her home overnight. He saw the indecision on her face and knew he had to let her off the hook. He wanted to sleep with her, but this was not the time or place.

"You have a guest room, or should I take the couch?" he asked.

He was a little pissed at the look of relief on her face. "A guest room. Yes, of course. Let me show you upstairs."

He shook his head. "Just point the way. I'm really tired and think I'll just go straight to bed. I need to be at the course tomorrow morning for the round of golf that was auctioned off." He'd been surprised and pleased how high the round had gone for. Several professional hockey players joined in on the bidding and raised the price. In the end, they had awarded the prize to the highest celebrity bidder, a hockey player named Pete Ryan. Knowing the locals couldn't outbid the professionals, Lizzie decided to raffle off a place in tomorrow's group—making it a threesome. They were just starting to sell the raffle tickets when Katie began to yawn and Darío insisted on taking her home.

"I'm ready to go up, too, I'll take you," Katie said as she turned off the kitchen lights and led Darío up the stairs. "Do you need me to wake you in the morning?" she asked as she climbed the steps in front of him.

His eyes on her swaying behind, he had to concentrate on what she'd said. "Uh…no, that is not necessary. I have a travel alarm."

She nodded and he watched her hair bob up and down against her shoulder blades. "Do you remember your way to the golf course? Do you want me to take you?"

"No. I can manage," he said. They'd reached the top of the stairs and she turned to face him in the hallway.

"Of course you can. What am I thinking? You travel all over the world, get yourself to golf courses all the time. Surely the Copper Country isn't going to be a problem."

No, navigating the Copper Country wasn't going to be a problem, but sleeping across the hallway from Katie and not being able to touch her surely would be. "Do you mind if I take a shower before I turn in?" he asked.

He didn't add that it would be a cold one.

Fourteen

—⟶—

I can tell right away if a guy is a winner or a loser just by the way he conducts himself on the course.

~ Donald Trump

LIZZIE HAD TOLD HIM last night that they'd tee off at ten, so Darío planned to be to the course by nine-thirty. There would be no need for his usual two-hour warm up. This was to be just a friendly round of golf.

He made his way downstairs after showering and shaving. There was no sign of Katie. When he went to the kitchen there was a pot of coffee made and a note on the kitchen table saying she'd gone to the *Ingot* offices to pick up a few things she'd forgotten.

Good, she was an early person, like himself. She would need to be on the Tour. It was an early to bed, early to rise life. Except for the caddies. Somehow, they managed to burn the candle at both ends.

She'd left a travel mug out for him and he gratefully filled it. He gathered his clubs and left Katie's home. He had no trouble remembering his way to the golf course. In fact, in just three days he had the small area practically memorized. He supposed once he and Katie were married they'd be spending a lot of time here. His child's uncles, aunts and grandparents were here, after all.

Thinking so easily of being married to Katie shook him. She

hadn't agreed to it. Yet. If Darío were honest with himself, he wasn't absolutely sure that it was the right thing to do. To raise a child in a loveless marriage. Oh, he and Katie had a mutual attraction, there was no denying that. And he liked her as a person—assuming she hadn't lied to him about her being able to get pregnant or the paternity. But he didn't love Katie. And he was quite sure Katie felt the same way about him.

But more important than his and Katie's feelings were that of his child. He would not have his child raised without a father. And without his name. There was no way that a marriage with mutual attraction and respect—if not love—wouldn't be better than his child never knowing who he was.

Like Darío and his father.

He pulled into the golf course parking lot, not surprised to see it full. Sunday morning was a heavy golf time for amateur players. Having been raised by a clubhouse cook, he knew the workings of golf courses. He had designed one himself, and constantly had offers to do more. Darío had thought he'd design courses when he could no longer be competitive. He had thought that to be many years off, after the regular Tour and several years on the Champions Tour after turning fifty.

It was a thought that bore more weight now that he would be a father.

He gathered his clubs and walked to the clubhouse. Lizzie met him halfway. Her stepson, Stevie, whom Darío met yesterday, took his bag from him and began heading to the first tee. Darío started to follow the boy, but Lizzie stopped him with a hand to his arm.

"Darío, I'm so sorry about this. I think it's wonderful that you're going through with it. Actually, I wasn't sure if you'd show or not, but…" She seemed nervous. In Darío's short acquaintance with her, Lizzie'd never seemed nervous.

"Why wouldn't I come, Lizzie? I told you last night, it would be my pleasure to help out."

"Well yes, but that was before the raffle. What a stupid idea.

I was just trying to get as much money as possible for that poor little boy's medical expenses," she explained.

Darío was still confused. "I don't understand? Was the raffle unsuccessful?"

"You weren't there for the raffle?" Lizzie asked.

He shook his head. "No. Katie was tired. We left right after the auction."

Lizzie groaned and raised her eyes skyward. "Oh, man. So you don't know. And Katie doesn't know."

"Know what?" Darío was concerned now that Lizzie mentioned Katie.

"Who won the raffle," Lizzie said.

Again, Darío shook his head. "No, we left before that. But why would it matter to me who won the raffle? I don't know anyone here, anyway. And why would Katie care who…" He didn't need to finish his sentence to know who won. With one look at the discomfort on Lizzie's face, his suspicions were confirmed. "Ron Lipton won, didn't he?"

Lizzie nodded. "I'm so sorry. We sold over a hundred tickets. What are the odds he'd win? We could cancel, if you want. I could say you got sick or something. We could reschedule Petey's round and, I don't know, I'd come up with some plan about the raffle entries."

Darío had never missed a scheduled round of golf in his life. Had not withdrawn from a tournament even with a dreadful flu and a temperature over one hundred and two. He would not mar that record here in the Copper Country.

"No, I will play with Pete and Ron."

He heard the sigh of relief that escaped Lizzie. "Thanks, Darío, you're a class act," she said, and was already moving away toward the first tee. Darío followed her.

At the tee were two men, both large, with strong, muscular physiques. Darío recognized the blond man as Ron. The one with black hair must be Pete Ryan. Darío hadn't met him yesterday but knew him to be a local who played for the Red Wings and was a close friend to Lizzie and Katie. Probably to Ron as well.

Well, it wouldn't be the relaxing round of golf he'd thought. Pulling Lizzie to his side and speaking low so the two men they approached wouldn't hear him, he asked, "Ron doesn't know about me, does he?"

"No. Just Al and I know about the baby. And just Katie's family knows the two of you are traveling together. I'm sure the whole town will know soon enough with Katie's sisters-in-law loving small town gossip, but nobody knows yet."

"And Pete Ryan?"

Lizzie shook her head. "Nope. He just got into town this week. He was in Florida visiting my brother Zeke. We haven't even had a chance to catch up yet."

Darío felt better as he stepped forward to meet the men. He could play dumb for one round of golf. Pretend to know Katie only as Lizzie's friend. That was how they'd met. The rest... well...these men did not need to hear the rest from him. He'd let the small-town gossip mill take care of that after they left town. The news of the baby could wait until they came back in a few months.

Lizzie made the introductions. Darío shook both men's hands, surprised at how firm and solid Ron's felt. What did he expect? That a man who cheated on his wife would somehow have an inferior handshake?

They stepped to the first tee and began play. All three shots were down the middle, with Darío's drive nearly even with the other two. He didn't mind. Length was not his game. Finesse around the greens and laser approach shots were what had won him his green jackets. Stevie had recruited a couple of buddies to caddy for the other men and they started down the fairway.

Lizzie pulled Darío back as he made to follow. "Do you want me to go with you guys? I hadn't planned on it, but I could walk the course with you."

Darío liked that idea. Some sort of buffer. He wasn't sure what he needed a buffer from, but the thought appealed to him.

Then he looked at Lizzie. Pregnant, large, Lizzie. Who had just spent who knows how many hours putting this weekend together. She looked worn out and Darío couldn't imagine her waddling over eighteen holes.

As if reading his mind she said, "I could go get a cart. I've arranged for beverages to be brought out to you later, I could just take that cart now and follow you the whole way."

Darío felt like a coward, needing this woman to protect him. He smiled and laid a hand on her shoulder. "There's no need. Most of the time in these situations, the men only want to talk golf. They want some pointers on their game, they want to hear stories from me about the Tour. If they don't know of my involvement with Katie, I see no reason why her name would even come up."

"Oh, her name will come up all right," she said. "Petey hasn't seen Ron yet either. I mean, hasn't seen him since Ron left Katie last fall. I would imagine Petey has a few choice words for him." She looked down the fairway to the group of golfers then noticed her stepson about halfway between, waiting on Darío. "And none of those words are ones I want Stevie to hear. Maybe I should come along after all."

Darío shook his head. "I'm sure it will be fine. Go home and get some rest, Lizzie, you look exhausted."

She sighed and rubbed her enormous stomach. "I am. I will. Petey said he'd bring Stevie home after you're done, so I thought I'd just go home and take a nap." She started to turn away, then faced Darío again. "If you're sure?"

He nodded. "Of course. Please, go home, we'll be fine." He watched her as she walked away, her full hips swaying side to side, her steps heavy, her gait uncomfortable. She put her hand to the small of her back and rubbed. "Lizzie," Darío said. She turned. "How far along are you?"

She chuckled. "Just six months, if you can believe that. I know. I look huge, like I could go at any minute." Darío said nothing, although he agreed with her.

"Don't worry about Katie, Darío. She and I have totally different body types. She'll love being able to walk the course with you on Tour. I'm sure she'll be one of those lucky people who won't show for a long time. And then when she does, she'll look like she's swallowed a basketball, not spread all over heck the way I am." Again, Darío wisely kept his mouth shut, which only made Lizzie laugh more. "That's okay, I made my peace with Katie looking like...well...Katie a long time ago. Besides, this time I'm putting on weight for all the right reasons." She walked toward the clubhouse and Darío started down the first fairway.

They were spread out enough on the fairway to only allow talk between each player and their caddy. But when they got to the green, all three men were standing in close proximity as they marked their balls and lined up their shots.

Darío didn't want to stare at Ron, but he couldn't help it. It was easy to see how a woman would fall for him. Darío had to admit, Ron was a very handsome man in the traditional blond, golden-boy type. His demeanor was easy, his movements fluid. Ron caught Darío staring at him and Darío quickly covered with a suggestion for Ron on his putting grip.

"Unless you would prefer I don't offer you advice," Darío added.

Ron shook his head. "No, I'd love anything you have to offer."

"I've got a few things I could offer," Petey Ryan said.

Ron looked at Petey, then nodded his head toward Darío. "Can we save this, Petey? I'd really just like to enjoy this round of golf. Watch Mr. Luna, learn what I can from him."

Mr. Luna? The man was the same age as Darío! "Please, call me Darío," he said.

"You honestly think you and I aren't going to get into it?" Petey asked Ron.

The men finished putting and started walking to the second tee, the three boys trailing along behind them. Darío was happy to see that they were not within hearing range. Stevie must have his stepmother's good sense.

Ron hadn't answered Petey and apparently the hockey star was not going to let the subject drop. "We can do it now, we can do it on the eighteenth, we can do it all over the golf course. But if you seriously think you're going to get off of this course without hearing it from me you're even more full of shit than I always thought."

He should just ignore them, Darío thought. Pretend that he's not getting it. But some perverse elf seemed to be sitting on his shoulder, egging him on. This would be his only chance to see the real Ron Lipton. A man's true personality came out on a golf course like no other place.

"Gentlemen," he said, "is there something bothering you?"

Petey snorted. Ron flushed and said, "I'm sorry, Darío, I don't mean to bring you into our personal issue."

This caused a laugh from Petey, though not a friendly one. "Issue? That's what we're going to call it? Our issue? Oh, we've got an issue all right."

"Perhaps we would be better off playing these rounds individually?" Darío offered, praying they would say no. The thought of golfing alone with Ron was not appealing, and he was beginning to enjoy Petey's jabs at Ron.

Both men shook their heads. "No. Sorry. I'm really looking forward to this. It means the world to me to play with someone of your stature," Ron said. It was not said with a fawning that would have turned Darío off, but with the understanding of a man who knows he can learn from another.

Darío turned to Petey who waved the thought away. "Whatever. I'll behave. I want a few pointers, too." Petey stepped up to the tee box and addressed the ball.

Darío nodded. "Well, then, you can start by standing six inches closer to the ball when you tee off."

Petey looked over his shoulder at Darío, who nodded his head toward Petey's feet. Petey furrowed his brows as if to argue and Darío nodded again to Petey's stance. Petey reluctantly moved his feet closer to the ball. "This feels really uncomfortable," he said.

"Try it."

Petey took his swing and the ball sailed at least twenty yards further than his drive on the first hole. "Holy shit," Petey said. Darío tried not to smile.

Ron teed off. Darío didn't say anything, even though Ron looked at him hopefully. Darío teed off and the three walked down the fairway.

They played the next several holes with Darío talking to Petey and Ron about golf, and Ron and Petey ignoring each other. Darío enjoyed talking with Stevie, asking him about the area, the schools, what kids his age did for fun. He usually talked with the sign bearers during tournaments, but never had he paid so close attention when talking with a child before. The thought that his child would most likely spend a good share of its time here in the Copper Country made Darío curious about the area.

He began to think about Katie and their child's future in more concrete terms. They would get married. He would cut back his schedule to maybe twenty or so tournaments a year. Get a house in Florida to have a home base closer to tournaments than the U.P. They could spend the summers here, the falls in Spain, and the winters and springs in Florida and at Tour stops. When the child started school, he would cut back even more and only play tournaments in the summer when Katie and the child could come with him. Eventually he would design courses for a living, only traveling when necessary.

He had it mapped out neatly. It was a lovely picture. Except for the fact that Katie didn't want to marry him. And he couldn't be absolutely sure the child was his until after it was born and they were able to perform DNA tests.

There were some snags.

That was what would hopefully work itself out during the next few months.

He was pulled out of his planning by Ron's angry voice. "Jesus Christ, Petey, I fucked up. Okay? Don't you think I know that?"

They were at the tee on the tenth hole. Near the clubhouse. They'd been playing smoothly but apparently while Darío was mentally picking out houses in Florida, Pete and Ron had started in again. Darío looked to find the boys, but they were gathered around the cart that had appeared, eating sandwiches, guzzling colas, and flirting with the girl driving the cart.

He walked over to the two men. "Please keep your voices down. I know Lizzie wouldn't want Stevie to hear that type of language." He felt like a schoolmarm scolding children. Not a tone he liked on himself. He silently cursed Ron and Pete for putting him in the position.

He expected the men to part, but they still stood toe to toe. Ron looked his way. "I'm sorry, Darío, you shouldn't be a party to this. But apparently Petey's not going to let it die."

"Let it die? Let it die? You fuck around on one of my closest friends, break her heart and you expect me to just let it die? I thought you knew me better than that."

Darío knew he should try to intervene again, but he didn't. They were taking the break at the turn that most golfers took and the boys would be busy at the beverage and sandwich cart for a while. Better to just let the two men get this over with now and then play the rest of the round in silence.

Assuming Ron could golf with two broken arms.

"I didn't fuck around on Katie," Ron said.

Petey raised his eyebrows at that. So did Darío, but thankfully Ron was looking at Petey and didn't see Darío's reaction.

"Yeah. Right. Seems to me there's a little kid out there who proves otherwise," Petey said. He took a step closer to Ron. The men were of equal height and width, both huge, hulking men. Darío didn't know who he'd put his money on if it did come to blows. Probably Petey. He looked like he knew how to play dirty.

Ron held up his hands. Not in surrender, but in a wait and see manner. "Listen, I don't expect you to understand. But you have to know I never intended to hurt Katie."

Petey took a deep breath, ran his fingers through his already tousled hair, and said, "Make me understand."

"What?" Ron said.

Petey took a step back, as if literally giving Ron room to tell his tale. "Make me understand. We go back a long time, Ron. But that long time is because of Katie. Nobody would tell me what all was going on up here last winter. I'm out on the road. I know there's a shit storm happening here and all I can do is call in. All Lizzie would say was that you were screwing some chick and got her knocked up. That Katie couldn't even function. That she was a total mess. I'm in freakin' Pittsburgh when I hear that. Do you have any idea how much I wanted to just chuck the whole season and come home?"

Darío saw Ron wince at that, but he wasn't sure if it was from the thought that Katie had been distraught or that Lizzie had summed up his indiscretions so bluntly.

"So tell me what happened, Ron. As you see it," Petey said. He took another step back, giving Ron more room.

Darío knew he should turn and leave. Join the boys at the cart. Give these two men, these one-time friends, the privacy they deserved. But he didn't. Couldn't. He wouldn't miss this opportunity to hear from Ron's own lips what type of total dick he'd been. The rationalizations he would give to his cheating on Katie. The excuses he would offer up.

"No excuses, if that's what you're thinking," Ron began. Darío was taken aback. Had he voiced his thoughts out loud? But Ron wasn't talking to him, he was addressing Petey. Both men had become oblivious to Darío's presence.

"Good, 'cause I wouldn't buy any anyways," Petey said.

Ron took a deep breath, let it out in a long sigh. "I slept with Amber once, Petey. Once. It was stupid and I hadn't intended for it to happen. But it was only once. I wasn't out screwing around on Katie. I wasn't having an affair."

Darío and Petey were both silent, waiting for Ron to continue.

"I don't expect you to understand how it was for Katie and me then. The doctor's visits. The shots. The hormones. The sex only when she was ovulating. The cold, clinical sex life we'd had for the last few years. Whenever Katie's period would come, she'd go into a three-day funk. She'd pulled away from me, Petey. She wouldn't talk to me about it. She shut me out. She'd only confide in Lizzie and Alison." He looked away, down the tenth fairway, as if the rolling green landscape could help him escape.

Darío expected Petey to jump in. To challenge Ron on his description of Katie, of their marriage. It certainly did not describe the Katie Darío knew. But Petey remained silent. Darío didn't know if that was telling or not.

"I felt so helpless. My wife was hurting and I couldn't help. Hell, I might have been the cause, they didn't know. So there was always that between us. The unspoken "whose fault is this?" question. We'd wanted kids so badly, for so long. It was something we talked about all the time when we were first married. By last winter it was like the elephant in the room. We couldn't even talk anymore. Can you imagine that? The woman you shared every waking moment with for seventeen years and you can't even thinking of something to say to her over breakfast that won't eventually turn to the subject of babies.

"She wouldn't take any kind of comfort from me. Didn't want it. Not from me, anyway. I suppose she got it from her friends.

"So, I turned away for comfort too," Ron continued. "Once. With Amber. The day Katie's period came and she shut down again. I went out. Got drunk. And there's Amber. She started coming on strong, telling me I'd been her favorite teacher, that she'd always had a crush on me. Really stroking me. What can I say? I needed to hear that. I needed to see myself the way Amber saw me. Not as the failure who couldn't get his wife pregnant. For one night I could forget the pain that Katie was going through. The pain I was going through."

He held his hands up as if to fend off the coming barrage, but Petey kept quiet. So did Darío. Ron lowered his hands. No attack had come, but he already had the look of someone defeated.

"I felt shitty about it. Really started trying to break down the barriers with Katie. Knew that we had to get past the infertility stuff or we weren't going to make it. That's when Amber told me she was pregnant."

He looked away again. Darío looked to see that the boys had remained on the benches some yards away, eating their sandwiches and talking amongst themselves. He caught Stevie's eye and knew the boy was the reason the men had been left alone so long. There were other golfers on the course, but none that had made the turn to the back nine yet, so they weren't holding anyone up. Darío nodded to Stevie and the boy nodded in return. Smart kid. Darío would tip him well.

Ron returned his gaze to Petey, but it looked to Darío that his sight was somewhere else. Miles away. Months away. "How fucked up was that? I couldn't make a baby with the woman I loved after trying for years and years, and I get some girl I barely know pregnant on a one-night stand. It shook me. I didn't know what to do. Amber was scared. Said she couldn't go through a pregnancy alone. That her family would turn their backs on her. That she'd have an abortion if I didn't want to be with her. I don't know if she was playing me or not. It could have been a bluff, but there was no way I was going to find out for sure."

Darío understood that. The minute Katie had told him she was pregnant, there was nothing he wouldn't do to make sure his child was taken care of. He could not fault Ron for ensuring the safety of his child.

Ron let out a snort of disgust. "I even tried to talk Amber into giving the child up to Katie and me. I didn't know how I'd get Katie to agree to it. I just couldn't bear the thought that I'd have to choose between my wife and my child.

"But, eventually, I realized that's exactly what I had to do. I knew Katie would survive. She would be devastated about the baby, and she'd hate me, but she had her family, and Lizzie and Alison. I knew she'd be taken care of. I…I wasn't so sure about my baby."

He cleared his throat, His voice cracked as he added, "I had to make sure my baby would have at least one parent in its life who was ready to be a parent. Who *wanted* to be a parent."

Petey and Darío remained silent. What could they add? Would Darío be able to choose between the welfare of his child and remaining with Katie? He was thankful that wouldn't be the case in his situation. He would never worry about his child with Katie as its mother.

"So I left Katie. God, that day. That horrible day." He shook his head, as if the memory would never leave his mind. "It was brutal. No. I was brutal. I was so pissed that I had to make this choice. That I had put myself in this position. And yet, I was so happy about becoming a father. I turned it all on Katie. Totally unleashed it. Was a total prick. But, maybe that was for the best."

"How?" Petey asked.

"She hates me now," Ron said. He waited for Petey to contradict him, but Petey didn't say a word. "That's probably better. At least we can both start over. Get on with our lives. Can you imagine the situation if she still loved me?"

A lump formed in Darío's throat. If Katie had heard all this would she feel differently toward Ron? Would it matter? It wouldn't change the fact that she was now carrying Darío's child. *Maybe* carrying his child. *Probably* carrying his child.

"You didn't say if you still loved her," Petey asked as Darío thought the same thing.

Ron barked a laugh. "Hell yes, I still love her. You don't spend seventeen years with a woman like Katie and not love her forever."

Darío held his breath. Was there a but coming?

"But," Ron said. Darío exhaled. "Now there's Crystal. I got to tell you, Petey, she's changed my life." He whirled to Darío. "Darío, do you have kids?"

Startled, Darío answered, "I...I...not yet." That was true. And all he was willing to say to these two men. For now.

Ron was shaking his head. "So you guys can't really understand. I know they always say you'll never be the same once you become a parent, and that no one ever really knows those kinds of feelings...protectiveness...fierceness...until you have a kid. It's true. There isn't anything I wouldn't do for Crystal. To make sure she was safe and happy and taken care of." He held up his hand and shrugged with the simplicity of it. "She's my life."

Petey turned and walked away. Ron looked at Darío. Darío met his gaze. He wanted to hate the man for the pain he'd caused Katie. But the man was simply trying to protect his child. Would Darío do anything less?

He was relieved he did not have to make a comment to Ron about his confessions because Petey turned around and said. "Ten bucks for closest to the pin on this hole, guys?"

They waved the caddies over to them and played the rest of the round in relative silence, only talking about golf swings and techniques. Darío told the story that amateurs most often wanted to hear—how he'd won the green jacket of the Masters.

They finished the round with Darío wining by double digits, which was no surprise. Petey and Ron had identical scores, which irked both men. It seemed a fitting end to the most exhausting round of golf Darío could remember playing in a long time.

Fifteen

The more I practice, the luckier I get.
~ Jerry Barber, professional golfer

THEY HADN'T DISCUSSED sleeping arrangements when they'd come up with their plan for Katie to travel with Darío. That fact became clear to Katie at their first Tour stop, in Denver, when they had an awkward moment at the hotel registration desk.

The hotel had a last-minute cancellation from a player who withdrew from the tournament and Katie was able to have a room of her own. The hotel receptionist remarked on how lucky they were to have found another room with no notice.

Katie wasn't sure if that luck was working against her or for her. Darío seemed amenable to separate rooms, and that too kept her wondering.

The altitude in Denver was a shock to Katie, but she rallied and walked the course each day with Darío's group. They had dinner the first two nights with Binky, who seemed delighted that Katie had joined Darío.

Darío easily made the cut and would have made the top ten, but he called a penalty shot on himself on Sunday that took him out of contention.

Binky was furious. "You can't be sure the ball moved," he spat out as the threesome drove from the course to Binky's hotel in the courtesy car the tournament provided.

"I can't be sure it didn't," Darío said softly.

Katie got that something had happened on the fourteenth hole and it cost Darío a stroke, a top-ten finish, and a great deal of money. She'd watched from the ropes as Darío and Binky shared words, then played the rest of the round in stony silence. "Explain this to me," she said, tentatively, not wanting to upset Binky even more. Oddly, Darío didn't seem nearly as upset as Binky.

Darío opened his mouth, but Binky beat him to it. "I'll explain it to you. When you're addressing the ball on the green for a putt, if the ball moves while your club is grounded, whether you touch it or not, it's a penalty stroke. That's why, if it's a really windy day, lots of golfers will take a long time in their pre-shot, but hit the putt as soon as they get up to the address, just in case the wind moves the ball."

"So, the ball moved?" Katie asked, not seeing why Binky would be so upset. Golfers lived and died by the rules. In no other sport did the participants call penalties on themselves. It was a fact of the game.

Darío again opened his mouth and again Binky cut him off from the backseat. "That's just it. Guv, here, can't be sure. He thinks it might have moved. Nobody saw it move. Even he didn't see it move." The exasperation in his voice was evident.

Katie looked from Binky in the back to Darío across the front seat from her.

"When I replace my ball after Binky cleans it, I always place it a particular way with the word Titleist at the very top of the ball reading left to right." Darío's voice was controlled, just like the man. His tone was patient, as he explained to Katie, and Katie suspected, to Binky as well.

Katie nodded. She had already witnessed some of the rituals that the golfers had. All different, but all consistent. Darío continued, "I placed my ball, took my practice swings, and walked to the ball and took the address. When I looked down, the word Titleist was at the bottom, near the grass. The ball had moved."

"But you don't know that it moved before or after you addressed the ball and grounded your club. It could have been while you were taking your practice swings," Katie said.

"Exactly," Binky added from the back. He crossed his arms over his chest and stared out the window. Katie turned back to Darío in time to see him glance in the rearview mirror at Binky with a stern look that Katie was sure Binky would ignore, if he even saw it at all.

"I cannot be sure that it didn't move while my club was grounded, so, I had to call the penalty on myself," he said, nonchalantly, as if losing $40,000 because of a penalty stroke were an everyday occurrence.

"That stroke cost you more than I make in a year," Katie said.

"It's not about the money. It's about being able to sign your scorecard with a clear conscience."

Binky snorted. "Meanwhile, there's a couple of guys out there who take every advantage on their drops, some outright illegal."

Darío only shook his head. "I cannot play their game for them. I can only play within the rules myself. I can look myself in the mirror while shaving. I wonder if they can."

The car fell silent as Katie wondered how Ron felt when he shaved his chiseled face every morning.

—⚉—

Darío was used to doing things alone. He traveled alone. He spent his evenings alone. Sure, a couple of nights a week he and Binky ate dinner together, but he always returned to the quiet tranquility of his hotel room.

It wasn't like he was starved for company. During the days he was at the course playing a round and then practicing on the range. He usually played his practice rounds with another Spaniard if there was one in town for that particular tournament. If not, there were several players on the Tour that he'd known for years that he played with. The camaraderie on the practice range was enough togetherness to suit Darío.

So it came as a great shock to him how much he enjoyed Katie's constant companionship. And there was no way it could be anything less than constant. Sometimes on a Tuesday or Wednesday she'd stay at the hotel and write, or she'd be doing an interview with a fellow player. But otherwise, she was with him.

Except for the nights when they both slept alone, his body aching for her.

After their first week in Denver, Katie's editor had emailed her applauding the story she'd sent him on a player who had missed the cut for the forty-second straight week and the perseverance of that player to keep on trying to make the cut, save his card, and stay on Tour. The wire service picked it up and the next week, in Flint, she wrote about a player on his fourth marriage, who was habitually in and out of rehab with a drinking problem. Much had been written about this player through the years as he was very popular amongst the fans, but Katie's story went deeper than a writer normally would, and it showed in the article.

Darío was not surprised at Katie's talent, though she seemed surprised at the success of her articles. He was glad that the sacrifice of leaving her home to be on the road with him was paying off for her professionally.

Most days she got up when Darío did and after breakfast at the hotel where she made sure to drink her dreaded milk, they'd go to the course together. She sat in the stands at the practice range, sometimes taking a book, sometimes writing in a journalist's notebook, sometimes just watching Darío.

He'd look up every so often, making sure she was okay, that the heat—or rain, or cold—wasn't bothering her. She'd sit on the top row, usually in a corner, distancing herself from the others who came to watch the players practice. She'd become quite tan from the days in the sun, though she was careful never to burn.

He gave her new Chapsticks all the time, but she always seemed to forget them when they left for the course. One night at dinner, trying to find something in her purse, she'd emptied the contents on the table, only to have several tubes of lip balm scatter across to Darío.

In the stands, she was like a beacon to Darío, calling to him on the ground. As if she were a golden angel, her white hair her halo, her presence hovering over Darío in a kind of peaceful blessing.

And that's how he felt with her watching over him. Peaceful. Blessed.

He noticed he didn't search out the galleries as much as he used to. Only to find her, which was never difficult. She was normally alone, walking ahead, her eyes more times than not on him. Sometimes she'd walk with the wife of the player he was paired with, but usually only if that woman made the first overture. She attracted men, but with a smile and a kind word or two, separated from them and walked the course alone during Darío's rounds.

If only he could do something about her sleeping in a different room.

The first week in Denver, it seemed like a fluke that there'd been an open room. The next week, in Flint, he'd asked at the desk when they'd arrived, more for show than actually wanting there to be an available room. He was taken aback when the hotel manager moved heaven and earth to find another room for his "honored guest" Mr. Luna. Too bad none of the big guns were playing that week or Darío was sure his stature would have slipped a few notches from honored guest to "one of those golfers".

He'd waited for Katie to jump in with a "No, no, don't go to any trouble. One room will be fine." But she hadn't. So he'd kept silent as well. And slept alone again since the night she'd left his room in Texas.

After watching her walk the course in front of him all day, gazing at her graceful sway, he could barely stand to sit across the table from her at dinner. The need to hold her again, to kiss her, was unbearable. She'd smile her brilliant white smile at something he'd say, and he'd nearly lose it. The steel control he used on the course was coming in handy off the course as well.

But, he didn't want to pressure her. It was enough that she'd agreed to come on the road with him, let them get to know each other so they could make the best decisions for their child as possible. Well, not enough, but it was what he'd asked for. The deal they'd made.

He was foolish enough to believe that once on the road, Katie would want to resume their physical relationship. That after leaving the Copper Country, leaving memories of her life with Ron, her thoughts would be only of Darío. Of that passionate night they'd shared. Of the intense release they'd brought each other to.

It had been good for her, hadn't it?

Darío refused to believe that anything so satisfying to him could have been one-sided. But then, he figured all men thought that at one time or another.

The third week out, in Chicago where the year's last major was being played, Darío was astonished to find out that he'd been put in a suite. So there was no need for Katie to get her own room—and there were none to be had anyway—but she did have her own bedroom. The management of the hotel was catering to past major winners by giving them suites instead of regular rooms. A nice perk that would have been appreciated any other time. But not this week.

Darío seriously thought about trading in his Claret Jug for one night in the same room—the same bed—with Katie.

—⚬⚬⚬—

The suite was beautiful. Huge. The bedrooms seemed miles apart. And that was not a good thing to Katie. She was happy to finally be sharing rooms—sort of—with Darío.

She enjoyed the time they spent together. He was a fascinating man. Very well-read, which surprised Katie. She knew she shouldn't generalize, but she'd figured Darío for the typical jock.

Never had she and Ron spent the entire time over dinner discussing the religious undertones of *Moby Dick*. Katie was fairly certain Ron had never even read *Moby Dick*, let alone picked up on undertones.

Darío brushed aside her admiration of his reading list. "There is much time on flights, or waiting for rain delays. There is always time to kill," he'd said.

That was true, but she now knew from experience that most of the golfers spent that time playing poker, chasing girls, and making investment deals with their brokers on their ever-present smartphones and tablets.

That was another thing. Darío didn't have a bunch of gadgets, just a basic cell phone to keep in contact with his mother. Nor did he have an agent, manager, coach, and trainer who traveled with him. Binky traveled separately, as most of the caddies did, to each event. Darío made one call each week to his manager back in Spain to check on flight arrangements and if there were any changes Darío should know about. Katie didn't ask about the details of her traveling with Darío. It seemed the manager handled that and there was plane reservation information waiting for them both at their hotel for their next stop.

Darío didn't have an entourage as many of the players of his caliber did. Well, Katie supposed, he did now…her.

The last major of the year. Darío had missed the cut at the Masters. Finished top twenty at the US Open. Top ten at the British Open. Katie knew he had high hopes for the PGA Championship. He didn't voice them out loud, but there was an intensity about him this week that hadn't been there the previous weeks. She wasn't surprised to realize she'd learned to read him so well in so short a time. That's what happened when you were together nearly 24-7.

Not quite around the clock. There were the hours she slept alone.

In a perverse way, she was slightly ticked at Darío for not pressuring her. Not making a bigger deal about her having her own room. Passive aggressive thinking on her part, she knew. If she wanted to sleep with the man, she should just come out and tell him so. But she'd never been able to do that—at least not while sober. Lizzie or Alison could. Heck, Lizzie had come out and done just that last year, telling Finn she wanted a summer fling with him.

The one night with Darío had been different—she'd never expected to see him again. And even then it had taken all her courage. Before that, she'd never had to be the aggressor, the one who moved relationships along.

She'd always depended on the men in her life to do that. And they had, right down to the day Ron left her.

Too bad Darío was a gentleman.

She accompanied him during his final practice round on Wednesday. The crowd was huge, even for a practice round day, with it being a major. But the gallery around Darío was not very large. He was playing with two little-known players who mainly played on the European Tour—one Spanish and one from Argentina—and most of the crowd elected to follow pairings with bigger names.

The players spoke Spanish to each other, the caddies content to keep their own conversations as they measured greens with their strides, marking everything in their yardage books. At each green they players would spend several minutes putting tees as markers where the different pin placements would be on each day and chipping and putting multiple balls at each target. It was an organized mess with balls whizzing past each other on the green as one player putted toward Thursday's pin while another tried to get out of the bunker and close to Sunday's target.

Physical yearnings, ones she was becoming used to, pulled at her as she watched Darío on the course. The way he exuded confidence over a putt. How his arms glistened with sweat magnified by the sun. How he smiled at her after a difficult shot.

As the players walked down the fairways, Katie could hear their rapid exchanges and once again silently thanked the stars that Darío was so fluent in English. One of the other players barely spoke a word of it.

As the golfers walked up the eighteenth fairway, nearly done for the day, Darío waved to Katie. She waved back, surprised. She'd felt his eyes on her during rounds, but he seldom acknowledged her while he played. Sometimes he would send Binky over to get her water bottle and refill it at the iced water stand that was inside the rope and for the players' use only. Or send him to dispatch a tube of Chapstick, which she always seemed to forget.

He waved again and she realized that he was summoning her to join them. Inside the ropes. On the fairway.

She'd never gone inside the ropes before. During practice rounds, club manufacturer reps, agents, coaches and even sometimes wives would walk with the players, but Darío always played with just Binky at his side.

She stupidly looked behind her, certain he must be calling to someone else.

"*Gata*, come, join us," he said.

Nope. Nobody else.

The three men had stopped in the middle of the fairway, apparently waiting for her to join them. She stepped under the rope, catching the curious glances of those gallery members next to her. A man in a shirt denoting his tournament volunteer status walked up to stop her, but Darío called out to the man, "It's okay. She's with me."

She was with him. Katie didn't take the time to think about what that meant beyond admittance to the fairway.

Darío introduced her to his playing companions. She was curious to see what he would say to them about her, but only said, "This is Katie." She didn't know if Darío had explained who "Katie" was earlier. She wished them luck in the tournament and walked the rest of the way to the green with the men. She stayed on the fringe of the green while they went through their various routines.

The bleachers were full at the eighteenth green and the crowd burst into applause when Darío sank a putt that traversed the entire length of the green. He smiled and doffed his cap to the crowd. When they quieted, he said loud enough for them to hear, "Here's hoping I can do that on Sunday." The crowd laughed good-naturedly and applauded the group as they left the green. There were some shouts of "Good luck, Darío!" and "Go get 'em, Darío!"

Katie felt a tingle race up and down her spine as they rooted for her guy. There was definitely a different feeling at this tournament than the others she'd attended. An electricity. An importance. A major.

As they headed to the clubhouse inside the ropes that separated them from the crowd, a dark-haired woman with a baby in her arms and a toddler at her knees headed toward them. As one of Darío's playing partners—the Spaniard whom Darío had introduced as Angel—stepped forward, it became obvious by the smile on the woman's face that they were a family.

Angel lifted the rope and the woman and children passed underneath. The adults gave each other a kiss that made Katie look away. It wasn't so much that the kiss was X-rated, but it telegraphed such a sweetness, such an intimacy between the couple, that Katie felt like an intruder watching.

The toddler switched his hold from his mother's loose flowing skirt to the pants of his father. Only his father had moved—to kiss his mother—and the pants the young boy had grabbed were Darío's. The little boy tugged and Darío looked away from the autograph he was signing to peer down at the boy. The child seemed startled that it was not his father's face he saw when he looked up from the pants he was covering with some substance from his hands.

Angel and his wife were transferring the baby to Angel's arms and didn't notice that their son was about to shriek in fright at the man whom he had mistaken as his father.

Katie was just about to intervene, to scoop the boy up so he could be on face-to-face level with his parents, when Darío bent down and did just that. The little boy's eyes—chocolate brown, just like Darío's—grew wide and his mouth opened. But Darío beat him to any words, speaking softly and low in Spanish to the boy. "Something, something, Alejandro," was all Katie could make out.

Darío turned the boy—Alejandro, apparently—so he could see that his mother and father stood next to him. Angel's wife started to take the boy, but the boy put his arms around Darío's neck— to everyone's surprise, it seemed—and Darío motioned to the mother that it was okay.

Darío and the other players continued to sign autographs and pose for pictures with fans. Practice-round days were the only days spectators were allowed to bring cameras onto the grounds.

Katie watched as Darío rubbed Alejandro's back in small, soothing circles. At that moment she felt the slightest fluttering in her belly.

It was the first time she'd felt movement. She was just at her four-month mark. She wasn't showing at all, yet, not even tightness in her waistband. It could have been anything. Gas. The heat. Not enough fluids. But Katie knew it was the baby. It wasn't a kick, not yet. But it was movement.

She looked over at Darío, laughing at something shared with little Alejandro. She put her hand on her belly and cursed herself for tearing up. But she couldn't help it.

Darío looked at her at that moment and handed Alejandro back to his mother, moving quickly to Katie's side. "*Gata*? Katie? What is it? What's wrong?"

Katie cleared her throat to speak. She smiled at Darío. "Nothing. Nothing's wrong. I'm just happy," she said.

—☙—

Hormones. Curious little things, Darío thought, as he put *What to Expect When You're Expecting* down on the bedside table next to him. He turned off the light and turned over to his side. He should be thinking of the tournament tomorrow. Of his strategy. Of his swing.

All he could think of was Katie's beautiful blue eyes filled with tears.

It was an odd situation. He really hadn't known Katie well

enough before she'd become pregnant to know what in her behavior was Katie and what was pregnancy-induced. It didn't matter, he supposed. She was what she was.

And what she was was alone in her own bed, just as Darío was.

He'd thought that maybe sharing a suite would raise the stakes, make it easier for them to act on their wishes. Or at least Darío's wishes. Katie had begged off from his dinner with Binky, saying she wanted to work on some ideas for a new piece and that she'd order room service. By the time Darío had returned, she'd turned in, the door to her bedroom closed.

Maybe she did want to get some work done. Darío had read all the pieces she'd submitted since they'd been traveling together. They were good. Really good. And it seemed to Darío that their being together long-term could be not only good for them and the child, but for Katie's career as well. He'd certainly been playing better since he'd met her.

And maybe she didn't want to interfere with his and Binky's discussion of strategy for tomorrow. Although she'd joined them for Wednesday night dinners before, keeping quiet most times during strategy talks. Sometimes adding a point or two that Darío always listened to. Most times she was right.

And maybe she was just tired after walking the course today. Practice rounds were much longer than competition rounds because players often times took two or three shots from each position. So much more time was spent on each green, reading it from every angle.

And maybe she just didn't want to sleep with him.

His body once again in knots, that thought stayed with him as he drifted off to sleep.

―⁜―

Something was off with Darío's game. Nobody else would notice it. But Katie did. And Binky could too, Katie could tell, because he shot her questioning looks every so often in the gallery. She shrugged, having no clue what could make Darío's approach shots—which had been like lasers the last few weeks—land on the opposite side of the green from every pin.

It wasn't disastrous. He would still make the cut, and if he had a good weekend perhaps a top-twenty finish. But by the end of the round on Friday, Katie could see the frustration on Darío's face as he struggled to make par on hole after hole.

They ate dinner in silence at a chain steakhouse and returned to their suite. They stood awkwardly in the living room, each ready to go to their respective corners—their own rooms—yet both hesitating to do so.

Finally, Katie broke the silence. "Darío, you're going to have to help me out here. What do you need from me in a situation like this?"

He turned to her, surprise on his face. "What…what do I need from you?"

"Yes. When you've had a bad round." She saw his shoulders sag. "Not that you had a bad round. Any time you can shoot par in major you're in great shape."

He snorted. "Unless forty players shot well under par."

She didn't concede his point, but knew it was true. He'd be in the one of the first pairings tomorrow. An early tee time on a Saturday and Sunday was not a good thing. It meant you were way down on the leaderboard.

"What can I do for you? Do you want me to leave you alone when this happens? Do you want me to be a sounding board? Let you vent about the round? Can I pep talk you or would that just tick you off?

"Pep talk me?"

"You know. 'It wasn't you, it was those crazy greens. You'll get 'em tomorrow. Shoot a sixty-five and you're right back in this thing.' Stuff like that?"

He shook his head. "No. I don't think I'd like that."

She smiled. "No, I didn't think that would be your style. Maybe you'd just like to forget a bad round." She looked around the room, saw the TV, her laptop, the small pile of books they were both reading. "Can I do something to distract you?"

He cleared his throat. Then it turned to a cough. After a moment Katie was afraid he was choking and stepped forward to slap him on the back or to do something, but he waved his hands up at her and stepped back.

"I'm sorry, Katie. This is new for me. When I have a bad day on the course, normally I am alone with my thoughts."

"Is that what you'd like? To be left alone? I can just go to my room. We do have an early start tomorrow."

He opened his mouth to respond but she held up her hand, stopping him. "It's okay, you're not hurting my feelings. This... us...it's a lot more togetherness than you're used to. I know it's not me." A flash of insecurity—not something she normally felt with men—came over her. "It's not me, is it? You'd let me know if you wanted our situation to change, right?"

He cleared his throat. "Wanted our situation to change?"

She nodded. "If you didn't want me to travel with you anymore."

He exhaled loudly. Katie wasn't sure what that meant.

"Katie, yes, I'm used to being alone. But please know that I am very happy that you're with me. I'm sorry if I haven't said that."

He hadn't, and she was happy to hear it. She felt the same way. She was just about to tell him that when he continued. "We'll just have to find our way. To figure out what works best when traveling like this. Between your changing hormones and my always changing game, there will be plenty of mood swings to learn to deal with." He chuckled and the warmth in his voice soothed Katie.

"Well..." she said.

"Well..." he said.

"Good night, then."

"Good night."

They both walked to their sides of the suite. She had her hand on the door handle when she turned around. "Darío?"

He turned, his eyes questioning. Was he asking the same thing she was? She couldn't be sure, and so she didn't take the chance. Instead, she smiled. "You shoot a sixty-five tomorrow and you're right back in this thing."

Did he look disappointed? He gave her a small smile. "Thanks for the pep talk, coach," he said as he entered his room.

—⁓—

He didn't shoot a sixty-five. And he didn't get back into contention. Saturday night was basically a repeat of Friday night and Sunday's final round was not much better. He had a late-round surge that ended up putting him right around the middle of the field. He'd gone another season without winning a major. Katie knew that majors were the measurement that the truly great golfers lived by. Darío had three. A career to be proud of. Still, she felt his disappointment. And felt helpless to comfort him.

When they were checking out on Monday, as Darío was getting the bags to the car and checking on the tickets to Akron—their next stop—Katie was summoned by the hotel clerk.

"Are you Katie Maki?"

"Yes." She was taken aback. They'd always checked in under Darío's name whether she'd had her own room or not. She'd never had to give her own name at any of the places they'd stayed.

"Ah, good, good," the man said. "The package said you'd be care of Mr. Luna." He pulled a FedEx envelope out from behind the counter. "This arrived for you this morning." Katie showed the man her ID, signed for the envelope and looked at the return address. Alison.

She tucked the envelope into a side pocket of her laptop case as Darío approached her. "We're all set," he said. He pointed to her laptop case. "Problems?"

She shook her head and started walking to the hotel entrance. "No. Just something from Alison. Probably clippings of my stuff for the *Ingot*."

But that wasn't what was in the envelope. Katie knew it then, and had it confirmed when she snuck the package out while

Darío dozed on their flight, his back turned to her. The first-class seats were spacious and she didn't worry about jarring or waking him.

Inside the FedEx envelope was another envelope, this one in legal office brown. She handed the FedEx wrappings to a passing flight attendant and stared at the heavy envelope sitting on her lap. Finally she placed the envelope—unopened—back into her laptop case.

A hand-written note from Alison had accompanied the envelope and Katie held it in her hands, her fingers tracing over Al's precise script. "Finally. Now you can dump the fucker once and for all and get on with your life."

That was Alison. No "miss you", no "I'm sure this is hard for you". It was always so cut and dried for Alison. Black and white. Yes or no.

Dump the fucker.

Alison knew Katie hated profanity. That, of course, is why she'd written it. Katie quietly chuckled at her friend's message. She wasn't sure what part of the Midwest they were flying over when her chuckles turned to quiet tears.

Sixteen

—◊◊◊—

Golf and sex are about the only things you
can enjoy without being good at them.
~ Jimmy Demaret, professional golfer

"IS THERE ANY POSSIBILITY of another room being available?"
Darío asked. "We've become a larger party than expected when
the reservation was first made."

He felt Katie at his elbow. "That won't be necessary," she said
to the hotel clerk. She looked at him, her eyes huge, blue pools.
She raised her perfectly arched brows. "Will it?"

"You know it is a room, not a suite?" he asked, not wanting
any misunderstandings.

She nodded. "I got that part."

He turned to the confused hotel clerk. "One room will be
fine. Thank you."

The clerk sighed in relief. "Great, because, much as we feel
honored to have you with us Mr. Luna, there simply isn't another
room to be had. In all of Akron, really."

Darío's hand shook as he filled out the requisite forms. This
could only mean one thing, right? He searched his mind for some
other explanation, but came up with nothing. They would be
alone. In one room. With one bed.

"You know, I was there," the clerk was saying to him. Darío

looked up, confused, as the clerk continued. "In ninety-eight. When you shot the sixty. I was in the stands at eighteen when you drained that putt. That was the most impressive round of golf I've ever seen."

Darío thanked the man, humbled that he would remember a round of golf played over fourteen years ago. Darío remembered it, of course, every drive, every putt, but that was because he'd never played a round of golf like that in his life. Never had again.

They turned and started to the elevators, the bellhop following them with their luggage and Darío's clubs. They were silent in the elevator and as they entered the room. As the bellhop unloaded their things he said, "I was there too, that day."

Darío's mind was filled with thoughts of being alone in a single room with Katie and he had to think for a moment about what the bell-hop was saying before it dawned on him. "Thank you. It was quite a day." Normally a generous tipper—his mother's hard life in service had taught him that—Darío was even more so now.

The bellhop looked down at his tip. "Thank you, sir." He turned to leave the room, then stopped and looked over his shoulder. "You know that sixty still stands as the course record at Firestone. Nobody's come close, even all these years later."

The man disappeared behind the closed door. Darío turned to see Katie standing in the middle of the room.

Yes, Akron was Darío's lucky city.

—⁓—

Katie looked around the nondescript room anxiously. She'd put this into motion. Did she need to make the first move? Would it be expected of her? Could she do it? Wouldn't it be enough for Darío that she had requested only one room? Couldn't he make the next move?

He wasn't. He had started to unpack his garment bag.

Of course, it was only mid-afternoon. What, did she think he'd jump her bones the minute they were finally in a bedroom together?

Would that be too much to ask?

The thought of being on edge until bedtime—she silently laughed at her own pun—was too much for her. It had to happen now or she'd never make it.

Okay. She could do this. She could be the aggressor. The starter. The one to set the tone. She took a deep breath and started toward him. He was pulling his sportscoat out from the bag, turning toward her just as she got to him. She ran into him and they both let out a small "oof".

Why was she so clumsy around this man when things turned physical? She considered herself a fairly graceful person and had never had this happen with other men. With Darío she suddenly turned into The Three Stooges.

Darío held onto her for longer than was needed. The heat ran up and down her arm, but still caused goose bumps. She raised her hand to his face, but he stepped back, a look of regret on his face.

"I have to go to the course," he said.

"Now?"

He nodded. "*Sí*, they're having a pre-tournament dinner that some of the players are invited to."

"They have those at every tournament, you haven't gone before," she said. She tamped down the thought that maybe he was attending this one to get away from the awkwardness she'd created by asking for only one room.

"Right. But I feel I should attend this one. They put on a clinic for club members and area youth charities and then a dinner afterward. I still hold the course record as you now know, and this is a tournament I have won three times." He shrugged. "These people have been very good to me. I'd like to show my appreciation."

That was so like Darío. Never forgetting those who helped him. Paying his debts. Being honorable.

"So, you'll be gone for a while?" She wasn't sure what feeling was greater, disappointment or relief at her reprieve. He pulled out his coral-colored Lacoste shirt, the one that was so striking against his dark complexion.

Disappointment. Definitely disappointment.

He nodded. He pulled out his dress slacks and light blue dress shirt, and put them with the jacket. Apparently he'd wear golf clothes to the course for the clinic, then change into dress-wear for dinner.

He looked at her again. Started to say something then stopped. He took a deep breath, let it out. He grabbed his shaving kit and the coral shirt, and retreated to the bathroom.

Katie sat down on the bed. She didn't move. Just sat, thinking about ordering room service for dinner. About sitting in this room for hours obsessing about what would happen when Darío got back.

He wasn't long in the bathroom. He came back into the room freshly shaved and wearing the coral shirt. Her eyes flashed over him in appreciation.

He cleared his throat. "Would you…would you like to go with me?"

"To the course?"

He nodded.

"For the clinic?"

"And for the dinner afterward," he said.

It shouldn't have felt so monumental to her. They had dinner together nearly every night. Practically lived together. But this felt different. This felt like…a date.

"It is a nicer affair…" he began.

"I have a nice dress. I brought one with me, I wasn't sure if I'd need one or not. I figured if I needed more than the one, I could buy another somewhere."

He nodded, looked at his watch. "I really have to get going to be there for the entire clinic. Why don't I take the courtesy car now and you come later in a cab, in time for the dinner. Around seven? Tell the driver to take you to the Firestone South club-house. I'll leave your name with someone there."

"That sounds good," she said. Her dress was somewhere at the bottom of her suitcase, getting pushed further and further down as shorts and tee-shirts rose to the top. She'd need some time to press it off, shower, maybe even put her hair up. She'd been wearing it in either ponytails on the course or loose in her hotel rooms. Life had been so casual the last three weeks, dressing up sounded appealing.

She tried to help him with his clubs, but ended up getting tangled between the shoulder strap and his slacks that were on a hanger.

He chuckled. "Katie, maybe you should just stand over there for a moment."

She stepped back, watching him effortlessly balancing his clubs against his shoulder and his shaving kit, its handle looped over the top of the hangers holding his dress clothes which hung from his fingers.

"Maybe you could just get the door for me," he said, stepping clearly out of her way as she walked to the door.

"You know, I'm not dangerous or anything," she said.

He passed her, paused in the doorway, caught her eyes in a hypnotizing stare. He leaned toward her. Her breath hitched. His lips met her…forehead! Forehead!

"Oh, you are most definitely dangerous, *Gata*. But to me or to yourself, that I have not yet decided." He was chuckling to himself as he walked down the hallway.

Katie let the weight of the heavy door close itself; she was already turning toward her suitcases.

—⁂—

The clinic seemed to be running long. That or Katie was early. Darío was nowhere to be seen in the clubhouse, although other players were there. She nodded to a few that she hadn't exactly met, but had seen in the past couple of weeks.

They were openly staring at her. First with looks of curiosity, then with admiration.

Another woman might look to see if a zipper was open or

something was in some way wrong with her appearance. But Katie was used to men eyeing her. Especially when she put some time and effort into her appearance, as she had tonight. It should make her feel good, but it never did. Strange men finding her attractive had never been particularly pleasing to her. It had only mattered that one man found her attractive. Her man.

The man had changed, but the sentiment had not.

She wanted to find Darío. For him to see her. For her to see him dressed up.

A player, one she knew was married, approached her, a cocktail in his hand, dressed in an open-necked dress shirt, jacket and slacks. "Looking for someone?" he asked in what wasn't necessarily a helpful tone.

"Yes. Thank you. Darío Luna, have you seen him?"

The man seemed disappointed. "Darío? Hmmm, he's probably still out on the range. He was when I left." He stepped closer. Closer than he should. "Can I get you a drink?"

Katie took a step back. "No, thank you. I think I'll make my way out to the range."

The man swept a look over her attire, raised an eyebrow at her heels and said, "It's down the slope if you turn right out of the clubhouse."

She thanked the player and made her way over to the range, cursing her heels and dress. It was definitely country-club garb, but not conducive to walking a course. Fortunately the range wasn't far from the clubhouse. The huge bleachers were already set up for tomorrow's practice rounds and Thursday's official start. The expansive rise of the bleachers eclipsed the range and she wasn't even sure if Darío was still out here.

She made her way around to the front and Darío was the first thing she saw. Made easy because he was surrounded by children.

There were a few other pro players on the range, but they were talking with what seemed to Katie to be club members. Older men who were showing the pros their grips, their swings, looking for help of any kind. Or just wanting to say they got a tip from a pro.

Darío, in that coral shirt Katie loved and black pants, was talking with the children, all of whom were wearing tee-shirts with the First Tee emblem across the front. These weren't children of members, country-club rats. These were kids from the urban parts of the city. The poor kids. Kids who didn't get chances to play on a course like Firestone. Kids who might never have had a golf club in their hands before, might never come to a course again.

That was the point of the First Tee program, to get these kids interested in golf. Give them a reason to come back to the game. Give them an alternative. An outlet. Their lives would be tough enough in the years to come—probably were right now—and this program gave them at least a few hours to be just kids playing a game.

The children were a true Rainbow Coalition, representing every color and race imaginable.

Darío was working with them all, one at a time. The kids had obviously had their time with the other pros earlier during the clinic, but Darío had stayed and was making sure each got a second or two of his time.

He was talking with a little girl of about eight years old. She had cornrows and her tee-shirt was huge, hanging nearly to her knees, her ebony skin glistening from either the heat or exertion, or most likely both. Katie watched as Darío knelt down to be on her level and listened to her. He nodded, giving her time to speak. He appeared to take whatever she had to say very seriously. He stood, stepped back and the little girl stepped up to the tee and took a good whack at the ball, which Katie was happy to see go a fair distance right down the middle of the fairway.

The other kids cheered for her, Darío leading the ovation.

He seemed to sense Katie's presence, and turned toward the bleachers. She walked to the front of the railing and he met her there. He leaned his golden-brown arm on the railing. She saw a tiny drop of sweat roll down his forearm, slide down his wrist and come to rest on the green metal railing.

She towered over him, the front platform of the bleachers starting at his waist. Her hips were even with where his arm rested on the railing, and she curbed the desire to lean there, against his arm, his hand.

"Sorry to keep you waiting," he said, his shoulders raised apologetically.

"Not a problem. This is more important," she said.

"Their bus is late for their pickup, so I thought I'd keep them company," he said. As if it had been summoned, the bus appeared in the parking lot behind them and the kids started to put their clubs down and make their way toward it, waving to Darío, calling out thank yous.

"It will only take me a few minutes to clean up," he said. "I'm sorry to make you wait. You look so…fresh…so lovely. I didn't wish for you to be out in this heat."

She shrugged her fresh and lovely shoulders, basking in his words. "It's okay, really. It's more important that these kids get your time. Your attention. They probably don't get that a lot."

He nodded his head, but seemed to be far away in thought.

"The First Tee is a great program for these kids," she said.

He nodded again, waving goodbye to the kids as they were herded away. He looked back at Katie, his eyes full of some emotion she couldn't quite read. Torment? Regret?

"These kids are me, Katie."

—❧—

The dinner was a blur to Darío. He couldn't taste the food. He drank very little except water. The speakers seemed to drone on and on.

All he seemed to see was Katie in that dress.

When he'd seen her in the bleachers he was once again struck by her beauty. He should be used to it by now, but he wasn't. And that dress. It was made of some type of material that floated, that shimmered. The part closest to her body—and it was very close to her body, skimming it deliciously—was light blue. There was a sheer, willowy layer; over that was a floral print, with creams, blues and yellows.

The dress was long, flaring after the waist into a billowy cloud, covering her long legs. Only her shapely ankles were exposed, leading to narrow, long feet. She wore sandals with more heel than Darío had seen on her before.

She had her hair up, her graceful neck exposed to him.

She wore ponytails quite frequently on the course, but this was different. Her golden hair was twisted in the back and held with some kind of thing that glittered when she turned her head. Small earrings dangled just below her luscious earlobes.

He'd never noticed her earlobes before. They were full and perfectly proportioned. Just right for nibbling.

Bah! He was not going to make it through dinner at this rate.

He tried to take his mind off of Katie, off of the night to come. The fact that when they returned to their hotel after this dinner—unlike their dinners every other night—they'd be returning to one room.

One bed.

He noticed she seemed restless too. Unfocused.

That was good.

He caught her staring at his hands as he cut his meat.

That was very good.

Finally, the evening wrapped up. Normally Darío would have stayed longer, talked to the club members, but after a quick conversation with the tournament director, Darío was able to make a semi-graceful exit. Last year's tournament winner was there, as well as a few other players. They would be enough for the group of clubmembers to talk with.

The drive back to the motel was like any other night, and yet it wasn't. Their conversation was like every other week. Katie asked about what players he thought would do well on this particular course. How he felt about his chances this week.

Her questions sounded half-hearted at best. His answers were barely one word.

When they entered the room, they both looked around as if it had gotten smaller while they'd been away.

Katie walked a few steps into the room. He closed the door and leaned up against it, content to watch her move.

She turned around. The only light in the room was the lamp on the desk at the far end of the room that Katie must have left on when she'd left. It lit her from the back, showing him the outline of her body, her hips, her legs.

He looked to her face. That striking, stunning face. Which right now looked apprehensive. He watched as she looked at the carpet, not meeting his eyes. She chewed on her lower lip.

Oh God, she'd changed her mind.

He'd have to do the right thing, of course. Offer to leave the room. Stay somewhere else. Give the room to her. It was the last thing in the world he wanted, but if she wasn't sure, he wouldn't press her.

If theirs was to be a short-term relationship he'd cajole, seduce, plead…whatever it took to get her into bed. But no, he'd be dealing with Katie—in some form—for the rest of his life; he had to be sure that she trusted him. That she wasn't leery of him in any way.

His child's future depended on it.

Dios mio, how he wanted her.

He made no move toward her, still leaning against the closed door. "Katie," he began. He dragged a hand through his hair, hoping the frustration wasn't obvious in his voice. She looked up at him, her eyes questioning. "If you rather I leave," he said, then stopped. Her eyes grew huge, the blue exactly matching the blue of one of the flowers on her dress. The one near her collarbone.

Her head began to shake. "No…no," she said and then she stepped toward him. Her heel caught in the hem of her dress and she fell into Darío, his arms barely able to catch her. He steadied her.

She let out a small groan. "Oh God, I can't do this," she said softly to herself, but Darío heard.

He dropped his hands from her. "It is fine. Really if you can't do this—"

She cut him off. "I want to do *this*." She waggled her hands between them, showing a form of togetherness. Darío pretended not to notice when she inadvertently hit him.

"God, how I want to. It's making the first move that I can't seem to do. Not without causing bodily damage, anyway."

"Making the first move?"

She nodded, her gaze still looking anywhere but him. "I've wanted to for weeks, but I just…I just… don't know how. That time in Texas was not the real me…I…" She finally looked at him, her eyes full of chagrin, her shoulders gave a tiny shrug. "I've never had to before."

He laughed. God, what an idiot he'd been giving her the space he thought she desired. He reached out and—gently, lest some body part of hers came into painful contact with his— pulled her to him.

"You'll never have to again," he whispered to her.

—❧—

He felt so good. Warm, strong. She knew she'd wanted to be with him again. Had known that since she'd left his bed in Texas. But she hadn't realized the physical ache to be with him was so strong until she was back in his arms again.

She slid his linen sportscoat from his shoulders, reveling in the curve of his shoulder, the strength of his arms. She tossed the coat aside and started working on the buttons of his shirt. She heard him gasp as her fingers brushed bare skin. Saw his stomach contract. Good, he was nervous too.

She shouldn't be nervous, she told herself. They'd done this before. And even if it hadn't been graceful, it had been exactly what she'd needed.

She'd needed an escape then. Now she needed—what? To cement a foundation with Darío? To see if they had what it took to sustain a relationship, at least in bed?

No. Too much pressure to put on this. She'd just enjoy it, and worry about the rest tomorrow.

She was certainly enjoying seeing his bare chest, his dark hair swirling across the golden brown of his skin. She pressed her nose to his neck and breathed in his scent. He'd showered after the clinic, but she could still smell grass, earth, the outdoors on him. He wore cologne, but it was slight, she couldn't make it out. Mixed all together it was heavenly.

And very arousing.

She nuzzled into him, trying to get closer. Get to the heart of him. Find a piece of his soul. Or at the very least, get his pants off.

She slipped the unbuttoned shirt off of him and reached for his belt.

He stilled her hands with his. "*Gata*, slow down. Please. Let me hold you. Let me feel you." His voice was raspy, husky.

She started to twine her arms around his neck, wanting that too. Wanting to be held. She realized how badly she wanted to be held by Darío.

But he took her hands and instead turned her around, pulling her behind, her back up against him, wrapping his strong arms around her waist. She moved a little too quickly, forcing him back. She heard his head crack against the door.

"I'm sorry—"

"Shhh," he whispered into her neck. His tongue traced a line up her neck to her ear. She let her head fall back to his shoulder as he nibbled on her earlobe. He then started kissing her neck. Some small, tiny kisses, some long, wet, pulling.

She bowed her head forward and his mouth continued along the nape of her neck. She'd have to wear her hair up more often. She opened her eyes and saw his arms encircling her, her hands lightly resting on them. She ran her hands along his arms, feeling them tense beneath her touch. Where muscle met bone, where wrist met hand, where fingers met palm.

Her breath hitched and she felt him chuckle into her neck.

"That's right, you're hot for my arms, eh?"

He took his hands from her and held them in front of them both, making an imaginary golf stance, setting up to an imaginary ball. "I wouldn't say I'm *hot* for them, I think..." Her response died in her throat as she looked down. Oh yes, she was hot for his arms. And completely turned on by what was not even her favorite body part on a man.

Until now.

She traced her hands down his arms, her stance taking the same as his, her hands making a grip on his hands as if they were a nine iron. She did a pretend waggle, her bottom grinding into him. She felt the air rush out of him, but offered no apologies. She wasn't sorry for that one.

"My girl, she likes to play games, eh?" he said, laughing.

He spun her to the side, then effortlessly swung her up in her arms and walked to the bed. He tumbled her down unto the middle of the huge bed. Katie pretended to be tossed around much more than she was, hands flopping about, losing her balance. Then she saw the look of horror cross Darío's tender face.

"The baby. *Dios Mio*, Katie I did not even think. I could have hurt...did I hurt you? Are you..."

She held her hand up for him to stop. She knelt up on the bed, her skirt tangling around her legs, her sandals hanging on by a strap. "I'm fine, Darío. The baby's fine. I was just kidding around." She slid the sandals off her feet, untangled her skirt and, figuring what the heck, pulled the dress all the way up and over her head.

She was rewarded by the sharp intake of breath by Darío. He mumbled something in Spanish that made Katie desperately wish she knew more of the language.

The rest of their clothes were off in record time, as was the bedspread. The feel of the cool sheets on Katie's back was almost as delicious of the feel of Darío's heat on her front.

They stroked each other, both trying to remember each other's bodies, but it had been a long time. They discovered each other anew.

How he grunted when she touched him there. How she shivered when he licked her here. Soon, they needed more, and by tacit agreement, and with Katie only bumping Darío in the head with her elbow once, he thrust himself inside her.

They both exhaled in slow moans, the fit was so excruciatingly perfect. Katie looked up at Darío to see his warm eyes on her. He smiled, that small, lopsided smile and Katie realized she hadn't even kissed him yet. Not on the mouth, anyway.

It was as if he thought the same thing, his eyes gliding down her face and resting on her lips. Knowing exactly what she was doing, she ran her tongue along her mouth, grabbing her lower lip with her teeth. Before she let go, his mouth was there, taking up the pressure, pulling at her lip, running his tongue along the outline of her mouth, making an exaggerated dip at the bow of her upper lip.

He whispered but Katie couldn't tell if it was in English or Spanish because his mouth was already back on hers.

The kiss was so heady Katie almost forgot that Darío was buried deep inside her. Almost.

Then he began to move and it was sensory overload. She tried to pull her mouth from his, to take in a badly needed breath, but instead of an inhale, she exhaled loudly as she came apart, her climax hitting her hard and fast.

Darío said something Katie didn't even try to hear, and his rhythm picked up speed. She was spiraling down when he put his hand between them and stroked her, taking her back up, taking her to him.

They exploded together. He nipped at her neck, she clawed at his back. Hips raised, arms clenched. Their bodies ground together, getting everything. Taking everything.

It wasn't beautiful lovemaking. It wasn't graceful.

It was exactly what they both needed.

Seventeen

—᚛᚜—

The longer you play, the better chance
the better player has of winning.
                    ~ Jack Nicklaus, professional golfer

"KATIE, LUV, C'MERE. There's someone I want you to meet."

Katie went over to Binky, sitting at the edge of the cad-dyshack. It wasn't a shack, of course—nothing was a shack at the courses the Tour played. It was a lovely, small building where the caddies went to eat, rest, play cards, do whatever, until their players met them for practice or tee times.

But all the caddies, and players, called such buildings caddyshacks. Caddies weren't allowed in the clubhouses, a rule Katie found abhorrent when she'd found out, but Binky didn't seem to mind. He'd said he'd rather hang out with the caddies than the hoity-toity in the clubhouse anyway. He didn't clarify that Darío was nowhere near hoity-toity, they both knew that.

Katie made her way to the gate of the enclosed area. There was an overhang area outside where a few of the caddies were smoking, but most of the caddies were in the shack where it was air conditioned, gathered around a television. They were all waiting to hear if the rain delay they were in the middle of was going to be upgraded to an actual postponement.

Darío was in the lockerroom. He had offered to come sit in

the clubhouse with Katie, but she didn't want him to break his concentration in case they got the call to get back on the course. Besides, it had slowed to a drizzle, so Katie made her way outside just to walk around, get some fresh air. She'd made her way to the caddyshack to see what Binky was up to.

Darío had introduced her to some of the player's wives, but most of them were busy with children or their husbands or whatever and didn't seem very interested in Katie. They probably saw her as just another groupie who was staying around longer than most. That was fine. She really had never made friends easily. Had never really had to because of having Lizzie and Alison.

It was a skill she hadn't acquired. It had never bothered her until now.

Binky moved aside and Katie saw that he meant to introduce her to a woman. A woman who Katie'd watched a lot in the past four weeks. A woman she'd come to admire from afar. If more for her shear endurance than anything else.

"Katie Maki, this is Franny Kowalski. Franny, Katie."

Katie shook Franny's strong hand. It was firm and her fingers were calloused. Probably from tossing endless golf balls to Rick Donaldson during the hours and hours they spent on the range.

"Nice to meet you, Franny. I've watched you on the range," Katie said.

Franny seemed taken aback at that, as if the thought that she'd stick out—a woman with incredibly long, curly, blond hair amongst a range filled with men—had never occurred to her.

Before Franny could respond, a caddy popped his head out the door and loudly declared, "Postponed. First round finishes up at six tomorrow." There were groans all around from the caddies whose players had yet to finish, meaning they'd be back at sunrise tomorrow and have to play the rest of the first round as well as the second.

Instantly, the caddies' cell phones and two-ways started going off. Their players calling from the clubhouse to tell them what time they'd tee off and what time they wanted their caddy on the range with their clubs.

Franny looked apologetically at Katie as she took her ringing cell phone from her belt. She turned away from them, taking the call. Katie watched her head bob up and down in agreement with whatever the caller was saying.

Just as Franny was signing off, Katie felt a warm hand on her neck. The touch was gentle, but firm. And familiar, she'd felt it plenty in the last few days.

Darío came along side of her, facing Binky and nodded to him. "You heard?"

Binky nodded. "Yep. You want your clubs in the car or should I store them here?"

Darío thought on that for a moment. Sometimes he took his clubs with them back to the hotel and Katie had imagined him practicing his putting across the hotel floor as she sat in her room alone.

But not anymore. Now they shared a room, a bed. They were lovers. The last three days since they'd arrived in Akron had more than proven that. They'd left the room only when Darío needed to be at the course and to eat. And as if they'd needed actually physical proof of them becoming lovers, much to her dismay, Darío even had a few little bruises and scratches that he laughed away.

Katie knew what Darío's answer would be before he spoke. "Leave them here. I won't use them tonight."

Katie ducked her head. Darío give a soft squeeze to her neck and watched as Binky's eyes passed between the two of them, figuring out the lay of the land.

"Ah, I see. 'Bout time, I'd say."

Katie met Darío's knowing eyes and flushed. She thought she heard Darío mumble "*Sí*," but she wasn't sure.

"So, you'll be wanting to skip our Thursday dinner then, Guv?"

Katie spoke up. "Don't skip that on my account. Don't change your routine now, you're playing so well."

Darío looked torn and Katie took secret pleasure in that, but she really didn't want to mess with his and Binky's rituals.

"Then you should come with us," he said to her. Franny had rejoined their group by then, cell phone back on her belt loop. "And you, Franny, please join us as well."

Franny looked at the three of them, the invitation obviously a surprise. But the thought of another woman at dinner while Darío and Binky talked course management was appealing to Katie. "Yes, please join us," Katie added.

"Sure, that'd be great. Rick wanted to practice another couple of hours but the officials won't let anybody on the range with the high chance of lightning." As if on cue, a thunderclap roared in the distance.

"And that stopped Prick?" Binky asked, using Rick Donaldson's nickname on tour.

Franny shrugged. "He tried to argue them out of it, but no go. So, I'm free as a bird till five tomorrow morning."

—⁂—

They had dinner at a steakhouse. One of those chain places that all ended up tasting the same to Darío. He couldn't wait for a break in his schedule so he could sleep without hearing people walking the hallways of the hotels. To eat something not ordered off a menu.

He and Binky managed to wrap up their course talk quickly and he turned to the women just in time to hear Katie say to Franny, "You know, there's a cameraman—camera*person*, I guess—for CBS that looks just like you. I've seen her on the course."

"That's my sister, Zooey."

"Franny and Zooey?" Katie said, raising her eyebrow. Darío had done the same thing when he'd met the twosome years ago.

Franny shrugged. "What can I say? My mom is a literature prof. A huge Salinger fan."

"Well it could be worse. You could have been named after a Stephen King character."

Franny chuckled. "Katie, where are you from originally?

Your accent sounds so familiar."

Katie laughed, her smile lighting up her face. "I didn't realize I had an accent. Guess you never really lose your Yooper drawl."

Franny nodded her head. "A Yooper! I thought so."

Katie looked surprised. "You've heard of Yoopers?"

"You betcha," Franny said. "I'm a Cheesehead."

"You are?" Katie said, like she'd found a long-lost friend. "What part of Wisconsin?"

"LaCrosse."

"Oh, that's a ways away from da Yoop. You're practically in Minnesota."

Franny nodded. "Yeah, but we spent our summers in the U.P. at my grandmother's. Just outside of Baraga."

"We were practically neighbors. I'm from Hancock," Katie added with great enthusiasm.

Darío listened with half an ear as the two women compared places in the Copper Country, families they might both know, places to eat. She spoke with such longing in her voice that Darío wondered for the first time if she regretted her decision to come with him.

She seemed happy. She appeared to love traveling. She found out things about the places they went that Darío, who had been to these same stops for many years, had never known. She'd dragged him to an aquarium in Chicago and a Tigers game in Detroit when he played in Flint. It was good for him to be taken away from the everyday grind of golf course, restaurant, and hotel.

He wondered if they'd still be taking these little excursions now that they had found the ultimate diversion.

"So, how did a Yooper hook up with a Spanish pro golfer?" he heard Franny ask. He turned his full attention back to the women, waiting to hear Katie's answer. They hadn't told anyone their story yet. Hadn't had to. They'd kept mainly to themselves. He'd introduced her to many people at the courses, in the club-houses, but they must have just assumed that...Darío didn't know what they'd assumed.

"I...I..." Katie looked to Darío for help, obviously not used to Franny's bluntness. Darío had known the caddy for years; she could be quite jolting if you didn't know her.

"Katie and I met on a Tour stop and have been together ever since." He took a deep breath, then added, "We're going to have a baby."

He couldn't believe he'd said it. Out loud. To someone other than Binky or Katie.

It felt good.

He looked to Katie for her reaction. Braced himself for her shock or anger at his blurting out something so personal to someone she'd just met.

Instead he saw a tenderness in her huge blue eyes that stopped him. She reached over for his hand, took it and squeezed. She turned her head back to Franny and nodded, her blond hair, still in its ponytail from the course, bobbing in agreement.

Franny seemed stunned. Looked at Katie, Darío, then to Binky—as if he'd had something to do with it. Binky, to Darío's amusement, sat back and nodded his head as he folded his arms across his chest, almost like he was the proud mastermind of the blessed event.

"Wow! A baby. That's so...so..." Franny stumbled.

"Wonderful," Katie whispered.

Franny picked up her cue. "Of course, wonderful. That's fantastic. When are you due?"

"Early January."

"A New Year's baby."

"Maybe."

"You look great, not even showing."

"No. Not yet," Katie said. Darío swore he heard disappointment in her voice. Her hand went to her stomach. He could now attest that her stomach had just the slightest of curves to it. But one you could only see when she was naked.

"How are you feeling?"

Katie's face lit up even more, the glow around her almost

giving off sparks. "Great. Super. Walking the courses has been great, all the fresh air. My feet get a little puffy on the flights, but it's been really great."

"No morning sickness at all?" Franny asked.

Darío was waiting for the answer to this as well. Not sharing a room until three days ago, he hadn't been a part of Katie's morning rituals. She could have been puking her guts out every morning and Darío wouldn't have known. And he didn't think she'd complain about it either. Every part of this pregnancy was a miracle to her.

Katie shook her head, then dipped her head in concession. "Well, the only thing is the smell of freshly squeezed toothpaste nearly makes me lose it. Every morning I put it on my toothbrush then run out of the bathroom for a few minutes for the smell to go away or I gag."

Franny nodded her head in understanding. "One of my friends had to change her deodorant while she was pregnant. She'd been wearing the same brand her entire adult life and then as soon as she was pregnant the stuff made her retch."

Franny sat back, crossed her hands across her chest, matching Binky who had not moved, and pointedly looked at Darío as she asked, "So. What are your guys' plans?" She had used the plural, but Darío felt the question was directed to him. Franny's keen eyes were certainly pinning him down. Anyone else he would have told to piss off, but Franny…well, Franny was not a woman you told to mind her own business.

"I've asked Katie—"

"We're working that out," Katie interrupted him.

He felt disappointment creeping down his back and then it was replaced by Katie's soft hand, rubbing up and down his spine, then resting on his arm. "There are lots of logistics to figure out. Where we'll live after the baby. How often the baby and I will travel with Darío. I have a house in the U.P., he has one in Spain. All that stuff needs to be worked out."

Franny nodded, seemingly accepting Katie's answer.

Darío was not sure he did. He was thrilled that Katie spoke of their future together with no qualms, but she didn't mention marriage; had in fact cut him off knowing full well he was going to mention it.

But he had agreed not to push her on it. On anything, really. And she'd willingly told Franny that they'd be together as a family, they were just working out the details. Logistics, she called them.

It felt to Darío that more than geographical details needed to be settled between them, but he finished his dinner in silence, happy, and looking forward to being alone with Katie again.

—⁓—

Akron went well. On the course, anyway. Off the course, Akron went very, very well.

Darío didn't come near his course record, but had a respectable showing placing in the top ten again. He had all but locked up being eligible for the Tour Championship, the last tournament of the season, played in November. Only the top thirty players from the money list got in.

They moved on to Connecticut. He skipped his practice round on Tuesday and they spent the entire day in bed.

Their next stop would be Boston and then Darío wouldn't play in the US again until the Tour Championship, electing to skip the lesser tournaments that filled the schedule from September to November. That would be the end of the trial period that they'd discussed when they'd come to their agreement of Katie traveling with Darío.

Katie wasn't sure what would happen after Boston. Would they head to the U.P.? Finally tell her parents about the baby? Would Darío want to head back to Spain? She knew from Binky that was what he usually did.

She wasn't sure what to suggest. She only knew she didn't want to be away from him now that they were sharing a bed.

More than a bed. Now that they were sharing the beginning of a life together.

In Connecticut, Darío had his usual Thursday night dinner with Binky. Katie elected to stay at the hotel and get some work done on her newest article. Darío was going to bring her back a salad from wherever he and Binky ended up for dinner. Maybe he'd forget the milk.

Her latest article was a feature on one of the players whose child was autistic. The nomadic life of a family on the road posed some unique challenges for the player, his wife and their children. It was a heartbreaking piece on the struggle these parents felt about being on the road or not being together. The player was one who annually struggled to keep his Tour card.

Their story tugged at Katie and she assumed it would also tug at readers' hearts.

She put the finishing touches on the piece and jotted herself a couple of notes on things she wanted to double check with the player's wife as well as the call she wanted to make to an autism center.

She applauded her timing as Darío walked in the hotel room just as she put her laptop away and sat down on the small couch in the living area of the room.

"How was dinner? Did you guys figure out the game plan for tomorrow?" she asked. Though Darío's round today of five under par wouldn't need much tinkering with.

He nodded. "*Sí.* I won't do too much differently, but will go with my three wood instead of driver on the fifth hole."

Katie nodded, agreeing with his and Binky's decision.

Darío brought Katie back the salad she'd requested as well as the dreaded milk she'd force herself to drink. He leaned over and gave her a quick kiss. It didn't satisfy either of them and he zeroed in for a longer, hungrier taste.

Finally he broke away, much to her disappointment and, pointing to the food, said, "Eat."

She noticed he also had a small package, which he tossed to her as he set out her food on the coffee table in front of her. The bag landed softly on her lap and she looked up at Darío questioningly.

"For you," he said. "Well, actually, for the both of us, but you can have the first look." He seemed embarrassed and Katie gave him a small smile, which he returned with a shrug and an "it's nothing" brush of his hand.

Curious, she opened the package to find a baby-name book. Touched by his thoughtfulness, she decided not to mention that she already had this same version at home as well as three other baby name books all ragged-eared from use.

He didn't need to know that. Besides, the names she and Ron had tossed around for years wouldn't necessarily be the names she and Darío would choose. It seemed almost tacky to her to consider naming Darío's child a name she and Ron had decided on. Somehow, she didn't think Darío would go for Ron Jr.

Instead, she thanked him. She patted the seat beside her on the couch and started to prepare her dinner. "Tell me what names you like while I eat," she said.

He sat beside her, took her hair and brought it to the back of her neck and stroked it down her back. She loved it when he did that. It felt both comforting and sexy.

"I don't really have any idea about names," he said.

"You've never thought about what you'd like to name a child?" she asked as she poured dressing on her salad and took the plastic knife and fork out of their cellophane wrap. She'd been thinking about it since she was fourteen.

He shook his head no.

"Well, we could do the traditional route," she said, "something Biblical or a family name."

He seemed to think that over. "We could do that. Is there a family name that you would like?" he asked.

She chuckled. "I come from a Finnish family, remember? There aren't too many Finnish first names that would go well with Luna. I'd never saddle a son with Urho Luna."

He smiled at the thought and she warmed at the sight of his lips turned up in that sly way. "Perhaps not," he conceded.

"What about you? Any family names you want to continue down the line." The moment she saw his smile fade to a grim line she regretted her words. He was probably thinking about his father – or lack of one. Quickly trying to bring back the lighter moment, she said, "Or, we could go the celebrity route. You are, after all a celebrity." At his raised brows she added, "At least in the golfing world."

"What, exactly, is the celebrity way of naming a child?"

"Sometimes an inanimate object, like Apple," she said. She laughed at his horrified look. "Or named after the place where the child was conceived. Just look at David Beckham and Posh Spice's Brooklyn." Their minds went back to Texas. Katie could see Darío's thoughts were the same as hers. "Irving Luna," they said together, laughing.

He nudged the milk toward her. "Drink," he said, still laughing. He got up and headed toward the bathroom.

She took a sip of milk. "So, Irving for a boy," she teased. "We haven't discussed girls' names."

He turned toward her, his hand on the doorknob. "Well, that does not need to be discussed." At her questioning look, he smiled and said, "She has been *Peaches* to me from the very first."

Eighteen

One minute you're bleeding.
The next minute you're hemorrhaging.
The next minute you're painting the Mona Lisa.
- Mac O'Grady, golfer, on a typical round of golf.

The next week was a whirlwind of days on the courses and nights in bed with Darío. She still was klutzy with Darío in bed, but she got better. And they practiced. A lot.

Their bodies relaxed, legs intertwined, arms around each other. Katie's head on Darío's chest. Hotel sounds of doors slamming and the occasional room service cart wheeling down the hallway were the only things they heard.

"Tell me about your father," Katie said. She felt Darío's chest stiffen under her hand. "Or what you remember about your father." His whole body tensed. She gently rubbed her hand across his chest, trying to infuse some of her warmth into him. "Please," she whispered. She heard his sigh, felt his soft breath float across her hair.

"There's not much to tell. I remember nothing because he was never a part of our lives," Darío said. Katie heard the leashed control in his voice. She hadn't heard that tone since the night she'd gone to Memphis and asked Darío to give up all rights to his child.

Because of their child, she forged on. "Never? He didn't leave you and your mother when you were young? Weren't there any pictures of him around?"

His arm tightened around her, then loosened, his hand soothing her skin. "You don't understand. It wasn't a case of my parents being together and then my father leaving. They were never together. My mother…" He sighed again, heavier, making Katie's hair flutter across her nose. Darío brushed it back behind her ear.

"When I was older, when I wanted to find out who my father was…I asked the women where my mother worked. They said they'd never seen her as much as speak to any men in the club, let alone spend enough time with one to become pregnant."

"Maybe they were protecting her?"

Darío snorted. "Not those old bitches. They hated my mother. They would have loved to tell me who she was whore to."

Katie gasped. "Is that what you think? That your mother is a whore?" She couldn't fathom the thought. Her own mother seemed so…asexual to Katie, as any mother should.

Darío's legs shifted under her knee. "No, no of course not. That is what they thought. My mother is a saint. She raised me alone. She did the best she could. When she saw I had a talent for golf, she moved heaven and earth to find a way for me to play. She loved me and fed me, and in her eyes, I was no bastard.

"But, when I was in my teens, I didn't know what to think. No one appreciates their parents as teenagers."

Katie thought of the fights she and her mother had when she was a teen. The same fights Katie's sisters-in-law were having with their teens now. "Yes, of course. What about your mother's family? Were they any help to her while you were growing up?"

She felt his chin against her as he shook his head. "No. It wasn't the dark ages, but it was still a very conservative, small resort area then. My grandparents told my mother she could go away to have the child, give it up for adoption and then come home. My grandparents are strict Catholics. Of course, abortion was out of the question."

"Thank goodness," Katie said. She couldn't imagine a life without Darío in it. The magnitude of that thought hit her full force. She pushed it away. Later. She'd deal with those thoughts later. Darío was opening up to her and she didn't want to miss a word of it.

"Yes, though there were times, very few, but times when I thought another choice would have been the better one. And I let my poor mother know it, too."

Katie tried to ease his obvious guilt. "Hey, what kid doesn't shout 'I wish I'd never been born' a couple of times at their parents?"

"Really? All children do that?"

"Of course. And ours will too. No matter how much love and security you give a child, they have to exert their independence at some point. They don't know how, and that's when they push you away. If you've done your job right, though, they always come back to you."

Darío didn't say anything, deep in thought, deep in remembering. "You're close with your mother now, right?" Katie asked.

"*Sí*, very close."

She brought him back to his story. "So, when she wouldn't give you up for adoption, what happened?"

Darío placed his hand over his eyes, as if trying to hide from the memories of a time he was too young to possibly remember. "She was working as a cook at the country club. San Barria is a resort town. Businessmen come to the area for conferences and to golf on our courses. She continued on at the country club, even though she took much abuse from her co-workers. The wife of the greenskeeper kept me during the days until I was old enough to go to school.

"Mamá would come home every evening smelling of wonderful herbs and saffron. Sergio, the greenskeeper, would come home at the same time. He smelled of grass and the outdoors." Darío chuckled. "To me they both smelled like heaven."

"So that's how you learned to golf? You grew up at the course?"

"*Sí*. Both Sergio and his wife, and my mother and I had small cottages that were just a pathway away from the course. In the evenings, Sergio would take me with him while he walked the course one more time. When I was old enough, he brought me some old clubs that had been discarded by a member. Sergio cut them down for my size."

Katie took Darío's hand from his eyes, kissed the calloused knuckles, the skin smoother around the fingers where he'd worn tape during his round. "And the rest is history."

She sensed, more than saw, his smile. "Not quite. But it became obvious when I was a teen that I had a natural ability for the game."

"I'll say," Katie teased. "Three majors to prove it."

He kissed the top of her head, and she burrowed in deeper to his warmth. "Sergio found ways to get me into tournaments. The amateur system in Europe is a very good building block. I had offers to attend college here in the States, and many of my peers were going. But I wanted to turn pro. Needed to turn pro."

"For the money. For your mother," Katie said quietly.

"*Sí*," came the just as quiet answer.

She didn't want to cause him any pain, and she thought that her next question might, but, in for a penny…she figured. She also had selfish motives. Whoever Darío's father was, he was also the biological grandfather to her child. Though the man had certainly gave up every right he had to claim Darío as his son, not to mention his grandchild, there were genetic health issues to wonder about.

"In all this time, your mother never told you who your father was? You never asked?"

"I asked all the time when I was younger. When I was very little she told me, 'Your father is someone who loves you very much but cannot be with you.' When I was old enough to question her further on that, she said he lived very far away. When I would not be put off with that she would become very upset, asking if she wasn't a good mother, why couldn't I be happy with just her, things like that. After a while, I learned not to ask."

"The poor woman, it must have been so hard for her."

"As an adult I saw that, and tried to make up for the hardships she endured for me. I tried to make up for the child who brought her pain when pestering her about his father."

"But that's a natural reaction, for a child to ask those questions. Did you ever guess who your father might be? What about this Sergio?"

Darío laughed. "Sergio was an old man then who only had eyes for his wife. He's a very old man now, who still only has eyes for his wife." He was quiet, thoughtful. "Of course I guessed. I measured my looks against every man who worked at the resort. Every man in church on Sundays. I never saw anyone look at me or my mother with any kind of deep emotion. That was when I vowed things would be different with me. No child of mine would ever spend their days looking at the men around him, looking to see if he has someone's nose or eyes. Even if it meant never having children at all."

"You never wanted children?" She was surprised. Apart from the odd circumstances, Darío seemed to be embracing the idea of fatherhood fairly easily. And she'd noticed his naturalness with the children of friends on the Tour.

"*Sí*, I wanted them. I just thought I'd have a few more things...settled before I had them."

"What kind of things?" The man was a stand-out in his career, had wealth for his, his children's, and his children's children's lifetimes. What more needed to be...settled?

"I wanted to be invited to the capital by the president of Spain. I wanted to have my picture on the cover of Sports Illustrated again. I wanted to..." His voice trailed off.

Puzzled, Katie said, "I'm surprised. Granted we haven't known each other long, but the time we've been together has been pretty...revealing."

His hand stroked down her arm and across her breast as if to emphasize her point. "Why are you surprised? You yourself have commented on my drive."

"To compete. To win. Yes."

"To get on the cover of magazines, to be invited to the capital, to do these things you must win."

"So, the winning is only a means to the fame?" She felt his chin as he nodded. "But you're such a private man. And you're so intelligent. Wanting something as fleeting and vapid as fame surprises me."

"You think I'm shallow to want my accomplishments to be known?"

An image of Ron, skating across the ice after a goal, his helmet off to his adoring fans skittered through Katie's mind. "No, I think you're the least shallow man I know. That's why I'm so surprised."

The room was quiet. No outside noises. No inside ones either. Finally Darío spoke, his voice no more than a whisper. If Katie's ear weren't just below his mouth, she never would have heard him. "I want him to know. I want him to see."

She felt the tension running through him, though where he touched her, he was gentle. "Your father," she said, seeing into his pain, seeing into his soul.

"*Sí*, my father. I want him to see that I did not need him. That I am a success without him. That I was better raised by a woman alone and a greenskeeper than by him."

Another moment passed, Katie smoothed her hand across his chest, his arms, his belly, trying to take some of the pain onto herself. An image of Darío on the course—focused, determined to win—came to her.

"That's who you're looking for. In the galleries. You're looking for him, aren't you?"

He shuddered, his stomach hollowing beneath her hand. He rubbed his hand across his face, wiping away…what? Katie wondered. "*Sí*. I suppose I am. Of course if my father ever were in a gallery, I'd have no way of knowing. Sometimes I see someone with a likeness to me and I think 'Is that him? Has he come to watch his son win?' Pathetic, eh?"

"No, not pathetic. Sad, but not pathetic."

"I suppose that is what I really want. To have it settled before I have children. But I don't know what settled would mean in this situation. And that is not to be, so I must settle it in here, eh?" His placed his hand on his chest, above his heart.

"We could still do it. Find your father, I mean. With the internet and my connections at news agencies, it probably wouldn't be that hard. We'd just have to get his name from your mother."

She felt his body tense and then relax. "No. I could not hurt my mother that way. She has given up too much for me, I will not cause her any pain."

Katie placed her hand on his. "I wish I could say I was sorry that things won't be settled for you, Darío, but of course I'm not. I wouldn't have waited another second to have this child."

A small smile played across his mouth. "No, I'm not sorry either."

Katie smiled back, her hand left his chest, moved down his belly and curled around his penis. "Let's change the subject."

A while later, she lay in his arms, sated, exhausted. Sleep soon to come.

"Marry me, *Gata*," he whispered as he drifted off to sleep. His voice was so soft, so tender, Katie wasn't sure if he'd really said it, or if it was part of a dream she was quickly losing herself to.

She wasn't surprised to find him gone when she woke up. They had agreed that he'd go to the course early to warm up and she'd take a cab later to arrive in time for his ten-thirty tee off. Looking at the clock and seeing it was already nine thirty, she jumped from bed and made her way to the bathroom. He must have gotten dressed in the dark, she thought, so as not to wake her.

Just as she was thinking how thoughtful that was, she looked down at the sink and stopped. Setting on the edge of the sink was her toothbrush, wetted and with a dollop of toothpaste on it. He had remembered that she'd mentioned to Franny that the smell of fresh toothpaste made her queasy, so he had put it on her brush for her. She was touched by his gesture. As she brushed her teeth for the first time in weeks without gagging, silent tears slid down her cheeks.

Must be the hormones. Something so small, so inconsequential wouldn't normally have her crying. It was just a nice thing to do, that's all. Nothing to get all worked up about. It was toothpaste on a toothbrush, for Pete's sake, not some grand gesture.

Grand gestures were for the young. The young had the innocence to carry off such drama without seeming flamboyant.

Ron had once made a grand gesture.

He had swept into the newsroom of *The Lansing State Journal* where Katie was interning her senior year, wearing his only suit, and brandishing a dozen roses.

As he passed the sports desks, he winked at Chris, the reporter who covered MSU hockey, then made his way to Katie, relegated to the back of the room with the features staff.

A hush fell over the newsroom—no small feat in the chaotic atmosphere—and all eyes followed Ron's towering physique as he made his way to Katie's desk. Instinctively, she knew why he'd come. Katie was both touched and horrified. Touched that Ron had gone to the effort of coming here for her. Horrified that he would take something so personal, so singular, like their future together, and put it on display.

She'd only been an intern at *The Journal* a few months and hadn't made any close friends. These were not the people she wanted to share the most special moment of her young life with. If he was going to propose in front of people—and that alone was a second choice to Katie behind being alone with Ron—she would want it to be Alison and Lizzie, or even Ron's close friends, or even their parents. Certainly not this group of people that she barely knew, and who were none too friendly to her to begin with.

No fault of theirs, the world of daily newspapers was just too hectic to make friends with an intern who'd be gone in a few short months. You came in, got your assignments, wrote your stuff, and hoped to heck it'd make it into print. She knew the drill.

When Ron reached her and dropped to one knee, she heard the gasps and oohs from the surrounding females. She wasn't surprised that Ron was proposing, they had talked about getting married after graduation, but she was surprised he was doing it now, in the middle of their senior year, and doing it here, in the middle of *The Journal's* newsroom.

"Katie Maki, you are the most beautiful woman I have ever seen and I worship the ground you walk on. Make me the happiest man on earth and say you'll be my wife," he said. His eyes never left hers, but his voice was loud enough to carry, and the oohs and aahs continued.

Dry eyed, but very pleased, she accepted his proposal and the newsroom burst into applause as he slipped the miniscule diamond ring on her finger. Seeing the looks of sentiment on the faces of hardened reporters who covered murder and corruption on a daily basis moved Katie almost as much as Ron's proposal did. Several flashbulbs went off—the photographers were always slinking around the newsroom, and always had a camera strapped around their necks.

They celebrated with their friends that night, and later, alone.

In the next day's *Journal,* a story of Ron's proposal ran with the heading, "Hobey Baker Hopeful Scores Big". A picture of Ron on his knees in front of Katie took up three columns.

Katie tried not to think about the timing of Ron's proposal with the ongoing hockey season and the fact that he was a candidate to win the Hobey Baker Award, college hockey's equivalent to the Heisman.

She'd thought it odd that Chris, who covered MSU hockey, was in the office that day. If he came in at all, it was in the evening, wrapping up the sports page. Most of the time, he didn't come in at all, posting his story from his laptop at a game or at home.

Katie wouldn't have known him from interning, but she had seen him covering hockey for the past four years, had watched him interview Ron countless times while she waited.

She ignored her doubts of Ron's sincerity. Maybe he had used the proposal to get a little press. Who cared? What mattered was he loved her and wanted to spend the rest of their lives together.

In the end, the Spartans got knocked out in the first round of playoffs, a player from Maine won the Hobey, and Ron and Katie planned a big September wedding.

Yes, grand gestures were for the young, the naive. It was the small things that mattered, the building blocks of a future. It was carrying in groceries from the car. It was letting you off at the door when it was raining. It was rubbing your feet when they were sore.

It was putting toothpaste on a toothbrush.

Brushing her teeth in a hotel bathroom, not even sure what city she was in, tears streaming down her cheeks, Katie decided to marry Darío Luna.

—⁓—

Darío couldn't believe it when the next night Katie agreed to marry him.

He made the decision right then and there not to question the paternity of this child again. It would do no good. And his gut told him the child was his. Had told him that from the start. And Darío was a man who listened to his gut.

Like Binky always said after a difficult selection of which club to use, "Don't look back, Guv, don't look back."

He played the Boston tournament in a fog, barely making the cut. In a way, he almost wished he'd missed it, then he and Katie could begin with their plans that much sooner.

They'd decided that she'd go home for the weekend without Darío while he stayed in Boston. She'd tell her parents about the baby and start tying up her loose ends in Hancock. After she was done with that, they'd fly to Spain so Katie could meet his mother and they could start making wedding arrangements.

Darío would join her in Hancock on Monday. He'd wanted her to put off telling her parents until he was there, he wanted to properly ask her father for his daughter's hand in marriage, but Katie wanted it this way.

He didn't push it. He also didn't say anything when she mentioned she wanted to get married in Spain, not in the Copper Country. He had a feeling it had something to do with her first marriage, with Ron still living in Hancock, but he kept silent. He tried to push the niggling doubts away, but they stayed with him.

Nineteen

—◊—

It's a marriage. If I had to choose between my wife
and my putter—well, I'd miss her.
                        ~ *Gary Player, professional golfer*

"YOU'RE SURE ABOUT THIS, KitKat? It's not the fifties, you
know, you don't *have* to marry the father of your child," Alison
said.

They were in the Commodore, having pizza and drinks. Alison was having drinks. Katie and the now immense Lizzie were having water.

"I know I don't have to marry Darío. That's the point I made all along. I was fully prepared to raise this child alone."

"So a few months away, some good sex, and now you're ready to shackle yourself to this guy?"

"Al, for Pete's sake, marriage is not a shackling," Lizzie said.

"Says you."

Lizzie leaned back in the booth, her huge stomach touching the table. She rubbed her belly, a small smile playing on her very happy mouth. "Yes. Says me."

Katie thought she looked the most beautiful she'd ever seen her and told her so.

"I can't believe I'm so happy at being so heavy," Lizzie said.

"Yeah, yeah, yeah. Lizzie's deliriously happy and about ready to pop, let's get back to Katie. How'd your parents take the news?"

Katie thought back to yesterday in her mother's kitchen. Lots of tears had been shed, lots of hands had been wrung, lots of words had been said. But in the end, Katie had walked out of the house that she'd grown up in with her parents' blessing.

"After the initial shock, they came around. Of course they were ecstatic that I was finally able to conceive…"

"Just not so ecstatic about the out-of-wedlock part," Alison said.

Katie nodded. "They like Darío and everything, that's not it…"

"They're just concerned that you're marrying a man—having a child with a man—who you've only known for what? Three? Four months?"

Katie placed her hand on her stomach, feeling the tiny roundness that was discernible only to her. And Darío when she was naked. "Four and a half," she said.

"You can't blame them, Kat, they are your parents. We're concerned for you too," Lizzie said.

"I know, and I love you guys for it. Just like I love my parents. But, I'm going to do it. I'm going to marry Darío."

She saw Lizzie and Alison exchange glances and then come to some kind of silent agreement. "Well, too bad you guys are on the wagon, because we really should toast this," Alison said, sipping from her huge fishbowl drink.

Katie let out the breath she'd been holding. "Wow. I thought I'd get a lot more argument out of you guys." She looked at Alison seated next to her in the booth. "Especially you."

Alison shrugged. "You went into this knowing you'd be fine on your own. I'm assuming Darío didn't put the screws to you—no pun intended—to get you to marry him?"

Katie shook her head. "No, he kept his promise and didn't bring it up." She didn't mention him whispering "Marry me, *Gata*" to her as they fell asleep. She wasn't even sure that he was aware he'd said it, or that she'd heard it.

"Then you obviously, for whatever reason, decided you want Darío to be a part of your life," Alison said. She and Lizzie, the subject apparently decided upon, returned to the half-eaten pizza.

"So, are you nervous about meeting his parents?" Lizzie asked as they were getting ready to go.

"It's just his mother, and yes, kind of nervous. They're very close. I'm not sure how she's going to like having an American for a daughter-in-law. An American who doesn't speak any Spanish. She could be really old school and want a little senorita for her son."

"Just the two of them while he was growing up?" Alison, ever the shrink, asked.

Katie nodded.

"Hmm, that's interesting. Darío doesn't seem like a mama's boy, so you should be okay. What did she do, when he was a kid, before he turned pro?"

"He said she was a cook at the country club. Has been since he was born." She didn't feel the need to tell her friends about Darío's upbringing. It seemed…unfaithful, somehow. It was probably the first thing she'd ever kept from Lizzie and Alison. She didn't let herself think about the significance of that.

"Great. Of course you'd end up having a mother-in-law who's a fantastic cook," from Lizzie.

"I picture this old woman with black stockings rolled down to her ankles rolling a grocery cart home from the market every morning." They all laughed. Katie admitted she'd had the same vision of Darío's mother. "And a kerchief, definitely a kerchief."

"She'll probably grab you and start shouting about the *bambino* and that you're too skinny and you need to *Mangia, Mangia!*" Lizzie said.

"I think that's Italian, Lizard," Katie said, although she wasn't sure.

—⁓—

He arrived two days later after a rather poor showing in Boston. He told Katie it had been because his good-luck charm wasn't there.

She met him at the airport. The minute she saw him her face lit up and Darío realized that two days away from this woman was two too many. He, who'd traveled alone for nearly fifteen years, did not want to be alone again.

He wanted to be with Katie. Forever.

When she wrapped her arms around him and kissed him hello, her body soft and yielding, she made him believe that was what she wanted as well.

But, deep inside he knew there was a difference. Katie wanted to be with the father of her child, and that happened to be Darío. Darío saw Katie as more than the mother of his child. She was the woman he wanted to be his wife. Share every moment with. Read her thoughtful news pieces. Stare at her beautiful face. Wince from the pain she inevitably invoked when making love.

Grow old together. That there was already a child growing out of this union was just another blessing.

He was in love with her.

It snuck up on him, but being in Boston alone, without her in the bed next to him, walking the course without being able to find her in the gallery, he had finally put it into words. He was in love with Katie Maki.

The summer tourists had left the area, schools had started, the university was back in session and the leaves were just beginning to turn color. As Darío watched the sleepy little town through the car window, he thought that it would be a nice place to raise children. His children. Their children.

There was no question this time that they'd be sleeping in the same bed. But which bed? When she led him upstairs, she paused at the door to the guest bedroom. She seemed unsure of what to do. His heart went out to her.

"Katie," he said softly, reaching for her.

"It's just…it's just…" Her eyes, her beautiful blue eyes, looked tentatively down the hall toward the master bedroom.

He stepped backward into the guestroom, gently pulling her

hand. He led her to the bed. "No ghosts in here, eh?" he asked as he slid her shirt over her head.

She sat down on the bed, reached for his belt. "No. No ghosts in here. No memories in here at all."

He pushed her backward, her feet dragged up his calves, her legs opened wide for him. He stepped into the space she created. "Then let's make some."

—⚬⚬⚬—

They spent the next few days making arrangements. Darío was on the phone with his manager telling him which events he would and would not play in the new year. This season, he'd only play the two tournaments in Europe he'd already committed to—one being the Spanish Open, hardly a tournament he could skip—and the Tour Championship back in the States in November. If all went well, when they came back from Spain for it, they'd be man and wife.

Katie gave her resignation to her boss at the newspaper. Darío was not surprised when Katie reported that they'd asked her to stay on staff as a freelancer, continuing with the articles that she'd written on tour. And possibly down the road, some features on new motherhood. She was thrilled that she would be able to continue to write.

He'd gone with her to her parents' for dinner and had survived. In fact, her parents had been very welcoming to Darío and he wondered if he would be the same if faced with a man who had impregnated his daughter. A fierce protectiveness of his unborn child rose within him, daunting him, humbling him.

They met her friends at the Commodore their final night in town. Lizzie and her husband, Finn, and Alison. The five of them were at a large center table in the place and there were many toasts and blessings for all the coming events. Babies—both Lizzie and Finn's and Darío and Katie's—and marriage.

"We know you're going to do it in Spain, but we'll do something here when you get back right? A reception or something?" Lizzie said, reaching for her datebook. "I'll plan it all, you won't have to do a thing. We're looking at the second week of November, after the Tour Championship, right?"

Darío felt Katie stiffen next to him. Before she could say anything, Finn said, "Babe, that's right around your due date, you can't be putting together something like a wedding reception then."

Lizzie looked at her husband like he'd never met her before. Finn threw up his hands in surrender. "I forgot who I was talking to. Of course you can. Go for it." Finn chuckled to himself, gave a shrug to the rest of the table and took a swig of beer. Darío liked the man.

"Finn's right, Lizard. Besides, we really don't want anything here," Katie said. Darío kept silent. If that's what she wanted, he would abide by it. He would have liked to announce it on the front page of Katie's paper, but he only nodded when she looked to him for agreement.

"Well you have to have something. For your family. For the people you're close with at the *Ingot*. For us," Lizzie said.

"For me," Alison said. "I haven't been to a good wedding reception in a long time."

"Hey!" Lizzie said.

"Except for yours, Lizard, and that was months ago."

"You'll have to keep your dancing shoes in storage a little longer, Al, because we're not going to do anything. I already did that once," Katie said quietly. The table grew silent as they thought about that. Darío could see them each remembering Katie's first wedding. Different expressions played over the different faces. Except for Finn, who only took another drink of his beer. Darío would have given anything to be able to read their thoughts.

As if Katie had conjured him up, Darío watched as Ron Lipton walked into the Commodore, carrying a baby. A woman—girl, really—walked alongside him. He felt the moment Katie saw them, her body grew taut, the hand that had rested on his thigh pulled away. She pretended to use it to take a sip of her water, but when she put the glass down, her hand fell into her lap, not his.

"Jesus. Just what we don't need tonight," Alison said.

"Small town. Popular restaurant. What're ya gonna do," Finn said, shrugging. "You want me to go talk to him?" He looked as if that was the last thing in the world he wanted to do.

Alison seemed to like that idea, but Katie shook her head. "No. Don't worry about it. It's not an issue anymore." She turned to Darío and smiled at him, but it wasn't the warm, knowing smile he'd come to love. It looked forced and did not reach her eyes.

Darío knew the second Ron saw them. The second he saw Katie. He didn't seem to notice anyone else at the table.

Darío watched Ron's eyes caress Katie's face, sweep over her body. He saw pain fill the huge man's eyes. He saw Ron tighten his hold on his daughter, as if reminding himself that the bundle he was carrying was what he had gained when he'd lost the woman he loved. Finally, Ron's eyes tore from Katie, it seemed reluctantly, and skimmed over the other people at the table. They stopped on Darío.

No shock registered. The man must have heard he and Katie were traveling together. Darío wondered how long after the day he'd golfed with Ron the man had found out about Darío and his wife. He felt a twinge of guilt for not having spoken up that day, for letting Ron vent his despair over losing Katie and not mentioning that he was now involved with her.

More than involved. Bewitched. Snared. Intertwined. He thought of the last few nights in Katie's guestroom. Most definitely intertwined.

The girl with Ron saw Katie and her friends and came over. Ron followed.

"Mrs. Lipto—Katie," the girl said, nodding toward Katie.

"Amber," Katie nodded in return. She looked to Ron and then the little girl Ron was holding. "You have a beautiful child, Amber, congratulations."

Darío felt a rush of pride that the woman he was marrying could handle herself with such dignity while inside...what?

Was her heart breaking to see her husband, the man she thought, hoped, would father her children, carrying the child of another woman?

Was the child growing in her own womb salve enough to ease that pain? Was Darío enough?

The girl, Amber, was not gracious in her imagined triumph. "Isn't she? Well, how could she be anything but with such a handsome daddy?"

"Oh, Jesus," Alison said.

Finn and Darío had risen as they had approached the table. Finn and Ron shook hands and then Ron turned to Darío. Darío stuck out his hand, expecting a crushing grip from Ron, but the shake was firm and quick.

"Darío," was all Ron said.

"Ron," Darío responded. He could have called upon his years of making small talk during pro-ams. He could have asked about Ron's golf game. About his swing. If the tips Darío had given him had helped. Instead he said nothing.

"You two know each other?" Katie asked.

The men nodded. Ron was the one to answer her. "I won the raffle to golf with Darío at Annie Aid. We played with Petey."

Katie looked at Darío with surprise. Then she turned to Lizzie. "You didn't tell me Ron won the raffle."

"I didn't see you after that. You left the next day," Lizzie said. "Besides, I guess I assumed Darío told you."

Katie's head swung around again to Darío, her hair flipping over her shoulder, baring her long, graceful neck. "Why didn't you say anything?"

Because he wanted her to think of him, not Ron. Because his thoughts were too consumed with being in her bed again. Because he was coming to terms with traveling with a woman he barely knew. Coming to terms with becoming a father.

Because, if he told her, he wasn't sure he wouldn't tell her the things Ron had said that day about losing Katie. About choosing to protect his child.

All of Darío's reasons were true, were valid, but it was the last that stung.

Instead, he shrugged at Katie, "Does it matter?"

She looked up at him, her blue eyes clear and penetrating, searching for something Darío may have left out. He met her gaze, held it.

After a moment, she sighed. "No, I guess not."

There was an awkward moment when Finn and Darío re-seated themselves. The moment when either Ron and Amber would leave, or the group would ask them to join them. Neither happened.

Ron started to turn away, but Amber grabbed his shirtsleeve and yanked.

"What do you want, Amber?" Alison asked for them all.

Amber ignored Alison, never taking her eyes from Katie. Eyes filled with jealousy and venom, Darío thought.

"I just thought I could give Katie a friendly reminder about the divorce papers. Our lawyer says you still haven't signed them and sent them to him."

Darío felt Katie tense beside him, but it was Alison who answered. "Oh, Jesus. It never occurred to me you didn't get them. I sent them to the hotel in Chicago over three weeks ago. They must have just missed you. I wonder where they are?"

"They're lost? You lost them?" Amber said in a petulant voice, showing her youth.

"Calm down," Ron said. Her mother's voice, more like yelp, made the baby fidgety. Ron crooned something into the baby's ear and she settled down, burrowing her little head into her father's chest.

Darío watched Katie watch Ron and the baby. Darío's instincts were purely male. He longed to put his arm around Katie, pat her flat tummy with pride, shout to the hulking man in front of them that Katie was to be his wife, was carrying his child. Instead, he did nothing, waiting for Katie to say something. Anything.

"I got the papers, I just haven't signed them yet," Katie said. That was not what he wanted her to say.

Darío noticed several things simultaneously. Amber's fierce look of mistrust directed at Katie. Lizzie and Alison's exchanging of glances. Finn's sudden attention to a piece of pizza.

But what he saw that terrified him most was the look of sheer hopefulness that played on Ron's handsome face.

"Why not?" Ron softly whispered while Amber bellowed the same words.

Though it was the visiting couple that asked the question, Katie turned to Darío for her explanation. "I got them just as we were leaving Chicago. I put them in a side pocket I never use in my laptop case. I was going to sign them the next day and get them out." She paused, leaned her head closer to Darío.

He could smell her shampoo, her light perfume. It would normally distract him, but what she was saying was too important. He shook away the thoughts of her in the shower, lathering up with the aromatic shampoo.

"Then we got to Akron," she said, her emphasis not lost on Darío.

"So what? They don't have pens in Akron?" Amber said, earning a stern glance from Ron, which she answered with a defiant grin.

Katie kept her eyes on Darío as she answered. "Everything changed in Akron."

It was explanation enough for Darío. He nodded his understanding to Katie. She smiled, her soft, sweet smile. She brushed her hand across his arm, then turned once again to Ron and Amber. "I'm sorry if I held anything up. I'll look for them tomorrow."

They were leaving for Spain tomorrow, but Darío kept quiet, as did the others at their table.

"No, it's not that—" Ron said, but was cut off by Amber's "Thank you. We'd appreciate it."

The couple started to turn away when Alison said, "Katie, why don't you tell Ron your news?"

A mistake. Darío knew that Alison had made a mistake. He knew Katie well enough by now that her news was not something she would rub in Ron's face in front of others. She would probably try to avoid that conversation altogether, assuming that the small town rumor mill would take care of it for her. Darío didn't blame her.

But Alison was a woman who didn't mind confrontation. Darío figured she'd probably been waiting for this moment – to strike back at Ron – since the man had hurt her best friend.

She sat with a devious smile on her face and Darío mused that the man who ended up with Alison would have to be very sure of himself, very strong, or else this small woman would walk all over him.

Alison looked at Katie, raising an eyebrow, only shrugging as Katie shot her an "I'll deal with you later" look. Darío thought it was a good thing for Alison that they were leaving the next day.

She looked at Ron. He seemed to steel himself for what she was about to say. His eyes slid over Darío as if he suspected he were a part of it.

Katie took a deep breath, let it out. "Ron, I've decided to sell the house. I just thought you'd want to know."

The sigh of relief from Ron was audible. As were the gasps from Lizzie and Alison. "No, I meant—" This time Alison shut up at Katie's warning look.

Ron looked at Alison, hoping she'd slip, but she kept still. He turned to Katie. "But you love that house. We worked so hard to get it just right."

Katie only nodded, she didn't say a word.

Darío thought of the mansions he could buy her. Would she love them as much as the little house she'd shared with Ron?

If the nursery of her new home were full, the answer would be yes. Again, Darío thought about the one thing Katie could get from him and not Ron. Her child. Their child.

Mansion. Shack. Florida. Spain. The Copper Country. It didn't matter to Darío where they made their home. Just as long as their child was safe, protected, loved. He knew Katie felt the same.

Ron searched Katie's face, but it was still, serene, beautiful. "Well, thanks for letting me know. I guess we should let you guys get back to your dinner."

They all made overly polite goodbyes and the new family went to a table out of hearing distance, but not out of sight, from the group's table.

Katie gave Lizzie and Alison warning glances. Alison stewed while Lizzie, God bless her, drew everyone in to listen to a story about one of her newest clients.

They finished their dinners, each telling their news or stories. None of them mentioning the family across the restaurant.

Darío, Katie, and Lizzie were at the side of the table that faced Ron and Amber. As soon as they'd sat down, Amber had gotten on a cell phone while Ron got the baby settled in a high chair wooden thing the waitress brought. He pulled toys out of a diaper bag, entertaining the baby while they had their dinner.

As the fivesome got up to leave, Darío heard Lizzie say quietly to Katie, "You've got to admit, he is great with that baby. "

Katie nodded, glancing at Ron and his child, then down at her purse as she gathered her things. "That's not surprising. I always knew Ron would make a great father."

Darío felt a stab of jealousy, then quickly pushed it away. Katie would see. He'd be a great father, too.

"It's a good thing, too. Because it looks like Amber doesn't have a lot of maternal instincts," Lizzie said.

Katie shrugged. "She's young. It'll come."

They made their way from the restaurant, Katie not looking back.

But Darío did. He couldn't help himself. He met Ron's eyes. Blue, just like Katie's. There were so many emotions going through them that Darío took a step back, startled. He turned and walked out of the restaurant feeling a strange sense of guilt.

Twenty

It was a friendly divorce.
She left me the piano and the lawnmower.
I couldn't play either one.
- Lee Trevino, professional golfer

KATIE REPLAYED THE SCENE in the Commodore over in her head as she packed her final bag later that night. She heard the moan from the pipes as Darío took a shower down the hall.

She tried playing it over with herself in Amber's part. She and Ron and their baby walking into the Commodore, seeing Lizzie, Finn, and Alison. Sitting down. Ron playing with the baby as she gossiped with Lizard and Al.

It was fuzzy, the image unclear, as if she couldn't bring the lens of her daydream into focus.

Instantly she knew why. Darío wasn't in the picture. And he should be. She wanted him to be.

She saw him so clearly, his brown eyes, warm, shimmering at her. His smile, crooked, lopsided, as if he knew a secret. The scent of him. The way his skin tasted after being on the golf course.

He was crystal clear, and thus the daydream, with him in it, became whole.

She put the packed bag next to her laptop case, reminding herself she needed to get the divorce papers out. She herself had felt legally free from Ron the minute she received them. And she'd felt bound to Darío ever since Akron. The papers were just a formality to her, but they were important for everyone to get on with their lives.

She started to reach for the bag, the papers, when she heard Darío yell from the shower, "*Gata*, come here, I have a very special place that needs personal washing."

There was music in his teasing voice. Katie left the bedroom, shedding her clothes as she walked down the hall.

—⚬⚬—

Katie listened to a couple seated down the row of airport chairs from her. They spoke both a smattering of English and Spanish. She closed her eyes and listened to the lilting voices, sounding so sensuous, even though they were probably only speaking of unpaid bills or who remembered to turn off the coffee pot that morning.

She realized she now equated spoken Spanish with words of arousal, words spoken in passion. Darío only spoke Spanish with her when they were alone, in bed. Words he whispered low in her ear as he entered her. Words he panted against her neck as he thrust deeply inside her. Words he could barely mutter as he climaxed within her.

Words she didn't understand.

Oh, she understood their meaning. At least, she thought she did. But, he could be reciting the rules of golf while whispering what she assumed were sweet nothings.

She looked across the gate area of the airport to see Darío in the newsstand, still trying to decide what book to buy. She liked that he was giving so much thought to his literary choice, even if his selection was limited to five or six bestsellers. She did the same thing. Whenever she got out of the Copper Country, the first thing she did was find a Barnes & Noble or some other bookstore and spend hours in the giant bookstore, surrounded by the written word.

Taking advantage of Darío being engrossed at the book rack,

Katie rose and walked over to the couple who had been speaking both Spanish and English.

They were in their mid-forties, Katie guessed, both wearing wedding rings. Nothing made them stand out in any way. They were neither attractive nor unattractive. Just your basic, nondescript couple sitting in plastic chairs in an airport, waiting for their flight.

Katie sensed an ease about them. This was a couple that had been together for a while. A couple used to traveling together. The man held the tickets, the woman both their books. It was a system that had been practiced many times, and Katie found herself envious of them. She and Darío did not have any sort of flow about them when they traveled. Yet.

"Excuse me," she said. When she had their attention, she gave them her friendliest smile, which they returned. "I couldn't help but overhear and realize that you're bilingual." The couple both nodded. "I was wondering if you would be so kind as to translate something for me?"

"Yes, of course," the man said, as the woman nodded her mutual assent.

Katie hesitated. What if what she wanted translated was too graphic for these nice people to translate? She didn't want to embarrass them. Or herself. She chose the one phrase that Darío seemed to use the most often. Several times he had whispered it to her while he thought she was napping. When he'd brush her hair back from her face with such tenderness that she'd think maybe she'd imagined it. Surely that wouldn't be something along the lines of, "my, what big hooters you have". She was hoping for something like, "your skin is so soft".

Committed to asking, Katie said, "I would like to know what *te quiero* means." Her accent was not bad, considering she'd never spoken Spanish before. She had certainly heard Darío say those words often enough to give a passable rendition.

The man gave her a bright smile. "Ah, that is an easy one. *Te quiero* means 'I love you'," he said.

He loved her! Darío loved her!

If he loved her, he must trust and believe her, right?

No, not necessarily, she told herself. If she was completely honest with herself, she had to admit that she still loved Ron, although she certainly no longer trusted him. Didn't even like him, really. But still loved him. Sometimes those old feelings never entirely go away, they're just pushed to the back by new ones.

There would be love in her marriage. To know he loved her filled her with joy.

Wanting to digest this information—that Darío had told her he loved her, albeit in a language she didn't understand—she told the couple thank you and made to return to her seat.

Something about the expression of the woman made her stop.

"Is there more?" she asked.

The woman looked at her husband, and then gave Katie a soft smile. "Well, it is true that *te quiero* means 'I love you', but it is meant in more of a…" She struggled for the words. She finally seemed to try to make her point using body language. Her hands curled into fists and her arms pulled into her chest, in almost a fit of angst. "It is more 'I want you' than 'I love you'. Does that make sense?"

"Perfect sense," Katie said, surprised at how deflated she felt at the clarification.

"*Te amo* is 'I love you' in the sense that I believe you are looking for," the woman added.

"Yes," Katie said, in almost a whisper, "I guess that is the sense I'm looking for." Still not willing to accept the lesser endearment, she said, "Which would mean more to you to hear?"

Knowingly, the woman gave Katie a sad smile. "It is always nice to hear *te quiero*. And it is not an emotion to be taken lightly. But, a woman longs to hear *te amo* from her mate."

Katie thanked them both again and walked back to her seat. From behind her, she heard the man whisper "*te amo*" to the woman, and the woman chuckle and reply the same.

She had only been back in her seat a short time before Darío joined her, but it was long enough for her to ruminate on the fact that never once had the words *te amo* come from Darío's mouth.

She seemed to have finally won his trust. Could she win his love? Did she even want to?

She had to protect herself. She never wanted to feel hurt like she'd experienced when Ron walked out. If she let herself fall in love with Darío—and let's face it, she was nearly there—and he never returned her feelings, she was setting herself up for another devastation. But this time it would be worse, because there'd be a child involved.

So, she would continue to care for him, sleep with him, raise their child together, but she would protect her heart, not fall in love.

Darío leaned over, brushed a strand from her face, tucked behind her ear, giving her earlobe a playful tug. His warm hand rested on her bare neck and she felt the heat seep into her skin.

Oh, yeah, piece of cake.

—⁓—

When she met them at the airport, Sofia Luna was wearing black stockings just like Katie and her friends had predicted. But they weren't wool, and they weren't rolled down to her ankles. No, it was more like black silk stockings that glided up her shapely legs and disappeared under the hem of her tasteful skirt, perhaps to be fastened by lacy garters.

The woman was beautiful. Breathtaking. And young.

Much too young to have a thirty-six-year-old son.

The woman had to be in her early-to-mid fifties, at the youngest, but she looked not a day older than forty-five. Her dark olive skin was flawless, with only the hint of wrinkles around her eyes and mouth. Laugh lines, Katie thought. That boded well.

Her black hair was pulled back into a low chignon, her brown eyes made up to their best advantage. She wore a long skirt of black linen and a white blouse tucked in with a beautiful, wide leather belt with a huge brass buckle. The silk stockings disappeared into tasteful leather pumps.

She looked like a woman who spent a lot of time at spas and with experts on the art of makeup application. She looked like she'd lived a fine and pampered life. Katie knew that hadn't always been the way she lived.

Katie stood frozen while Darío rushed forward and kissed his mother on both cheeks and then embraced her in a long, warm hug. "Mamá," he said. Katie was touched by the tenderness in his voice.

"*Mi corazón*," she cooed into Darío's ear, then rained kisses all over his face. She clutched her son tight to her and Katie felt as though she were intruding on a private moment. Looking behind her, she wondered if she could gracefully exit and pretend to be busy with the luggage until the mother and child reunion was over.

Sensing her movement, Darío broke away from his mother and reached for Katie's hand. "*Mamá*, this is Katie Maki. Katie, my mother, Sofia Luna."

Katie felt Darío's squeeze of encouragement on her hand and squeezed back. She stepped into the circle the two had created, hoping they'd let her join in. They both took a small step back to allow her entrance.

"Señora Luna, it's an honor to meet you," she said in Spanish. She'd practiced the few words the whole flight over, daring to say it out loud only after Darío fell asleep. She had envisioned saying it to a much older woman. She thought she'd got the pronunciation down pretty well, but she knew it didn't sound half as sexy as Darío's accent, but then, she wasn't going for sexy right now. She was going for daughter-in-law material. Mother of her grandchild material. Upstanding. Forthright. Nurturing. Honest.

Katie wasn't sure what Darío had told his mother, other than Katie was pregnant and they planned on getting married. Had he told her of his suspicions that Katie had tricked Darío into getting her pregnant? That after the baby was born, he would probably demand a paternity test? That Katie was a woman who would sleep with a man she had known for twenty-four hours with absolutely no protection, and with no intention of ever seeing him again?

Whatever he'd told her, it wasn't enough for her to have a tainted view of Katie. This was made obvious when Sofia pulled Katie into an embrace as tight as she had held Darío and started answering Katie's words with her own, in a Spanish that seemed faster than a speeding bullet. Katie recognized a word here and there, was pretty sure she made out "*bueno*" and "*bebé*", but wasn't positive. But when Sofia pulled back and looked at Katie with tears in her eyes, then touched Katie's slightly rounded stomach with gentle hands, Katie understood.

She felt the same way as Sofia about the miracle of this baby.

"*Mamá*, Katie doesn't speak Spanish," Darío said. He looked at Katie questioningly, as if maybe she'd learned the language without him knowing it. Katie was pleased that he thought her capable of learning a second language covertly and so quickly.

"No I don't, I had one of the caddies on tour write that out for me phonetically. I've been practicing it for a few days, but I'm afraid that's the extent of my bilingual talents." She offered up this information to Sofia almost apologetically.

"*Sí, Sí,* I understand. Don't worry, Katie, I am almost as proficient at *Inglés* as my son."

Katie felt sheepish that she didn't know Spanish, hadn't learned more by now. But how was she supposed to know she'd be impregnated by a Spaniard someday back when she was in high school and had to choose between taking French and Spanish?

"Forgive me, but I'm having a hard time believing Darío is your son. You look much too young." She could have been trying to score some brownie points, but she wasn't. It was true.

Sofia seemed to know that Katie's shock was genuine. "I was only sixteen years old when I had Darío, but there is no doubt that he is my son," she chuckled. "I can't even claim a mix-up at the hospital that your American soap operas love so much. Darío was born right here. Not in this house, but in the one that stood on the same spot, thirty-six years ago. I wouldn't let him out of my arms for nearly a week, I was so afraid he'd be taken from me." She touched her son's cheek with her fingertips. "He is most definitely my son."

The woman's warm brown eyes shone with pride and love as she looked at her son.

Darío's eyes returned the warm sentiment to the woman who was only a child herself when she'd given birth to him.

The stress of the past few weeks seemed to catch up to Katie. Jetlag and nervousness at meeting Darío's mother didn't help either, and she wasn't surprised to find herself moved at the tender moment between Darío and his mother.

As Sofia moved aside to wipe at her tears, turning her back to the couple, Katie took Darío's hand and laid it on her stomach, placing it in the exact spot that Sofia had touched only moments before, her warmth still evident.

She met his questioning glance with sure eyes.

"He is most definitely your son," she murmured to him.

He comprehended what she was saying to him, that the baby was his. He nodded, and lightly kissed her cheek as he whispered, "*Sí*," in her ear.

Flooded with relief, and afraid that this sweet moment, coupled with her emotional state and those pesky hormones, might send her into a crying jag, she attempted to lighten the mood. "Or, *she* is most definitely your *daughter*," she said, teasing, her voice now on surer ground.

He laughed. "No. No. If she is a daughter, let her be yours. With your hair, your eyes, your beauty. And certainly not my nose."

Sofia, now composed and once again facing the twosome, swatted good-naturedly at her son. "Bah! I love your nose. It gives you character."

"I could make do with a little less character. And a little less nose."

Katie laughed along, but her thoughts were on Darío's words

about a daughter having her beauty. Did she wish that for her daughter? Being beautiful in today's society was definitely an advantage, but was it an advantage she wanted her child to have? She knew the saying, "I want my child to have every advantage…", but was that really something parents should want for their child?

Without certain advantages, do children work harder? Develop other skills? Find other ways to achieve their goals? And would having to achieve those goals without advantages be, like living with a big nose, bringing out character that would otherwise go undiscovered?

Would being a beautiful girl, then woman, make her daughter's life better? Easier? Katie knew firsthand that the answer to that was a resounding no.

She knew that Darío was just being nice, giving her a compliment. She didn't believe for one second that Darío would love his child any more or less because of its looks. But the thought of her own issues with looks and how they would translate to their child found a little drawer in her mind and climbed in, waiting, as if kept in storage. Katie knew that the drawer would surely open up many more times in the future.

"So that's where Darío gets his 'bah!' from. He uses it on the course all the time," Katie said, acknowledging Sofia's use of the word she could often hear Darío booming halfway down the fairway while she stood on the green two hundred yards away.

"I'm sure that is not the only loud word he uses, eh?" his mother said, giving her son a knowing smile.

Darío hung his head. "Katie does not like profanity, *Mamá*, so I am trying to limit my…outbursts," he said, chagrinned.

Katie hadn't even realized that Darío noticed she didn't care for foul language, let alone that he was trying to curb his.

Sofia eyed Katie. "I think that maybe you are to be a good influence on my Darío, eh?"

The thought stunned Katie. It seemed she was getting so much from Darío, could she possibly be giving something to him in return? A good influence? He said he golfed better when she

was in the gallery, but she figured he was just being polite by saying that. Though his recent playing proved him correct.

Sofia turned, leading the way into the huge house. "Come
in, come in. Let's get you settled. Katie you probably want to rest
before dinner. A siesta, eh?"

After the emotional flight when she'd decided she needed to
guard her heart, only to have it tweaked by Darío's obvious adora-
tion of his mother, a siesta sounded like heaven. She followed the
woman into Darío's home.

Twenty-One

—⁕—

Dan would rather play golf than have sex any day.
- Marilyn Quayle

KATIE'D SPENT THE NIGHT in a different bedroom than Darío. He'd tried to talk her out of it. The suite of rooms Darío inhabited when he was home encompassed nearly half the large house. There were three bedrooms, all with their own bath, a spacious sitting room, dining area, and office. There was also a kitchen, but Darío rarely entered it, preferring to eat with his mother when he was here; certainly preferring to eat her cooking to his own. After weeks in America, or elsewhere in Europe, Sofia always prepared her paella for Darío's first night home. She hadn't disappointed him last night.

The level of privacy he and Katie had was as though they were staying in another city, and yet, Katie insisted on staying in one of the other bedrooms. Maybe she was just nervous about meeting his mother. Maybe after a full day with his mother and in his house, she would be comfortable enough to sleep in his room with him. Maybe he'd be moving into the guest room with her.

Because Darío had no intention of sleeping without Katie next to him another night.

Since Akron, he'd become used to having her in his bed. Beyond the sex—which was incredible—he liked holding her next to him while he fell asleep. The warmth of her body molded against his, the tickle of her hair against his chin, the way her sweet little behind fit in the cradle of his hips.

He woke in the mornings with the scent of her in his nose whether she was still in the bed with him or not.

His thoughts of her were interrupted by a soft knock at his door, and as if his thinking of her had summoned her to him, she entered his bedroom.

"I didn't wake you, did I?" she asked.

He shook his head and patted a spot next to him on the bed. She came in, closing the door behind her, but didn't cross the room to the bed. Instead, she circled the perimeter of the room, looking at the things scattered on his dresser and bookshelf. He watched her as she fingered cufflinks and watches, mostly gifts from tournament sponsors that he'd never worn. His body tensed watching her stroke a gold lighter that he'd never used. Her fingers stroked along the lighter and he went hard thinking of the stroking she'd done to him in the past few weeks.

Her hair was mussed from sleep. He knew exactly what she'd smell like if only she'd get close enough for him to confirm it. She wore a nightgown he'd never seen her in before. It was soft and demure, long, past her knees with a high collar. She looked sweet and virginal in it.

He hated it.

"*Gata*, come here," he said, his voice hoarse from sleep and arousal.

She smiled at him and shook her head. "What would your mother say?" She continued her perusal of his room.

"First of all, she would never know, she's over on the other side of the house, no way for her to hear us."

"What if she came over? Came in on us?" She had reached his walk-in closet, opened the door and entered the large room. She left the door open. Darío could still hear her, but couldn't see her.

He spoke a little louder so she'd be sure to hear him. "She

never comes to my side of the house when I'm in town."

He thought he heard something, a gasp, a soft "Oh" from her, but when she answered him all she said was, "Never?"

"Never. I go over to her."

The door opened wide. "Well, okay, then."

Darío's breath caught in his throat. Maybe lower. Katie had shed her prim nightgown and was wearing his green jacket from his Master's victory.

And nothing else.

She walked to the bed. "Is it okay that I wear this? It's not sacrilege or anything, is it?"

Her blond hair hung in front of her, falling across the lapels of the jacket. The deep vee of the front exposed her tan chest, then the whiteness of her breasts, and belly, mostly concealed by the button in front. The roundness of her breasts and cleavage were visible, but her nipples were hidden behind the jacket. The emblem of the United States wavered over the curve of her left breast. The flag that represented Augusta rippled and waved as she moved.

No flag had ever claimed a more valuable territory.

"*Sí*," was all he could answer, and that came out rough and short.

She smiled knowingly, her confidence building as she looked down and saw his sheet tenting at his arousal.

She climbed on at the foot of the bed. Darío started to sit up, to come to her, but she put her hand up. He stayed where he was. Waiting. Dying.

She was on her hands and knees, crawling up the length of him. "*Gata*," he said. She had never embodied her nickname more. He pressed his legs together so she could easily straddle him as she padded her way up to him.

"Meow," she purred.

Dios Mio.

She wrapped her fingers in the bed sheet at his knees and slowly pulled down. The cotton, so smooth normally, seemed rough and jagged against his skin. It prickled against the hair of his chest, across his stomach, along the line of hair snaking downward. Just an inch or two further and she'd be able to see what her feline antics were doing to him. Though the bulge in the sheet was evidence enough.

She stopped.

She bent her head down with the grace of a panther, still on her hands and knees, most of her torso even with his legs. She purred—growled, really—from the back of her throat and ran her tongue along his skin, following the line of hair up. She got to his belly button, which she ran her tongue around twice. She continued on to his stomach, which shuddered when her hot tongue lapped his sensitive skin. She seemed to like that, nuzzling her whole face into him, breathing deep, as if taking in the scent of him, savoring it, making sure to remember it.

Darío could think of nothing better than to be tracked by Katie.

He placed his hands on her calves, ran them up to behind her knees, slid his fingers in the juncture created as she crawled. Pressure as the back of her thigh came down, then release as she moved forward. Pressure. Release.

Feeling the pressure, and definitely needing release, Darío moved his hands up the back of her thighs to her round, firm butt to confirm what he already knew. Absolutely nothing on under the green jacket.

He slid his fingers into the soft cleft, his big palms kneading the taut cheeks of her bottom. She raised up on her hands, her soft hair skimming across his chest. Her blue eyes staring down into his. He moved his fingers. Her eyes grew huge. He swung one hand down, around the front, finding her drenched. Her tongue peeked out from her mouth, wetting her bottom lip. One hand held her open from behind while the other played over her. Stroking her, finding the spots she liked. Staying away from the one that sent her over.

She began to rock against his hand, her arms moving her

forward and back, her dangling breasts caught and held tight by the jacket. Her eyes closed and she began to nod. "Yes. Yes," she panted.

Her head dropped, a blond curtain falling in front of her face. As she moved, and the curtain parted, he would catch glances of her eyelashes, her nose, her lips. Her breathing grew shorter, louder, pained. Soon would come the three short breaths that she took right before she came.

He heard them as well as felt them. Then she came, her muscles clenching around his fingers, her wetness seeping over him, her arms quivering as if she couldn't hold her weight any longer. Her moan sounding more feline than human.

Her head knocking into his chin, eliciting a grunt from him.

She didn't notice, just kept spasming, spiraling. As she came down, her toes dug into the sheet and dragged it backward, as if kicking her little paws over some dirt, baring Darío. She came up on her haunches and Darío led himself to her. She came down on him hard, gasps coming from them both.

His hands moved to her thighs, skimmed them up and down, watching as his hands disappeared under the tails of the green jacket. He had a sudden flash of having the jacket put on his shoulders the first time he'd won golf's most coveted prize. He'd run his hands along the sleeves, just as he now did along Katie's arms. He'd smoothed down the lapels, the buttons, treated it with reverence. He did the same to Katie, his fingers tracing where her skin met lapel. His hand not quite able to run flat along the buttons because of her bulge.

The baby. She was showing enough now that the jacket pulled across her tummy, the button nearly popping.

Emotions roiled through him as he looked up at the woman he loved, carrying a child he already loved, wrapped in the ultimate symbol of his success.

The jacket became a blur and all he could see was the woman he would spend the rest of his life with. He rose up to meet her, to kiss her, taste her. She wrapped her arms around his neck, kissing him back, playing with his tongue, her hips finding a new, faster rythym. He buried his face in her neck, his hands sliding under the jacket to play with her breasts.

He began mumbling in Spanish as he often did when buried deep inside Katie. What she meant to him. How good she felt. That she was precious, cherished. He knew she didn't understand him but he was so mindless when he was this close that there was no way he could translate. She seemed to like when he spoke to her that way. Even now, her hips ground deeply into his, her legs spread more widely, allowing him to go deeper.

"*Te quiero*," he gasped as he spilled himself inside her. "*Te quiero.*"

He felt her tense. Expected her to follow but she didn't. He tried to hold back, but he was already coming. Nothing could stop him now. He tried to hold on, make it last, get her there again, but she collapsed against him, her face turned away.

When he could finally catch his breath, he reluctantly pulled out of her. He turned them over, laying her down next to him. He undid the button of the jacket, surprised it had held. He spread the sides of the jacket wide, Katie's body limp, allowing him full access. He gently laid his head on her hip, his hand coming up to stroke her belly.

It seemed to have grown in the one night they'd been apart. He ran his hand across her heated skin, following the rise that protected his child.

He looked up at her, expecting to see her looking back with that soft smile she wore when he did this to her.

But she was not smiling back at him. Nor were her hands playing in his hair, smoothing his shoulders. Katie laid flat, hands at her sides, staring straight up at the ceiling, as if she were somewhere else. A million miles away.

Darío thought he knew where she was. In the Copper Country. He hoped to hell she wasn't thinking of Ron.

—⁂—

Several days passed. Days that Darío took Katie sightseeing

through the northern part of Spain. San Barria was a resort town that sat nestled between the Pyrenees and the Bay of Biscay. The area was breathtaking, so rich in color. The people treated Darío as a long-lost war hero. It was obvious he was their favorite son. He was polite to all, even those whom he told Katie later had given his mother a hard time when she was raising him alone.

Katie didn't sleep in the guestroom again. She moved her things into Darío's room, figuring either Sofia wouldn't know, or, if she did, so what.

Their lovemaking became frenzied as Katie tried to hold her emotions in check, to only respond to Darío physically. As if he sensed it, his claim on her took on a desperation, as if their time was limited. They would lay tangled in bed afterward, and then Katie would turn away, trying to keep her heart separate, knowing she was fighting a losing battle.

She was in love with him. She couldn't deny it any longer.

He was attracted to her. Cared for her. Wanted to be a part of his child's life. But that was it. It was *te quiero*, not *te amo* that he whispered to her, that he moaned in her ear while he came. And it wasn't just the words. Though they seemed to be beyond it now, Darío had not trusted her, and the bottom line was he only fought for them to be together to give their child his name.

The thought she had back in the airport—about a marriage where only one party loved—mocked her now, as she realized that indeed would be the case. Only she would be the one who loved. Could she do that to herself? To her child? Make Darío give up his chance to possibly find someone he loved? Would he ever come to love her?

—⁊⁊—

Darío was out back on the small putting green area, practicing, while Katie and Sofia shared iced tea in Sofia's living room. They had formed an alliance of sorts, since they'd arrived, based on the baby Katie was carrying.

And their mutual affection for Darío.

"I love how you've decorated, Sofia. The house is so warm, it captures your culture so well, and yet is so comfortable."

Sofia graciously nodded her thanks.

"And huge," Katie added.

Sofia chuckled. "Yes, I know, it is too much house for just two people. One, most of the time. But it was important to Darío to have this house. To have it here."

"I don't understand."

Sofia settled into her chair, placed her glass on the table beside her. "This is where he grew up. Where he endured life in poverty, being called a bastard. It was important that he show these people that he had…made it, is how I think you say it."

Katie nodded, waited, hoping the woman would go on. Instead the woman rose, walkinged over to a beautiful antique desk and rummaged through a couple of drawers until she found what she was looking for. She brought a piece of paper over to Katie.

A letter, Katie realized. It was addressed to the San Barria Golf and Country Club. The club that Darío's mother had been a cook at. The club you could see from the balcony of Darío's suite.

"One of the maids at the club found this in the trash of the director's office. We worked together many years, she and I." Sofia's eyes were soft, remembering. "She thought I might like to see it." She handed the letter to Katie. "Apparently, a few years ago, the club invited Darío to be a lifetime member, gratis. It is a very expensive and exclusive club." She nodded at the paper as Katie took it out of the envelope. "Here is the best example of the kind of man my Darío is."

Katie read the letter. It was polite and gracious and read just like Darío spoke. He thanked them for the invitation, but declined. Stating that the invitation would have been welcome when he was younger, when his mother was in their employ and they'd struggled and scrimped so that Darío could play the course from time to time. When they were in need. Now that he could well afford to become a member, he was no longer interested in becoming one.

Proud. Honorable. Making his point. So Darío.

Sofia's voice was soft. "The course he designed is only a few miles away. A beautiful course, one to rival San Barria. He has made it public, with very inexpensive greens fees. So that the people who live here, not just those who can afford to come to the resort, but those who *work* at the resort, have a grand course to play." She sat back in her chair once more. "And yet, he made sure that this house was the finest in the area, and that it sit high on a hill over the club. So that all there would know where he lived.

"That is my Darío."

That *was* Darío, proud and honorable, yet needing to prove that he'd succeeded. He never flaunted, but he made sure people were aware of what he'd achieved. "You must be very proud of your son," Katie said, proud of him herself.

Sofia's stately head bobbed. "*Sî, sî.*"

Sensing a softness in the woman, Katie said, "May I ask you something, Sofia?"

The woman's demeanor did not change, but there was a sharpening of her eyes, a slight raise of a perfectly arched brow. "Of course."

"Is there anything you could share with me about Darío's father?"

Sofia didn't seem surprised by Katie's line of questioning, had probably been waiting for it. "We do not speak of Darío's father," Sofia said softly.

A few months ago Katie would have let it go. But not now. She wanted to find out about Darío's father. "Yes, Darío told me you don't talk about it—talk about him. But, you see, I thought that…" Even the new, stronger Katie wilted as Sofia's other brow shot up.

"Of course. You must be curious because of the child you carry. You are wondering about genetics, illnesses, things like that."

Katie had been, but that was only a small part of it. She'd also assumed that Darío's genes, like hers, were just fine. And honestly, it didn't really matter to her anyway. She'd love and cherish this baby no matter what. Illness and accidents can happen at any time. She chose not to think about those things until faced with the real possibility of them.

Katie shook her head, proceeding cautiously. "No. It's not that, although certainly I'm concerned about the baby's health. It's really more for Darío that I'm curious."

Sofia looked confused, gave her head a tiny shake. "I don't understand."

"Darío's feelings about his father are still unresolved. He was hoping to have some closure about it before he became a father himself." Katie patted her belly. "Obviously time is running out to that end. I just thought if he knew more, maybe he could find some kind of peace with it all."

Sofia was stunned, Katie could easily see that. She looked around the room as if trying to orient herself. She took a long sip of tea, put the glass back on the table. Katie waited.

"Darío does not have...how do you Americans say it... 'issues',"— she raised her hands, making air quotation marks— "with his father. His father has never been a part of his life. He was curious as a child, of course, that is natural. But as he grew older, his questions stopped."

"That doesn't mean he doesn't still have them. He just assumed it was too painful for you to talk about, so he never brought it up."

"He has told you this?"

Katie nodded. Sofia looked at her closely, as if seeing her for the first time. "And it is so important for you to know?"

Katie nodded again. "Because it's important to Darío."

"You love my son." It was a statement more than a question.

"Yes. Very much," Katie answered.

"You would do anything for his happiness?"

"Yes. Of course."

Sofia nodded. She looked away, at a painting on the wall. It was of a cove along the beaches. Katie assumed it was the Bay of Biscay. It certainly looked like the same terrain she'd walked with Darío the other day. Sofia's eyes took on a dream-like trance. "That is how it was with me and Darío's father. He was older than I was, but still young. We were both so young. He was wild. Impetuous. I loved him deeply and he loved me. I would have done anything for him. Anything except give up my child."

Katie let out a gasp. Sofia glanced her way and then looked back at the painting. "It was different then, this was a very conservative place. Still is in some ways. My beloved wanted to get out, to see the world, he said this town was killing him, sucking him dry. It was, that's true. He was the kind of spirit meant to roam.

"He wanted me to go with him, and I was ready to. Sixteen years old and I was going to leave my mamá and papa and see the world with the boy I loved." Her voice was wistful; it had a girl-like quality. Her eyes grew damp at the memories and Katie's heart went out to the woman.

"And then you got pregnant," Katie prompted after a moment of silence.

"*Sí.*"

"And you had to choose. Have and keep your baby against everyone's wishes, your family's, your boyfriend's. Or leave with the man you love. Without your child." She didn't elaborate, was not sure how Sofia's parents and lover would go about taking her child from her. Whether they were talking abortion or adoption. She didn't want to know.

"It was no choice. Not really," Sofia said.

—⁂—

Darío came into his mother's quarters for something to drink, parched from being in the intense sun for too many hours. He heard Katie and his mother in her living room and made his way there after getting himself some tea.

Their voices were low, their cadence slow. Long pauses between hearing another voice. This was not a conversation about decorating or clothes or anything insubstantial.

He should announce himself. Cough or something. But Darío kept still as he approached the room. He was behind the entranceway, couldn't see the women, but could now hear them clearly.

"It was no choice. Not really," his mother said.

He took a sip of tea, trying to figure out what they were talking about from that. He couldn't.

"No, of course not," Katie said.

"You will see, Katie, perhaps you already do, there is nothing a parent would not do for their child. No sacrifice they would not make."

"Even to give up the man you love?" Katie asked, but it didn't sound like a question to Darío, more like a stated fact. He'd give anything to see her face right now, but he stayed in the alcove.

Was she talking about Ron? Would she have told his mother about Ron? Darío didn't think so, but what else could she be talking about? What other man had she had to give up for the sake of her child?

"Yes. Even that. Especially that," Darío's mother said.

"But that's so unfair," Katie said. Darío felt the wind knock out of him.

"*Sí.*"

"I'm so sorry, Sofia," Katie said.

Sorry for what? That she couldn't love Sofia's son? That she was still in love with another man? That life was so unfair as to finally give her a child while taking the man she loved?

He could hear no more. Didn't think he could take it. He stepped back a few paces, then cleared his throat and made a loud entrance into the room.

"*Darío,*" his mother said. She looked at him with tender eyes, filled with compassion. Or pity?

He looked at Katie, who smiled softly then ducked her head. Guilt?

He took a seat on a chair placed between the two of them.

Sofia slapped her hands down on her lap. "So. Enough. When are you two thinking of marrying? We will have to start planning right away, eh?"

"We'd hoped in the next few—" Katie started.

Darío interrupted her. "There is no hurry, Mamá."

Katie swung her head to him. Sofia motioned to Katie's belly. "No hurry? Are you sure about that?" There was no censure in her voice, more like amusement.

"If it is before or after the baby, it does not matter. The child will still bear my name." He turned to Katie. "Is that not so?"

She nodded. "Yes. Of course. But I thought we'd…" She looked at Sofia and stopped, obviously wanting to have this discussion without Darío's mother in the room.

Darío excused himself, saying he wanted to finish up practicing, that they'd talk about it later. He ignored Katie's questioning look as he left the room.

Instead of going outside, he made his way to the other side of the house, to his suite of rooms. He went into his office. Katie had been using the room as her work area since they'd arrived.

He went directly to her laptop case. It was against his nature to pry, but he could not stop himself. He looked in the main compartment. Laptop. Address book. Tablets with notes on story ideas. One of the side compartments held CDs and flash drives. Another held power cords and other electrical things.

One side pocket remained. He fingered the wide zipper teeth. He finally grabbed the tab and pulled. There was only one thing in the pocket. A brown envelope.

He knew what it was, he didn't have to pull it out. But he did. From a legal firm. He pulled out the papers. The divorce papers. He flipped to the last page, knowing what he'd find.

On the last page, about a third of the way down, Ron's signature read firm and bold. Next to it was a blank.

Katie hadn't signed them.

Twenty-Two

Golf is like a love affair. If you don't take it seriously, it's not fun.
If you do take it seriously, it breaks your heart.
- Arnold Daly, author

HE WAS HAVING SECOND THOUGHTS. He had to be. Katie
could think of no other explanation for Darío not wanting to set
a date. They had planned on getting married in Spain before going back to the States for the Tour Championship. That was now
just two months away. If he wanted to be married by then, they'd
surely have to start making plans soon.

She looked over at him behind his desk, going over a contract his manager had sent that day from his club manufacturer.
His head was bowed over the papers. Katie sat on the sofa in his
office, reading. It was comfortable here, the two of them like this,
just a quiet evening at home. Sofia was at some gathering in town,
but even if she'd been home, they'd still be alone. Darío had been
right, his mother never ventured over to this side of the house.

They could easily turn the guestroom—the one Katie had
foolishly spent their first night in Spain in—into the nursery.
Katie would sell her house in Hancock and look for something
on the water there. Maybe build. Darío had mentioned buying
something in Florida or Arizona to use as a resting place between
Tour events when traveling to the U.P. wouldn't be feasible.

They would spend the winters in Spain. She looked around the room at the huge fireplace, which was bare now. To have the fire roaring, holding their child here, with Darío at his desk, Sofia not far away. Yes, winters in Spain. Lovely.

If he still wanted to marry her. To be a family.

The phone rang, pulling Katie out of her thoughts. As Darío answered, she returned to her book. Darío soon walked over, handing the phone to her.

"It's for you. Alison."

That was surprising. She stayed in touch with Lizzie and Alison and her family mostly by email, because of the time difference. Besides, Alison was busy with a new semester starting at Tech and Lizzie was busy with…well, Lizzie was always busy, so she hadn't called them since she'd arrived in Spain. She hadn't even turned her cell phone on over here.

"Hey, Al, what's up?"

"Hey KitKat. God, it's good to hear your voice."

Her voice sounded weary and Katie was on instant alert. "Al? What is it? What's wrong?" Darío had returned to his desk but Katie could feel his questioning eyes on her. She turned to him and shrugged.

"Oh, I'm just tired that's all. I just finished teaching and have to get back to the hospital."

"What happened? Are you all right?"

Alison sighed. "It's not me. I'm only visiting." She let out a deep breath. "It's my dad."

Ah, Alison's father. Katie realized she'd been waiting for this call for some time, as Alison must have known she'd one day be making it.

Alison's parents were much older than Katie's and Lizzie's. Alison had been a change-of-life baby who'd surprised her parents. More like shocked them senseless. Having raised two older daughters, seen them through college and out of the house, and then finding out another one was on the way.

Alison's father was older than her mother, in his early eighties now. He'd been diagnosed with Alzheimer's seven years ago. He'd lived a relatively normal life since then with the help of Alison and her mother.

But they'd all been waiting, knowing there'd be the day when Alison and her mother wouldn't be able to do the job alone. Apparently, that day had arrived.

"He didn't hurt himself or anything did he? Is he okay physically?" Katie asked her friend. Again, she felt Darío's eyes on her.

"He's fine physically, but we had to put him in the longer-term care wing at the hospital. Mom just couldn't...I couldn't..."

"It's okay, Al, you did the right thing. It was all you could do."

"Yeah, I know. So why do I feel like such a shit?"

Katie smiled. "Because you're a good, caring person, that's why. And this is eating you up. How's your mom doing?"

She heard Alison's breath go out of her. "Well, that's the other thing. Not so good. We...I...decided to put Dad in the hospital because Mom's not doing so hot."

Katie could hear Alison take a sip of something, then clear her throat. "They've just diagnosed Mom with dementia too."

"Oh, God, Al. I'm so sorry." Katie wished she could climb through the phone wire and be with her friend, wrap her up in her arms and smother her with hugs. Alison would hate that, but she probably desperately needed it.

"Yeah. It's just the total shits here, KitKat."

"Maybe I should come home," Katie said. She turned to Darío. He didn't know what was going on, but must have realized it was something serious. He nodded his understanding, that Katie should go if she needed to.

"No. There's nothing you could do. Mom and I are just trying to get some things in order, in case she can't...make decisions...later." It was the only time Katie had ever known Alison to cry. She heard Alison blowing her nose, could almost see her pulling it together. "I just needed someone to talk to. I need to call my sisters and I wanted to say it out loud to someone besides them first, you know?"

"Sure, Al, I know."

"Anyway, it's been a long week. I've been either at the hospital or at Mom's every evening, after teaching in the morning and seeing patients in the afternoon. It just took its toll, that's all. No need for you to come home, KitKat, it'll all be…" Her voiced trailed off. Katie didn't finish the sentence for her. She couldn't.

"Hang in there, Al. Don't forget to take care of yourself," Katie said.

"I will. Don't worry KitKat, you just have a good time with your Latin lover. Are you married yet?"

Katie snuck a glance at Darío, his head down, reading the papers on the desk in front of him. "No," was all she said.

"Oh, I almost forgot the other reason I called," Alison said.

"That wasn't reason enough?"

"I was going to call you about my parents later, I didn't want you worrying about me while you were off doing the blushing bride thing."

Katie laughed at that. "So why the call?"

"At the hospital yesterday. There was a car accident. Amber and little Crystal."

Katie gasped. "And Ron?"

"No, he wasn't in the car. It wasn't too bad, but the baby had to have surgery. And they needed blood for her and Amber was kind of hysterical so they got Ron in there…and…and…"

"And?" Katie said loudly, worrying about that little baby going through surgery.

"And the baby is fine, she came through the surgery just fine, but they realized that Ron wasn't a match."

"Huh?"

"He wasn't a match. Which isn't so unusual. Except, I don't know, something about rare blood types and no possible way… bottom line, he's not Crystal's father."

A chill swept through Katie. A picture of Ron playing with Crystal in the Commodore flashed through her mind. How he'd gently placed the plastic keys on the tray of her highchair after Crystal repeatedly knocked them to the floor. "Oh God. Poor Ron."

"Yeah, I know. I was coming from seeing my dad after it all happened. Cindy Pietala was there because one of her kids had some surgery or something and heard the whole thing. She said Ron was shouting there must be some mistake. Amber was causing a scene. I guess it was nuts."

Cindy Pietala was a woman that she and Alison had graduated with and known forever. Though she'd been Cindy Kilpela in high school. She had five children now. A fact Katie knew because she'd seen a pregnant Cindy many times when Katie'd gone to the hospital to see her doctor about conceiving.

"So, I go up to the post-op area. Just to see how Ron's doing. I don't know why I should care after what he did to you," Alison said, as if she needed to defend her actions.

"You've known Ron a long time, Al. Whatever his and my situation, he was in pain and you wanted to help. It's okay."

Alison cleared her throat. "You should have seen him, Kat. The poor guy looked like he'd been run over by a truck. He was torn up with worry about the baby and shock to find out she isn't his. I felt so bad for him."

Katie felt Ron's pain too. How could she not? She, more than anyone, knew how much he wanted to be a father, what steps he would take to become one. Then to find out one day it was all a lie. Yes, she knew what he was going through.

They were both silent for a moment.

"Well, I've got to get going. I've got to head back to the hospital, then to my mom's. I'm sorry to dump everything on you, KitKat, but I needed to tell someone about my parents, you know?"

"Of course. I'm glad you called, Al. If there's anything I can do on this end…"

"I know, and thanks. Love you, Kat."

"Love you, too, Al."

She hung up the phone, stunned by the overload of information. Her heart went out to them all: Alison, her parents, Ron, the baby. Even Amber. Sort of.

—⁓—

Darío was going insane only being able to hear Katie's side of the conversation. He knew Ron was involved somehow. That something had happened.

That she wanted to go home.

No, he told himself, don't get carried away. She didn't say she wanted to go home, she asked Alison if she *should* go home. A slight difference, but one that Darío was hanging on to for dear life.

She brought the phone back over to his desk, placed it in its cradle. She looked a million miles away. Or at least an ocean and half the United States away.

He waited for her to start, but she just stood there, her long, elegant fingers tracing the buttons on the phone.

"Trouble?" he finally said.

"Not exactly trouble, but not great news, no."

She took a seat across the desk from him. Like he was interviewing her or some damn thing. He longed to go over, pull her to him and soothe her. He just wasn't sure what the problem was. "Alison's father is in the hospital with severe Alzhiemer's, and her mother isn't doing so well, either. They just diagnosed her with some form of dementia. I didn't get if it was Alzhiemer's too or not."

"Ah, poor Alison. That is quite a blow."

Katie nodded. "Yes. She's pretty stressed about it as you can imagine."

"And you'd like to be home, to be with her?" He asked, holding his breath, hoping Alison was the reason she wanted to leave Spain. Leave him.

"I guess there's nothing I could do, really. And this is just the beginning; it's going to be a long haul. I'll be there for her later." She started to get up, to leave the room.

Let her go, he told himself, don't ask. But he couldn't help himself. "Did I hear you mention something about Ron?" He hated himself for how desperate his voice sounded.

She turned around, her shoulders sagged, she let out a breath. "There was a car accident. Everyone is okay, I guess, but what came out of it is that Ron is not Crystal's father."

Darío was silent. He had pity for the man. To find out the child you loved, the child you gave up so much for is not yours. To realize the woman who bore you that child lied to you. Darío could not imagine such a thing, even though early on with Katie he had wondered if that was to be his fate. No longer. He knew Katie would never lie about such a thing.

But would she lie to him about her true feelings about Ron? If it were to protect Darío? To protect her child's future?

Then the weight of what this meant hit him. "Ron will no longer wish to be with Amber then, eh?"

"No, probably not. I hadn't thought of that."

But now she was.

"Well, I'm going to turn in. You coming?" she asked.

He wanted nothing more than to go to bed with her now. Hold her, make love to her, let her know he loved her. But he had to think. "You go on ahead. I need to finish reading these contracts."

She nodded and left the office, softly closing the door behind her.

He tried to keep his emotions in check, focus on the facts. Like he did on the course.

He thought back through the week they'd been in Spain. Things had definitely been different. Katie had pulled away from him. It was subtle, the difference, but he'd noticed it. He tried to pinpoint when exactly that had happened. She'd insisted on spending that first night alone, so it actually could have been from before they got to Spain.

He thought back to their last night in the Copper Country. They'd made love in her shower. And then again in the guest room.

Before that. At the Commodore. Ron being a good father.

Darío leaned his elbow onto the desk, resting his head in his hands.

Of course, she'd begun to pull away the next day. The day after seeing Ron and his family.

And now he was no longer a part of that family. Ron was free. Free to be with Katie.

He got up from the desk and went into the bedroom. The bedside lamp was on, Katie on her side—the most comfortable position for her to sleep in now—a book resting on her hip. Asleep.

He stood over her, watching her. She was so breathtakingly beautiful.

And she loved another man.

The words he'd overheard his mother say today when he'd been eavesdropping came back to him. Something about sacrificing for your child. Even if it meant giving up the one you love. Katie had agreed with his mother.

Is that what she was doing? Giving up the man she loved for the sake of her child?

Ron had done that.

Could Darío be that strong? Give up Katie for their child? It wasn't quite the same. Darío knew he'd be a good father if he and Katie stayed together. This was about Katie loving Ron, not Darío. About being in a marriage with a woman he loved desperately, who cared for him, but did not love him back.

Could he set her free to be with the man she loved to raise his child with Ron?

She shifted in her sleep, her eyes fluttered open. She gave him a soft smile, then drifted back to sleep.

He moved away from her, heading for the bathroom.

She was everything to him. And he had to give her up.

—⁓—

"What are your plans for the day?" Katie asked him over

breakfast. They were fending for themselves, Sofia having gone to one of her women's group meetings. Katie made them omelets.

She didn't bring up her disappointment that Darío hadn't awakened her last night when he'd come to bed. What was one night, after all, in the lifetime of nights they had ahead of them.

He put down his fork, pushed the half-eaten omelet away. Oh, oh, this wasn't going to be good.

She put her own fork down, grabbed the napkin in her lap as if to brace herself.

"Actually, I thought maybe we could look into flights for you to go home," he said.

He was watching her carefully, but for what she didn't know. So, she kept her face passive, serene, even though she was dying inside.

"Go home?"

"*Sí.*"

"Alone?"

"*Sí.* I have the Spanish Open next week, I must stay."

"And then you'll come over?"

He shook his head and she felt a little piece of her heart shake off as well. It must have shown in her eyes, because he reached across for her hand. "*Gata,*" he said softly, like he did when they made love.

She kept her hands where they were, needing to hear him out. He leaned back in his chair, let out a heavy sigh. She would have done anything for him to smile that lopsided smile of his, for his warm brown eyes to shine. But neither happened.

He looked away from her, couldn't meet her eyes.

Oh God, he was dumping her. She was being dumped again. And even though they'd been together so short a time, even though she'd only known him five months, the hurt she felt this time cut so much deeper than it had with Ron.

He must have realized she was in love with him. She'd tried to hide it, but how could she hide her feelings that well? The thought of marriage for the baby, with a mutual attraction and caring for each other was one thing. But a marriage where she loved him desperately was not what Darío had signed on for.

So he was pulling out.

"I see," she said, her voice cracking. She cleared her throat. "But you'll be coming back to the States for the Tour Championship?"

He nodded. "*Sí*, I have committed to play there."

"And you would never break a commitment, would you?" Her voice sounded shrill, even to herself.

He leaned forward, his elbows on the table. He waited till she looked at him. "I am committed to our child, Katie. I have been since the moment you told me you were pregnant."

To the child. Not to Katie. But if she was honest with herself, it was what she'd first proposed to him, when she'd brought the papers to him in Memphis. That they do what was best for the child. It was she that had said being in a loveless marriage was not the best option.

But it wouldn't be loveless now, at least not on her part.

She loved him. But he didn't love her. She was only a commitment to him. A noble gesture. The honorable thing to do.

She had to let him go if that's what he wanted.

"Perhaps you were right, those months ago in Memphis. Perhaps our child would be better off raised by you in the Copper Country. I have now spent some time there, with your friends, your family. I know our child would be happy there, as you were."

"And your part in our lives?"

"That doesn't have to be decided now," he said. She wanted to scratch his eyes out for being so calm and cool.

She needed to be away from him. She couldn't keep herself from falling apart and that wouldn't help the situation. She rose to leave and, like the gentleman he was, he rose also. She waved him back to his seat. "Sit. Sit. I'm going to go pack."

"I did not mean that you should leave today," he said.

"I might as well. Maybe I can be some help to Alison while she gets things with her parents squared away."

"Yes, of course. Alison. You'd want to be with her now."

There was something in his voice…sarcasm? But that was so unlike Darío. She stared at him a moment, trying to read his face, but he was impassive. Like he was on the course. Focused. Determined. You never really knew what he was thinking, what he was feeling inside.

—⁓—

As if the airlines were in cahoots with Darío to get her out of the country as quickly as possible, there was an open seat that afternoon. The ride to the airport was excruciating. The only saving grace was that Sofia hadn't come home before they left. Katie didn't know how she'd explain she was leaving to the woman whom she told only yesterday how much she loved Darío.

That seemed like months ago, not just yesterday.

Their goodbye was dismal. An awkward hug, a chaste kiss on both cheeks. Not the bone-melting kisses Darío had given her only nights ago.

Katie held it together at the gate, got situated in her seat, received a blanket and pillow from the flight attendant, then proceeded to cry the entire flight home.

Twenty-Three

You are meant to play the ball as it lies, a fact that may help to touch on your own objective approach to life.

~ Grantland Rice, sportswriter

BINKY WAS SHAKING his head. Again. It seemed that's all the wiry man had done since Darío began his tale of why Katie was not with him in Madrid for the Spanish Open.

The story didn't take Darío long. He wouldn't go into the details. There weren't many anyway. He'd felt Katie wanted to be at home. He'd suggested she go. She went.

But of course, Binky would not be satisfied with that. As Darío started his warm-up routine on the range he waited for the questions to start.

He'd not even gotten his glove on his hand when they did.

"So, the getting-married part?"

"On hold," Darío said as he took his pitching wedge out of the bag. He waited for Binky to set some balls up for him. Binky stayed at the bag with his arms folded across his chest. Darío sighed and went to the bucket of balls himself, tipping it over, scooping a few forward with the blade of his club. "You are still an employee, yes?"

Binky snorted at that, kicked a few more balls forward. "This 'on hold'. Her doing or yours?"

"A mutual decision."

Another snort. Darío picked his head up and looked around the range. "It sounds like a wild animal is around. Do you see it? Perhaps a wild boar." He put his head back down and did some warm up swings.

Binky, perhaps remembering he had a job to do as well, started going through Darío's bag, counting clubs, checking the ball count, the normal pre-round routine.

"Let me just ask this. Did she say she wanted to go home, or did you suggest it?"

Darío hit the ball. It was a good fifteen yards off target, not great when the shots he was practicing first were only fifty yards to begin with.

"I believe I suggested it." At Binky's "aha" look, he quickly added, "But only because she would not have asked herself. She wanted to go."

"How do you know that?"

What to say? How much to tell? It seemed unfair to Katie to impart the details of their breakup to anyone, even Binky. Besides, his pride wouldn't let him tell Binky that Katie was still in love with her ex-husband. Husband, he mentally corrected himself, remembering the unsigned divorce papers.

Did he tell Binky that the last week without Katie had been hell? That putting her on the plane was the hardest thing he'd ever done? That he wouldn't let the cleaning lady he'd hired for his mother change the pillowcase that Katie'd slept on? That he had horrifying dreams of a baby in distress that he couldn't save that woke him up in the middle of the night?

"I could tell she wanted to go home," was all he said, hoping Binky would let it go at that.

"How?"

Darío sighed and hit another ball, which was even further off target. "She was different once we got to Spain. She began to pull away. I think she finally realized what she'd committed to, and it wasn't what she wanted."

Marriage to him had never been what she wanted. She'd been upfront with him about that from the beginning. It was he who'd pressed, who'd said his child would not be born a bastard. Somewhere, for some reason, she'd agreed, but it was clear to Darío now that it was not what she wanted.

"Because she started to pull away? That could be a hundred different things. Your imagination, for one."

Darío raised an eyebrow at Binky. He switched to his nine iron. Binky brought the balls to him this time, took the wedge from Darío, cleaned it, then set it outside the bag.

"I did not imagine it."

Binky nodded, willing to concede the point. "Could be she was nervous around your mother? Or about being in your house, your country. Wondering how'd she fit in. If she'd fit in."

Darío shook his head. "She got along very well with my mother. And she seemed to love San Barria."

"Okay…could be…" Binky was searching for answers.

Darío decided to end this discussion. It was like picking at a scab to him. A newly formed, very fragile scab.

"Could be she is still in love with her husband, and now he has become available to raise her child with her."

"Did she tell you that?"

"That her husband was now available? In a way."

"No, that she still loved him? Did she tell you that herself?"

Darío turned away, not answering. He took a couple of quick swings with the nine iron, both shots going way right.

"Bloody hell. You know what this is? This is just like in Denver, calling the penalty shot on yourself when you didn't see the ball move."

Darío looked at Binky, waiting. "You didn't see the ball move with Katie, either, Guv," Binky said, his voice low, insistent.

Darío looked at Binky for a long moment. His caddy—his friend—seemed to be silently pleading with him. Darío would have liked nothing more than to agree with Binky's analogy. But it was Katie they were talking about, her happiness. And that was much more important than any golf tournament.

He lowered his head and, as he had in Denver, said only, "I cannot be sure it didn't."

—∿—

"Thanks for stopping by," Katie said as Ron stepped through the doorway of her home. Their home.

"Of course. No problem," Ron answered.

He'd sounded surprised when she'd called him earlier and asked if he could swing by the house. He was composed now, used to the idea, but she could see the questioning in his eyes. He looked tired, but Katie guessed that's what worrying about a child—even if it turned out not to be your own—did to you.

And of course, as always, he looked gorgeous. His hulking frame took up the most of the breakfast nook that Katie led them to. He pulled out a chair—his chair—and sat down. Katie put down a Bud for him and an iced tea for herself and seated herself across from her husband.

It seemed so familiar, so safe sitting here with him now. As if nothing had changed.

This was the room where they'd had all their important talks. And the unimportant ones. All the "how was your day?" conversations took place at this table. As well as "pass the salt". And the baby discussions. So many of them. When they'd first started trying, the talk was all of names, and college funds and fixing up the nursery. Then the conversation slowly turned to concern. Then calendars would be on the table with doctor's appointments and best conception days circled. After a while the table would be littered with infertility information, the baby name books moved to the lesser-used den.

Here, at this circular cherry table, in this circular room with windows all around, they had formed a life together.

Katie pushed the brown envelope across the table toward Ron, prepared to legally end that life.

He put his hand out to take the papers, then pulled them back, as if they might burn. He looked at Katie. His blue eyes, so like her own, were filled with an emotion she couldn't quite read. Remorse? Tenderness?

"I'm so sorry about forgetting these. That night we saw you at the Commodore, I came home and started to get them out of my bag and then…" She would skip that part about joining Darío in the shower. Ron didn't need to hear it, and it was too painful for her to remember anyway. "I got called out of the room. I left town the next day. I thought I'd taken care of it."

Ron's shoulders sagged. "Oh. You thought you'd signed them?"

"Yes."

"So it wasn't intentional? You not signing them and sending them on to the lawyer."

"No."

"Not intentional, but maybe subconsciously you didn't want to sign them?"

"Now you sound like Alison."

He barked a laugh. The last person Ron wanted to be compared to was Alison as they'd always rubbed each other the wrong way. "Does she think there's a bigger reason for you not signing the papers? Does she agree with me?"

"She doesn't know I didn't send them to the lawyer. She probably assumes that I went home that night after the Commodore, signed them and put them in the mail the next morning. It's what I'd assumed until I was unpacking my laptop case the other day."

He leaned across the table and took her hand as he had done hundred – thousands – of times before. "But you *didn't* sign them. And whether it was unintentional or a subconscious decision or, hell, an unconscious decision, the fact is we're still married."

She looked at his hand placed over hers, so familiar, keeping hers safe and warm. She should take it back, but she didn't. It was comforting, in a way, just to be touched. With her other hand, she nudged the papers closer to Ron. "They're signed now."

"But not delivered to the lawyer, not posted or whatever it is they do to make it legal, make it final."

"I thought you could drop them off at your lawyers. That's why I asked you here. I thought it better to do this face to face."

"Or we could just run them through the shredder."

She should have been stunned, but she wasn't. She didn't play dumb, either. "You're saying this now because you're hurt, and you're feeling alone. It's easy to fall back on the familiar, the safe." She sure knew what she was talking about. Just having him here in the nook, holding her hand, made the ache she felt from Darío's absence dull a tiny bit.

He nodded. "That. And the fact that I never stopped loving you, Katie."

She took a deep breath, let it out. "Ron…"

He held up his free hand to stop her. He gently squeezed her fngers, then let her hand go and sat back in his seat. "I know I screwed up, Katie. You have to know I know how much I hurt you, what me having a child with someone else would do to you. But when Amber told me she was pregnant after only having been with her once, I—"

"You only slept with Amber once?" Katie interrupted.

Ron slowly nodded his head, his blond hair tumbling across his broad forehead. "One drunken night, when I was so hurt that you'd shut me out again and I was feeling so useless…" Katie put her head down. "I'm not making excuses, Katie, really, what I did was so wrong, but I want you to know that I never looked at another woman. Before that night. You were all I ever wanted. All I still want."

"I know I shut you out, Ron," she quietly added. "I felt like such a failure, I just couldn't face you sometimes. I know I turned away from you, that we should have worked through it together. It should have made us stronger, a team. Instead, it…"

"Yeah," he whispered. He took a deep breath, as if steeling himself. "But it's not too late, Katie, not for us. Now that I'm not with Amber."

"What about Crystal?"

"I told Amber I would help out with her. I love that little girl like she was my own, and if I could raise her without Amber, I would in a second, but I can't take a child from its mother. I wouldn't have a legal leg to stand on anyway, with Crystal not being mine."

"I'm sorry about that, Ron, I really am. I've seen you with that baby, I know how much you love her."

He let out a soft sigh. "Thanks, but I guess I got what I deserved. I knew I should have questioned Amber more, demanded an amnio, or blood tests after Crystal was born." He brushed his hand through his hair, the lock on his forehead tumbling back into place. "I just wanted to believe so badly, you know?"

Katie only briefly let herself think about Darío questioning the paternity of his child. At some point he had come to believe her. Was it because he'd gotten to know Katie, knew she wasn't capable of a lie of that magnitude? Or did he just want to believe, like Ron?

Ron shook her out of her thoughts. "I'll always want to know what's going on with Crystal, be a part of her life if I can, but there's no way I can be with Amber after what she did."

"What about Crystal's real father?"

"She was sure it was mine, she says. She's not talking, anyway. Not giving up a name. Hell, this town is full of blue-eyed blond Finns, it could be anyone." He leaned forward again. "Let's talk about us, Katie. Do we have a future? Is there something we can build on? Start over?"

She leaned back and put her hand on her tummy. She was showing now, there was no mistaking. Ron hadn't commented thus far on the baby, but she'd seen his eyes on her stomach. He didn't look surprised, but then she'd figured someone in town had let him know. She'd been counting on it.

"You're forgetting about this," she said, rubbing her belly.

He smiled. His perfect, even smile, with beautiful, white teeth. "I'm not forgetting about it at all. It makes even more sense for us to be together now that you're going to have a baby."

"But it's not yours," she said, stating the obvious.

He didn't say anything for a moment. He looked around the nook, as if the faded wallpaper held the secret to what he was trying to say. "I was—am—fully prepared to raise Crystal even though she's not my own. I know you can love another man's child as much as you do your own. I do. But with Amber in the picture, that's not going to happen.

"But to love *your* child, Katie, that's a no-brainer. To raise that baby as our own, together, to be a family like we'd always talked about…" His voiced trailed off.

"What about Darío?" The question was more to herself, but she muttered it out loud.

"You tell me. Where does he play into all of this?"

"He's the father."

Ron nodded.

"He wants to be a part of his child's life."

Ron nodded again. "And yours? Does he want to be a part of yours? Because I do, Katie, I do so much."

Katie was finding it hard to breath. The nook seemed smaller, somehow, as if all the air was being sucked out. "I…I…"

Ron held his hand up. He pushed the papers back to her side of the table and stood up. He pushed his chair back in, and stepped behind it.

"Don't answer right now. Just think about this. I know I screwed up. But I'm here now, Katie, and I want to start over. I want you to be my wife, to raise your baby together.

"I'm here, Katie. Where's Darío?"

When he passed her, he touched her softly on the cheek. So softly it barely registered. But the tingle stayed with Katie for a long time afterward. As did his words.

Twenty-Four

The right way to play golf is to go up and hit the bloody thing.
~ George Duncan, Scottish golfer

THANK GOODNESS THE Tour Championship didn't have a cut. He'd have been flying back to Spain on Friday night if that were the case. But because the Championship only included the top thirty players on the money list for the year, there was no cut—all the golfers played on the weekend—and so Darío was making the turn to the final nine on Sunday tied for twenty-ninth place.

It would still be a nice payday, but Darío didn't feel he deserved the money playing as poorly as he was.

He had expected to play better. He'd spent the last month and a half since the Spanish Open practicing on the course he'd built in San Barria. For hours. And hours. It was the only time he didn't think of Katie, when he had a club in his hand and was poised over a ball, so he spent much more time on the course and practice range than he ever had before.

And even then she'd creep in. He'd be addressing the ball and he'd remember the night they'd first met and her drunken request that he take the same stance in the elevator so she could admire his forearms.

He'd put on sunscreen and remember the spot on her forehead that she always missed which would end up bright pink.

He'd brush his hair back, and replace his cap and picture her doing the same, adjusting her blond ponytail through the back hole.

He considered it a cruel joke that the Championship this year was being played in Texas. At least it wasn't Irving. But even Houston still felt too reminiscent to him.

Only nine more holes and he could leave. Return to Spain for the remainder of the year. Wait to hear from Katie that their child was born.

After the tenth hole, moving away from the clubhouse, their gallery, which was sparse to begin with, thinned out even more. The leaders were teeing off now, and the fans would want to follow those groups, not the players competing for last place.

As they teed up on eleven, Darío saw a flash of a bobbing ponytail down the fairway ropes that caught his eye. The woman was walking down the fairway, too far away for Darío to see her face, even if she had been facing him and not walking in the other direction. To where his ball would probably land.

To where someone who knew his game would most likely stand.

Dios Mio, it couldn't be.

His playing partner hit his ball and Darío stepped to the tee for his turn. He teed the ball then took his normal four paces behind it to line up where he wanted to hit his shot. But his eye did not find a place in the fairway where he wanted his ball to land. Nor did it look out for any obstacles to avoid.

His gaze was solely on the woman walking down the fairway. She was the right height. And the ponytail swayed across her back in a rythymn that Darío certainly recognized. But perhaps that was the way with all women and ponytails? Darío didn't think so.

The marshal mistook Darío's hesitance for a waiting of the people moving along the fairway ropes to settle. He stepped up to the tee box and lifted his "Quiet" sign. "Hold, please," he said loudly enough for those halfway down the fairway to hear him. He stepped back and gave Darío the "all clear" signal.

The woman with the ponytail stopped and began to turn. Finally, Darío would get to see her face. It was a distance away, but Darío knew he would never mistake Katie's face for any other.

But it wasn't her face that Darío saw first when the woman turned. It was her belly. Her large, beautiful, swelling tummy.

Darío's arms went weak. The club fell right out of his hands. He looked to Binky for help. For confirmation that he wasn't losing his mind. Binky had followed his line of vision, must have seen Katie. He looked at Darío with a smirk. "Don't like the club selection, Guv?"

Darío looked at him as if he spoke a foreign language. Binky nodded toward Darío's club on the ground in front of him.

The marshal came back to the tee box. "Sir? Is every thing all right?"

Embarrassed at his unprofessional behavior, Darío nodded to the marshal, picked up his driver and stepped to the ball.

He heard the club make contact but had no idea where it had gone. It could have been skidding four feet in front of him for all he knew. But by the way the other player, his caddy, and Binky all set off down the fairway, Darío knew he'd at least hit it in the right direction.

By the time Darío came to his ball, Katie had moved up to the green. To be at his approach shot as it landed. Just as she had done when they'd been together.

It was then that Darío realized she wasn't alone. A man stood next to her, talking with her. She pointed things out to the man. It didn't appear to be just a stranger talking golf with her. They appeared to be together.

Darío couldn't clearly see the man from this far away, but a sigh of relief rushed through him as he realized that man couldn't possibly be Ron. He was dark, for one thing, and only about Katie's height. And older.

A lawyer? Would she bring a lawyer to him? She'd shown up in Memphis with papers for him to sign, was she doing the same thing now, but with more legal weight behind her?

He didn't remember hitting the approach shot, just Binky handing him the club. But there was a smattering of applause from the sparse crowd so he figured he'd hit the green.

It was a large green and the pin was placed at the farthest corner from where Katie and the man stood. His shot had landed only about three feet from the pin and Darío made an easy birdie.

He teed off on the next hole in the same fog, staring down the fairway at Katie and the man she was with. As they walked together down the fairway, Darío pulled on Binky's sleeve.

"Go over and talk to her. Ask her why she's here. I can't concentrate, can't focus."

Binky snorted. "You just played the best hole of the tournament, maybe you should stay unfocused."

Darío shot him a glare and Binky said no more. When they got to the green, Binky cleaned Darío's ball, gave him his putter, then dropped the bag next to the walkway to the next hole and made his way over to Katie at the ropes.

Darío's playing partner was in trouble in the bunker and Darío stood on the green staring at Binky as he gave Katie a big hug, patted her tummy, then shook hands with the other man as Katie, presumably, introduced them.

When it was Darío's turn to putt, he did so quickly, taking no more than a cursory glance at the line. He made the putt and turned toward Katie but she and the man were moving away, back toward the clubhouse.

Binky had taken his bag and was walking to the next hole's tee.

Darío nearly sprinted to him. "Well? Why is she here? Where is she going? Who is that man?"

Binky checked his yardage book, then got out Darío's driver and handed it to him. "She'll meet you at the clubhouse after the round and explain that all to you."

Darío looked at the man, dumbfounded. "That's it?"

Binky nodded. "Oh yeah, she asked me to give you this." Binky held out his hand, his fist wrapped around something.

Darío looked at Binky's hand as if it might strike him. He'd not given Katie a ring, so it was not that. No legal papers would fit in Binky's closed fist. Cautiously, Darío put his hand out, palm out.

Binky placed the item in Darío's hand and stepped back beside Darío's bag.

For the first time in two months, he felt a glimmer of hope, as he stared at the Chapstick in his hand.

—∞—

Katie sat with her companion in the shade at the eighteenth hole drinking a lemonade and hoping she hadn't made a huge mistake.

She would have loved to watch Darío complete his round, but Binky suggested waiting at the clubhouse, and honestly, she was probably getting too big to be walking so far in the Texas heat. Though the heat in early November was definitely not as bad as her first visit.

She stretched her legs out on the bleachers—nearly empty now because the first groups were still a few holes from finishing—and thought about her first time in Texas.

It seemed an eternity ago, but her little bundle was the accurate timekeeper. Seven months. She rubbed her hand across her stomach and saw the man with her watch her movements, seemingly mesmerized by the life growing inside of her.

"Are you okay? Can I get you something?" he asked.

Katie shook her head. "No, thank you. This lemonade is just what I needed. Please don't feel you have to sit here with me. I know you'd like to watch him play. I'll be fine here."

She could see the man struggle with the decision. He wanted to watch Darío play, but didn't want to leave a pregnant Katie alone.

"Really, it's fine. We're close to the clubhouse, if there's any problem."

The man stood to leave, his decision made. He took a step away, then turned and took Katie's hand. Katie thought for a moment that he might kiss it, but he just held it in his for a moment, giving it a gentle squeeze. He then set it upon Katie's stomach. "Thank you for bringing me here today. It means more to me than I can say." The emotion in the man's voice conveyed his feelings. Katie only nodded, and the man walked away.

She rubbed her back and sat alone in the bleachers, her thoughts going back to the steps she'd taken to get here.

After Ron had left her house that day she'd sat down and done some thinking. How could she not when the man she loved didn't want her and the man she had loved did. Taking Ron back would be so easy. So safe. The strain of not having a baby gone, they could return to the marriage they'd once had.

But Katie knew that once she saw her child, Darío's child, she would be haunted by her love for him. If their child had his chocolate eyes, how would Katie ever be able to look at them and not feel the ache of emptiness she'd felt since losing Darío?

Ron was not the answer. Safe was not the answer.

She'd made the first move with Darío before and it hadn't killed her. In fact, she was getting a baby—what she'd always wanted—because of it.

If she made the first move again, would she get what she now wanted most—a life with Darío?

The next day, she'd put the legal envelope in the mail, started doing some internet research, and called Sofia, hoping that Darío wouldn't answer.

She was shaken from her thoughts by the sound of golf balls being hit. The tee on eighteen was not visible from the bleachers, but she saw first one, then another ball land in the middle of the fairway. She took the last sip of her lemonade and rose to meet the group—Darío's group—and her future.

The golfers finished out at eighteen and made their way to the scorer's tent. Katie made her way to the ropes on the other side, where the men would come out when they were done. Binky made his way over to her, as did the man she'd come with.

"Did you enjoy the golf?" Binky asked the man.

The man nodded, cleared his throat. "It was...it was..."

Katie couldn't imagine what types of emotions the man was feeling. He couldn't finish his sentence, but neither Katie nor Binky pressed him.

"Do you think I should stick around for the introduction?" Binky asked Katie.

"It probably wouldn't hurt," Katie said, feeling like a coward, but wanting as much moral support as possible when she talked to Darío for the first time in two months.

And for what would come next.

Darío was the first player out of the trailer used as a scorer's tent. His eyes swept the area and rested on her. Katie felt the familiar tingle go through her body as his warm eyes raked over her and his crooked smile showed up.

He came over to them, ignoring—for the first time that Katie had ever noticed—the autograph seekers along the ropes.

When he reached her, his hands reached out to her tummy then stopped, midair. He dropped his hands. "Katie," was all he said.

"Darío, I have someone I'd like you to meet."

He took a deep breath, as if bracing himself, and nodded for her to go on.

"Darío Luna, meet Miguél de la Sol."

Darío instinctively reached out his hand to shake the other man's, but Katie saw it freeze as she added, "Your father."

—❦—

Three hours later Darío's head was still spinning.

His father.

Katie had bowed out of dinner, saying he and his father needed time alone. He'd balked at that, wanting some kind of support when talking for the first time with the man who fathered him. But Katie had been insistent. Darío had wound up in a restaurant with a man he'd never met before. One who he'd thought he'd never meet.

His father had never known he'd existed.

Darío had sat and listened as Miguel de la Sol poured out his story. He'd been young and scared when Sofia had told him she was pregnant. When she'd said she was going to keep the baby and stay in San Barria instead of traveling the world with Miguel, he left town, hurt and confused.

But several months later he'd returned. He'd come to realize he wanted Sofia to be his wife; wanted to raise their child together. When he went to her home, her parents had told him she and the baby had died in childbirth. There was such a pallor over the house, a sense of death, that Miguel had never thought to question what he was told.

Darío knew that the last was true. There probably was a sense of death in the Luna household because by that time they had thrown Sofia and her large belly out. They'd never spoken to her again, and certainly had never acknowledged Darío.

The greenskeeper at the resort, Sergio, and his wife had taken pity on Sofia. They took her in and sheltered her—and then Darío—until Sofia was able to work at the country club and support herself and her baby.

When Darío had told Miguel of these events he had seen the pain in the man's eyes and knew that Miguel spoke the truth.

If he had known Sofia was alive, that she'd had his child, he would have been there. Been a part of their lives. Given Darío his name.

They'd sat in the restaurant, years of unshared lives between them. At one point Miguel had broken down in tears. At another, Darío had.

All those years of searching galleries or wanting his face on the covers of magazines so that his father would know he'd done well and hadn't needed him. All for a man who didn't know he was alive. Who'd mourned the loss of an unborn child years ago.

Now, driving to Katie's hotel, Darío was emotionally wrung out. He must somehow summon the strength to see Katie, to fight for her as he hadn't in Spain.

His evening with Miguel had shown him that he had to

seize what he wanted while he could. It could be taken away at any moment.

He'd thought he was doing the right thing letting Katie return to Ron, the man she loved. But now his yearning for the family he'd never had, the family Miguel and Sofia had had ripped away from them, and his love for Katie, meant more to him than his honor.

He must win her back from Ron.

He just prayed it wasn't too late.

—⚭—

Katie opened the door of her hotel room to Darío. God, he looked so good. But tired, and he looked like he may have lost some weight since the last time they'd seen each other. She quickly shook the memory of that bleak day in the Spanish airport out of her head.

They were starting over.

She hoped.

She waved him into the room, careful to step back as he passed, not wanting to get too close in case she felt the overwhelming urge to launch herself into his arms.

He seated himself on the bed of the small room and she took the chair opposite him.

She couldn't read the emotion on his face. She waited. Soon, his eyes, his beautiful chocolate eyes, filled with tears.

"Thank you," was all he said.

She could sense him trying to gain control and waited. It took several minutes, but she sat quietly, watching him. Memorizing him in case her plan backfired and this would be the last time they'd see each other.

When his voice was under control, he looked at her and asked, "How?"

She shrugged. "It wasn't that hard. I told you that with the internet and my connections with news agencies that I could probably find him fairly easily."

"But you needed a name to do that."

She nodded. "I got the name."

He raised an eyebrow over a chocolate eye.

"I got the name from Sofia."

That sent the other eyebrow up. "You spoke to my mother?"

"Yes."

"She didn't tell me."

"I asked her not to."

"But why, *Gata?*"

Gata. He still called her Gata. Katie's confidence rose.

She could do this. She'd set out to seduce him in Irving. She'd made the first move in Akron. She could go after a man.

Her man.

"I thought it was important for you to find out about your family before you started a family of your own. You told me once you'd wanted to have that behind you before you became a father."

He nodded, but said nothing, waiting.

"And you're about to become a father," she needlessly added.

His warm eyes settled on her belly, a look of peace crossed his face. "*Sí*," he said.

She took a deep breath. "And I hope you are about to become part of a family." That wasn't how she'd meant to say it, and she could tell by the confused look on his face that he hadn't understood her meaning.

"*Sí*, Miguel and I made plans. We'll stay in touch. He is even going to see my mother in San Barria, to explain to her."

"That's good. That's great, in fact. But that's not what I meant."

Again his brow shot up in question.

"I meant *our* family. You. Me. And the baby."

He said nothing. The room was silent. The sudden whir of the hotel room's air conditioner made her jump. It seemed a thousand years to Katie, but finally Darío cleared his throat and said, "And what role do you see me playing in our family, *Gata?*"

Katie stood up and walked to the bureau, to her laptop case and got out the envelope she'd brought with her. She turned to

Darío and saw his suspicious glance at the legal-looking papers.

"It's not what you think. It's not like Memphis and these aren't papers asking you to give up rights to your child."

"Some sort of custody settlement, then?" His voice was resigned.

He was getting the wrong idea. She'd botched this up. She quickly took the papers and put them down, away from them.

"They have nothing to do with the baby. It's my final divorce decree. I am officially divorced from Ron."

His head shot up, his eyes narrowed at her. "Surely he is not staying with Amber after what he has found out?"

"No, he's not."

"Katie, he wants to be your husband. I know this. Maybe he just hasn't found the way to—"

She cut him off. "He told me. He came to see me. To talk about a reconciliation."

"And yet you can't forgive him?"

"I forgive Ron. He wasn't the only one to blame for our marriage falling apart. I forgive him, but I don't love him. And a marriage without love is not one I want."

She heard the whoosh of breath leave his body and it gave her the will to forge on. She walked to him and knelt on one knee in front of him. His hands instinctively sprang out to help her, but she waved them away. "I love you, Darío Luna. With all my heart. You and no other."

She took his hand in hers and met his warm gaze. "Will you marry me?"

He didn't say anything.

Defeated, humiliated, she started to get up, but she caught her foot in the leg of her shorts and tumbled headfirst into Darío, causing him to sprawl backward on the bed, Katie draped on top of him.

"Are you okay?" His hands instinctively went out to protect the baby, but the fall was a short one and with a very soft landing—Darío.

"I'm fine. Fine. I'm so sorry." She tried to get up, get away from him, but he gently clasped her arms and held her to him.

"I said many months ago that making love with you would be *muy* dangerous, *Gata*. I now amend that to a *life* with you will be *muy* dangerous."

Her head sprung up. Did he mean it? "Do you mean it?"

He rolled them so that Katie was on her back. He propped himself up on an elbow looking down on her. "*Sí*," he said.

"*Sí* to what?" she asked.

He smiled, that warm, crooked, she'd never get tired of looking at, smile.

"*Sí* to all of it. Meaning what I said. And *sí* to your proposal. Most definitely *sí* to that."

He kissed her. He tasted just as she remembered. Exotic. Warm. Hungry. She kissed him back, their tongues tangling. He moved over her just as she put her arms out to reach for him and she punched him in the chin. "Oh, I'm so sor—"

"Shhh," he whispered in her ear, sending a chill through her. His hands were on her belly now, measuring, soothing, feeling. He looked up at Katie. "She is such a miracle," he said, mirroring her thoughts.

"She?" she teased.

"*Sí*. Peaches," he said, gently kissing her belly. Then he returned to her mouth with less gentleness and Katie's urgency matched his.

He began whispering Spanish in her ear and her body went taut.

"*Te amo, Gata*," he said. "*Te amo*."

Katie's body relaxed, and she held him close. She thought back to the Spanish woman in the airport telling her about the difference of words. The woman was right. *Te amo* was the phrase Katie longed to hear.

She cradled Darío's face in her hands, meeting the gaze of the man she'd raise her child with. The man who'd given her this miracle that was growing inside her. The man she'd spend the rest of her life with.

The man she loved.

"*Te amo*," she whispered, raising her lips to his.

—⋘—

The Worth Series continues with

WORTH THE FALL
THE WORTH SERIES BOOK 3: THE SMART ONE

Try Mara Jacobs's romantic mystery series

BROKEN WINGS
BLACKBIRD & CONFESSOR, BOOK 1

AGAINST THE ODDS
ANNA DAWSON'S VEGAS, BOOK 1

AGAINST THE SPREAD
ANNA DAWSON'S VEGAS, BOOK 2

Find out more at
www.MaraJacobs.com

After graduating from Michigan State University with a degree in advertising, Mara spent several years working at daily newspapers in Advertising sales and production. This certainly prepared her for the world of deadlines!

Most authors say they've been writing forever. Not so with Mara. She always had the stories, but they played like movies in her head. A few years ago she began transferring the movies to pages. She writes mysteries with romance, thrillers with romance, and romances with…well, you get it.

Forever a Yooper (someone who hails from Michigan's glorious Upper Peninsula), Mara now resides in the East Lansing, Michigan, area where she is better able to root on her beloved Spartans.

Mara first published in October of 2012 with 2 romantic mystery series and the contemporary romance Worth series. You can find out more about her books at **www.marajacobs.com**

CPSIA information can be obtained at www.ICGtesting.com
Printed in the USA
LVOW052337200313

325317LV00003B/167/P